FAME GAME

Also by Claudia Pattison

WOW!

FAME GAME

CLAUDIA PATTISON

PAN BOOKS

First published 2002 by Pan Books
an imprint of Pan Macmillan Ltd
Pan Macmillan, 20 New Wharf Road, London N1 9RR
Basingstoke and Oxford
Associated companies throughout the world
www.panmacmillan.com

ISBN 0 330 48795 7

1 3 5 7 9 8 6 4 2

A CIP catalogue record for this book is available from
the British Library.

Typeset by Set Systems Ltd, Saffron Walden, Essex
Printed and bound in Great Britain by
Mackays of Chatham plc, Chatham, Kent

For Rachel

Acknowledgements

Thank you to: my friend Soz Hilton for sharing her memories; John Adams for his fabulous artwork; my agent Luigi Bonomi; and all at Pan Macmillan, especially Mari Evans, Lucy Henson, Caroline Turner, Richard Ogle, Liz Cowen and the Ray Fidler super squad.

ONE

The last time I saw my husband, he said he was popping out for a newspaper and some cigarettes. That was two days ago. I'm not worried . . . pissed off, but not worried. It's all par for the course when you're married to a celebrity. *Celebrity* . . . I still find it hard to think of him like that. To me he's just Toby – not Toby the sex god (although he is fantastically good-looking) or Toby the indie rock king. Three years ago when I first laid eyes on him he was Toby Nobody, a struggling singer-songwriter with an unsigned guitar band called Drift, whose fame was limited to the north London pub circuit. I always knew he would make it – after all, he had the looks, the talent, the charisma and, more important than all of that, a pure, unshakeable self-belief. I just wasn't prepared for how much his fame would change our lives. I'm not talking materially, although we do have a shamelessly luxurious lifestyle and obviously I'm not complaining about *that*. I'm talking about the way it's affected our relationship.

'*Theee-yah!*' The shrill voice of Ivy, my cleaning lady, echoes down two flights of stairs, making me jump. Bugger, *and* I've dropped a stitch ... bet you didn't know knitting was the new rock 'n' roll did you? I'm making my husband a stocking-stitch sweater in midnight blue merino. He'll probably never wear it, but it's the thought that counts and anyway it gives me something to do.

Setting the half-formed jumper aside on the sofa, I walk out into the hall. Looking upwards, I can see Ivy hunched over the top banister, a shank of platinum hair falling over each shoulder. 'Do you want me to dust the chandelier or leave it till next time?' she hollers down the stairs.

The vast crystal monstrosity she's referring to is suspended from the ceiling above the upper landing. It cost four and a half grand in an antique shop on the Brompton Road. Toby and I saw it one afternoon after we'd staggered drunkenly out of a boozy record company lunch to celebrate Drift's Mercury Music Prize nomination. We didn't buy it because we fell in love with it or because we thought it would be an investment. We bought it just because we could – which was a bit stupid, really. It's an ugly old thing and a bitch to keep clean. Toby won't let me take it down because he thinks it looks 'classy'. I keep hoping Ivy will send it flying one day when she's up there on her stepladder doing the monthly dust. What I wouldn't give to see it shatter into a thousand glittering fragments.

'Next time's fine, Ivy,' I shout back up to her. 'It's gone six, you know. Isn't it time you were off?'

Her reply is drowned out by the ringing of the phone and I sprint back into the lounge to pick it up before the answerphone clicks in, just in case it's Toby. I try to tell myself I don't care when he goes on one of his marathon benders, that I'm grateful for a bit of time to myself, but after two whole days and nights without so much as a text message I'm beginning to feel a tad neglected. I snatch up the receiver with one ring to spare.

'Hello?' I say breathlessly, hoping to hear my husband's voice, thick with hangover, reverberate down the line.

'Thea, hon, it's me.'

A wave of disappointment wells up inside me, but I do my best to hide it.

'Oh, hi Kim. How's it going?'

'I'm in the throes of hunting down a ten-foot gold Buddha and four dozen bonsais. The trees shouldn't be a problem but the fat bloke's doing my head in.'

Kim runs her own party planning business, Party On! (we thought up the name together – it only took us three hours and two bottles of Frascati). Not kiddies' parties or crappy dos in church halls, but grand themed balls and posh wedding receptions. She runs her one-woman operation from home and sometimes, when she's really up against it, I give her a hand.

'Do you need some help? I can come round and put in a few phone calls if you like.'

'No, honestly, I'll be fine. I was just ringing to see if you wanted to meet up for a drink later on. Tim's out with the boys from the bank, so I'm all on my lonesome tonight.'

'I'd love to, but Toby's parents are expecting us for dinner. Mind you, I might have to cancel, seeing as the prodigal son has gone AWOL,' I say glumly, twirling the phone flex round my index finger.

'Christ, Thea, the man's never at home. How long has it been this time?'

'Two days. He went out to buy the *Sun* and a pack of Marlboros and that was the last I saw of him. I guess he took a little detour and ended up at some party. No doubt he's sleeping it off on someone's floor as we speak. I expect he's just letting off steam; that studio session last week totally wiped him out,' I say in a lame attempt to justify my husband's absence.

'Yeah, well, there's letting off steam and there's plain inconsiderate. I know he's got this great rock 'n' roll reputation to live up to, but he might include you in his plans, or at least phone to let you know where he is and what time he's coming home. I don't know how you put up with it, I really don't,' Kim says crossly. 'Tim would never dream of staying out all night, never mind two on the trot.'

Not many people are allowed to criticize my husband to my face, but after fifteen-odd years of best friendship Kim is one of them. What's more, she is well qualified to dispense advice, given that the lucky cow has got one of the happiest, most stable relationships I know of. She and Tim are crazy about each other – have been for six whole years (two of dating, four of marriage). They've only ever spent three nights apart and that was when Tim was strong-armed into attending some ghastly merchant banking conference. Even their bloody names rhyme.

'But then Toby's not exactly your typical husband, is he?' she continues. 'He's an artiste, he needs constant stimulation, adoration, excitement,' she says, tongue firmly in cheek.

Ivy walks past the open door of the lounge, pulling on her coat and mouthing the word 'goodbye' at me. I wave at her departing back. Trustworthy staff are so hard to find and I hit the jackpot with Ivy. She sees nothing, hears nothing. Just clears up the drug paraphernalia without batting an eyelid (I only allow weed in the house and if Toby wants to do something stronger when he's out, well, that's up to him) and she'd commit hara-kiri before she'd read a personal letter I'd left lying on the kitchen counter.

'Yeah, tell me about it . . . fuck it, Kim. I *will* come out with you,' I say with sudden conviction. Well, while the cat's away the mouse ain't gonna sit around moping. 'We're due at Toby's parents' at eight, so even if he turns up now we'd be cutting it fine, and anyway I doubt he'd be in any fit state to spend an evening with mummy and daddy,' I say bitterly. 'Can we go somewhere low-key though, I don't feel up to the West End tonight. How about Pablo's on Liverpool Road?'

Pablo's is a dingy little Mexican bar in Islington where Toby and I sometimes go when he doesn't want to be bothered by fans. It's about halfway between Itchycoo House – our place in Belsize Park (the Small Faces are Toby's biggest musical influence; at least that's what he always tells interviewers) – and Kim's house in Highbury.

'That's cool with me . . . shall we say seven-thirty, first one at the bar gets 'em in?'

'Done.'

I sometimes wonder what I'd do without Kim. We met at drama school. I envied her then and I still envy her now. As a kid, she was a living, breathing Sindy doll, with these amazing white-blonde corkscrew curls and a little snub nose to die for. She always looked so serene and well groomed and everybody wanted to be her friend. I was the oddball in the class, the skinny kid with the straggly blue-black hair and the mad purple leotard (black was the regulation colour, but my mother shunned conformity). For some unfathomable reason Kim gravitated towards me, actively sought out my friendship by inviting me to her house for tea. That was followed by a trip to the ice rink and a fantastic matinee at Sadler's Wells . . . *The Nutcracker* I think it was. I was both bemused by and grateful for her friendship and we've been inseparable ever since.

The great thing about Kim is that she always says

exactly what she means – none of this pussyfooting around, treating me with kid gloves because I just happen to be married to somebody famous. For example, she's never made any secret of her disapproval of Toby. It's not that she doesn't like him – because she does and the three of us have had some great nights out together. It's just that she doesn't think he's husband material and sometimes, depending on my mood, I'm inclined to agree with her.

Of course Kim's not my only friend. I've got an address book as fat as you like, but she's one of the few who honestly have my best interests at heart. It's tough making friends when you're in my position; real friends, I mean. So many people just want to know me because of what I might be able to do for them. One minute I'll be having a perfectly nice time at a party, chatting away with some woman, and suddenly she'll produce her boyfriend's demo tape for me to take home, or ask if I can get her backstage passes at Glastonbury. In the beginning I used to do it just because I hated saying 'no'. Then Toby told me not to be so naive, to learn to put my foot down, and nowadays I'm much choosier about who I socialize with.

I take a deep breath before I pick up the receiver again to call Toby's mum with the bad news. Lucy Carson and I aren't exactly bezzie mates and this last-minute cancellation is hardly going to endear me to her, even though it's not my fault. I can't be bothered to invent a white lie, so I just tell her straight.

'What do you mean you don't know where he is?' she says in that imperious way of hers. She thinks her son married beneath him, that much is obvious. In spite of his rough 'n' ready image, Toby Carson is a nice middle-class boy from the Home Counties, whose GCSE passes run into double figures (except he likes to keep that quiet). I think his mother was hoping he'd marry a supermodel or a high-ranking record company executive; not a nonentity like me. She was fleetingly interested when she heard about my early career as a child actress, but the novelty soon wore off when she realized I hadn't spoken to Bill Forsyth in over a decade.

'I'm sorry I can't be more specific, Lucy,' I say through gritted teeth. 'I assume he's at a friend's house. His mobile's permanently switched off, so I've no way of getting in touch with him.'

'So my rack of lamb's going to go to waste then?'

'Perhaps you could pop it in the freezer. Anyway, I must dash. I'll ask Toby to give you a ring when he rematerializes.'

'Yes, and when he does I'll be sure to give him a piece of my mind.'

No you won't, you daft old bat. You'll be doting and forgiving like you always are, I think to myself as I put down the phone. That boy's been spoiled rotten his whole life. No wonder he expects every woman to dance to his tune. Actually, that's a bit unfair of me – but what the hell. I'm in a cruel frame of mind.

Checking my little gold Tiffany watch – a first

wedding anniversary present from Toby – I realize I've only got half an hour to get ready, so I order a cab on account (our monthly bill regularly runs into four figures, so I'm always guaranteed a car at short notice) and jog up two flights of stairs to our bedroom on the second floor. This is my favourite room and I put a lot of time and energy into decorating it. Toby was all for hiring an interior designer to do the entire house, but I insisted on keeping the master bedroom for myself. After all, it's a very intimate place. I didn't want some jumped-up tosser waltzing in and pressurizing me to pick this *gorgeous* curtain material and that *fabulous* reproduction four-poster. Even though it's a huge great room with a high ceiling and half a dozen sash windows, I wanted to make it as cosy and comfortable as possible; not like those chi-chi hotel-style bedrooms you see in the pages of celebrity magazines with their coordinating pelmet/curtains/bedspreads and gold ceiling fans the size of a helicopter rotor. Yes, I'm very pleased with the finished result, I think to myself as I survey the room: white-lime waxed floorboards, soft lilac walls, swathes of vanilla muslin at the windows and a king-sized sleigh bed made up with crisp white linen sheets and heaped with velvet cushions in shades of purple and cranberry.

Sitting down at my découpage dressing table (one of my favourite Portobello market finds), I stare at the reflection in the mirror. I look tired and my face has a hard, pinched look. Leaning closer, I smooth a hand over my forehead. Despite all the facials and CACI treatments, I'm sure I've got more frown lines than the average 27-year-old. I shouldn't complain . . . for most of my adult life, people have been telling me how pretty I am, although it's something I've always found both embarrassing and mystifying. I suppose I do have my good points: I'm tallish – around five feet nine – and a size ten. I've got olive skin that tans easily and Cherokee cheekbones, as Toby calls them, and shoulder-length hair that's a proper raven colour and dead straight, so I don't have to spend hours with product and hot brush. But there are loads of bad bits too. My upper lip requires regular waxing and I've got knock knees and monstrous size seven feet and no bust to speak of. Toby's offered to pay for implants on more than one occasion, but I don't think I want to go down that route. I couldn't bear being photographed by a paparazzo with these enormous new knockers and having all the papers run those stories . . . *Has she or hasn't she?* when it's bloody obvious that she has. Actually, I try my hardest not to be photographed at all; I can't stand all the fuss, but sometimes it's unavoidable if we're attending an awards ceremony or an after-party. I'd be more than happy to stay at home on these occasions and let Toby go on his own, but when requested I dutifully play the part of consort, smiling and looking pretty and stepping out of the way when the photographers want a picture of Toby by himself . . . oh yes, I know my place all right.

Unbelievably, I've had a few approaches to do solo

interviews and photo shoots – usually those toe-curling 'Me and My Wardrobe' features, where a so-called 'personality' shows off all their designer labels and their mammoth collection of footwear. Some of the requests come through the record label, but others are sent directly to the house – pretty much everyone in the media knows our home address, or at least that's the way it seems. I turn them all down flat. I just can't be bothered with it all. It's like, OK, so I'm married to somebody famous and maybe I do scrub up pretty well, but that still doesn't give me the right to pose across three double-page spreads. And I just couldn't bear to answer all those voyeuristic questions about our sex life and what kind of pants Toby wears. No, I like to keep in the background as much as possible and if you saw me in the street you probably wouldn't even give me a second glance. I'm not a Bianca Jagger; my husband's the celebrity, not me.

Flipping back the lid of my make-up box, I search for my favourite BeneFit foundation stick and some blush. I don't usually wear much slap, just the basics. A touch of charcoal eyeliner, black mascara and nude lipgloss and I'm ready. My Earl jeans and cowboy boots will do, but I swap my grey Gap T-shirt for a soft cardigan in lavender angora. I absolutely love clothes, always have. I get that from my mum. As a kid I spent hours dressing up in her gear, wearing a poncho as a skirt or tying a headscarf round my undeveloped chest like a boob tube. Even so, it took me a while to get used to spending Toby's money when the royalties started rolling in. I remember when we were invited to our first film premiere – some Tom Cruise action-adventure blockbuster as I recall. Having splurged on a fantastic burnt orange Ozwald Boateng suit, Toby tossed a handful of fifties at me (in the early days he had a thing about carrying wads of cash, he said he liked the smell of it) and told me to buy myself something nice. I headed off to Knightsbridge and spent a good hour wandering the streets. I peered through the windows of Gucci, Armani and Versace, but I didn't have the nerve to go in. I found them all so intimidating with their minimalist interiors and impossibly chic assistants hovering by the door, ready to pounce on the next *nouveau riche biche* who set foot inside. In the end I plumped for a little Kookaï number, a pretty floral slip dress that I knew would go with some suede mules I already had at home. Toby went mad when he saw what I was planning to wear.

'It's a celebrity premiere for chrissakes,' he raged at me. 'You can't go in a fucking chain store frock. I do have an image to maintain you know.' He said that last sentence so seriously I had to bite my lip to stop myself laughing. Come to think of it, Toby's ego has grown in direct proportion to his fame. Don't get me wrong: I love my husband 'the man', I just have a few problems with my husband 'the celebrity'.

In the end I gave in. There was no time to buy

another outfit, so I got Kim to rifle through her own impressive wardrobe for something suitable. The backless, thigh-skimming Ben de Lisi number she picked out was just what Toby had in mind and he was delighted when the two of us were splashed across the pages of both the *Sun* and the *Mirror*. Nowadays I'm totally at home in designer shops. The staff at Gucci greet me like an old friend and I get a decent discount at Prada *and* Nicole Farhi.

Half the time I only go shopping to alleviate the boredom. I hate being stuck at home on my own. Thank God for my job. I work two mornings a week as a PA for J.C. Riley. J.C. is an actors' agent. He doesn't have any big-name clients, just a sprinkling of pantomime stalwarts and a couple of minor league soap stars – people whose faces you'd recognize if you watched a lot of daytime TV. My job's not in the least bit glamorous and consists largely of filing, answering the phone and chasing up invoices, but I do enjoy it – it gives me a sense of purpose, a reason for getting up in the morning. Toby doesn't approve. 'We don't need the money,' he says. 'So why not knock the job on the head?' I've tried to explain that I don't do it for the money, but he still doesn't get it. I've already gone from full to part-time at his request, but I'm not giving it up. No way.

Anyhow, I'm going to forget all about my errant husband for one night and lose myself in a frozen margarita or six. Maybe by the time I get back he'll even be at home – *him* waiting for *me*, imagine that. Then again, maybe he won't.

A delicious Ricky Martin lookalike in tight leather pants and a billowing white shirt is leading me in a seductive salsa. Drawing me towards him, he waits till our hip bones connect before pushing me away and spinning me round and round so my full skirt flares out in a bright poppy-coloured arc. A huge crowd has gathered to watch our sexually charged fandango. Some are beating out a rhythmic tattoo with their hands and feet, others are whooping encouragement. Above the loud beating of my heart and the rush of blood in my ears, I hear their handclaps start to build into a great crescendo. But somewhere among our audience is a dissenter, a person who is not clapping or cheering but, rather bizarrely, ringing a hand bell. As its peal starts to rise in pitch and volume, my dancing slows and my movements become clumsy and haphazard. I try to block out the sound, to find my rhythm again, but the ringing continues until it fills my head completely.

Fuck it; there's someone at the door. My eyes flicker open and a glance at the digital alarm clock on the bedside table tells me it's gone ten already. Kim and I really caned it last night. I lost count after the fifth margarita and I have only a faint recollection of the journey home, sprawled out across the back seat of a black cab. No wonder I feel like shit. My head is stuffed with kapok and my mouth tastes like something crawled inside to die. Downstairs the front-door bell continues to toll mercilessly. What on earth possessed us to get one of those ostentatious chimes that sound like a church bell? If whoever it is doesn't take their finger off the button right now, I'm going to have to pick them off with an air rifle. Throwing back the covers, I heave my leaden limbs out of bed and hobble over to the window to see which idiot is responsible for yanking me away from my Latino love god. Peering through the glass, I can just make out the back of a chocolate suede jacket and a tousled head of strawberry blond hair . . . I might have guessed.

Unhooking a cream silk wrap from the back of the bedroom door, I pull it around my naked body and stomp irritatedly down two flights of stairs. Swinging open the heavy oak door, I'm greeted by the sight of my smiling husband, who looks remarkably fresh-faced for someone who's been larging it for two days and nights.

'Hiya, babe,' he says good-humouredly, ignoring my stony expression. 'Sorry if I woke you up, I forgot to take my keys out with me.'

'Where the hell have you been?' I snap, warding off his attempt to hug me by folding my arms in front of my chest.

'At Nick's place. I forgot it was his birthday till Stefan called me on the mobile. A load of us met up at the Met Bar – Pete, Tim, Robbie, the usual suspects . . .'

The north London mafia, I might have known. A motley all-male crew of musicians, *meeja* types and assorted hangers-on, these are the people Toby likes to party with. They're not friends as such, not in the true sense of the word . . . more partners in crime. He only goes out with them every couple of months or so, but when he does they really raise the roof. I know because I've seen the photographic evidence in the pages of the tabloids . . . Toby putting up two fingers to a photographer through the window of a limo, Nick throwing a punch at a lippy doorman. I dread to think what else goes on away from the prying lenses of the paparazzi.

'We ended up at the Red Room for drum 'n' bass night,' he continues, kissing my neck and grazing my cheek with two days' worth of stubble in the process. 'Then Stefan invited us all back to his place for a smoke. I was going to come home the next day, but one thing led to another . . .'

'Oh spare me the excuses,' I say wearily.

'I meant to phone you, but the time just flew by and anyway I knew you wouldn't be interested in joining in. It was all lads and a sackful of Charlie . . . not really your scene.'

'No, Toby, getting off my face with a bunch of dickheads isn't my scene,' I say tightly. 'But I would've appreciated a call to let me know where you were. I tried your mobile countless times but all I got was: *the number you are calling is unavailable, please try again later.*'

'Oh yeah. Sorry, babe, the battery's dead. Don't be

angry with me. I'll make it up to you. Why don't I take you out to dinner tonight, anywhere you like?'

I shake my head. He's bloody naive if he thinks an expensive meal is going to make everything all right.

'Forget it, Toby, I'm not in the mood. I've got a killer hangover and I'm planning to stay in bed at least until tomorrow.'

'What did *you* get up to last night then?'

'I went out for a few drinks with Kim.'

'Get chatted up did you?'

'No, I did not,' I say indignantly.

'I'm surprised, a gorgeous-looking babe like you.' He makes another attempt to hug me and I let him nuzzle my neck while he runs his hands over my bum. 'Have you got anything on underneath that robe?' he whispers in my ear.

'You'd better call your mum,' I say, removing a hand from each buttock. 'She wasn't too pleased you blew her out last night.'

'Fuck it, I forgot about that. What did you tell her?'

'I told her the truth of course – that I hadn't seen you for two days and I didn't have the faintest idea where you were.'

'Shit, Thea, you could've made up an excuse.'

'I'm sick and tired of covering your arse, Toby; it's about time you did your own dirty work.'

I turn my back on him and march back up the stairs to the sanctuary of bed, slamming the door behind me –

a move I instantly regret because it sends a sick wave of pain shooting through my head. Rummaging in the medicine cabinet in the en suite, I manage to locate a pack of paracetamol and wash down a couple of tablets with a tooth mug of tap water. I half expect Toby to appear at the bedroom door with more apologies and promises, but he doesn't. He's probably on the phone to Lucy, begging forgiveness. He might be Mr Macho in front of his mates, but he's still a mummy's boy at heart.

I wonder how much longer I can put up with this ridiculous situation . . . I see more of the cleaner than I do of my husband. When he's not partying, he's ensconced in the studio or tied up with interviews or filming a new video, and pretty soon the band set off on the first leg of their UK tour. Toby did ask me if I wanted to go, but only in a half-hearted sort of way, so I said no thanks. I wouldn't want to be a burden. I seem to come pretty low down on his list of priorities these days. It's not that I mind Toby having a life away from me, I just wish he'd be a little more thoughtful and let me know where he is and what time he's coming home – just those normal courtesies that normal people expect in normal relationships. Except our relationship ceased being normal around the time Drift had their first Top Twenty hit.

I shouldn't admit this, but I can't help wondering what Toby gets up to when we're apart. I mean to say, there's temptation in his way practically twenty-four hours a day. Many's the time we've been at a club or restaurant and some girl's pushed right past me to get to him, and I'm not just talking bimbos, although Toby does get his fair share of those. I'm talking attractive, intelligent, expensively dressed women – some of them are even celebrities themselves, although I'm naming no names. These Drift chicks as I like to call them, sidle up to him – well, more march up to him, actually – and shove their cleavages in his face, whisper in his ear, slip him their phone numbers. He normally smiles at them, concedes two minutes of polite conversation and then disentangles himself, walks up to me and gives me a big kiss on the lips. 'Come on, babe,' he says. 'Let's blow this joint.' You should see their faces. But how does he treat the Drift chicks when he's out with his mates? I haven't got a clue.

Slipping back between the still warm sheets, I close my eyes and try to remember what it was like before Toby became famous. Things were very different then. Better different or worse different, though? That's the big question. Then the bedroom door opens and Toby walks in, wearing a sheepish smile.

'I phoned my mum,' he says, walking over to the bed and perching tentatively on the edge, like he's not sure if he's welcome or not. 'I've told her we'll go round there tonight. Is that OK with you?'

'I suppose it'll have to be,' I reply in a flat voice.

'Don't stay mad at me, babe. I know it was selfish and thoughtless of me to disappear like that and I'm really sorry. Sometimes all this music business shit just gets on top and I need to go off on one. I thought I was going to self-combust last week, trapped in that studio day after day with the same bunch of guys.'

'If it's that bad, perhaps you should think about easing up a bit. Why don't you take a sabbatical? Maybe we could go abroad for three months – Italy or the south of France, say. It's not like we're short of a few dollars. Oh, let's do it, Toby, just you and me. We could get a lovely villa on the coast and leave our mobile phones behind—'

'Nah, it's not that bad,' he says, cutting me short. 'And anyway I can't afford to be off the scene for too long or people will start to forget who Drift are. I'm fine now, honestly, babe. And from now on I'm going to be spending a lot more time at home. I can't have you feeling all lonely and neglected.'

'I just wish we could spend a bit more time together, you know, recapture a bit of the old romance. Do the kind of things we used to – go for long walks and boat rides down the Thames and day trips to Camber Sands.' Eughh, my voice has developed a horrid plaintive edge. I must try not to whine.

'I don't know why you wanna do crap like that when we can afford to go any place we like, babe,' he says dismissively.

''Cos I just do, OK?' I reply.

He stretches across the bed and rests his head on the soft region just above my pelvis. In the light that's streaming through the muslin drapes I can pick out four or five different colours in his hair, the 'lion's mane' as an adoring female interviewer wrote recently. I've lost my appetite for this particular conversation, so I say nothing and start to stroke his head in a rhythmic motion. In a few minutes his eyelids close. My sweet boy looks so vulnerable lying there. All of a sudden I feel a warm rush of love, washing away the anger and the hurt. I shouldn't be so sensitive, letting these little things upset me. I'm very lucky, after all, having such a good-looking, generous husband and this lovely big house and a wardrobe full of designer clothes and complimentary memberships to all the hottest clubs in town. But still I can't help feeling that there's something missing.

TWO

I've been looking forward to today for ages. My friend Suzy – another graduate of the infamous Lucy Jaeger School of Dramatic Arts – is getting married. To a professional footballer, no less. They met in the VIP lounge at Brown's when he was enjoying his first season at Wimbledon and she had found fame (after a fashion) as a *Price Is Right* hostess. She's a sweet girl, Suzy, and great fun, but not exactly overwhelmed in the brains department. Actually, that's a bit unfair. She *does* have brains; it's just that most of the time, for reasons best known to herself, she chooses not to use them. At school, while everyone else was fantasizing about a call-up from the RSC or a lead role in *EastEnders*, Suzy had just one ambition: to marry a rich man. And now that she's bagged Dons striker Michael Moody she is, understandably, over the moon. He's a flash git, with his Aston Martin convertible and his home cinema – it's got remote-controlled red velvet curtains *and* a Mr Slushy machine – but he absolutely adores Suzy, and that's the important thing. And of course she's totally in love with him. At least she will be so long as she never has to suffer the ignominy of Division Two.

Today is doubly special because Toby has magnanimously agreed to escort me to the nuptials. This, I should explain, is something of a coup, given that my husband seems to find it increasingly difficult to interact with mere mortals. He shuns everyday activities like trips to the supermarket, evenings at the pub or, indeed, friends' weddings. When the invitation arrived in the post, Toby said point-blank he wasn't coming. He took one look at the parchment scroll featuring the happy couple's specially designed insignia (consisting of two Wombles – I'd hazard a guess at Orinoco and Madame Cholet – with 'S&M' in italic script underneath) and muttered the words, 'I'd rather go on kids' TV than take part in this freakin' circus.' In an effort to persuade him otherwise, I pointed out that Suzy and Michael were bonafide celebrities and therefore Just Like Him.

'Fucking D-list celebrities,' he said cruelly.

'Yes, well, D-list or not, they're still my friends,' I retorted.

Then I tried a different tactic. 'Kim and Tim are going, so it's not as if you won't know anyone.'

The bored look on his face told me I was going to have to sell it better than that. And so I played my trump card.

'If you don't come, you can forget about me posing for the CD sleeve.'

I had foolishly agreed to be photographed (strictly in silhouette) for the cover of Drift's next album. I don't know why they couldn't just hire a model, but apparently I, as the frontman's wife, would add an extra frisson; a little harmless titillation for Toby's adoring public. Do I mind being prostituted in this way? Not really. Not if it helps the band shift a few more records. Besides which, it's proved to be a useful bargaining tool. More and more, this is the way our married life operates – on a ridiculous and resentment-forming system of bartering. I don't like it, but I suppose it's preferable to leading totally separate lives. Anyhow, this threat did the trick, as I knew it would, and Toby grudgingly said he would grace the wedding with his presence. However, there was one proviso: 'The minute some fucker asks for my autograph, I'm outta there.'

The venue for the wedding is Castleford House, a stately home deep in the heart of Kent commuter land. Toby was all for hiring a chauffeur-driven stretch limo to take us there, but I overruled him, saying that a cab was perfectly adequate. I mean, there's no point in throwing money away. That said, it *is* a bit of a squash with Kim and Tim in the back too and I'm relieved when we finally reach our destination after spending nearly two hours fighting our way out of London.

'This is pretty impressive,' says Tim, as we drive up

a long gravel road towards an imposing grey-stone mansion, built in the style of a castle, complete with battlements and mullioned windows. Blue and yellow pennants flutter atop each of the four corner turrets and, as we draw nearer, I can just about make out Suzy and Michael's Womble crest imprinted on each one.

'How romantic is that?' I say, pointing out the flags through the windscreen. Kim smiles in agreement, while my darling husband makes a loud gagging noise.

'Check out the fucking welcome committee,' says Toby as we pile out of the cab. Beside the castle's portcullis entrance, half a dozen youths sporting matching pageboy wigs and thigh-length blue-and-yellow-for-Wimbledon tunics are playing a bugle fanfare, their cheeks rosy with effort.

'What a bunch of pricks,' sneers Toby as we follow another group of newly arrived guests through the portcullis. I have to bite my lip to stop myself snapping at him. Why is he always so bloody rude about events involving *my* friends? He wouldn't like it if I took the piss out of one of his precious music industry functions.

'Actually, Toby, I rather like them,' says Kim lightly, sensing the tension between us. 'And, anyway, I expect it's all done tongue in cheek.' Toby raises his eyebrows doubtfully by way of reply.

Inside the castle's lofty entrance hall a second reception committee awaits us, in the shape of a pair of beefy security men in dark suits, their thick necks bulging over the tops of their off-white collars.

'Good afternoon, ladies and gents,' says monkey number one. 'Before you join the wedding party we need to check your bags and pockets. It won't take a minute.'

The woman at the front of our group opens her handbag obligingly and offers it up for inspection.

Toby, clearly irritated, shifts from one foot to another and then calls out, 'What's this in aid of, mate?'

I dig him with my elbow, but he ignores the hint. 'I've left my Uzi at home today, promise,' he continues.

A few titters break out, but the security guard remains straight-faced.

'We're acting on the instructions of the bride and groom,' he says coolly, pausing just long enough to let Toby know who's running the show, before adding, 'sir.'

Monkey number two, caressing the antenna of his walkie-talkie in an almost sexual fashion, expands on this explanation. 'Guests are not permitted to take cameras into the ceremony or the reception.'

'Fuck me, and here was I thinking this was a wedding,' says Toby defiantly. He absolutely hates being told what to do. 'It *is* traditional to take photos of the happy couple on their big day – or didn't you know?'

The first security guard smiles placidly, refusing to rise to the bait. 'Yes, sir, but in this instance the *happy couple* have a magazine exclusive to protect, which means that if any unauthorized photographs are leaked to the press the deal's off.'

'Oooh, how exciting!' squeals the woman with the handbag, as she hands over three disposable cameras. 'Is it *Wow!* magazine? Oh, I do hope so, I buy it every week.'

'Yes, madam, I do believe it is.'

Toby turns to me, a scowl spoiling his perfect features. 'Did you know about this?' he says, his eyes burning into me accusingly.

'No, I didn't,' I say, looking across at Kim for confirmation. 'We met Suzy for lunch just last week and she never mentioned any magazine deal, did she Kim?'

'Uh uh,' says Kim, shaking her head. 'But I can't say I'm surprised. Our Suze always did have an eye on the main chance. I wonder what she got for it. Let's see, professional footballer plus game show dolly . . .' she cocks her head, doing the mental arithmetic. 'Gotta be worth ten grand at least.'

'And what if I don't want my photo appearing in some shitty mag?' says Toby.

'Well, they can hardly force you to pose,' Tim points out sensibly. 'I'd just keep out of the photographer's way if I were you. Personally speaking, I can't wait to see my ugly mug beaming out from news-stands across the country. The boys at work will be green with envy.'

Toby releases a derisive snort. 'You'll be lucky, mate.'

'Toby!' I exclaim, incredulous at his lack of tact.

'No offence, Timbo,' he says hastily. 'But I daresay

the people at *Wow!* are only interested in shots of the rich and famous, so I doubt you and Kim will even get a look in.'

'Charming,' mutters Kim under her breath.

I have a feeling this is going to be a long old day.

Once our cameras have been bagged, tagged and stowed away, ready to be reclaimed on our departure, a pair of buxom Page 3 types wearing Wimbledon football strips (even *I* will concede that this is stretching the boundaries of good taste) escort us to the Upper Chamber, where the civil ceremony is due to take place. The wood-beamed room boasts a bizarre and mismatched assortment of decorative items: a suit of armour; a moth-eaten moose head; a couple of wall tapestries; a spinning wheel, complete with dwarf-sized waxwork perched on a stool. To add insult to injury, garish blue and yellow bunting has been strung along the backs of the ornately carved wooden pews in a kind of village fete meets *Antiques Roadshow* effect.

As we take our seats, I notice a few sidelong glances and furtive nudging of neighbours as the guests clock Toby. One young female can barely contain her excitement at the sight of a living, breathing indie rock god and I see her mouth the words, 'He's gorgeous,' to the friend sitting next to her. I have to admit Toby's looking particularly tasty today in his powder-blue corduroy Paul Smith suit, a chunk of blond hair flopping sexily over one eye. Looking around the room, I recognize a few more famous faces: the GMTV weather girl, a former *Blue Peter* presenter and a tight group of shaven-haired geezers all done up like dogs' dinners, who can only be footballers. The groom is sitting in the front row, nervously adjusting his cravat and whispering in the ear of his best man, legendary Wimbledon hardman Ashley Harris (although personally, I've always found it hard to believe that a man called Ashley could be anything other than slightly fey).

Kim points out the *Wow!* photographer, who is standing at the front of the room, next to the registrar's table and anxiously repositioning his tripod, a half-moon of sweat clearly visible under each armpit. 'And I'll bet she's the reporter,' says Kim, gesturing discreetly at a pretty redhead – markedly under-dressed in a simple beige shift dress and flat sandals – in an adjacent pew. 'Check out the notebook on her lap.'

As I crane my neck to see for myself, the girl turns in my direction and our eyes meet. She smiles at me and then looks away. Poor kid, having to cover this tacky old shindig – and on a Saturday too. Wonder if she gets paid overtime. Probably not.

All eyes turn to the front as the registrar and his clerk take their seats behind the table, and suddenly the room is filled with the familiar jangling chords of the *Match of the Day* theme tune. Toby shakes his head despairingly, while Kim and I exchange horrified looks. The groom stands up and I witness the full splendour of his wedding regalia – notably a hideous cream-coloured frock coat, embossed with giant fleur-de-lis. The doors at the back of the Upper Chamber swing open and the bride makes her entrance on the arm of her proud father.

'My God, what *is* she wearing?' whispers Kim.

I'd always thought Suzy had reasonable taste when it came to clothes, but this froufrou creation in flamingo pink tulle makes her look like a fairy godmother – and a very pornographic fairy godmother at that. The dress's back-laced bodice is so tight that Suzy's breasts are spilling over the top in a most unappetizing fashion, while the monstrous diamanté-and-feather headdress does her no favours at all. The two teenaged brides-maids have suffered an even worse fate, however. Their simple strapless satin gowns *would* be quite nice, were it not for the fact that one is canary yellow, the other being only marginally less conspicuous in dazzling royal blue.

The ceremony is brief but unforgettable, thanks to the couple's customized wedding vows (he promises not to interrupt while she's watching *Changing Rooms*, she promises to make his favourite lasagne at least once a fortnight) and the intrusive flash photography from the *Wow!* snapper. As we file out of the Upper Chamber – chivvied along by the two football babes – Toby drapes an arm around my shoulders and plants a kiss on my jaw.

'You know, I think I might enjoy this wedding after all,' he says, his lips pressed close to my ear. 'I haven't laughed so much in ages. I can't wait for the reception. I can see it now . . . tablecloths made of Astroturf and a cake in the shape of a giant football.'

The two of us start sniggering like a couple of kids. 'And we'll all be forced to do a Mexican wave before we're given any food.'

'Stop it,' I tell him, wiping tears of laughter from my eyes. 'People are going to think we're taking the piss.' Which, of course, we are.

The football babes lead us to a second room, where waiters dressed in Friar Tuck-style cassocks are serving champagne. An adjoining room, linked by an open set of double doors, has been converted into a makeshift studio with lights and camera gear and a pair of assistants are busily erecting a backdrop. Suzy and Michael are also there, chatting to the *Wow!* reporter.

'What do you think she's asking them?' asks Kim, arriving at my elbow with two glasses of champagne in her hand. 'Was it love at first sight for you two?' she says in a put-on posh voice.

'Well it was certainly lust,' I say. 'If my memory serves me right, she shagged him in the toilets at Brown's, didn't she?'

'Yeah, that's right,' agrees Kim. 'As soon as our Suzy heard the magic words *professional footballer*, she was like a rat up a drainpipe. And the rest, as they say, is history.'

Three-quarters of an hour later and the happy couple are *still* holed up in the 'studio', posing for endless photographs. At regular intervals the redhead reappears to usher selected guests into the room for various picture combos – the best man and bridesmaids, the bride and groom's parents, the weather girl kissing Michael (she must be an ex-girlfriend), Suzy showing off her garter, surrounded by the drooling footballers. Finally, Toby and I are invited to pose. 'No thanks, love,' Toby tells the girl from *Wow!* 'It's not really my thing.'

Her face falls. 'It'll only take five minutes,' she says. Toby shakes his head firmly. 'Two minutes then? Please. I'll even send you some prints in the post,' she pleads.

'Are you deaf?' Toby hisses. The girl looks shocked and then upset. She'll have some explaining to do when she gets back to the office. Her editor was probably banking on Toby with the happy couple for the centre spread. 'Sorry to have troubled you,' she says in clipped tones before walking away, head bowed.

'Was that really necessary?' I say.

'You've gotta be tough with those journalists or they won't fucking leave you alone,' he says, gulping back the dregs of his third glass of champagne. 'Anyway, when are we gonna eat? I'm starving.'

It's another half an hour before the guests are finally invited to take their seats in the Banqueting Hall, a long narrow room with a vaulted ceiling, which features the ubiquitous blue and yellow bunting draped incongruously over the ceremonial swords and battleaxes that line the walls. The tables are covered with thick cream cloths and scattered with pink rose petals, although the effect is rather spoiled by the novelty football candle in the centre, which nestles on a small square of genuine turf. Toby, Tim, Kim and I are sharing a table with a middle-aged couple who introduce themselves as Suzy's parents' next-door neighbours, Bob and Maggie. Despite being not of the record-buying generation, it's obvious that they know exactly who Toby is. Indeed Maggie is visibly awestruck, clutching the edge of the tablecloth and wearing an inane grin, whilst shooting nervous looks at Toby from under the brim of her enormous hat. Suddenly I have an overwhelming urge to put her straight, to tell her, 'He's only human you know. He burps and shits and farts in his sleep just like the rest of us.' I don't, of course, and it's Tim who puts her at ease, complimenting her on the hat and patiently drawing her out by asking what Suzy was like as a kid. He's such a thoughtful man, I can see exactly why Kim married him. Toby, meanwhile, stares boredly into the middle distance until he discovers that the little drawstring bags adorning each place-setting contain chocolate footballs, whereupon he begins flicking them across the table Subbuteo style, shouting 'Goal!' every time he gets one in between the salt and pepper shakers. It's a blessed relief when the starters arrive and we can all start behaving like adults again – although I have to kick Toby under the table when he starts eating before Bob's own slices of spit-roast pork in Calvados jelly have even arrived.

The rest of the afternoon passes pleasantly enough.

The food is adequate, the wine flows, the speeches are moderately amusing. But for me the biggest laugh of the day comes when coffee and wedding cake (a grotesque blue and yellow six-tiered affair, studded with fondant football boots) are served. Toby is so busy trying to drill a hole in the side of the football candle with the tip of a butter knife that he fails to see the waitress come up behind him with a stack of commemorative paper napkins, each bearing Suzy and Michael's 'S&M' insignia. As she reaches over Toby's shoulder to place a napkin on the table in front of him, he erupts. 'No fucking autographs!' he snarls, flinging the butter knife across the table. Turning round to confront the foolish guest who has had the temerity to approach him, his jaw falls open as he sees the bemused waitress standing there, a pile of napkins in one hand, a plate of sliced wedding cake in the other. Everyone around the table falls about laughing. Even Maggie.

Toby doesn't want to stay for the evening disco, so I call the cab company on my mobile and ask them to come and collect us. Kim and Tim are going to stay to the bitter end and will make their own way home. By this stage Toby is looking a little green around the gills, so when we've said our goodbyes and retrieved our camera, we go outside to wait for the cab and get some fresh air.

'Did I behave like a total arse today?' Toby says, as we settle down on a rickety wooden bench in the castle grounds. He's very pissed and I suspect he's had a few furtive tokes in the gents' because he kept disappearing in between courses and now his eyes are all red-rimmed.

'Well yes, frankly,' I say. 'I do wish you'd make more of an effort with people. You could do a lot worse than take a leaf out of Tim's book. He's been the perfect gentleman all day long.'

'Timbo, himbo, schwimbo,' Toby slurs drunkenly, then gives a big sigh and rests his head on my shoulder. There's no point trying to have a serious conversation when he's in this condition, so I let him drool on my shoulder while I sit there, gazing up at purply sky. As dusk falls, the stillness is spoiled only by the faint strains of speed garage and Toby's soft snores.

THREE

I'm pleased to see signs of life in last week's orange gerbera. A little bit droopy perhaps, but at least they're not dry and crispy like the posy of papery roses adorning the adjacent plot. Mum would never forgive me if I didn't keep her grave bright and cheerful. Kneeling on the freshly cut grass, I scoop up the old bunch of blooms from the metal vase, half buried in the ground, and replace it with this week's offering – big 'n' bold purple gladioli. The florist's on Haverstock Hill always has something different on a Tuesday afternoon when I pay my weekly visit, but they know I'm strict about my colour themes – orange and purple, mum's two favourites. I wish I could have marked her last resting place with something more ornate, something befitting her flamboyant personality – a gargoyle or two, or some gold italic script at the very least. But when my mother lost her battle with breast cancer, this plain lump of cold grey granite with its stark black lettering was the best I could afford. Mum didn't have much to leave me in her will, bless her. Toby's offered to buy a new headstone, but I don't like the thought of disturbing Mum's peace.

In loving memory of Shirley Parkinson: may her light continue to shine. Reading the inscription always brings a lump to my throat. Mum and me were more like best friends than mother and daughter and it's one of my biggest regrets that she didn't live to witness my wedding day. Toby's the only family I've got now; there's an uncle and a couple of cousins in New Zealand, but we've never met and they didn't even bother to come over for the funeral, so as far as I'm concerned they don't count. I hope that one day, in the not too distant future, Toby and I will have children of our own, children who'll have the love of two parents and not just one, like me. Not that I was starved of affection, far from it. My childhood was pretty unconventional, but Mum couldn't have been more loving or supportive.

I grew up in Greenwich, south-east London, where home was a two-bedroom maisonette nestling by the side of the railway line. From the outside our house was fairly shabby, with peeling paintwork and rotten window frames, but inside it resembled a maharaja's palace. Mum, ever the mistress of disguise, filled the place with vibrant clashing colours and a multitude of different fabrics and textures . . . silk cushions studded with little mirrors, embroidered hessian wall hangings to hide the stained woodchip and great flowing voile window dressings in sky blue and lilac. Mum's clothes were equally outrageous. Some days I'd come down to breakfast to find her dressed like a gypsy in black peasant skirt, fringed shawl and massive hoop earrings. Other times she'd go for the flower-power look in hand-embroidered bell-bottom jeans and a tie-dyed cheesecloth shirt. Clothes were her business; she started out as a dressmaker, running up copies of little Chanel suits for middle-class ladies who couldn't afford the real thing. Later on she gave free rein to her creativity and branched out into funkier hippy stuff, selling from a stall at Greenwich market. Over the years she made quite a name for herself and even counted several minor pop stars among her regular clientele. One time we even saw Ray Dorset of Mungo Jerry fame wearing one of her cotton daisy-print blousons on TV.

One of my clearest childhood memories relates to an incident during my second year at primary school. The teacher – a brusque woman with wispy ginger hair and an arse the size of a Sherman – asked us all to bring in a photograph of ourselves, our mummy and daddy and any brothers and sisters, so that we could make a 'family tree'. I listened excitedly as she explained the project, which involved painting a tree on a big sheet of cartridge paper and sticking a family snapshot on each branch. I loved painting and this project sounded like heaven to my six-year-old's ears. There was just one small hitch – and when the teacher asked if anyone had any questions my hand was the first to shoot up.

'I can't bring in a photo of my daddy because I haven't got one, Miss,' I declared boldly.

'I'm sure your mummy can help you find one,' she replied. 'It doesn't have to be a recent picture.'

'No, Miss, what I meant was I haven't got a daddy.'

Two or three of my classmates began to snigger and Miss called for hush.

'Don't be silly, Thea – everyone's got a daddy,' she said dismissively.

Today, of course, single-parent families are commonplace and I'm sure plenty of kids don't have any contact with their fathers, but back then it was a different story. Until that moment I'd never thought it was odd or unusual that I didn't have a dad. It had never even occurred to me that you needed two people to make a baby. I was an only child and as far as I was concerned Mum was the sum total of my family and that was fine by me. But now a seed of doubt had taken root in my mind, and that night I went home and over our cauliflower-cheese tea I broached the question.

'Mum,' I said, 'Miss said that everybody's got a daddy – but I haven't, have I?'

I knew I'd hit a raw nerve by the look on her face – a strange combination of panic and hurt – although, goodness knows, she must've known the question was going to come one day. She recovered quickly, however. Forcing her features into a tight smile, she pulled her chair closer to mine, put an arm around my shoulders and said, 'Well, it's true that you need a woman and a man to make a baby, but *making* a child and being a *father* to that child are two quite different things.'

I was confused, very confused. Mum was saying that somewhere out there I did have a dad, but that he wasn't interested in caring for me – in fact, wasn't interested in me at all. After all, I'd never had a single birthday card, gift token, phone call or indeed any communication from a man calling himself 'Dad'. There were other questions I wanted to ask – like what was this man's name and where did he live – but it didn't seem to be the right moment. I got the distinct impression that digging deeper would only upset Mum and I didn't want that. Giving me a reassuring hug, she put her lips to my ear: 'I chose the name *Thea* because it means "gift of God" and that's exactly what you are,' she said in a low voice, which made the tiny hairs in my ear tingle. I knew that already, it was something she often said, even though she wasn't particularly religious. 'I love you, sweet pea, and I'll always be here for you . . . that's all you need to know.' Then she stacked the dirty dishes on the table and carried them over to the sink. That was the last conversation we had about my father until I was a teenager.

As I begin to tear away the long grass around Mum's headstone which the lawnmower has missed, I think of all the times when I was growing up that I wished I had a dad – like the year the Christmas tree lights went on the blink or when I needed picking up from ballet class on a cold dark night (Mum didn't drive) or when the chain came off my bike for the umpteenth time. More often than not, whoever happened to be Mum's current boyfriend would happily oblige. Some of her relationships lasted a matter of weeks, others ran for years, but none of them ever reached the moving-in stage. Mum never seemed ready for that level of commitment. There *was* one special man, however. And even though he and Mum never lived together, he was the closest thing to a dad I ever had.

Mum moved with a colourful bohemian crowd, who included other fashion designers as well as local musicians and artists. Sometimes they went out in a big gang – to riverside Greenwich pubs or up to Ronnie Scott's in Soho – and I was left at home with a baby-sitter. Other times they all came round to ours and I would be sent to bed early so Mum and her mates could skin up and down a few bottles of Mateus Rosé. Marty was part of that crowd. He was a friend of Val, who ran a leather stall at the market, right next to Mum.

A tall beanpole of a man with a goatee beard and long chestnut hair, tied back in a ponytail, Marty was smitten with my mother. That much was obvious. I was only ten years old when they met, but I saw how he fussed around her, telling her how beautiful she looked, how he was going to be the envy of every other man at whatever pub/club/party they were going to. And he never turned up at our house empty-handed. He always came bearing gifts – a pretty scarf or a bottle of wine for Mum – and sweets for me – fruit gums usually or a sherbet dab.

Marty talked to me like I was his equal and not some irritating little kid he had to be nice to so he could keep her mum sweet, and he always took an active interest in my latest obsession – be it Tony Hadley or making my own ra-ra skirt or my plan to run away and join Hot Gossip. I was gutted when Mum and Marty eventually split up after three years. Mum said the relationship had run its natural course and that, of course, she and Marty would always be friends. And she was right; in fact, Marty was one of the last people she saw before she died. He was a real rock during the funeral, sitting beside me in that cold church with his arm around my waist, and later, as we stood right where I am now, I clung to him for support as I stared down at that flower-strewn mahogany coffin, unable to believe Mum lay inside it.

Anyway, back to happier times . . . Marty was a casting director for TV commercials – an impossibly glamorous job, or so it seemed to me. One day, not long after he and Mum had started seeing each other, he came to our house for tea and said he had something to ask me.

'Now I've already discussed this idea with your mum and she doesn't have a problem with it. However, the final decision is yours and yours alone and I'll understand totally if you don't fancy it.'

I didn't have a clue what Marty was talking about, but I put down my knife and fork so I could give my full attention to whatever it was he was about to say.

'The thing is, Thea,' he continued, 'I'm casting a TV advert for a new breakfast cereal. I've managed to cast the mum and dad, no problem, but I'm having real trouble finding the right girl to play their daughter. I need someone about your age, with dark hair like her screen mum – and the long and short of it is I think you'd fit the bill perfectly.'

I was taken aback, gobsmacked in fact. I'd never harboured any ambitions to be a star. I attended a local ballet class and I liked performing in front of an audience at the Christmas show, but appearing on TV – that was serious stuff.

'It's completely up to you, love,' said Mum. 'Marty says you'll be paid, so maybe you can buy those roller skates you've been hankering after.' That was all the incentive I needed and without a second thought I said, 'Yes please, Uncle Marty.' And that was the beginning of my acting career – simple as that.

Doing the advert was a doddle and required minimal acting ability. All I had to do was take a mouthful of cereal, flash a big toothy smile and utter my one and only line: 'I love my Crunchy Snaps!' The only downside was the endless hanging around in between takes, but Mum was chaperoning me and we passed the time knitting or playing my Frustration Pop-a-matic. When the ad was finally aired on TV, I became Miss Popularity at school almost overnight. It did go to my head at first and I developed a sassy Charlie's Angels swagger and an affected way of tossing my hair over one shoulder. However, Mum soon brought me back down to earth by telling me I wouldn't have any friends at all if I carried on like that.

More ads followed – for Ski yoghurt and Soda-Stream – and Marty, who had become my unofficial agent, arranged for me to have a professional photo card made up with details of my age, height and eye colour. But then I got offered a bite of a much bigger cherry. A TV director approached Marty to ask if I was interested in auditioning for a children's drama series he was making for the BBC, a four-part adaptation of an E. Nesbit tale. Mum was a bit hesitant – I think she was worried about my schoolwork suffering – but I pestered and pestered her until she gave in. The audition was pretty intimidating – at least two dozen other wannabes crowded the studio in west London – and this was only the first day of casting, but I swallowed my nerves and gave the audition my all. Before I knew it I was being called back for a screen test and then, all of a sudden, the role was mine and I was the happiest little girl in south London.

Shooting was confined to the long summer holiday, which met with Mum's approval, and I had a ball on set. I loved everything: the period costumes, the make-up lady, who dusted a fat brush of powder across my nose in between takes; the grip, Phil, who used to shout, 'See-ya Thee-ya' every time he saw me. I was an *act-or* and I was in my element. And when that E. Nesbit drama hit the small screen . . . I was absolutely beside myself. A big article in the *Radio Times* heralded the series and ran mini-interviews with me and my pre-pubescent co-stars – about our favourite food and our hobbies and our ambitions. At school my form teacher organized a question-and-answer session in front of the whole class, so they could ask me how TV shows were made. And on each of those four Sunday teatimes a posse of my friends would come round to our house and Mum would pile floor cushions in front of the box and hand out home-made carob cookies and hot chocolate.

We'd sit in a row, noses inches away from the screen, and for half an hour nobody spoke a single word. After it was over and the credits had rolled (when my name appeared, we all cheered), we'd spend the next few hours dissecting the episode . . . which was our favourite scene, who was the best-looking boy actor, which girl's dress was the prettiest. I really and truly thought I'd found my vocation in life. I didn't waste time thinking about other careers and I certainly didn't give too much thought to the shockingly low number of child actors who went on to enjoy even a modicum of success in adult life. Show business, after all, has a nasty habit of eating its young, but I never saw myself as Bonnie Langford – I was always a doe-eyed Elizabeth

Taylor. I used to spend hours dreaming about how I'd spend my inevitable riches – a new house for Mum, a truckload of Milky Ways for me.

When I was twelve, I won a place at the Lucy Jaeger School of Dramatic Arts in Bethnal Green, which was no mean achievement, although the place wasn't half as well known as it is now. I got a partial scholarship, but Mum still had to tighten her purse strings to pay the remainder of the fees and I think good old Marty may have dipped his hand in his pocket as well. From Mondays to Wednesdays Jaeger's was just like any other school, with conventional subjects like English and geography. Thursdays, Fridays and Saturday mornings were reserved for ballet, tap, drama and singing classes. Rest assured, it was nothing like the kids from *Fame* – forget breaking into spontaneous song in the canteen or high-kicking our way round the playground. Our noses were well and truly to the grindstone, what with having to cram a week's worth of lessons into three days and giving up part of our weekend to boot. But I made some good friends during my four years there, including Kim, of course, and most of us managed to get a few jobs under our belt along the way. I played Tinkerbell two years running at Croydon's Fairfield Halls, did a couple of catalogue shoots and, most excitingly, won a walk-on part in a Bill Forsyth film – although my scene ended up on the cutting-room floor so I never made it to the big screen. Nothing ever rivalled my moment of glory at the Beeb – but, to be absolutely honest, I wasn't that bothered. By the time I left Jaeger's, with a perfectly respectable clutch of GCSEs and a couple of A levels, my enthusiasm for the showbiz life had waned considerably. I didn't think I had the necessary competitive streak to make it in the industry – and I got fed up with being told to smile all the time. I felt duty bound to hawk myself round town for a couple of weeks, trying to find an agent, but my heart so obviously wasn't in it I didn't get a single taker.

By this time Kim was earning good money as a stage director's PA and encouraged by her tales of wild nights at the Limelight Club and her handbag full of Max Factor goodies, I decided to become a working girl too. I took the first job that came my way – working as a telephonist in a car hire firm. It was only ever meant to be a temporary arrangement, something to tide me over until I decided what I really wanted to do with my life. That's where I met Adam. Actually, he was my boss. He wasn't that good-looking and, at thirty-five, he was a good bit older than me, but I was young and easily impressed. Within a month of our first date I'd moved out of Mum's house and into Adam's three-bed semi in Barnet. Mum warned me about making a rash decision, but I thought I knew better. Deep down, I knew me and Adam would never work, but I hung on in there. I enjoyed the security of being in a steady relationship, plus I didn't want to admit defeat and go running back to Mum's. However, six months into the relationship my hand was forced when Adam proposed.

Despite his obvious affection for me, it came as a bolt from the blue. I got the works – nice meal in a posh restaurant, champagne, back home, down on one knee, diamond ring in a little padded box. I almost said yes when I saw the look of expectancy on his face. But I knew I couldn't go through with it. I had to pull the plug. He was heartbroken – and angry too. Angry that I'd been stringing him along, as he put it. I moved out the next day, chucked in my job, and we haven't spoken since.

The stupid thing is, I never really learned my lesson. Other unsuitable relationships with other unsuitable men followed and ended inevitably in cohabitation, followed six to twelve months down the line by tears and bitter recriminations. I was desperate to meet the One, I really was . . . but I always seemed to pick the wrong guy. The trouble was I couldn't bear being on my own, not even for a couple of months. In between these love affairs I'd move back to Mum's – although I'm ashamed to admit that I actually moved out of one bloke's house and straight into the next bloke's on more than one occasion. I pulled my weight by working in a series of dead-end temping jobs, but I always had the safety net of a bloke in the background.

Standing up, I brush the damp grass cuttings from my knees, before taking a step back to admire my handiwork. I sometimes wonder if it's all tied up with my dad – or rather with not knowing who my dad is. And the fact that most of these blokes have been older than me – that's no coincidence. Perhaps subconsciously I'm looking for a father figure, someone to take care of me and treat me like his little princess. Terribly unhealthy, I'm sure. Thankfully, I managed to break out of that self-destructive cycle when I met Toby. *He* certainly isn't a father substitute, no way. In fact, sometimes *I* feel like the surrogate parent; I put a lot of effort into making sure his life runs smoothly – organizing cabs, booking his hair appointments, taking his stuff to the dry cleaner's . . .

I can remember the first time I laid eyes on my future husband like it was yesterday. It was the summer before last, 24 August to be exact. Three weeks earlier I'd split up with my boyfriend, Marcus, who owned a chain of discount mobile-phone shops and was doing very well for himself thank you very much. Our eight-month relationship had been stormy right from the start and one day, fed up with Marcus's endless criticizing, I walked out of his Spanish-style bungalow in the Kent countryside and moved into Kim and Tim's spare bedroom. So that was the state of play on that blazing hot August day when I persuaded Kim, who had launched Party On! the year before, to abandon the Come as Your Favourite Dead Celebrity ball she was arranging for a mob of teenage Trustafarians and join me on a picnic.

Dressed in cut-off denim shorts and bikini tops, Kim and I headed for Highbury Fields, where we found a nice child-free spot to spread out our blanket and unpack our food. We'd just got comfortable when seemingly out of nowhere a Frisbee came skimming across the tops of our heads and right into our M&S spinach and gruyere quiche, splattering eggy gunge everywhere. Needless to say, we weren't best pleased. Seconds later the culprit came jogging over to apologize and retrieve the offending weapon. And after I'd given him an earful with my hands on hips, all stroppy and indignant, I suddenly realized what a gorgeous-looking bloke he was. He was tall and slim with this tousled head of red-blond hair and big greeny eyes, flecked with gold, and he had this great mouth with full red lips that were sooo kissable. Although he was quite scruffily dressed in combats and a Mambo T-shirt, I could see he had a good body with well-developed pecs and strong forearms that showed the beginnings of a tan. He was H-O-T all right.

To cut a long story short, the Frisbee flinger (Toby, of course) and his mates joined our little picnic and later on that night, after an evening's pub crawling along Upper Street, Toby took me home to his rented one-bedroom flat in Finsbury Park. I never went back to Kim's. Right from day one I knew I'd found my soulmate in Toby. For the first time in my life I'd met a man who didn't try to mould me or dominate me or treat me as mere arm candy. He was caring and protective, but respectful at the same time – and I liked that. Within a couple of weeks I'd met all his friends. He wasn't one of those blokes who try and hide you away – they pretend it's because they want to keep you all to themselves, but really it's because they're embarrassed of you or they think you're going to give their mates the eye. Toby didn't give a shit what his friends thought of me . . . I mean he wanted them to like me, but if they didn't – and I'm pretty sure a couple of them weren't too keen – it didn't bother him. He loved me and I loved him and that was all that mattered.

Four months after our first meeting Toby went down on bended knee outside the Forum, where we'd just seen Travis play, and asked me to marry him. We didn't see the point in a long engagement and one month after that we were married at Islington register office. It was a pretty low-key affair with just a handful of our closest friends plus Toby's mum and dad in attendance. Lucy Carson's still smarting from the indignity of it all. 'It's the first register office wedding on *our* side of the family,' she told me at the reception. She couldn't believe it when I told her I *wasn't* pregnant – in her eyes that would've been the only reasonable excuse for such hasty nuptials. Now that we've got a bit of money, she's forever dropping hints about us renewing our vows in some fancy-shmancy church do, all beautifully choreographed for the pages of a glossy mag. No, thank you. *My* mum wouldn't have minded me having a register office do. 'So long as you're happy, Thea love, that's all that matters,' she would've said. Sadly she missed it, having passed away two months before Toby and I met.

For the first six months of our marriage Toby and I

lived hand to mouth, but they were happy times, really happy times. Home was a pokey flat above a kebab shop in Kilburn. Around five-thirty every night they'd spark up the grill and the smell of greasy lamb from that revolving elephant's leg would come wafting up the stairs. It wasn't unusual to find a pool of congealed vomit on the street by our front door in the morning, where some pissed geezer had puked his guts up – whether this was the result of the alcohol or the kebab I couldn't say, but it was enough of a deterrent to ensure I never ate at Dave's Doners myself.

I was the main breadwinner. I'd started temping at J.C. Riley's just before we got married and then, when I'd proved my worth, J.C. took me on full-time. I wasn't earning a fortune, but at least it paid the rent. Toby meanwhile had casual work on a building site – what his mum described as 'a complete waste of an expensive education'. But she didn't understand her son's commit-ment to his music. He always said there was no point in getting a proper job because pretty soon he'd be earning a living doing what he loved best. All this time Drift were quietly building a following for themselves, playing three or four nights a week at gigs and private functions – although their earnings were pretty meagre, split as they were between four band members. The guys had been together for years after meeting at sixth form college. Callum (the nutter) was on drums, Steve (the moody one) played bass and lovely sweet Luke was on rhythm guitar. Toby was the natural front man. He has a unique voice, strong and deep with a slight vibrato edge – 'Tom Jones on acid' as an eminent *NME* critic later wrote. And he has great stage presence too – in fact the first time I saw Drift play I hardly recognized him. Offstage, he's softly spoken and quite thoughtful, but onstage he's all trousers and testosterone.

The turning point came the night that Sonny McGregor, A&R man for Run Records was in the audience at Drift's Camden Embassy gig, where they were bottom of the bill. Ironically Sonny was there to see the headline band. They were so bad he almost left after the third song, but something kept him hanging on to see what the support act was made of. I was there at the side of the stage as usual. Toby and I were still in our clingy can't-bear-to-be-apart phase and we lived as closely as a pair of mittens on a string. Minutes after Drift came offstage, this guy came barging into the dressing room – well, when I say dressing room I mean a boxroom with one cracked mirror and four guys passing round a bottle of Jack Daniel's.

'You were fucking brilliant,' said the intruder, a short stocky geezer with a pierced eyebrow and number two haircut.

'Cheers, mate,' says Toby, wiping the rim of the Jack Daniel's and proffering the bottle.

'No thanks, I don't drink on the job. I'm Sonny. Sonny McGregor, Run Records,' said the man – and I watched as four jaws drop to the floor. The name meant nothing to me, but to these boys Sonny McGregor =

God = TOTP = fame. After a few minutes of chit-chat, during which he established that the band were still unsigned, Sonny handed over his business card and set up a meeting at his plush Soho offices the very next day. When he left the room all of us were jumping up and down, practically wetting ourselves, unable to believe the band had finally got a break – a bloody big break, in fact.

'Just think of it, babe,' Toby whispered to me in bed that night. 'This could change our lives.' He was right . . . by the end of the week Drift had a three-album deal and they were rock stars in waiting.

As I fold the now-redundant gerbera into the gladioli wrapping and carry the package to a nearby wastebasket, my thoughts turn once again to my father. During my teenage years I had tried to extract information from Mum on several occasions, but it was clear she felt uncomfortable talking about it. 'It wasn't a serious relationship,' she told me when I was thirteen and a half, soon after she and Marty had split up. 'Just a fling.'

'So I was an accident?' I asked in a wounded voice.

'Well, no, not really. I desperately wanted a baby, but I'd given up hope of ever finding the right man. I was well into my thirties by the time you were born and at the time that was considered quite old for a first-time mum.'

'So you deliberately used some poor bloke to get you pregnant?'

'Not quite . . . it's a bit more complicated than that. I suppose I threw caution to the winds, let things run their natural course,' she replied vaguely – but I thought I knew what she was saying.

'So did my dad even know you were pregnant?'

'No, I never told him.'

'You never told him . . . don't you think he had a right to know?' I said angrily.

'We'd already split up by the time I realized I was pregnant. I didn't see the point. I had no interest in sharing you, he had no interest in sticking around. I didn't even put his name on your birth certificate.'

'What was he like? Tall or short? Dark or fair? Do you have a photo of him?'

'Oh Thea, darling, it was a long time ago . . . and no, there are no photos.'

'Honestly, Mum, anyone would think you were trying to hide something,' I said aggressively, fed up with what I perceived to be her deliberate unhelpfulness. I think that particular conversation ended up with me storming off to my bedroom to sulk.

A couple of years later the subject came up again when I registered at a family planning clinic and they asked me loads of questions about my family medical history – any cancer, heart conditions, diabetes, and so on. Of course, I didn't know anything about my paternal background and I all but convinced myself I was carrying some hideous hereditary disease that I knew nothing about. I put this to Mum and she told me not to worry, said she was sure I was perfectly fit and healthy. It was at that time she made a rather shocking confession. For the first time, she admitted that even she, who had conceived me and carried me for nine months, wasn't 100 per cent sure who my father was.

Basically Mum was saying that she'd shagged a lot of people – possibly more than one person in a very short space of time. I couldn't help feeling something like disgust when she told me that; this was my mother for goodness sake. But I tried not to be judgemental – after all, back then in the early Seventies it was still free love and all that shit.

'You must be able to narrow it down to a couple of likely lads,' I suggested hopefully.

'Well, two – or maybe three,' she said, a bright crimson flush spreading up her neck. It wasn't very often I saw Mum get embarrassed.

'Three? What are their names?' I demanded. 'Do you know where they live? Maybe I should try and track them down. Perhaps I'll be able to find out which one of them's really my dad.'

'I don't think that would be a good idea at all,' she said quite tearfully. 'They'll have their own lives by now, wives, other children. You might end up getting hurt and I couldn't bear that.' She started crying for real then, big, noisy gulping sobs. So that's where we left it. I put my dad – the one of two, or was it three? – to the back of my mind and set off on my career as a serial monogamist.

FOUR

The last Friday of every month is a significant date in my social diary. It's when I make my one and only token gesture at networking, the day I drag out my most expensive designer daywear and haul my arse over to the Ivy or Momo or Nobu or whatever other joint in town guarantees a bunch of celebrity wives maximum exposure.

If I had to pick one of them, I'd say Patti was my favourite. She's older than the rest of us – maybe forty-eight or forty-nine, no one knows for sure – she 'mislaid' her birth certificate a long time ago. Back in the Seventies, Patti was one of the most infamous rock chicks in London. As a catwalk model with tenuous aristocratic connections, she had access to all the happening clubs and parties. She took full advantage of every opportunity that came her way, bagging a succession of rich musician boyfriends until she finally landed Rich Talbot, bass player for Rough Ryder. The band split up a long time ago, but Rich remains a cult figure among head-bangers and is still greatly in demand as a session musician, or at least that's what Patti's always telling me. They own this amazing eight-bedroom Gothic pile in Surrey's *rockbroker* belt (that bit between Guildford in the north and Horsham in the south) and for a rock 'n' roll couple they are remarkably clean-living. Forget wild all-night parties and chucking drum kits into swimming pools – these two seem to spend most of their spare time playing polo and clay-pigeon shooting with the local green-welly brigade.

The worst thing about Patti is her propensity to dispense unasked-for advice. No matter what dilemma a celebrity wife might find herself in – unsightly tattoo, unreliable domestic staff, genital herpes – Patti has a fast, discreet, no-nonsense solution for everything. It does come in handy once in a while, but it can also be fucking irritating as well. She once turned to me in the ladies' at the Atlantic Bar and announced, 'I can give you a number for a great cosmetic dentist, Thea. You'd be amazed what a difference whiter teeth can make.'

But Patti's got plenty of good points too. I'd say her best quality is the fact that she's totally comfortable with who she is and never tries to pull rank. She has this been there done that don't have anything to prove and if you don't like it you can fuck off attitude that I find rather refreshing.

Unlike Stella. Not content with being a stunning size 8 and a fully trained make-up artist to boot, Stella is constantly battling to go one better than every other woman within a fifty-mile radius. But then she's under a great deal of pressure from her husband – Sky TV newscaster Stephen Morrison (and a latent homosexual if ever I saw one) – to be the most beautiful, organized, popular trophy wife in town.

'Is that collagen?' she asked the first time we met, looking at my mouth and touching her own Chanel-slicked lips with one perfectly French-manicured hand.

'Er no, they're all my own.' I replied.

'Oh,' she said, sounding disappointed. 'I was going to ask you which clinic you used. I'll ask Patti, she'll be able to recommend someone.'

And that set the pattern for the rest of our friendship, such as it is. Every time we meet she'll comment on some facet of my appearance – not because she wants to pay me a compliment, but because she wants to have the information which will help her go one better. I'm sure it's just insecurity, but if you didn't know any better it would come across as pure vanity.

Stella's best friend and the third member of our monthly lunch club is Angela. Angela is . . . how can I put this politely? Fuck it . . . she's a cokehead, there's no nice way of saying it. She'll pay at least two visits to the khazi during the course of a single lunch and come back with cold symptoms. She's in the throes of a bitter divorce battle, so I guess she needs a little help getting through it. Her ex is Titus Collier, star of veterinary daytime soap *Pet ER*. They split up shortly after she caught him doing something unspeakable with one of his canine extras . . . you'll forgive me if I don't elaborate. Angela used to be a receptionist at LWT, but she hasn't done an honest day's work in the past three years, and she's not planning to change her routine now. I think she's hoping to live off the proceeds of her divorce settlement, which is perfectly plausible given that she's threatening to go to the press with the story of her marriage break-up if Titus doesn't cough up.

I met this motley trio at last year's Showbiz Woman of the Year luncheon at the Dorchester, where we found ourselves sharing a table. It's not the sort of event I would normally grace in a million years, but I was at a bit of a loose end that day. I think Toby had done one of his disappearing acts and I was stuck at home with Ivy, who was singing an out-of-key version of 'Total Eclipse of the Heart' as she dusted Toby's collection of toby jugs (his parents give him one for every birthday and Christmas. I've always considered it a spectacularly tasteless tradition). Faced with these two options, lunch with a bunch of bored, rich, well-connected women seemed the lesser evil.

As soon as I took my seat in the Dorchester ballroom, I knew I'd made the wrong choice. Glancing at my dining companions, I realized that my cherry velvet trouser suit wasn't nearly glam enough – and there's nothing worse than feeling under-dressed. What's more, everyone else seemed to know each other. Two of the women on my table were so engrossed in conversation

with their mate at the next table that they didn't even
bother to acknowledge me. The other three diners –
Patti, Stella and Angela – were at least polite enough to
introduce themselves, however. After a few minutes of
polite chit-chat about the chilly weather and the lovely
table arrangements, during which time all three women
managed to let slip their husbands' names, one of them
– I think it was Angela – asked me what I did. This was
my opportunity to declare smugly, 'I'm the wife of a
pop star don't you know?' Drift weren't as big as they
are now of course, but their debut album had just
entered the charts at number eleven, so they were definitely coming up to the boil. However, not wanting to
seem pushy, I said that I was a PA in an actors' agency.
Well, that just about killed the conversation. I might as
well have said I worked in an abattoir. Having established that I was nobody remotely worth bothering with,
the three women formed a huddle at their side of the
table and got down to some serious bitching among
themselves.

'Have you *seen* the size of Kiki Benson's chest?' I
heard Stella exclaim to the others, nodding towards the
prominent wife of a prominent talk-show host. 'I swear
to God those bazookas get bigger every time I see her.
She'll topple over if she has any more work done.'

'Quite, darling. And you'd think that husband of
hers would at least pay for a decent surgeon. Anyone
can see her left tit's bigger than the right,' added Patti
spitefully.

Staring fixedly at the corn-fed chicken breast on a bed of baby spinach that the waiter had just laid before me, I plotted my escape. Looking around, I located the nearest exit, which was on the other side of the vast ballroom. I decided I would bolt down my main course, then excuse myself from the table, saying I was going to powder my nose, and do a runner. The afternoon wouldn't have been a complete waste of time, I comforted myself . . . it would be a good story to tell Kim. She loved it when I ripped the piss out of the showbiz set.

I had just put my knife and fork in the six o'clock position, dabbed at my mouth with the linen napkin, and was feeling around my ankles for my handbag when Stella stretched across the table and asked me if I had a light. 'Sure,' I said. Retrieving my bag, I plonked it on the table and began to rummage for the Cartier lighter Toby gave me last Christmas (I don't smoke myself, but it's always nice to be prepared). As I pulled out the lighter, a plastic wallet containing Drift's latest promo CD, which Toby had given to me a couple of days before, slithered onto the table. It was the band's new single, due to be sent out to the music press for review at the end of the week.

'Oooh, Drift, they're my absolute fave band right now,' squealed Stella, pouncing on the disc hungrily. 'What I wouldn't give for a night of passion with that lead singer. He'd be an absolute animal in bed. You can tell just by looking at a man's eyebrows, you know. His are thick and arched, which is an absolute guarantee of a Grade A shag.'

I know that Toby has this effect on women, so I wasn't embarrassed; in fact I found it rather amusing, so I just smiled, flicked the little button on the Cartier and held it to the end of Stella's baby cigar.

'Hang about,' she said, exhaling a cloud of thick stinky smoke right in my face. 'This is the new single, it isn't released for weeks. How the hell did you get your mitts on it?' she said accusingly.

Even then I wasn't going to admit the marital connection. I was poised to make my getaway and didn't plan on being waylaid. I started to say that a friend of mine worked for Run Records, when Stella practically shouted at me, 'Oh, my fucking God! You're her, aren't you?'

I stared back mutely, not knowing whether or not the cat was out of the bag. Patti and Angela stopped bitching and stared at their friend questioningly.

'I knew your face was familiar,' Stella declared. 'You were in *Heat* magazine last week ... they had a photograph of the two of you at the MOBOs.'

'I'm sorry, we appear to have missed something,' said Patti. 'Perhaps you could bring us up to speed, Stella.'

'It's only his bloody wife!' said Stella.

'*Whose* wife?' said Angela.

'Toby Carson's wife, you idiot. *Thea* Carson, the woman who went and snared the best-looking bloke in pop.'

At that precise moment the entire atmosphere changed and there was absolutely no way I was going to get away from the Dorchester until the bitter end. After firing a seemingly endless stream of questions at me (Where did I live/eat/shop? Who was my aroma-therapist? Did Steven Woodham or Jane Packer do my floral displays?), the three women proceeded to drag me round the room, showing me off to all their mates like I was a new handbag.

'You really should have told us you were Toby Carson's wife,' said Patti as coyly as she could manage, as we returned to our seats for the prize-giving cere-mony. 'We always look after our own, you know.'

I wasn't entirely sure what she meant, but by the end of the afternoon I had a pretty good idea, having been overwhelmed with invitations to fundraisers, char-ity polo matches, ashtanga yoga classes and more besides. I managed to wriggle out of most of them, but I did agree to meet Patti, Stella and Angela for lunch the following Friday. I figured I owed them that much after they'd lavished so much attention on me.

Somewhere along the way our lunch date became a regular thing – which is why all these months later I find myself in a cab, en route to this week's rendezvous. Sometimes hard work and frequently bitchy, these lunches are always highly entertaining. They're my chance to see how the bona fide celebrity wife really lives and catch up on all the latest gossip. But I don't count myself as one of them, not really. And what do *they* get out of it? Well, it gives them a certain cachet I suppose ... improves their collective cool quotient being on kissy-kissy terms with the wife of an indie rock god.

Walking into the restaurant, I spot the girls right away. They're the noisiest, brashest bunch, yapping away at one of the best tables in the house – not the very best, you understand (we are only the wives, after all).

'Thea darling, wherever have you been? We'd almost given up on you,' says Patti, standing up to deliver an air kiss that won't muss her hair.

'Yeah, sorry I'm late, my cab got stuck in traffic,' I say, moving round the table to greet Stella and Angela in turn.

'That's a fab dress,' says Stella, catching my arm. 'Last season's Betsey Johnson isn't it?'

'How clever of you to recognize it,' I say through gritted teeth.

Angela pours me a glass of Krug as I take my place at the table.

'Cheers everyone,' I say raising my glass and taking a big swig of the ice-cold champagne. 'Mmmm, that tastes fab. So what have you all been up to since I last saw you?'

'Well, the big news is Angela's going into rehab,' announces Stella, swishing her mane of golden hair over one shoulder and practically taking my eye out in the process.

'Yeah, but I'm trying to keep it quiet,' says Angela in a low voice. 'I don't want the *News of the World* on my doorstep, trying to steal a shot of my ravaged septum.'

'It looks all right to me,' I say, squinting at Angela's nostrils.

'I was joking, there's nothing wrong with my nose. I'm not *that* much of a junkie, thank you very much,' she says tartly.

'Well, I think it's great you've decided to get some help,' I say. 'Which clinic are you going to?'

'The Anderson Center in California. It's costing an arm and a leg, but I've heard their shiatsu therapist is the best on the west coast, and anyway Titus is footing the bill, so who cares?'

'Well, good luck, Angela – and don't forget to send us a postcard.'

'I only wish I could, darling . . . Contact with the outside world is absolutely forbidden at the Anderson. I don't know how I'm going to cope without my mobile. Just the thought of being shut up in that place for three weeks sends shivers up my spine. In fact, if you ladies will excuse me, I'll just go and powder my nose. If the waiter comes to take our order, I'll have the Caesar salad – hold the anchovies and the Parmesan. Oh, and I'd better not have any dressing either, it's far too fattening,' she says, patting her stomach, which is totally flat, if not concave. Stuffing her Fendi bag under her arm, she whooshes off to snort a line of Charlie off the top of the toilet cistern. Patti, sitting opposite me, shakes her head in despair, but she doesn't say anything in front of Stella, who is fiercely protective of her best friend and won't tolerate criticism of any kind.

We give the waiter our order – three salads and ridiculously over-priced sausage and mash for me, plus another bottle of Krug for good measure.

'Do you know what you're wearing to the Brits yet?' Stella asks me as she lights up a Consulate, ignoring the fact that we're in the restaurant's no-smoking area. 'Drift are nominated in two categories, so you'd better be looking good for the cameras, girl. You don't want to let down that delicious husband of yours.'

'Actually, I think I'll give it a miss this year. Those awards ceremonies always bore me rigid. And I'm sure Toby will have a much better time without me hanging on his arm. He'll be able to get off his face with his mates, do the wild man of rock 'n' roll bit and get plenty of press coverage into the bargain.'

'I don't understand you at all, Thea. If I was married to a pop star I'd be out every night of the week. You wouldn't catch me sitting at home knitting or whatever it is you do. Why don't you let your hair down, make the most of life on the A-list while you still can? It's a wonder you and Toby ever got together – him so extrovert, you so, so . . . well, you like a quieter life don't you?' says Stella, with a vague attempt at tact.

'Well, I think Thea's got exactly the right attitude,' says Patti, springing to my defence. 'It's best to give these musicians a long rein. I should know – I've been married to one for the past twenty-odd years.' (Note the lack of specifics . . . it's so we can't make an educated guess at her age.)

'It's no good acting clingy,' she continues. 'It just cramps their style and leads to resentment. I've always let Rich do his own thing – and I found my own interests too. I joined the polo club, launched a writing career . . .'

I should mention here that Patti has her own letters page in one of the upper-crust women's glossies – a question and answer thing about etiquette and entertaining. It's amazing the kind of inane questions people send in: 'Should the salt cruet be passed to the left or the right?' 'Is it acceptable to eat asparagus with one's fingers?' You'd think people would have more important things to worry about. I'm often tempted to send in an anonymous letter of my own, just to see if they'd publish it. 'If I accidentally break wind at the dinner table, should I apologize or blame it on the dog?'

'Yeah, but what good is a famous husband if you can't reap the benefits?' says Stella, flicking cigarette ash onto her side plate. 'You get to give up work, spend all day shopping, hang out at all those great after-parties . . . not that Stephen gets invited to many of those. Newsreading's hardly showbiz is it?'

'So I suppose love doesn't come into it at all?' I ask her.

'What the hell's love got to do with it?' she giggles. 'Stephen and I have the perfect arrangement. I take care of his diary and play consort when he needs me and in return I get a comfortable house and a generous clothing allowance. Don't get me wrong . . . I'm very fond of the man, but I'm not *in love* with him.'

Angela, returning from the ladies', catches the tail end of the conversation. 'And best of all Stella gets to shag around as much as she likes,' she says with a knowing look at her friend.

'Yeah, but I'm very discreet. I wouldn't dream of causing Stephen any embarrassment. He knows I'd never shit on my own doorstep.'

'You mean Stephen knows you've been unfaithful?' I ask, somewhat taken aback by Stella's admission. I knew she was a flirt – and, like I say, I've always suspected Stephen bats for the other side – but I didn't have her down as a wanton adulterer.

'Sure he does. And he's cool about it. We don't even sleep in the same bedroom at home. Now if I was married to a hot piece of ass like Toby, I wouldn't let him out of my sight.'

I suppose I should feel flattered that my husband's considered such a catch, but something about Stella's way of talking makes me feel uncomfortable.

'I don't know how you can live like that. What if

you meet someone else and fall in love with them? You'd leave Stephen then, wouldn't you?'

'That would depend on the new bloke's salary!' she says, giving a great dirty laugh.

The waiter arrives with our food. He removes Stella's soiled side plate without a word. He's not going to jeopardize a hefty tip for the sake of a No Smoking sign.

'*You're* not in a marriage of convenience, are you?' I ask Patti when he's gone. 'I've seen the way you and Rich act around each other and I'd say you were definitely in love.'

'Yes I am. But it's not the hot, throbbing passion you probably feel for Toby. After all these years together we've slipped into a comfortable relationship – it's rather like going home and easing on an old pair of slippers.'

Bloody hell – is that what I've got to look forward to, I think to myself. Over my dead body. Toby may be unreliable, selfish and thoughtless at times, but he's crazy about me, I know he is. I feel the same way about him and I'm gonna work damn hard to make sure it stays that way.

'Sorry to be such a misery, but I've come to the inescapable conclusion that true love rarely, if ever, lasts,' says Angela, spearing a leaf of iceberg with her fork. 'Take me and Titus. I thought I'd found the man of my dreams, I really did. He was everything I'd ever wanted – kind, intelligent, good in bed, rich . . . And then after three years of blissful wedded life he goes and lets me down in the worst way imaginable. But don't worry, I'm going to get my own back. Boy, is he ever gonna wish he made me sign a pre-nup.' The three of them share a conspiratorial laugh. But I can't see the funny side. In my opinion, there's nothing remotely humorous about the end of a marriage.

By the time we get to dessert (Italian chocolate mousse for me, passion fruit sorbet for the others) the conversation has turned to Patti's children. Daisy, her eldest, has become something of a handful since she left boarding school and returned to live at home. Patti had hoped her daughter would go to university – or at least enrol on a nice Lucie Clayton course – but Daisy had other plans. She's spent the last six months doing fuck all, sleeping all day and partying with the polo set by night. By all accounts, she'll shag anything in a pair of jodhpurs and Patti is terrified that before too long some pretty youth with well-muscled thighs is going to impregnate her eighteen-year-old daughter and bring disgrace on the family.

'I'm at my wits' end,' she tells us. 'Rich doesn't seem to see anything wrong in her behaviour, just so long as she uses condoms, but I don't want my daughter getting a bad reputation. Actually, I think it's a bit late for that. According to my gardener, Daisy is known in the village as the *chukka fucker*. Charming isn't it? And when the nice man from *Country Life* came to do the *at home* shoot, she insisted on being photographed in the most inappropriate outfit – a shocking pink dress with a waist-high split and a neckline that was practically cut to the navel. I don't care if it *was* Julien MacDonald, she still looked like a cheap slut. You three should thank your lucky stars you don't have children ... you wouldn't believe how many sleepless nights I've had to endure.'

'Well, the chances of Stephen and I reproducing are practically non-existent,' says Stella. 'And I can't say I'm too upset. Think of all the money we'll save not having to fork out on nannies, designer trainers, school fees, not to mention a flash car for their eighteenth. No, it wouldn't bother me if I never had children. You've always wanted a couple of brats though haven't you, Angie?'

'I absolutely adore babies,' gushes Angela, who has perked up considerably since her trip to the ladies'. 'And I think I've got an awful lot of love to give. Remember Mr Baggins, my pet Yorkie? I spent a fortune on him – diamanté collars, custom-made Aran sweaters, fresh turkey suppers ... that dog wanted for nothing. I was devastated when he was crushed to death by the electronic garage door. I can't believe Titus was so careless.' Or maybe Titus was worried Mr Baggins would talk, I think unkindly.

'Not having kids with Titus is one of the biggest regrets of my life,' she continues. 'Just think of the child support I could wring out of him.'

'What about you, Thea?' asks Patti. 'I bet you and Toby are planning a family, aren't you?'

'Not just yet,' I say, embarrassed. The truth is, I can't wait to be a mum, but Toby doesn't share my enthusiasm for parenthood, not yet anyway. He says he wants to live a bit before he gets tied down. I want at least three children and given that I'm twenty-seven already and I'd like a two-year gap between them, I'd say we need to get cracking pretty soon.

'We'll probably start trying next year,' I say optimistically.

'You'll be a great mum; you won't mind staying at home in the least, will you? It's not as if you've got a career or anything,' says Stella, smiling patronizingly.

'Let's get the bill shall we?' I say, feeling my jaw constrict. We nearly always have coffee and liqueurs, but I may have to resort to physical violence if I don't get out of here in the next ten minutes.

FIVE

It's absolute bloody bedlam in here. On one side of the hangar-like arena half a dozen effing and blinding workmen are struggling to erect a series of flimsy bamboo beach huts. Each one will house a Photo-Me booth, so guests will be able to capture the spirit of the evening. On the opposite side of the room, a skinny girl in voluminous orange maharishi pants grapples with a six-foot inflatable shark. I watch as she mounts a tall stepladder and attempts to attach the pneumatic monster to a fine wire suspended from a rafter. Just behind her, on a raised stage area, two spotty youths standing ankle deep in fine yellow sand are in the throes of creating a splendid faux beach with a couple of garden rakes. Close by, a pile of wooden recliners and a great heap of brightly coloured plastic buckets and spades wait to be distributed.

In the midst of all the mayhem stands Kim, looking utterly unruffled and effortlessly chic in a well-cut black sheath dress, a garland of tropical flowers dangling from one hand, a crackling walkie-talkie in the other.

'Thea!' she yells out as soon as she spots me.

I negotiate my way around the various soldier ants until we finally make contact under a full-sized artificial coconut palm.

'Fuck me, you've certainly got your work cut out today,' I say, giving her a peck on the cheek.

'It looks worse than it is,' she says with a grimace. 'Believe me, everything's under control . . . it wants to be, I've spent the best part of two months planning this event – watch it, Tony! That tank cost an arm and a leg,' she shouts as a man pushing a trolley laden with a mammoth perspex fish tank almost collides with a pile of scaffolding poles heaped carelessly on the floor.

This, darlings, is showbiz. At least it will be when Kim's carefully orchestrated party plan falls perfectly into place in approximately three hours' time. The venue is a former tobacco warehouse in Docklands, the occasion is the eighteenth birthday of pop diva Amba Lazenby. All the best celebrity shindigs have a theme and this one is no exception. In a nod to Amba's half-Fijian heritage the warehouse is being transformed into a South Sea island paradise, thanks to a £20,000 contribution from her record company. And all the greats will be turning out to play tribute to Britain's pop princess – three-fifths of Westlife, two Rolling Stones' daughters, the cast of *Hollyoaks* . . .

Toby was a bit miffed when I told him I was going

to be helping Kim today. Normally he wouldn't care less. It's just that, in this instance, he happens to be an invited guest and doesn't like the thought of his wife being one of the hired hands. I mollified him last night with a mega blow job and a pledge to stop working the instant the party kicks off; so now everything is sweet. Actually, I'm rather looking forward to tonight. It's ages since we partied together and Toby has promised that none of his druggie friends will be in tow.

Kim wants me to meet, greet and brief the posse of waiters and waitresses, who will be plying the two hundred or so guests with a selection of drinks and canapés, all gratis of course. When I work Kim's parties, this is one of my regular jobs, so I know the spiel off by heart: 'No drinking or smoking on the job, no accepting of tips, no slipping off to the broom cupboard for a quickie with one of the guests, and above all, smile, smile, smile.' Kim has a kazillion things to do, so she hastily fills me in on costumes and cocktails before whooshing off to see a man about an aquarium.

The waiting staff are due any minute so I make my way to the makeshift dressing room to sort through the mound of costumes heaped on the wooden floor. The men are going to be transformed into Fifties' surfer dudes, with Brylcreem quiffs and hipster swimming trunks, while the women will become grass-skirted, bikini-topped hula girls. Plastic flip-flops and garish garlands of plastic flowers will add the finishing touches.

With half an hour to go before the party starts, all the staff are dressed and genned up on the various cocktails – sea breezes, banana daiquiris and the custom-made South Sea sling, a potent mix of tequila, pineapple juice and lime, served with a raspberry lipstick rim.

There's just time to change into my own party gear – a velvet-trimmed Voyage dress and Gina sandals – and freshen up my make-up before the first guests start to arrive. Toby never ever arrives at a party until it's in full swing, so I don't expect to see him for another couple of hours at least. I just hope he's in a dancing mood. It's ages since I tore up the dance floor. Who am I trying to kid? Toby doesn't 'do' dancing, at least not in public. Still, maybe if I get him drunk first . . .

'Thanks for all your help, hon. This one's been a real toughie,' says Kim as we enjoy a well-earned glass of champagne at the bar just before the party kicks off.

'Well, it looks awesome. And when people see the photos, you're going to get loads more commissions – what magazine did you say was coming tonight?'

'*Night & Day* – they're doing "An Insider's Guide to Party Planning". Amba's press officer is thrilled – the piece is running the week of the album release, so the timing couldn't be better as far as they're concerned. I did a phone interview with a journalist last week and their photographer should be here any minute. Actually I'd better just ask the door staff to let me know the instant he arrives. Will you be all right here on your own?'

'Course I will. I've propped up plenty of bars in my time. I'll catch up with you later.'

I hoist myself onto a wicker bar stool and settle down to a spot of people watching. It's only early, but the place is half-full already and judging by the amazed looks on guests' faces, they're well impressed with the exotic decor. Before long the party girl herself wafts past, accompanied by her man of the moment, Ministry of Sound DJ Milo Moston. According to Kim, it's not a genuine love affair, but a carefully planned PR stunt – the idea being that Milo will give Amba kudos on the club scene, while she will help ease *him* into the mainstream. As the pair make their way across the dance floor, I can't help noticing that Amba, dressed in an unforgiving silver catsuit, looks a bit wobbly on her feet. I know it's her birthday, but surely she can't be drunk already. Come to think of it, I'm sure I remember reading that she was teetotal – *and* a virgin too. Bollocks to that.

I'm so busy watching her unsteady progress that I don't notice a certain tall, black-haired pop star take the bar stool next to mine until I feel a light tap on my shoulder. I turn round to see him sitting there with a big grin on his face and two South Sea slings in his hand.

'I thought you could use a drink,' he says, offering me one of the tall glasses.

'Well, hello there, Stan,' I say, accepting the drink. 'I didn't expect to see you here. I had no idea you and Amba were friends.'

'We're not. The record company invited me. And you know me . . . I'll go anywhere for a free drink – they don't call me Lord Ligger for nothing. How 'bout you? Don't tell me Toby's let you come on your own.'

'Absolutely not. He'll be putting in an appearance later,' I say, like Toby and I never go anywhere without each other (hah!). 'I've been here all afternoon, helping my friend Kim. She organized this whole event . . . pretty impressive wouldn't you say?'

'Yeah, not bad. That beach is cool and I really dig those hula chicks,' he says, leering at a passing waitress.

Stan plays drums in a band called Tanner. They're big on the festival circuit and they've had a couple of Top Forty singles, but they're not massive like Drift. Last year Stan and Toby almost came to blows at Glastonbury – something to do with Tanner's set running over I think. They squared up to each other backstage and a couple of roadies had to break it up. I don't know if Stan was serious – he *has* got a bit of a reputation as a trouble-maker – but it was mere posturing on Toby's part, he wouldn't hurt a fly. Some geezer from one of the tabloids with an Access All Areas was loitering nearby and he was obviously desperate for material for his gossip column because he made it his lead story the next day. He jazzed it up a bit, though – made out the pair were kicking the shit out of each other, when in actual fact not a single punch was thrown. Toby didn't really mind – as he's always telling me, all publicity is good publicity. And besides which –

to use another cliché – it's all tomorrow's fish-and-chip paper.

I came face to face with Stan myself a couple of months ago at a party in a private members' club in Mayfair. I'd got talking to this Amazonian blonde in the queue for the ladies' and she turned out to be Stan's girlfriend Sonia. By the time we'd powdered our noses and returned to the party, our other halves had disappeared, so we got ourselves a couple of drinks and spent a good hour chatting away in the chill-out room. Sonia had me in stitches with the story of her Brazilian bikini wax nightmare. She'd gone to some hot new Californian beauty therapist, who told her to take off her 'pants' and then turned her back while she prepared her hot wax concoction. Sonia did think the request a little strange, but nevertheless dutifully eased off her CK jeans and removed her G-string before making herself comfy on the couch. Only then did it occur to her that, in American-speak, 'pants' actually means 'trousers'.

By this time the therapist was coming back over and Sonia decided the best way to cover her embarrassment was to brazen it out and make like taking off one's knicks pre-wax was the most natural thing in the world. The therapist gave her a barely concealed look of disgust before pulling a paper tissue from a box and handing it to her. Poor Sonia then spent the entire session with the hanky cupped over her private parts.

We were both pissing ourselves laughing when Stan eventually materialized. He didn't bat an eyelid when

Sonia told him I was Toby's wife – although he was obviously drunk or stoned or something, so maybe the name just didn't register. After five minutes or so, I made my excuses and went off to track down Toby, who I eventually found smoking a spliff in the DJ booth. He wasn't best pleased when I told him whose acquaintance I'd just made. 'He's an ignorant little shit,' he snapped. 'You should keep away from him.' He can be so childish sometimes.

'Is Sonia with you tonight?' I ask Stan now.

'Nah, I came with Alan from the band, 'cept he spotted some Page 3 bird he once shagged and I think he fancies a rematch, so I left 'em to it. Then I saw you sitting here at the bar on your lonesome and decided to come and keep you company.'

'Well, that's very sweet of you. Next time I see Sonia I'll be sure to tell her what a gentleman you've been.'

'She won't give a monkey's . . . she dumped me a coupla weeks ago.'

'Oh, I'm sorry to hear that. She seemed like a really nice girl.'

'She was. She just got fed up with always coming having to come second to the band.'

'I know the feeling,' I mutter.

Stan turns out to be rather good company – which is just as well because there's still no sign of Toby. Despite his media image as a mouthy little git, Stan is really an OK guy when you get him on his own. Like a lot of bad-boy pop stars, he plays to his audience. Deprive him of that and he's Mr Normal. Much to my delight, he even proposes a turn on the dance floor and we spend a sweaty half-hour shaking booty. Later on we're downing more South Sea slings, while he fills me in on his new loft apartment in Shoreditch when we're rudely interrupted by a bright white flash which goes off practically in our faces. I spin round in time to see some photographer looking very pleased with himself. Then he spots the beefy security guard bearing down on him and tries to do a runner. A second guard closes in, with Kim close behind.

'Get back out on the street, matey boy,' Kim tells the shutterbug. '*Night & Day* have got the exclusive tonight. You stick to arrivals.'

'I'm so sorry, people,' she says to the group of us who are clustered round the bar as the disgruntled snapper is manhandled towards the door. 'The door staff are supposed to check everyone for cameras, but this character obviously slipped through the net.'

I flash her a sympathetic smile. Poor Kim. She won't be able to relax until the very last guest has departed.

'D'you know if Toby's arrived yet?' I ask her.

'Not as far as I know. What time did he say he'd be here?'

'Before twelve – and it's already half past.'

'Why don't you give him a ring on his mobile? Here, use my phone if you like,' she says, producing a silver Nokia.

'Thanks, but I won't bother. I don't want him to think I'm on his case.'

'I'm sure he'll be here soon,' she says, giving my arm a little squeeze. 'Anyway, I gotta dash. There's been some sort of incident in the ladies' – no doubt someone's chucked up everywhere.'

'Who was *that*?' asks Stan, who has been standing silent and slack-jawed throughout my brief conversation with Kim.

'Don't even think about it,' I warn him. 'She's married.'

'So what? I'm sure she'd like to get jiggy with Stan the Man,' he says, grabbing his crotch Michael Jackson-style.

'You know, not every woman finds you irresistible,' I say witheringly.

'Yeah, but most do,' he laughs.

Five minutes pass and then all hell breaks loose. Kim comes running past us, shouting, 'Is there a doctor in the house?'

'Hey, what's wrong? Can I help?' I say, catching her arm as she passes us.

'It's Amba . . . she's collapsed.'

The music's so loud I don't think most people have even heard Kim's request for help – certainly, no one seems to be responding.

'I'm a trained first-aider, maybe I can help,' says Stan.

'Great. The paramedics are on their way, but perhaps

you can put her in the recovery position or something. Follow me.'

As we jog across the room behind Kim, I ask Stan doubtfully, 'Do you really know first aid or are you just trying to get into my friend's knickers?'

'Both,' he replies, flashing me a mischievous smile.

Outside the ladies' a security man is redirecting full-bladdered female guests to the men's facilities next door. 'One of the toilets has flooded,' he tells them. Inside, Milo Moston is gazing in the mirror above the hand basins and squeezing a blackhead on the side of his nose, seemingly unconcerned by his pseudo-girlfriend's collapse. A dishevelled-looking Amba is sitting on the tiled floor, her back resting against a cubicle door. Above her right eyebrow a blue-tinged lump the size of a quail's egg is throbbing nastily. Kneeling next to her is a petite Asian woman I recognize from earlier in the day as Amba's publicist, Suki Tang. Last time I saw her she was kicking up a fuss because Kim hadn't set aside a VIP area. I can't see the point frankly – why throw a birthday party, invite all your mates and then spend the night closeted behind the proverbial velvet rope with a load of famous people you barely know?

'Who the hell are these people?' Suki snaps, giving Kim a filthy look.

'Stan's a first-aider and Thea is my assistant,' Kim replies. 'Don't worry, they're both utterly discreet.' She shoots us a warning glance and on cue we both nod emphatically.

'They damn well better be. I don't expect to see this little incident recounted blow by blow in the tabloids.'

'We oughta get some ice on that head,' says Stan, crouching down and gently fingering the ugly swelling. Amba winces in pain. 'Sorry, sweetheart, didn't mean to hurt you. Do you feel dizzy at all?'

She shakes her head.

'Any blurred vision?'

'No, I'll be fine.'

'What happened?'

'I was coming out of the toilet and I just, er, lost my balance. As I fell I must have hit my head on something. I blacked out for a second or two, but I'm all right now.'

A highly unconvincing explanation – particularly when the evidence in the cubicle points in another direction.

'Luckily I was with her,' pipes up Milo.

'Really?' says Kim, shooting him a quizzical look. 'This is a *ladies'* toilet, you know.'

'Right, yeah . . . anyway, if I'm not needed I think I'll get back to the party.'

'No you fucking well won't,' snaps Suki, glaring at him. 'I want a word with you – in private.'

'I didn't *make* her take it,' he retaliates – and then, under his breath, 'It *is* supposed to be her birthday.'

'Shut up, you idiot!' Suki shrieks.

'Please, can you not shout? My head is killing me,' says Amba, attempting to stand up.

'Take it easy now,' warns Stan. 'I think you should stay right where you are until the paramedics have checked you over.'

'I don't think there's any need for that now,' says Suki. 'She's obviously going to be OK.'

'I think we should let them take a look at her, just to be on the safe side,' says Kim.

'She's fine,' barks Suki. 'Now I'd be grateful if you'd head them off. The last thing we want is men in green jumpsuits wandering across the dance floor, ruining the party and causing tongues to wag.'

Kim purses her lips, like she's deciding whether it's worth her while to contradict one of the best-known pop publicists in town. She obviously thinks better of it because she calls security on her walkie-talkie and instructs them to cancel the 999 call, or if it's too late for that, meet them at reception and apologize profusely. 'I suggest you take Amba to the staff dressing room – it won't be needed until the end of the night and I can post a couple of security guys outside. If anyone asks, we can just say Amba's just had a little too much to drink.'

'But Amba doesn't drink,' squeals Suki. 'Not officially, anyway.'

'I dunno why you made me say that in the first place,' complains Amba. 'Nobody believes it anyway.'

'Britney doesn't drink,' says Suki primly. 'And it hasn't done *her* career any harm. We'll say you're suffering from a recurring kidney infection.'

'Kidney infection – do we have to?' groans Amba. 'Why don't you just go for maximum embarrassment and tell everyone I've got the shits?'

'You ungrateful little madam. After all I've done for you . . .'

'Now then, ladies. I think we'd better get a move on,' says Kim. 'We need to get these toilets back in operation.'

Stan and Suki help Amba to her feet and walk her slowly towards the door. Kim lags behind to scoop up the tell-tale paper wrap lying on top of the toilet cistern.

Everyone files out, the rest of us forming a tight-knit group around Amba on Suki's instructions, to make her less conspicuous. Once star and publicist are safely deposited in the dressing room, Kim thanks us for our assistance and heads off to check the whereabouts of the *Night & Day* photographer, just to make sure he's safely out of harm's way. Glancing at my watch, I see that it's already two a.m. The party finishes in half an hour. There's no way Toby will turn up now. You know what I can't understand? Every time Toby lets me down like this, I'm disappointed. He does it time and time again and yet I'm always surprised. Stupid, isn't it? I should toughen up, try not to take it to heart, he is a famous rock star after all, with lots of demands on his time. But then again I *am* his wife.

'Tell me something, Stan,' I say.

'What's that then?'

'Did you love Sonia?'

'Fuck. That's a bit of a heavy one. I'll have to think about that . . . as much as I've ever loved any woman I suppose. We had some good times, some bloody good times,' he says.

'So when she said she was leaving you, how did you feel?'

'Pretty cut up actually. I kind of knew it was coming. She was always going on about the band and how much time it took up. And the fact that I went out so much – without her.'

'Did you try and persuade her to stay?'

'Nah.'

'You didn't offer to give up some of your boys' nights out?'

'Nah. Why would I wanna do that?'

'You don't consider the love of a good woman to be a big priority in your life?'

'I suppose so, but not the main priority. It's band, booze, birds – in that order.'

Yeah, that's what I thought.

SIX

I've spent most of the night – well, the early hours of the morning anyway – riding the porcelain pony. I can't remember the last time I puked so violently. I didn't even drink that much last night because I wanted to be reasonably sober when Toby arrived. But the bastard didn't turn up. In fact, he still hasn't turned up, although right now I'm feeling far too fragile to dwell on the possible reasons for his absence. I wonder how Amba's feeling this morning – worse than me probably.

By the time Ivy arrives I've managed to drag myself out of bed and onto the squashy velvet sofa downstairs, so I can watch *Trisha* from a semi-prone position. I must be looking rough as arseholes, dressed as I am in a fleecy dressing gown and a pair of Toby's woolly socks, because instead of saying a quick 'Hello, dear' before she gets the Hoover out, Ivy stops in front of the TV, cocks her head to one side and gives me a long hard look.

'Your face is all funny and grey,' she says, frowning. 'Are you poorly?'

'I've just got a bit of a dicky tummy,' I say with a grimace. 'I went to a party last night and I think I OD'd on cocktails. Or maybe I ate a dodgy canapé – I doubt it, though, seeing as it was one of Kim's dos and her caterers are always scrupulous about hygiene.'

'Why don't you take yourself off to bed, then? I can leave the Hoovering till later so as not to disturb you.'

'It's not that bad, really, Ivy . . . a nice long soak in the bath will sort me out,' I say, dragging myself up from the sofa, eyes still glued to the TV screen, where Trisha is trying to prevent two feuding sisters from punching each other's lights out. 'Do you mind keeping an ear out for the phone?'

'No, dear. Are you expecting someone in particular?'

'Not really. Can you take a message – unless it's Toby, in which case give me a shout. He's gone missing in action for the millionth time.'

She doesn't pass comment, but raises her eyebrows in a gesture of sympathy before setting off to Mr Sheen the dining-room table.

Upstairs in the master bathroom I strip off and run a warm bath, adding a few drops of clary sage aromatherapy oil, which promises to 'soothe, relax and uplift' – exactly what I need right now. I float in the scented water for half an hour or so with my eyes closed and gradually my stomach pain recedes. I'm pickling nicely when my reverie is rudely shattered by the thud of heavy footsteps on the stairs outside. Seconds later the bathroom door bursts open and in walks Toby with a face like thunder.

'Oh, the mighty wanderer returns,' I say sarcastically, staring up at him.

'You've got some explaining to do,' he snarls, his voice trembling with emotion.

'Likewise,' I retort. 'I hope you had one helluva good time last night because you missed a brilliant party.'

'Oh I know *you* had a good time,' he says bitterly and thrusts a copy of the *Sun* in front of me.

It's the lead photograph on the 'Bizarre' column. A full-colour shot that takes up almost half the page. It's me and I'm wearing my Voyage dress and I'm leaning towards some guy and talking into his ear and there's a kind of half-smile on my face. Oh, and the guy's hand is resting on the small of my back. His face is in profile – and it takes a couple of seconds before I realize that it's Stan. The headline reads: 'Hands off, Stan – that's Toby's missus!' I don't bother to read the two paragraphs of copy underneath. I think I get the gist.

'What the hell were you playing at?' demands Toby, flinging the newspaper into the bath and splashing me in the face in the process.

'Oh, for God's sake, grow up,' I say coldly, standing up and reaching for a big white bath towel from the pile on the shelf. 'You know how the tabloids love to twist things. It's quite simple: I was at the party, I bumped into Stan, we got talking, end of story. And if you'd been there like you were supposed to be, I probably wouldn't have been talking to him at all.'

'How do I know you're telling the truth?' he says petulantly.

'If there was anything going on between us, we'd hardly do it in full view of half the record industry, now would we?' The idiot knows full well I wouldn't cheat on him. He just hates to be cuckolded in public; it's not good for his image.

'S'pose not,' he concedes reluctantly. 'But you would have to go and be photographed with him of all people, wouldn't you? Now I'm gonna be a laughing stock.'

'Don't be ridiculous. Anyone who knows us will take the story for what it is – a meaningless piece of fluff,' I say, placing the flat of my foot on the soggy paper and pushing it to the bottom of the bath as I climb out.

'But what about the fans?' he whines.

'What *about* the fans? The story will probably just increase your popularity – the public loves a good pop rivalry.'

He makes a grunting noise, then turns his back on me and makes to go out to the bedroom.

'Er, excuse me, Mister Big Stuff, but this discussion isn't over yet,' I say sharply.

'Isn't it?' he says, turning back to me.

'You still haven't told me where you got to last night. You swore you'd come to the party and I was really looking forward to a night out together.'

'Yeah, well I had every intention of coming, but I said I'd meet Callum at Black's for a few pre-party drinks. Then we bumped into a couple of session musicians we worked with on the first album, really nice geezers, and we got talking and I kind of lost track of the time. By the time I looked at my watch it was nearly one o'clock and I figured the party would practically be over by the time I got there.'

How highly unimaginative. I wish I had a Tiffany necklace for every time I've heard that excuse – I'd be able to open my own jewellery shop by now. And that's exactly what it is: an excuse. Nobody's that bad at timekeeping. If he really wanted to come to that party, he would've booked a taxi to pick him up from Black's . . . which leads me to the inescapable conclusion that my husband would rather spend time with his friends than me. He's not content with a romantic meal for two or a quiet drink in a local bar, not any more. It's almost as if I'm not stimulating enough for him. These days he has to be surrounded by people, copious amounts of alcohol and no doubt assorted pharmaceuticals too, in order to have a really good time. He's hardly ever at home and when he is he mooches around the place like a bored teenager, not quite knowing what to do with himself . . . fiddling with his Play Station, flicking through the satellite channels, picking up a men's style magazine and putting it back down again five minutes later.

'So why didn't you just come home? Where have you been all night?' I continue my cross-examination, biting my lip in a bid to stop the tears from coming. I'm not usually this emotional – I must be pre-menstrual.

'After Black's we all went back to Callum's to carry on drinking. I thought about coming home then, but I didn't want to be the first one to bail out. I guess I must have passed out. I woke up at ten in the morning on his living-room floor.'

Same old, same old. Pushing past him, I walk through to the bedroom to dry myself. Toby remains standing at the entrance to the bathroom, hands in his pockets. He hasn't even got the decency to apologize. He may as well be saying, 'This is the way I am: like it or lump it.'

Tossing the towel on the bed, I open the chest of drawers and rummage for a pair of knickers. 'If I ask you a question, will you answer it truthfully?' I say, fishing out a pair of silky La Perlas and then rejecting them in favour of a sensible cotton G.

'Course I will, babe. Fire away.'

'Do you think I'm boring?'

He hesitates for a second.

'What the hell kind of question is that to ask your husband?' he says.

'Just answer it,' I say, suddenly weary of all his procrastinating. 'Do you think I'm boring? Yes or no?'

'No, of course not. I wouldn't have married you if I didn't think we could have fun together.'

'But you never include me in your plans. It's almost as if you're embarrassed by me or something.'

'Don't be silly, babe. You're a stunning, intelligent woman. How could I be embarrassed by you?'

'Well, I do wonder that I'm not rock 'n' roll enough for you these days – that you'd prefer it if I was a bit more Marianne Faithfull.'

'I dunno about Marianne Faithfull . . . in her heyday she'd probably have drunk me under the table, but I would appreciate it if you made a bit more effort.'

'And what exactly do you mean by *effort*?'

'Well, you never want to come to awards ceremonies for starters – or launches, or premieres, come to think of it.'

'That's because they're full of pretentious twats who are busy licking each others' arses. I hate the idea of being on show, dangling off your arm like some stupid Barbie doll. Why can't we just do normal things like go to the pub or have dinner parties?'

'Dinner parties?' Toby sniggers. 'You'll be suggesting bridge evenings next.'

That just about does it. I'm sick of being Mrs Put Up and Shut Up, it's time I stood up for myself.

'You obviously don't give a damn about this marriage because if you did you'd be taking me a bit more seriously,' I scream at him in a sudden fit of temper. 'I'm telling you, Toby, if things don't start improving between us, I'm packing my bags. You've changed. I hardly recognize you any more.'

'I don't need this shit,' he says, walking towards the door. 'Call me on the mobile when you've calmed down.'

Grabbing a pillow from the bed, I hurl it at him, but Toby's already out the door and, even if he wasn't, the pillow is totally off target. Collapsing into self-pitying sobs I fling myself on the bed in true drama queen fashion. A few seconds later I hear the loud slam of the front door. What a fucking marvellous day this is turning out to be. I wish I'd stayed in bed.

When I get up the next morning, the first thing I do is vomit. Profusely. That's the alcohol-poisoning theory out the window, then. I must have a touch of gastric flu. The second thing I do is check the house for signs of Toby. He might have come home in the dead of night and crashed out in one of the other bedrooms or even downstairs on the sofa. He's nowhere to be seen however. I shouldn't be surprised; I haven't spoken to him since he walked out yesterday. I didn't bother calling his mobile because: *a*) I found his suggestion that I call him when I'd 'calmed down' incredibly patronizing and *b*) his phone probably would have been switched off anyway – or the battery would've been flat, or some other mysterious technical problem would have conspired to prevent me making contact with him.

Ivy's not coming today because she's visiting her sister in Romford, so I've got the place to myself. It's

not one of my work days and I'm bored already, so
I run through a list of possible activities: shopping
expedition (feeling too delicate), trip to the nail bar
(life's too short), meet Patti or one of the other wives
for lunch (liable to induce further nausea). In the end I
decide to embark on a tedious, but thoroughly necessary
task I've been putting off for ages: a grand clear-out of
the built-in wardrobe in the smallest bedroom. It's
absolutely chock-a-block with junk, all the stuff I can't
bear to throw away, but haven't yet found a proper
home for. Ivy has offered to tackle the job on more than
one occasion, but I don't want to take the piss – she's a
cleaner, not a dogsbody, and anyway she wouldn't
know what to keep and what to chuck.

Dressed in a T-shirt and an old pair of jogging
bottoms, I arm myself with a roll of black bin bags and
get straight down to business. 'Did I really wear these?'
I say out loud in disbelief as I unearth a pair of rhine-
stone-studded palazzo pants. They may be Versace, but
they're fucking tasteless; still, they'll do for the charity
shop. Ditto a pair of white knee-high patent leather
boots and a purple polka-dot pussy-bow blouse. I am,
however, very pleased to rediscover my once-treasured
record collection, which Toby refused to allow to 'disgrace' our mammoth music library downstairs. There
are a few dodgy albums I concede as I flick through
them, but nothing in the Black Lace league. I think Toby
was probably just pissed off that I owned a copy of
Tanner's first CD.

By midday I've made excellent progress. My ruthlessness has paid off and I've managed to fill five bin bags – three for the dustbin men, two for Oxfam – and I've also made a pile of things I want to keep and have vowed to find a permanent home for. I'll finish off sorting through the two unexplored cardboard boxes that remain in the wardrobe and then I'll have a spot of lunch, something bland and warming, like lentil soup.

The first box proves rather disappointing, containing as it does manky old Christmas decorations that haven't been used in years. Quite why I decided to hold on to this collection of broken baubles and moulting tinsel, I have no idea. I kick it towards the rubbish pile disdainfully. The second box, however, yields something far more precious.

The week after Mum died I held a kind of open day at her house in Greenwich and invited all her friends to come and choose whatever bits and pieces they wanted. I think she would've liked that – the idea of each of them having something to remember her by. I was living with Marcus the mobile-phone entrepreneur at the time, whose home was equipped with every conceivable luxury (brand-new Aga, cappuccino maker, electric floor polisher), so you see I really had no use for Mum's well-worn furniture and jazzy soft furnishings. I did retrieve a few personal keepsakes, however – some photo albums and a few pieces of costume jewellery. I also rescued her old diaries. I don't really know why – they weren't of any practical use to me, but they seemed too intimate to throw away. As soon as Toby and I moved into this place, I found new homes for the photo albums and the jewellery, but I just shoved the diaries in a box, along with some dusty old paperbacks, and chucked the whole lot in the wardrobe.

Reaching into the box, I pull out the black leatherette diaries, which are bound together with an old hair scrunchy. I'd forgotten how many there were, they must go back years. Mum could never bear to throw anything away and I know they were useful when it came to working out her tax returns. I've never really looked at them; I suppose I was frightened they'd bring back too many memories. Peeling off the top volume, I flick through the pages, which are filled with day-to-day appointments as well as random thoughts and jottings – directions to places, books she wanted to buy, shopping lists even. She was a bit scatty, my mum, and she wrote down everything as a kind of aide-mémoire. Tears prick the back of my eyes as I notice a series of pencil sketches, designs for a dapper little waistcoat she was doubtless planning to make and sell on her market stall.

I miss her so much. I still think about her every day, every hour sometimes, especially on days like this when I've rowed with Toby. She'd tell me to stop feeling sorry for myself and tackle the problem head-on, pin Toby down and force him to discuss things. She never took any shit from her men, that's for sure. And she always stayed independent, she never allowed herself to be dominated by any guy. Not like me. I need to be in a relationship, it gives me strength, makes me feel more confident. Mind you, Toby spends so much time away from home I might as well be on my own.

By the time I've had something to eat and dragged the rubbish sacks out to the wheelie bin at the side of the house and Hoovered the carpet at the bottom of the wardrobe, it's still only two o'clock. I give Kim a call, just to gossip really, but she can always tell when I'm at a loose end and invites me round, despite the fact that she's just started work on a big society wedding that *Tatler* is supposed to be covering.

'Don't mention the T-word,' I tell her the minute I walk in the door.

'Don't tell me . . . that photo in yesterday's *Sun*?'

'You've got it in one. That stupid picture sparked off a massive row and he stormed out.'

'Oh, come here,' says Kim, hooking an arm around my waist and pulling me towards her. 'You two'll make it up, you always do.'

'Thing is, I don't know if I want to this time,' I say into her shoulder.

'Oh, come on, you can't mean that,' she says disbelievingly.

'I just feel like we're leading completely separate lives these days,' I say, drawing away from her. 'I was really hurt when he didn't turn up to Amba's party the other night. I tried to discuss it with him and he just gave me a whole bunch of excuses, just like he always does. Every time he lets me down like that, it kind of eats away at my love. I'm scared that one day there won't be any left. I dunno what to do, I just feel really confused . . . maybe I'm coming down with something. I've been really sick the last couple of days.'

'What do you mean? Vomit-sick or poorly-sick?'

'I puked my guts up this morning – and yesterday. Come to think of it, I haven't felt a hundred per cent for the past couple of weeks; not ill exactly, just odd.'

'You don't think you might be pregnant, do you?'

I laugh out loud. 'Definitely not,' I say with absolute assurance. 'My boobs certainly haven't grown; mind you, that would be a bloody miracle. And my period's not late . . . at least, I don't think it is.' I mentally count back the days. 'Well, now I come to think of it, maybe a week or so late. Christ, Kim, I can't be – can I?'

'There's only one way to find out.'

Kim kindly offers to procure the necessaries. It's a sensible precaution – you'd be surprised how much a person could earn for tipping off one of the tabloids regarding the purchase of a Clear Blue by a pop star's wife. On her return, I disappear into her downstairs loo with the white plastic wand. I don't really think I can be pregnant, even though my methods of contraception are a bit ad hoc.

The deed done, I pop the cap on the Clear Blue, wash my hands and walk into the lounge, where Kim is pacing up and down in front of the big bay window. She's even more nervous than I am. 'This is sooo exciting,' she says, as we sit together on the sofa, knee to knee, staring at the wand, which has ceremonially been placed on the glass coffee table atop a stack of *Elle Decos*. Well, prepare to be disappointed, I think to myself.

'Ohmigod, it's turning!' she squeals after about a minute.

'No it's not,' I say squinting at the see-through plastic window.

'It is, it is – look!' she says, squeezing my forearm so hard I yelp in pain.

Fuck me. She's right. A blue line. A definitely positive no-room-for-doubt blue. I open my mouth like a stranded fish. No sound comes out. Kim looks at me. Bloody hell, her eyes are glistening with tears.

'I'm pregnant, Kim,' I say in a Stepford wife monotone. Then I lose it completely.

'Aaaarghhhhh!' I scream, jumping up from the sofa.

'Yipp-eeeee!' I start doing a silly jumping from side to side dance on Kim's parquet floor.

'Ha ha! Toby's put a bun in my oven!'

Kim jumps up, wraps her arms around me and right on cue I burst into tears.

SEVEN

I take a deep breath and give it to him straight. 'I'm sorry, Alex, but you weren't what they were looking for this time.' Alexander Gaffney releases a tirade of abuse into my right earhole. Thankfully, it is not directed at me, but at the Yorkshire TV casting director who doesn't think Alex can cut the mustard as a 'brilliant but troubled young neurosurgeon, haunted by the untimely death of his wife in a suspicious drowning incident'.

'That part was made for me,' Alex fumes. 'I've got the looks, the maturity, the emotional range. What more do they want, for chrissakes? Nobody in TV appreciates my talent. I may as well go and hang myself.'

Tucking the phone receiver firmly under my chin, I begin to construct a necklace from the pile of coloured paperclips in my desk tidy. For the next seven and a half minutes I remain silent, save for the occasional, 'Uh huh,' or 'Poor you,' while Alex gets it all off his chest.

Being a good listener and having the patience of a saint are just two of the many qualities you need to be a PA for an actors' agent. The task of telling a client that he's failed an audition would usually fall to my boss, J.C. Riley, but J.C. is out of the office all morning on appointments and so the unenviable task has fallen to me.

I might have known Alex would take it badly. These former soap actors are always the worst. One sniff of fame and they think they've got it made. Alex was convinced he'd hit the big time when he landed the role of Darren the mechanic in the daytime drama *Relative Values* (although it has to be said the part didn't require an awful lot of acting ability, just the capacity to look good in a pair of overalls). Ten months and one *TV Quick* award nomination later, Alex decided he was destined for bigger and better things and – much against J.C.'s advice – he quit the soap and announced his intention to become, quote unquote, 'the new Robson Green'. That was nearly a year ago and Alex hasn't worked in television since – not unless you count a one-off guest presenting spot on *Wish You Were Here*. He's still smarting from the fact that they only sent him as far as Tintagel.

After assuring Alex that I will dedicate the rest of the morning to investigating fresh audition possibilities on his behalf (only a small white lie), I finally get rid of him. Normally, I like chatting to clients – even suicidal ones – but today I have more important things on my mind.

I hardly slept a wink all night. I kept stroking my belly and thinking about the unformed creature who's taken root inside me. I feel like I'm going to burst with excitement, I can't wait to tell the world I'm pregnant, but obviously not until I've delivered the news to Toby. I haven't seen him since he walked out after our row two days ago. I tried his mobile several times last night – and again this morning – but as usual it was switched off, so I had to content myself with leaving a message. I know he'll materialize eventually and actually I'm glad of a little breathing space, a chance to work out the best way to break the news. You see, I'm not entirely sure how he's going to take it. He'll be stunned, I should think. Stunned, but pleased. Stunned, pleased and maybe a little apprehensive. Parenthood is a big responsibility, after all, and Toby's used to doing his own thing. I'm not sure how easily he'll adapt to the arrival of a tiny dependent.

I try to visualize my husband with a baby in his arms, a pink sweet-smelling bundle wrapped in a soft blanket. That image comes to mind readily enough; in fact it's quite heartbreaking. Okaaay . . . now, can I see him pushing a pram along Camden Parkway? That one's more difficult. It's the pram that's the problem. How about a baby carrier? Nah, too effeminate. Right, let's try something totally different. It's the middle of the night and the baby's crying because its nappy needs changing. Squeezing my eyes tight shut, I try to imagine Toby jumping out of bed, scooping up the squalling infant, removing its soiled nappy and gently wiping its shitty arse. Hmmm, it's just not happening; instead, my mind is filled with a vision of Toby turning over and pretending to be asleep. I'm probably being unfair; I'm sure he'll be a great dad.

His mum is going to be overjoyed when she hears I'm expecting. Lucy Carson may be a witch of a mother-in-law but she's an ace grandmother; she spoils Toby's sister's kids rotten and she's always lamenting the fact that they're growing up so fast. I wish my mum had lived to meet her grandchildren. It fills me with sadness to know that my baby will only have the love of one set of grandparents. Of course, there probably is another grandfather out there somewhere. I wonder how he'd react if I turned up on his doorstep one day. Totally unannounced, just bowled up and said, 'Hi, Dad. It's me; your long-lost daughter.' Of course that's not likely to happen. After all, I don't know who my dad is, so I don't know why I'm even bothering to fantasize about him. Mum was the only one who could've helped me find him and she's not here any more.

The phone trills into life, interrupting my melancholy train of thought.

'Good morning, J.C. Riley,' I say in my chirrupy PA's voice. It's only Kim, wanting to know if I've spoken to Toby since we did the pregnancy test.

'I haven't been able to get hold of him,' I explain. 'He's probably still pissed off with me after our argument.'

'God, that man certainly knows how to pick his moments,' says Kim reproachfully. 'Here's you gagging to tell him he's about to become a dad and he's sulking in a corner somewhere.'

'Oh, he'll turn up sooner or later,' I say with exaggerated nonchalance. 'Although, when I break the news, he's going to be so shocked he'll probably turn around and walk straight back out of the house.'

Kim thinks I'm joking. She laughs. 'Seriously, though,' she says, 'you're not worried about how he's going to take it, are you? Toby wants kids as much as you – right?'

'Well, yes. At least he's always given me that impression.'

'There you are, then. So what if this has come sooner than you both expected? Toby will be over the moon, trust me.'

'Yeah, course he will,' I say with rather more conviction than I feel. 'But I can't help feeling worried about the division of responsibilities. Toby spends so much time away from home, I can just see myself bringing up this child single-handedly.'

'But he'll adjust his lifestyle accordingly,' says Kim. 'He's going to have to. I mean once the baby's born he won't be able to disappear for days at a time or go off on tour at the drop of a hat.'

'But I wouldn't want the baby to . . . you know – cramp his style.'

'Darling, having a baby will only serve to *enhance* Toby's godlike status,' says Kim, putting on her *Ab Fab* voice. 'These days, fatherhood is practically de rigueur for any self-respecting rock star of a certain age.'

At this juncture, the *call waiting* light on my phone begins to flash, forcing me to cut Kim off after having promised to brief her on Toby's reaction to the pregnancy, as and when I get it.

'Good morning, J.C. Riley.'

'Hi, babycakes, it's only me, Danny Boy. Just wondered if you fancied an early lunch. A liquid lunch that is. I'm having the shopping trip from hell and I could murder a Malibu and Coke. I can't *belieeeve* that no one in London stocks purple reinforced-gusset pantyhose in XXL.'

Just what I needed, a bit of light relief. Danny Newman (stage name: Lady Dee) is absolutely and positively my favourite of all J.C.'s clients. He's a 6ft 4in drag queen, or *performance artiste* as J.C. prefers to describe him, and the sweetest, funniest man I know. Danny's bread-and-butter money comes from his twice-weekly cabaret at Zsa Zsa's, a Soho nightclub staffed entirely by transvestites. The show is fantastic; I've been three times – once with Toby and twice with Kim. But Danny is clearly destined for bigger and better things and, since signing up with J.C. last year, he's had a nonspeaking role in a Brit flick, plus a couple of pop videos and a TV ad for sanitary towels (don't ask me to explain – it was all terribly surreal).

'Sorry, Danny, no can do. J.C.'s out on appointments and I can't desert my post till he comes back.'

'Never mind, babycakes, another time. Are you going to the Mulberry accessories launch on Friday?'

'Ugh,' I say, shuddering. 'I wouldn't go if my life depended on it. All those ghastly jabbering women practically climaxing over a fucking Filofax cover.'

'Yes, but think of all that free champagne,' coos Danny. 'And I hear the goodie bags are going to be to die for.'

'I'd rather stay home and descale the kettle quite frankly.'

'Oh, Thea, you are awful,' Danny says playfully in his best Dick Emery impersonation. 'Most girls would be tripping over their Manolos to go to a nice free party, but you, you just don't give a shit, do you? Have you ever thought that maybe you're in the wrong profession, that you're just not cut out to be a celebrity wife?'

'Every day of my life,' I say, unable to keep a twang of rancour out of my voice. 'But what choice do I have? After all, I'm married to the job.'

'What's this? Do I sense a whiff of disharmony at Château Itchycoo? Surely not.'

'Oh, it's nothing. Toby and I had a bit of a row yesterday and now he's done one of his disappearing tricks and there's something really important I need to—Oh Danny, I'm really sorry but I'm going to have to go, I've got a call waiting.'

'OK, babycakes, and you tell that husband of yours that if ever he needs an escort, I'm always available at short notice. I can be anything he wants me to be – blonde, brunette, redhead . . .'

'Good morning, J.C. Riley.'

'Hi.'

'Toby! Where on earth have you been?'

'Around and about,' he says coolly; cruelly. 'I thought we both needed some time on our own. Give you a chance to cool down.'

God, he can be so arrogant sometimes; but I don't want to start another argument, so I tell him to get his arse back home by the time I return from the office at two-ish because there is something we need to discuss. As soon as I put the phone down I panic, realizing that I only have two hours to compose and rehearse my 'We're going to have a baby' speech. I do so want it to be a special moment, I mustn't just blurt it out, excited as I am.

I arrive back at Itchycoo to find Toby in the kitchen, snaffling cheese and anchovies on toast. I'm full of nerves already, but the sight of him slouched against the fridge sets my heart racing even faster. Putting my tote bag down on the kitchen table, I walk over to him and kiss him on the lips. He gives my waist a quick squeeze with his spare hand. He smells stale and smoky and he's wearing the same clothes he left the house in.

'D'you want some?' he asks, raising a slice of toast to my lips.

Normally I love anchovies, but in my current delicate state the smell alone is enough to induce an attack of nausea.

'No thanks,' I say, wrinkling my nose and drawing away. 'I'm going to make a cup of tea. Why don't you take that into the living room?'

'OK,' he says with a shrug.

Once he's safely out of the room, I pull two champagne flutes from a cupboard, before going to my bag and retrieving the already chilled bottle of Veuve Clicquot that I bought at the upmarket offie three doors down from J.C.'s office. I spend thirty seconds mentally playing through the little speech I have prepared, before picking up the champagne and glasses and taking them into the living room.

'Jesus Christ.' Toby raises his eyebrows as I plonk the bottle down on the long wooden coffee table. 'Bit early isn't it?'

'We're celebrating,' I say with a knowing smile.

'What?'

Perfect. He's following the script exactly.

'This,' I say simply, lifting up my Joseph T-shirt and running a hand back and forth across my stomach.

'Sorry, angel, you've lost me.'

If I didn't know better, I'd say he was being deliberately obtuse.

'The baby,' I say. '*Our* baby.'

His eyes widen. He does a big swallow and I see his Adam's apple bob down and then up again.

'Are you saying what I think you're saying?'

I nod my head slowly, a big grin spreading across my face. 'I'm pregnant.'

'You're not?'

'I know, I can hardly believe it myself, but I've got the evidence right here.' I walk up to the mantelpiece and recover the Clear Blue from its hiding place behind a pewter photo frame.

'See,' I say, handing it to him. 'I did two, just to be sure and it was positive both times.'

He holds the plastic stick at eye level and squints at the little window. 'Stone me,' he says. Then he breaks into one of his lovely smiles – the one that makes all the Drift chicks weak at the knees. 'That's fantastic,' he says, rising to his feet. 'I can't believe it, I'm going to be a dad.'

He wraps his arms around me and pushes his face into the hollow above my collarbone.

'Have you told anyone else?' he says, his hot breath burning into my neck.

'Just Kim,' I say lightly. 'She was with me when I found out. In fact it was her idea to do the test. It hadn't even crossed my mind I might be pregnant. I just thought I had a tummy bug, I didn't dream it could be morning sickness. I don't even know how far gone I am. I've got an appointment at the doctor's tomorrow—'

He cuts me short. 'We can't tell anyone else yet; at least not until you've cleared the three-month stage – 'cos that's when you're most at risk of a miscarriage.'

'I didn't realize you were such an authority on the subject,' I say teasingly. 'But surely we can tell your mum and dad?'

'No way. You know what Mum's like, she'll never be able to keep it to herself. She'll tell her best friend, who'll tell her next-door neighbour and the next thing we know the press will be closing in like flies round shit.'

'OK, have it your way, they're your parents. But the press are going to find out sooner or later and when they do we'd better have some sort of statement prepared.'

A sudden thought crosses my mind. 'Hey, you know what we should do?'

'What?'

'Forget the statement. Let's set something up with one of the Sunday supplements; a nice interview with somebody decent like Chrissy Iley, and maybe a couple of photos too. Not at home – I couldn't bear a load of strangers trampling through Itchycoo; in a hotel perhaps.'

'But you never give interviews.'

'Yeah, but I'd make an exception just this once.

You see that way we'd get everything out in the open in one fell swoop. You won't be hounded for quotes and I won't be trailed by paparazzi trying to get a shot of my developing bulge.'

'Clever girl, like it,' he says nodding. 'Listen, angel, I just gotta make a couple of phone calls and then we'll crack open this champagne, shall we?'

'Toby, you are pleased, aren't you?' I say as he walks towards the door.

'Pleased isn't the word,' he says over his shoulder. 'I'm fucking delirious, babe.' And with that he disappears upstairs.

It suddenly occurs to me that neither one of us has mentioned the argument that caused him to walk out on me the day before yesterday. Oh well, I don't suppose it matters; now there's a baby on the way, things are going to be so much better between us.

EIGHT

I've abandoned Toby's merino jumper in favour of another project: an adorable angora shawl for my baby. I stood in the wool shop for a good half-hour this morning, agonizing over the colour until finally I plumped for a delicate androgynous lavender. I know it's early days – I've just entered the sixth week of pregnancy according to my GP's calculations – but I can't help making plans. I've even got a shortlist of names: Diva for a girl, Hendrix for a boy. Only joking. About the names, that is – I was serious about the shortlist. Kim and I have had lengthy discussions on the subject.

'Naming a child is a big responsibility when you're in the public eye,' she told me last night over tapas and drinks at Pablo's. (I was sticking to Coke, determined that from now until the birth my body will be nothing short of the proverbial temple.) 'So I hope you're not going to pick something really flaky like Dandelion or Satchel.'

'As if!' I snorted. 'Although Toby might, given half the chance.'

After hours of debate, we finally decided that short and simple was best, so we've settled on Leo for a little boy and Ellie for a girl. I put the names to Toby this morning and he said he'd have to think about it and get back to me. It's been two weeks and three days since I discovered I was pregnant and Toby is still trying to get his head round the idea. To tell the truth, I think he's a bit scared. It's perfectly understandable, especially for someone like him who's used to having a bunch of record company flunkies attend to his every need. He's a bit like a child himself in that respect, so it's no wonder he's worried about taking care of somebody else. You should have seen the look on his face when I told him I wasn't planning to hire a maternity nurse *or* a nanny to help out.

'She doesn't have to live in,' he said, as if that made a blind bit of difference.

'That's not the point,' I told him. 'The point is, why *have* a child if you aren't prepared to look after it yourself?'

'But bringing up a child is an awful lot of work for one person.'

'*One* person?' I said imperiously. 'I thought there were two of us in this marriage.'

'Oh yeah, course there are, angel. I just meant that you'll probably be doing the lion's share because . . . because you're a woman and there's all that breastfeeding stuff you gotta do. But I'm gonna do my bit, don't you worry about that.'

I was pleased to hear him say that, especially as he doesn't seem to share my enthusiasm for advance planning. A couple of days ago, for example, he caught me poring over baby bouncers in a catalogue.

'Which one should we go for?' I asked him. 'This one, with three-speed vibration unit and two removable covers, or this one, with two-speed vibration and interactive sound console?'

'What's the big rush? We've got ages yet,' he said, not even bothering to humour me by taking a cursory look at the catalogue. 'You'll be asking me what colour we're gonna paint the nursery next.'

He was wrong. I had already worked that one out. 'I thought we could commission a mural,' I said. 'Something really fun and original. What d'ya reckon?'

He burst out laughing. 'You kill me, angel,' he said, shaking his head and walking away.

I think it's just that he doesn't want to tempt fate, and maybe he's right, maybe I should hold off making any purchases until I've passed that crucial three-month threshold – which reminds me, I *must* organize a scan. I'll be going private, of course. Not that I have any qualms about the quality of care in NHS hospitals, but this is one instance where I do think it's worth splashing out. I'll have to talk to Toby later on, find out when he's free to go to the hospital with me. I bet he can't wait to catch the first glimpse of his son or daughter. I know I can't. He's been at the record company all afternoon, meeting with stylists and art directors and goodness knows who else to discuss the band's forthcoming video. They want to shoot part of it in Trafalgar Square, which seems to be causing all sorts of problems to do with permits and security and crowd control. Toby's been quite tense with it all.

Never mind, he'll be able to relax tonight. We're supposed to be going to the cinema. It's one of the few 'ordinary' things we still do together, although it's not quite as straightforward as it used to be. For a start, we always have to pre-book (Toby doesn't 'do' queues); and we always arrive under cover of darkness a couple of minutes after the main programme has begun so nobody gets a chance to recognize Toby. Ergo, we always leave the instant the credits start to roll. Glancing at my watch, I see that's it's five past six already. I've booked tickets for the seven o'clock show, so Toby had better get a move on.

Ten minutes later I'm sitting in the living room flicking through a copy of *Practical Parenting* when the phone starts ringing. It's Toby and he's in a record company Range Rover, on the way home. 'I was just checking to make sure you were there,' he says.

'Of course I'm here. Where else would I be?' I say. 'We're going to the pictures, aren't we?'

'Are we?'

I sigh impatiently. 'We discussed it last night in bed. I've booked the tickets and everything.'

'Shit, I forgot all about it.'

That man has a memory like a sieve. 'Don't tell me you've gone and arranged to meet one of your mates instead,' I say. 'Because if you have you can bloody well blow them out.'

'No, no. I haven't arranged anything.' He pauses. 'It's just there's something I need to talk to you about.'

'Well, you can talk to me about it after the film, can't you?'

'Nah, I gotta tell you before.'

'Why can't you just tell me now?'

'Look, I'll be home in fifteen minutes. See you then.'

The phone goes dead before I even have a chance to say goodbye.

When I see the Range Rover pull up outside the house, I go to the front door to let Toby in. He looks tired and edgy.

'How'd it go?' I ask, kissing him on the lips.

'How'd what go?' He pulls off his denim jacket and hooks it over the polished mahogany knob at the foot of the stair rail.

'The meeting, of course.'

'Fine.' He walks towards the kitchen. 'I'm getting a beer. D'you want one?'

'I'm off alcohol – remember?' I say, pointing to my stomach. He doesn't reply.

I return to my spot on the sofa in the living room. A few seconds later Toby comes in with a bottle of Beck's and sits down next to me.

'You'd better drink that quickly because we have to leave in a minute,' I say.

'I don't think you're gonna want to see the film when you hear what I've got to say,' he says, his voice steady and even.

For one ridiculous second I think he's about to tell me that he's left the band. That he's had a big row with the record company and walked out.

'Toby?' I say, pulling his arm back to force him to look me in the eyes. 'What's happened?'

He sighs and starts picking at the label on his beer bottle.

'I've been doing a lot of thinking,' he says. 'About the baby.'

'Go on.'

'And I know this is going to make me sound like a total cunt, but—'. He pauses and takes a swig of lager. 'I don't think I'm ready to be a dad.'

'Oh, darling,' I say, putting an arm around his shoulders. 'I know you're scared, but if it's any consolation so am I. It's a big deal, having a baby, and it's going to be tough at first – I'm not going to pretend otherwise – but we'll get by; we'll be *fine*. And you're going to be a great dad.'

He shrugs off my arm and puts his head in his hands. 'Shit, Thea. You're gonna hate me.'

'What on earth are you talking about? Of course I don't hate you.'

'I can't go through with it – that's what I'm talking

about,' he says. He stands up abruptly and walks over to the window. Then, with his back to me, he says calmly, 'I want you to have an abortion.'

'What did you say?'

'I-want-you-to-have-an-abortion,' he repeats, spitting out the words staccato-style.

A great wave of nausea wells up inside me and for a second I really think I might be sick. Right over the very expensive handwoven Heal's rug. I lean forward, clutching my stomach with both hands, desperately trying to take in what Toby has just said. He can't mean it; he *can't*. He's standing there, not facing me, but gazing out of the bay window. I want to go over there and shake him, make him retract that evil, unspeakable word, but I'm certain my legs would buckle underneath me.

'What the hell are you talking about?' I say, my voice wavering with emotion. 'You said you were pleased about the baby, you said – and I quote – "I'm fucking delirious."'

'I had to say that, didn't I?' he says, finally turning to face me.

'No you didn't. You could've said you were unsure, that you needed time to think about it.'

'I was in shock, I was confused, I thought maybe I just needed time to get used to the idea. But the more I thought about it, the more I realized that it isn't what I want, not at this stage in my life.'

He walks over to me and squats on the floor in front of me.

'I know this is going to sound really shitty, but to be honest this pregnancy has come at the worst possible time for me. This is a big year for the band. We've got the UK tour coming up and the new album to write. I just don't see how I can fit fatherhood into the schedule.' He strokes his index finger down the side of my cheek. 'Maybe next year.'

'We're not talking about a fucking car,' I shriek. 'This is a baby, *our* baby.'

'Well, it's not even really a baby yet, is it?' he says. 'Just a bunch of cells.'

'And this *bunch of cells* as you so callously describe it has been growing inside me for the past few weeks.'

'I'm sorry, Thea, I didn't mean to string you along. I just wanted to get things clear in my own head, make sure this is what I really wanted. And it is.'

'Look, let's not make a rash decision, let's leave it for a couple more weeks,' I say tentatively.

He shrugs and purses his lips so they form a thin cruel line. 'It's up to you, but I'm telling you quite categorically my feelings aren't gonna change. Why drag this out? You'd be better off booking yourself into a clinic and getting it over and done with as soon as possible.'

His words seem to squeeze the foetus inside my womb like an icy hand. 'I don't know if I can go through with an abortion,' I say shakily.

'It's nothing to worry about, you'll be in and out in

an afternoon, you won't even need to have a general anaesthetic,' he says.

'And what if I refuse? What if I go ahead and have this baby?'

'Well, that's your right, it's your body after all. I can't force you to have an abortion.' He looks me directly in the eye. 'The thing is, Thea, I don't know how I'd feel about you . . . about us . . . if you just went ahead and kept the baby regardless of my feelings. It would change everything.'

I grit my teeth and squeeze my hands into fists till the knuckles turn white.

That I suffered no pain made it worse. If it had hurt, I would have felt happier in the knowledge that I was being duly punished. As it was, the whole procedure was ridiculously straightforward: Toby drove me to the Riverview Clinic in leafy Harrow and I lay on the treatment bed, my feet in stirrups, while the nine-week-old foetus was vacuumed from my body. It was all over in less than five minutes and I was fully conscious throughout. Some mild cramps and a little light bleeding ensued, but by the following day I was right as rain.

I had put off phoning the clinic for two whole weeks in the vain hope that Toby would change his mind. He didn't. Instead, he seemed to grow ever distant, refusing to discuss the issue with me and absenting himself from Itchycoo even more than usual. In the end

I knew I had to go through with it because much as I wanted that baby, my marriage means more to me. We can always try for a baby next year, Toby's 'schedule' permitting. After the abortion Toby revealed an unexpected sensitivity. He cleared his diary for two whole days, which included postponing a big magazine shoot that I knew he was looking forward to. He volunteered to phone J.C. to tell him I had an ear infection and wouldn't be in till next week. He tucked me up on the sofa and brought me tea and toast and held me when I cried. But I know he didn't feel guilty; not the way I do.

Kim was taken aback – no, stunned – when I told her I was going to have an abortion. 'But I don't understand, you were so happy when you found out you were pregnant,' she said. Then her voice took on a sharper tone: 'Has Toby pushed you into this?'

I told her it had been a mutual decision. 'When we thought it through properly, we both agreed it wasn't the right time,' I said. I couldn't tell her Toby was the instigator because I would have felt so terribly disloyal. And I *did* have the final say – as Toby said, it's *my* body – and it's a decision I have to live with for the rest of my life.

In the two weeks after the abortion, I had the same dream three times. I am sitting in a doctor's surgery, holding a small baby in my arms, tightly wrapped in a soft lavender shawl. The receptionist tells me, 'The doctor will see you now, Mrs Carson,' and I go through to the consulting room. I tell the tall man in the white coat that my baby is ill. He takes the child from my arms, places it on a theatre trolley and turns his back to me while he rummages in an instrument tray. When he turns back to face me, I see that he has a huge knife in his hands. I open my mouth to scream, but no sound comes out. I try to scoop my baby to safety, but my feet are stuck in quicksand. I watch in horror as the doctor raises the knife above his head with both hands and brings it down towards my baby's chest. It's at this point that I always wake up, trembling and sweating.

When I told Kim about the dream, she suggested I might benefit from talking to somebody. I took her advice and went to see a counsellor, a woman the Riverview had recommended. It was a real catharsis. We talked about loads of stuff – my feelings about the baby, my feelings about my husband, my feelings about myself. We even talked about my relationship with Mum and the fact that I grew up not knowing who my father was. I admitted that I still felt a certain degree of resentment towards Toby – and disappointment too, in the sense that he had somehow failed to live up to my expectations. And then the counsellor said something that really struck a chord.

'You seem very angry,' she said. 'Of course that's perfectly normal after going through an experience as traumatic as abortion. However, do you think it's possible that some of that anger stems from a feeling that you were abandoned by your own father?'

At first I wasn't sure what she was getting at. 'My

father doesn't even know I exist,' I told her. 'So how can I possibly resent him for not sticking around?'

'Well, that's right – *if* you regard your situation from a rational standpoint. But people's emotions don't always behave in a rational way,' she said. 'I was just wondering if you felt a certain lack of resolution in that area of your life; if you'd ever thought of trying to find him.'

I answered as honestly as I could. 'I've often wondered about him, if that's what you mean, and yes, I've sometimes thought my life would be better, richer somehow, if I knew who he was. But as for trying to find him . . . I wouldn't know where to start. The thing is, Mum wasn't sure which bloke got her pregnant. She once told me he could be one of several men, but I don't even know their names. And now that she's gone, I don't have a snowflake's chance in hell of finding him.'

NINE

Early morning and I am sitting in the dining room with Mum's old diaries spread across the table in front of me, the usual centrepiece of heady stargazer lilies now relegated to the windowsill. Looking at the innocuous black volumes, laid out in chronological order, I am unexpectedly nervous, almost as if I'm doing something I shouldn't, and I can't help feeling relieved that there will be no witnesses to my transgression. Ivy's not due until midday and Toby's gone clothes shopping with Callum (the Bond Street branch of Versace has opened an hour early just for them).

It's nearly a week since I visited that counsellor, during which time my thoughts have returned time and time again not only to the baby I lost, but also to my father. I know I brushed off the suggestion that I might track him down, but the more I think about it, the more I'm excited by the possibility of finding him – or *trying* to find him, at least. And so, just out of curiosity, I decided to subject Mum's old diaries to a thorough scrutiny. At this stage, I don't know what, or who, I'm looking for, but I've already made one surprising discovery: the diaries go back a long way, much further than I thought – to three years before my birth, in fact.

The obvious starting point is the year of my conception. I've already done the maths: my birthday is 16 May, so nine months before that is 16 August. But it's a bit more complicated than that because I was born premature, a piddling 3lb 8oz; they kept me in an incubator for the first week of my life. Was I days early – or weeks? Mum did tell me, but I can't remember. I had better be generous and consider the whole of August and September as a possible time frame for my conception.

Reaching across the table, I draw the relevant diary towards me and, in doing so, I notice that my hand is shaking ever so slightly. Suddenly I am struck by the potential enormity of my actions and I take a couple of moments to compose myself before lifting the leatherette cover. As I turn the thin yellowy pages, snapshots of Mum's life flash before my eyes – an appointment at the hairdresser's, a gig at Ronnie Scott's, a football match at Gunnersbury FC and then . . .

1 August
Roy, Coronet 7.30p.m.

The name Roy doesn't mean anything to me, but I'm well acquainted with the Coronet. It's the old cinema in Woolwich, a red velvet, gold-trimmed, old-fashioned picture palace. Mum and I used to go there all the time when I was a kid; it was one of my favourite weekend treats, and on the way home we'd stop off at the local Wimpy for a Brown Derby and a cup of tea. Brushing a tear from the corner of my eye and swallowing hard, I continue through August, seeking other references to Roy. He couldn't have been that hot because he only gets two more mentions and neither is accompanied by the name of a meeting place. But while I've been tracking Roy's romantic progress another name has caught my eye.

7 August

Kevin, my place, 8-ish

Sounds like an intimate dinner for two – although I suppose there is the chance Kevin was only coming round to fix the washing machine. Maybe not ... turning the pages forwards, I count his name another six times. Turning back, I find that he gets his first mention in mid-July. I note that they always met on a Tuesday night and each 'date' was spaced exactly two weeks apart. Clearly they had some sort of relationship, but given the time lapse between dates, maybe it was just a sex thing. Next to one of the entries is an address:

83 Hermitage Road. He was obviously a local boy. Hermitage Road is in Greenwich. I used to walk past the bottom of it every day on my way home from school.

Returning to August, I come across a couple more guys, both of whom I am able to discount with reasonable confidence. 'Andy' was the teenage son of a neighbour who used to babysit me sometimes, while 'Pete' was one of Mum's mates from art college. During my childhood both men were regular visitors to the house – and Mum did tell me that my father had never laid eyes on me.

There is, however, one final likely lad:

10 September
Barney 8p.m.
Rules, Maiden Lane, WC2

This Barney must have been a class act if he was taking Mum to posh restaurants like Rules. Toby and I ate there once – the sticky-toffee pudding was to die for. Barney's modus operandi reminds me of an entry I noticed earlier. It caught my eye because of the upmarket venue. I retrace my steps back through August and there it is:

22 August
B – Simpsons-in-the-Strand

Could 'B' be Barney? If so, he seems to have wined and dined Mum at some of London's finest eateries. And here he is again, although this time it's a restaurant I've never heard of.

12 August
B – Pierce & Hussey

In all, 'Barney' or 'B' makes more than fifty appearances in the diary. He first emerges in mid-April – a date at Claridge's, no less – and bows out some six months later in the dying throes of October when Mum would've been more than a month into her pregnancy. A number of different meeting places are given, but 'Pierce & Hussey' is the clear favourite.

Resting my chin in my hands, I stare at the diary lying in front of me, its plain black cover belying the writhing Pandora's Box of secrets inside. A mere fifteen minutes of detective work and I have my contenders: Roy, Kevin and Barney. Are *they* the three could-be fathers Mum alluded to all those years ago? Could it really be that simple? Of course it bloody can't. The words 'clutching' and 'straws' spring to mind. I don't have the smallest scrap of evidence that Mum ever exchanged bodily fluids with any one of these three characters. And there's always the possibility that my father didn't even merit a mention in her diary. He could've been a one-night stand, a drunken encounter at a party, a quick fumble in a back alley after the pubs had shut. Yuck! I don't even want to think about that.

What I have in front of me is a starting point, the first clue in the treasure hunt. But do I have the balls to pass *go*, to grab those three Christian names in both hands and try and turn them into something real? It's a big challenge and one I'm not sure I can live up to. Then, of course, there's always the risk of rejection. Just say one of these three guys does turn out to be my father, but he's got a family of his own and doesn't want anything to do with me – what then? I suppose what it boils down to is can I live with myself if I just walk away, or will there always be that little creature gnawing away at my conscience, telling me to take a chance just once in my life?

TEN

This morning I waved goodbye to my husband. Over the course of the next four weeks he will be entertaining capacity crowds at premier venues on what is Drift's biggest UK tour to date. I, meanwhile, will be keeping the home fires burning – after a fashion. I had thought we could meet up in Leeds at the halfway stage, but Toby says my presence would be too distracting. Leeds is a very big deal in gigging terms, apparently, and he needs to keep his mind on the job. But I am hoping that once he's had a couple of weeks to miss me he will weaken and change his mind. We'll see.

Our last night together was really special. We both got Gucci-ed up to the eyeballs and headed off to the Sanderson for a fantastically extravagant meal: aperitifs, three courses, champagne, wine, coffee, liqueurs, the works. It's very rare to have a night out on our own, just the two of us, and it was wonderful to have Toby's undivided attention for once. We didn't get hassled by a single person all night long – other than an autograph request from the cab driver who dropped us off in Oxford Street, but he was so polite he didn't really count. Not that Toby doesn't appreciate his fans – far from it – but unless you've experienced fan worship first-hand, you can't understand just how wearing it can be, especially when people get abusive because Toby hasn't got time to stop and chat.

We left the restaurant around midnight, stuffed to the gunnels and in a pretty advanced state of inebriation. I was glad when Toby didn't suggest going on to a club, like he normally does. He's such a night owl, I don't know where he gets his energy from. I need my eight hours a night, but he can survive on five or six. On the way home, snuggled up in the back of a black cab, Toby sprang a surprise in the shape of an Asprey & Garrard gift box. Inside was the most beautiful silver charm bracelet I've ever seen; so delicate and pretty. He has very good taste in jewellery, my husband. And as I gave him a thank-you kiss, he held me close and told me he loved me. It's been a long time since I've heard those three little words – well, a couple of months anyway – and I can't tell you how good they felt.

We'd got pretty frisky in the back of that cab, so when we arrived home both of us had one thing on our minds. Without a word to each other, we headed straight upstairs. I was peeling back the covers on the bed while simultaneously trying to kick off my Emma Hope slingbacks when Toby suggested a precoital candlelit bath. So we ran round the house collecting every candle we could find – the fat church candles from the fireplace, little tea lights, Jo Malone vanilla-scented sticks, the hideous glass bowl with floating gobs of wax that Toby's mum got us for Christmas. And we lined them all up all around the bathroom and climbed into the huge bubble-filled roll-top tub with a couple of Remy Martins. We lay there for ages, talking and giggling and kissing, just like the old days. And when we were both horny as hell we dried off and got into bed and made love for over an hour. And do you know, it's the first time since the abortion that I've actually enjoyed sex. Yeah, it was a good night all right. A very good night.

But now he's gone and I'm all alone. I have no intention of rattling round Itchycoo for a whole month, however, so I've moved in temporarily with Kim and Tim. They're amazingly generous friends, they wouldn't dream of asking me for any kind of contribution to the household expenses, but I've insisted on paying my way by helping out with Party On! Kim's got loads of work at the moment – the publicity for Amba Lazenby's party has practically doubled her commissions. And I don't need to worry about Itchycoo – the security system is state of the art and Ivy, whose Camden council flat is only a ten-minute walk away, has agreed to keep an eye on the place for me and give it an occasional dust.

I've spent the afternoon closeted in Kim's home office, sourcing props for a C-list It girl's Wild West party. It sounds straightforward, but it's proving pretty damn challenging, I can tell you. I've sorted the hay bales, the billycans, the stetsons – even the bucking bronco mechanical bull – but I'm stuck on the cacti. I mean, where on earth am I going to find two dozen six-foot cactus plants, spines removed? Maybe Kew Gardens can point me in the right direction.

I'm very relieved when Kim turns to me from her desk by the window and says, 'I dunno about you, but I've had enough for one day. How about we put the phones on voicemail and pour ourselves a couple of ice-cold gin and slims?'

'Sounds wonderful. These cacti are really doing my head in.'

'Yeah, that's one tall order. Maybe I could persuade Jacinta Doomes-Braithwaite to settle for inflatable cacti – they'd be a piece of piss.'

'Or Joshua trees, or those great balls of tumbleweed – anything but fucking cacti.'

'I'll give her agent a call tomorrow and see what I can do.'

'Ta, Kim, that would be much appreciated.'

We go through to the kitchen and Kim fixes two drinks in tall highball glasses. 'Cheers,' I say. 'To the continued success of Party On! and Drift's UK tour.'

'I'll drink to that,' she says, taking a slug of G and T. 'I expect Toby and the guys will be in Newcastle by now, won't they?'

'Let's see,' I say, looking at my watch. 'Six-thirty –

they'll have checked into their hotel, Callum will be screaming blue murder if he hasn't got the hypo-allergenic pillow he requested; Steve will be chasing the chambermaids; Luke will be searching for the nearest McDonald's and Toby will be exploring the minibar. In another couple of hours they'll hit the town with the roadies and crawl from bar to bar and then club to club, getting progressively drunker and picking up assorted hangers-on as they go. I don't expect they'll hit the sack much before five a.m.'

'But the gig's tomorrow. Shouldn't they be getting an early night?'

'Come on, Kim, this *is* rock 'n' roll. Do you think Keith Richard ever climbs into his jammies at ten p.m. and falls asleep to *Book at Bedtime*?'

'S'pose not. But don't you ever, you know, worry about Toby when he's on the road?'

'Worry about him copping off with someone else, you mean?'

'No, don't be stupid. I mean worry about him getting into a fight or suffering alcohol poisoning or accidentally overdosing.'

'I used to, but not any more. I figure Toby's old enough to look after himself – and, anyway, the guys always stick together; none of them would go off on their own, not in a strange city.'

'You know something, Thea, Toby's very lucky to have a wife like you. Not many women would give their husband such a free rein, let him go off gallivanting round the country. I couldn't bear to let Tim loose like that – not that I don't trust him one hundred per cent, I'd just miss him like mad, that's all.'

'And I'm going to miss Toby. But when you're a rock star's wife, you have to take the rough with the smooth. And I don't have it too bad – I mean just check out my house and my wardrobe, darling!' I say with mock pretension.

'Yeah, but does that stuff make you happy? I mean *really* happy?'

'Put it this way: I'd rather shop at Next and live in a two-bed semi with a husband who comes home every night at six p.m. than live this weird, fragmented existence. But you know how I feel about Toby, he means the world to me. Sure, our lives have changed beyond all recognition over the past couple of years, but I'd say we've still got a good marriage – most of the time.'

Kim tilts her head to one side and gives me a long appraising look.

'What?' I say.

'Can I ask you something? You can tell me to mind my own business, if you want.'

'Sure.'

'I know you said that having the abortion had been a mutual decision,' she says tentatively. 'But you really wanted that baby didn't you?'

I knew that she knew. 'Yes, I did. But Toby obviously wasn't ready for fatherhood and so I had to make a choice: the baby or him.'

Kim nods her head in a gesture of understanding.

'I really think our relationship would've suffered if I'd gone through with the pregnancy and, anyway, I'm only young, so there's plenty of time for kids.' I stare down at my hands and absent-mindedly twist the gold band on my ring finger. 'Now, if you don't mind, can we change the subject? I get weepy enough after a few gins as it is.'

Tim is working late, so after our aperitifs I help Kim prepare a pasta carbonara and a stick of garlic bread and we settle down to eat in front of the TV. My favourite show, *The Salon*, is on tonight. I absolutely love docusoaps, there's something utterly compelling about observing the minutiae of someone else's life. Take this hairdressing mob, for instance – they're bitchier than a bunch of celebrity wives, or should that be a 'lunch' of celebrity wives?

'You know what would make a *really* riveting docusoap,' I say to Kim.

'What's that then?'

'*A Day in the Life of a Celebrity Wife*. Nobody would believe how incredibly humdrum my existence is. Just think, they could film me watching *Trisha*, putting the world to rights with Ivy, getting my moustache waxed . . .'

'Sorting out your smalls for the wash, pumicing the

dead skin on your feet, trying to get through to Toby on his mobile,' continues Kim. 'You should write a proposal and take it to Channel 4 – they'd snap it up, I'm telling you.'

'If I wasn't so camera-shy I might be tempted. At least it would be a challenge,' I say, mopping up the last dollop of carbonara with a hunk of garlic bread. 'I wish I had a proper career like you, Kim. Working at J.C. Riley's doesn't exactly stretch me.'

'Why don't you launch your own range of designer undies – or become a modern-day Bardot and set up an animal sanctuary in Itchycoo's back garden?' says Kim facetiously.

'Very funny. Seriously though, there is an idea I've been mulling over. I've been meaning to talk to you about it.'

'Ooh, do tell.'

'I thought I might look for my dad.'

'Your dad – but you don't even know who your dad is.'

'Not yet, but I unearthed Mum's old diaries recently and they yielded some interesting information.'

'Go on.'

'Do you remember me telling you ages ago that, when I was a teenager, Mum said my dad could be one of two or maybe three men?'

'Yeah, and I remember being quite shocked.'

'Well, I worked out a rough timescale for my conception and looking back at Mum's diary entries for that year I've managed to identify three men she was seeing at the time: Roy, Kevin and Barney.'

'You mean one of them might actually be your father?'

'Perhaps, I don't know for sure. All I've got so far is their Christian names.'

'So how do you know Shirley actually slept with them?'

'I don't.'

'But she *was* going out with them – right?'

'It certainly appears that way. According to the diary, she was meeting them regularly for dinner and dates at the cinema. The relationship with Roy seems to have fizzled out after just three dates, the one with Kevin lasted a couple of months and good old Barney was on the scene for almost six months. Crucially, however, they all overlap.'

'And you think you can find these men – with only their Christian names to go on?'

'I know it's a long shot, but I thought I might give it a go.'

Kim looks at me doubtfully. 'So why the sudden urge to find him?' she says. 'You've never been even remotely curious up to now.'

'It was something that counsellor said, about me having pent-up feelings of anger and lacking a sense of resolution because I didn't know who my father was.

And the more I thought about it, the more I wondered if there might be some truth in that.' I pause, giving Kim the opportunity to contradict me, but she remains silent.

'I've often wondered about him – what he looks like, where he lives, whether he's got any more kids. Hey, just think, Kim, I could have loads of brothers and sisters I know nothing about. Wouldn't that be great? I always hated being an only child.'

'Hang on a minute. It could all end in disaster, you know. Even if you do manage to find him, he could slam the door in your face. I'm not trying to put you off, it's just you've had enough upset this past month. I don't want you setting yourself up for more disappointment.'

'I've given it a lot of thought and, the way I see it, what have I got to lose? I've got time on my hands, plenty of money if I need to hire a private investigator and, even if I can't find him, at least I'll know I've tried. And if I do find him, but he doesn't want to know me . . . well, I've managed perfectly well without a dad up to now.'

'Well, if you're sure it's what you want . . .'

'I'd like to at least give it a go. I love being married, looking after the house and stuff, but this is my chance to be totally selfish, to do something just for me.'

'What does Toby think about the idea?'

'I haven't mentioned it to him. Things have been so fraught lately with all the rehearsals for the tour that I didn't want to dump anything else on him.'

The look on Kim's face tells me she's not impressed. But then people don't always understand that when you're married to a celebrity your own needs have to come second a lot of the time.

The smell of bacon frying lures me from my bed. That's one of the things I love about staying here – Tim never ever leaves for work without first making himself a bacon sarnie: fat removed, well done, thick-sliced Mother's Pride, lashings of brown sauce, just the way I like it. And if yours truly can get her arse into the kitchen before he's done the washing up, he'll happily add another couple of rashers to the frying pan. It's been twelve days since Toby abandoned me for the delights of life on the road, and on eight of those days I have been seated at the breakfast table by 7.45a.m. For a true-blue lady of leisure like me, that's quite an achievement. It's become a kind of running joke between Tim and me. He's even started calling me Miss Piggy.

It sounds as if Kim will be participating in today's early morning porkfest because as I descend the stairs, I can hear voices – voices that seem unusually animated for this time of the morning. The moment I push open the kitchen door, however, the conversation suddenly and suspiciously dries.

'What's up with you two?' I ask, staring at Tim, whose jaw is actually hanging open, as though in mid-sentence. 'Talking dirty were you? I didn't mean to interrupt anything, I'll just grab some breakfast and I'll be out of your way in two ticks.' As I walk past the table, I catch Tim raising his eyebrows questioningly at Kim. 'What?' I say, looking from one to the other.

'It's nothing,' Tim blusters, clearly lying.

'Oh, I get it. You were talking about me, weren't you? Have I outstayed my welcome? Are you wondering how to get rid of me without hurting my feelings?' I am, of course, only joking, but neither of them laughs, which is odd. Tim, in particular, has a very well-developed sense of humour, which is one of the things I like most about him. And he's good-looking in a ruddy-cheeked Prince William sort of way. And very handy round the house too – his fitted wardrobes are a veritable work of art.

'Don't be silly, you know we love having you here,' says Kim.

'Well that's a relief because I don't get breakfast cooked for me at home, you know, and I've rather got used to this five-star service.'

Tim gives a funny, strained, half-smile, but I detect a definite tension in the air. 'Come on guys, 'fess up,' I command. 'I know something's going on.'

'We ought to tell her. It's better that she hears it from us than anyone else,' says Tim.

'Ooh, sounds ominous,' I say a little too cheerily. I can't imagine what they're about to tell me.

'I think you ought to sit down first,' says Kim, gesturing at the chair next to her. Fuck, it gets worse. I tighten the belt of my white towelling robe in the manner of Jackie Chan preparing for combat and plonk myself down. Kim glances across at Tim, who nods encouragingly and then pushes a copy of the *Mirror* across the table towards her.

'There's a story,' she says. 'In the newspaper.' She releases a little sigh. 'About Toby.' She puts a hand on my arm. 'And it's not good.'

'Really?' I say. 'I spoke to him on the phone only yesterday afternoon – we were making plans for me to join him in Leeds at the end of the week and he didn't say anything about a story.'

'It's not exactly the kind of news a wife wants to hear,' says Tim.

'What do you mean?' I say, my hackles starting to rise.

'I think it's probably best if you read it for yourself,' says Kim. She opens the paper and turns the pages till she gets to page seven. She pushes it towards me. 'Take a deep breath,' she says. 'And remember, Tim and I are here for you.'

The story is spread across half a page. 'Alexa gets the Drift' reads the headline above the photo. It's a black and white picture, the classic celebrity in back seat of black Merc with leggy blonde scenario, a snatched shot taken through the car window, the glare of the flash reflecting on the glass. At this point, I'm reasonably calm. There could be any number of reasons why Toby is with this girl, whose face I recognize, but can't quite place. Maybe it's his Manchester publicist or some competition-winning fan. The accompanying words put paid to all my theories.

> *With his wife safely at home in London, Toby Carson spent five hours cosied up in a Manchester hotel room with MTV presenter Alexa Hunt. The pair left the Humbug Club together at four a.m. before heading back to the Drift frontman's suite at the ultra-trendy Malmaison. According to our man on the scene, Alexa, 23, had a big smile on her face when she finally departed a full five hours later. Drift are nearly halfway through their UK tour and it looks as if Toby is playing away from home in more ways than one. Let's hope his wife Thea is the understanding sort.*

I'm glad I'm sitting down because my head goes suddenly swimmy, forcing me to grip the edge of the table with both hands.

'Are you all right, hon?' says Kim gently.

I manage a small nod, but my wobbling lower lip's a dead giveaway.

'I know it looks bad,' she continues, 'but I'd take this story with a large pinch of salt, if I were you. You know what the tabloids are like.'

'Yeah, but there's no smoke without fire,' I say bitterly. 'Five hours is an awfully long time and I'm damn sure they weren't playing tiddlywinks.'

'How could he do that to you?' Tim mutters, shaking his head.

Kim shoots him a warning look and taking the hint he gets up and says it's time he was getting off to work. As he walks towards the door, he stops and kisses the top of my head. 'There'll be a perfectly reasonable explanation, you'll see,' he says.

'Yeah, right,' I manage to say in a hoarse whisper before bursting into tears.

ELEVEN

The rest of the day passes in a blur. Despite the pressing matter of Jacinta Doomes-Braithwaite's six-foot cacti (the difficult bitch refused to compromise with inflatables), Kim puts her own life on hold in order to sort out mine. Her first priority is protecting me from the tabloid hacks, who will inevitably try to follow up the *Mirror*'s scoop by pursuing the 'wronged wife' for an interview. And they haven't wasted any time – a phone call to Ivy reveals that a mob of baying reporters are already camped outside Itchycoo. 'I told them to eff off, bloody scum,' raged Ivy, never one to mince her words. And apparently there's a string of messages on the answerphone – everyone from Channel 5 News to *Wow!* magazine, all wanting a quote or an interview. Our number is unlisted, of course, but these journalists have ways and means. Kim instructs Ivy not to reveal my whereabouts to a single person – and that includes 'concerned' friends. In situations like this, you don't know who you can trust.

I'm hoping that none of the papers will be able to track me down to Kim's. In public, I've always been quite guarded on the subject of our friendship and I can't think of a single occasion when we've been photographed together. She in turn has never namedropped *me* in the course of her business dealings, even though the Carson connection would doubtless open a few doors.

Heaven knows what I'd say to any reporters who did find me. 'My husband shagged a ridiculously attractive TV presenter and hasn't even had the decency to phone me to offer a half-baked excuse.' That would certainly guarantee me a few column inches in tomorrow's paper. You see, I haven't been able to get in touch with Toby. I've tried his mobile twenty times or more, but it remains resolutely switched off. I called the hotel and they told me he'd checked out. I dialled Callum's number and got voicemail. Finally I called the tour manager's mobile and got his assistant, who has promised to get Toby to call me the minute she sees him.

All day long I've been going over and over it in my mind, trying to conjure up a plausible scenario that would exonerate my husband, but in truth he's probably guilty as hell. Even if penetrative sex to conclusion didn't actually occur, there's no denying that he took another woman back to his hotel – the photograph was taken as they arrived at the Malmaison – and in my book that still qualifies as betrayal. What sickens me

149

most is the memory of our last night together before he hit the road – the meal, the Asprey & Garrard bauble, the candles, the lovemaking ... it must've meant nothing to him, it was just a ploy to keep the little wifey sweet while he went off and shagged his way round Britain. No wonder he didn't want me coming on tour with him. He wasn't even that keen to meet up in Leeds on Friday, but I managed to persuade him by saying I'd only stay one night. What a total fool I've been, I feel so humiliated.

Straight after *News at Ten* I head for bed, desperate to slip into the arms of Morpheus so I can put an end to this hateful day. But the sleep god proves even more elusive than my errant husband. An hour and a half later I'm still wide awake, staring at the ceiling and visualizing Toby going down on the lovely Alexa when there's a gentle knock at the door. It's Kim and she's carrying the cordless phone. 'Guess who?' she says simply, before handing me the phone and walking out of the room, closing the door behind her.

'Hello,' I say into the handset from my prone position.

'It's me, babe – and before you kick off will you just give me two minutes so I can tell you my side of the story?'

'I'm all ears,' I say sarcastically.

'First of all, I'm sorry I haven't called before. I didn't even hear about that thing in the *Mirror* till lunchtime.

I tried to call, but I couldn't find your mobile number and Kim was permanently engaged. Then the band had to do a soundcheck and halfway through some local radio station turned up to do an interview . . .'

'Toby,' I interrupt, 'cut the crap and just get to the fucking point, will you?'

'Sorry, babe. OK – I know this is gonna sound far-fetched, but I'm telling you it's the God's honest truth. First off, Alexa Hunt is a friend of mine, it wasn't like we met for the first time the other night.'

'That's funny, you've never mentioned her.'

'I must've done . . . Drift guested on her MTV show last month. We did an acoustic set.'

'No, I have no recollection of that whatsoever.'

That seems to have thrown him because there's a long silence. I don't even attempt to fill the gap. Why the fuck should I make things easy for him?

'Right. Well, anyway, I've bumped into her a couple of times since at various parties and launches and we've talked a bit, you know, just industry stuff mainly, not flirting or anything.'

'Go on.'

'Well, Lexy was at the Manchester gig . . .'

'*Lexy* is it, then?'

'C'mon, Thea, give me a break. All her friends call her Lexy.'

'Right.'

'And we met up backstage afterwards – she just

wanted to congratulate us on a great gig. And she was right, we tore the fucking place up, Thea. I wish you could've seen us.'

'Well, somebody forgot to invite me.'

'Oh, yeah. Sorry, babe. Anyway a big group of us decided to go on to the Humbug Club. We had a right laugh, the DJ was wicked . . .'

'Toby, I swear I'm going to hang up if you drag this out much longer.'

'OK, OK. All the lightweights started peeling off around two a.m. and by closing time there was just me and Lex . . . Alexa. Neither of us was ready for bed – that is we weren't ready to go back to our hotels – so I invited her to come back to the Malmaison and raid my minibar. I know it was a bad move, taking a girl back to my room like that, I should've known there'd be photographers hanging round after the gig, but I was pissed and I'd done a bit of Charlie, I wasn't thinking straight. I just fancied some company . . .'

'You mean you didn't think you'd get caught.'

'Yes, I mean no . . . I wasn't doing anything wrong. I'd never be unfaithful to you. You've got to believe me.'

'But five hours, Toby . . . don't tell me you were drinking solidly for five hours.'

'We caned the miniatures and then we fell asleep – not in bed or anything. I was in an armchair, she was on the sofa.'

There is a long silence while I silently weigh up the likelihood that my husband is telling the truth, the

whole truth and nothing but the truth. The verdict: not
very likely. I may be in love, but I'm not stupid. He's
bound to have glossed over some details. Like the bit
where Lexy disappeared to the loo and came back
wearing nothing but a smile and a spritz of CKbe – OK
I'm only speculating, but this is rock 'n' roll so anything's possible.

'You haven't spoken to the press have you?' he says
suddenly.

'No, but they're camped outside the house.'

'Fuck. You'd better give Itchycoo a wide berth for a
couple of days. They'll soon get bored and go off to
hassle some other poor bugger. And if they do track you
down, you will say "no comment", won't you?'

'I may . . . I haven't decided yet.'

'Well, it's up to you, but if you give the story legs
it'll just run and run, you know.'

'Whatever.'

'You *are* still coming up to Leeds on Friday aren't
you?' he says plaintively.

'I don't think so.'

'C'mon, babe, don't be like that.'

'Like what – like a person who actually has some
self-respect?' I snap. 'I'm sick of this bloody lifestyle.
Not knowing where you are or who you're with. What
kind of marriage is that?'

'So what are we going to do about it?'

'What are *we* going to do? What are *you* going to
do, more like? I've always supported you, always played

the good little wife, and all you've done is take advantage of me. I think you should use this time on tour to think about whether you're prepared to change your ways, spend more time at home, start acting like a proper husband instead of the big I Am.'

'Or else?'

'Or else I'm leaving you, Toby – and I mean that most sincerely because otherwise I'm in danger of losing whatever precious shreds of self-respect I still possess.'

'Right, well you've made your feelings perfectly plain. I'll see you in a couple of weeks' time, then. I won't bother calling you again because you probably don't want me to, but you know where I am if you need me. And, Thea, I never meant to hurt you, I want you to know that.'

I switch off the phone without replying because there's a lump the size of a football developing in the back of my throat. And I musn't show any weakness or Toby will know I'm bluffing.

I sleep extremely well, considering. In many ways it's a relief finally to have delivered my ultimatum, which is something I should've done months ago. I just hope it has the desired effect. I don't want to break up with Toby – I've always believed that marriage is for life – but at the same time I'm not happy with things the way they are, not happy at all. I've done my share of supporting and understanding and I really think it's

about time someone else besides me put a bit of effort
into our marriage.

'Do you think he's telling the truth about that girl?'
Kim asked me when I'd given her the blow-by-blow
account of our conversation.

'I'd like to think so, but I don't know, I really don't
know. Put it this way – the words "faithful" and "rock
star" don't usually go hand in hand.'

'I see your point, but I hardly think Toby's capable
of serial adultery. Having said that, I do think you've
done the right thing putting a firework up his arse like
that. You need to start putting yourself first instead of
always dancing attendance on him. I'm sure he'll come
to his senses, and when he comes back to London, he'll
be a changed man, you'll see.'

I hope she's right. And in the meantime I'll keep
myself as busy as possible, so I won't have time to dwell
on things. Despite Kim's concerns, I plan to start trying
to trace my father tomorrow, even though I have precious little to go on. This afternoon, however, I intend to
lose myself in the utter vacuum of lunch with the
celebrity wives. If one thing will help take my mind off
Toby, it's the bitchy, but utterly addictive prattle of
those three gossip queens.

The route into town is unusually traffic-free and for
once I am the first to arrive at the appointed restaurant
– an overpriced French joint in South Ken and a regular
venue for our little lunch club. As soon as I push open

the heavy glass door, the hideously obsequious maître d' comes rushing to greet me. 'How wonderful to see you again Mrs Carson,' he gushes, clumsily attempting to relieve me of my alpaca wrap.

'It's fine, Bertrand, I'll keep it with me.' I say, wresting it off him.

'Very good, Mrs Carson,' he slimes. 'Now, if you'd like to follow me, your usual table is ready.' He shows me to a seat by the window and makes a big fuss of pulling out my chair and shaking my napkin. 'I do hope everything will be to your satisfaction,' Bertrand says. 'Philippe, our head waiter, will be looking after you ladies today, so if there's anything you need, anything at all, be sure to let him know.' He gestures to an angular chap hovering by a giant yucca in the corner of the room.

'Thank you, Bertrand. But I'm fine for now, honestly,' I say through gritted teeth. Thankfully he takes the hint and pisses off back to his little desk by the restaurant entrance. I really can't bear being drooled over and I find myself wishing I was just an ordinary punter, even if it meant being stuck with the table next to the toilets.

Within ten minutes the others have all arrived – Patti first, followed by Angela and Stella, who waft in together, borne on a suffocating cloud of very expensive perfume.

'You really should have rung me right away, you

poor darling girl,' says Patti when we're all present and correct.

'Pardon?'

'I know an excellent divorce lawyer – not that you're actually going to get divorced of course, but the mere threat of it can work wonders. Toby will soon toe the line when he realizes how much money he stands to lose. What is it now – one year? That's gotta be worth a couple of mill even without a pre-nup.'

'Oh,' I say. 'You've seen the story then.'

'Who *hasn't* seen the story?' says Stella, reaching over to squeeze my shoulder patronizingly. 'I feel for you, I really do.'

How naive of me to think I could enjoy a nice quiet lunch without reference to Toby's indiscretion. I bet this lot have really been looking forward to today. This is going to be the hottest piece of prandial gossip since Angela's colonic irrigationist turned down her kind offer of oral sex. I mean, she's a gorgeous-looking woman, but the guy *had* just stuffed a hosepipe up her arse and watched a month's worth of shit shoot out. A blow job was probably the last thing on his mind.

Philippe appears at our table. 'Would you care to order some drinks *laydeez*?' he smarms.

'I'll have a Bellini,' says Stella. Angela plumps for champagne and I go for a white-wine spritzer. Philippe looks expectantly at Patti, who doesn't say a word, but simply pulls a cream-coloured business card with gold italic lettering from her Kelly bag and hands it to him. He looks at the card, raises his eyebrows in surprise, and says, 'Very good, madame,' before mincing off in the direction of the bar.

'What's the matter, Patti? Don't you converse with the hired help these days?' I ask.

'You'd be surprised how many bartenders don't know how to mix a decent cocktail,' she says in clipped tones. 'I'm just making life easy for them.' Seeing my quizzical look, she fishes an identical card from her bag and hands it to me.

'Smirnoff martini, straight up, extra cold, one olive, stirred not shaken,' I read aloud. 'How terribly organized of you.' How terribly fucking anal more like it.

'Now, let's not waste time on small talk,' says Patti, swiping the card out of my hand. 'I vote we get our menu selections out of the way immediately and then we can concentrate on helping Thea.'

'I don't need your help, honestly,' I protest. 'I'm perfectly capable of salvaging my own marriage.'

'Darling, there's no need to be brave. You're among friends here – and what Stella, Angie and I don't know about unfaithful husbands simply isn't worth knowing. Now, I'm going to have the consommé, followed by, let's see . . . a nice mangetout and quail's egg salad . . .'

'Hang on a minute, I don't actually know that Toby *has* been unfaithful. As a matter of fact, he insists that he hasn't – he says he met this girl backstage, they hit a club and then they went back to his hotel room for a drink and nothing more.'

'Oh, c'mon, Thea. Get real,' says Angela unkindly. 'They probably humped the living daylights out of each other.'

'Now, now,' Patti interjects. 'The truth is probably somewhere in between.' She takes a big thirsty gulp of the martini that's just been delivered. 'Hmmm, not bad. Right, everyone, let's get down to business. The unsavoury fact is that any woman in our position expects her husband to be unfaithful, which is fine so long as she is adequately compensated.'

'Compensated?' says Stella.

'Furs, jewellery, five-star Caribbean holidays – all perfectly acceptable currency in my book,' says Patti, smiling smugly. 'What we won't stand for, however, is having our noses rubbed in it. Gossip among one's friends and acquaintances is bad enough, but a nasty little newspaper story' – at this point she looks at me sympathetically – 'is a different matter altogether. Now, as I see it, Thea has several options open to her. The first one is to give Toby a taste of his own medicine. May I illustrate by using a personal example?'

'Please do,' I say. Despite my distaste for this very public dissection of my marriage, I must also admit to a certain morbid curiosity about Patti's own marital traumas.

'Rich and I had only been married six months when

he was unfaithful to me for the first time. It was the early Seventies and Rough Ryder were on the South American leg of their Bridges to Nowhere tour when it came to my attention that my husband was fucking one of the backing singers – an American girl with an enormous Afro and tits like melons.'

'But didn't you go on that tour?' interrupts Angela.

'Yes, that's right. I kept a diary for *Vogue* – it was one of the best-selling issues of 1972 – I have half a dozen spare copies at home if you'd like to borrow one sometime.'

'How awful for you,' I say. 'I can't believe Rich would be so tacky.'

'Are you kidding? This is the man who recently commissioned a guitar-shaped swimming pool for the garden,' says Patti witheringly, before continuing with her tale. 'Everyone on that tour knew about Rich's fling, and I mean everyone – the roadies, the stage crew, my personal masseuse . . . I was mortified.'

'What did you do?' asks Stella. 'Confront Rich? Demand the backing singer be ditched from the tour?'

'No,' says Patti. 'I did better than that – I fucked Danny D'Silva.'

'Danny D'Silva . . . Rough Ryder's drummer,' Angela gasps. 'The man with a dick the size of—'

'A broom handle,' says Patti, smiling at the memory. 'I rode him like a Derby winner. In fact, I can honestly say it was the best sex I've ever had and of course I didn't keep it a secret.'

'Rich must've been furious,' says Stella.

'Oh yes, he went absolutely berserk – trashed the hotel room, the tour bus, his favourite Fender ... And that would've been the end of it of – he had cheated on me and I had wreaked my revenge. There was just one teensy complication: that stupid, selfish husband of mine had only gone and got the backing singer pregnant. An illegitimate child would be too much to bear. I arranged and paid for the abortion and gave her £5,000 in cash, which was a lot of money in those days. It was worth it, though – she stuck to her side of the bargain by keeping her trap shut. Rich and I reached a new understanding after that little episode and he never flaunted his affairs in front of me again. He's the soul of discretion these days.'

'But you aren't seriously suggesting I should shag one of Toby's bandmates?' I say incredulously. 'Because I'm telling you now, they wouldn't take it if it was offered to them on a plate ... they've all known each other since sixth form college, for heaven's sake.'

'It doesn't have to be a guy from the band, just somebody close to him – a brother, say, or someone at the record company,' she says.

'Absolutely no fucking way. I don't agree with this eye-for-an-eye mentality. And anyway, as I keep telling you, I don't know that Toby *has* been unfaithful.'

'Well, perhaps you should go for option two then: a six-page spread in *Wow!* magazine.'

I point two fingers at my open mouth and make a gagging noise.

'Come on, Thea, what could be better than a nice *at home* with a sympathetic journalist and full copy and picture approval? You'd probably make the front cover and you could even insist on Terry O'Neill and a set of complimentary prints. I can see it now: you and Toby clinking Waterford crystal glasses over that beautiful walnut dining table. The pair of you lounging on that kingsize sleigh bed ... you could wear those darling Donna Karan pyjamas. Interview-wise, you could play it one of two ways: Toby could either *a*) come clean and put his misdemeanour down to a moment of sheer, alcohol-fuelled madness and publicly declare undying love and fidelity to you, his beautiful wife, or *b*) deny everything. Either way you'd emerge with your dignity intact and earn yourself a nice thirty grand into the bargain.'

'I'd shoot myself before I'd open my front door to that sycophantic mob. And I don't think it would do much for Toby's street cred.'

'Well, that just takes us back to my original suggestion: empty the joint account, then get yourself the best divorce lawyer you can and take him to the fucking cleaner's. And if you can get him to impregnate you first, all the better – it'll double your alimony.'

I should point out at this juncture that Patti doesn't know about the abortion – nobody does, just Toby and Kim – or else she wouldn't have said that.

'But I don't want to get divorced,' I say petulantly.

'I don't blame you,' says Stella. 'If I was married to

that stud bunny, I'd hang on for grim death. If you let
Toby out of your clutches, he'll be snapped up in
seconds . . . that's if Alexa Hunt hasn't already got her
claws into him.'

'Stella, do you have to?' hisses Patti. 'We're trying
to cheer Thea up, not send her plummeting into a
suicidal depression.' She turns back to me. 'Although if
you did feel in need of a little pick-me-up, I know where
you can get a limitless supply of Prozac, no prescription
required.'

'Well, I'll be sure to let you know the minute I hit
rock bottom,' I say sarcastically, 'but for the time being
I would like to assure you all that I am perfectly OK.
Now can we please talk about someone else's love life
for a change?'

'Spoilsport,' says Stella under her breath. 'Only
kidding!' she trills when I glare at her.

'Let's talk about me then,' say Angela. 'I've started
seeing the most gorgeous man.'

'He's her personal trainer,' adds Stella.

'I didn't know you worked out,' I say.

'Oh yes, it's all part of my new health kick. My
sojourn at the Anderson Center has really helped me
reassess my entire lifestyle. Toxins are out, exercise is
in. I can't tell you how alive I feel,' she gushes.

'And no doubt you've been notching up plenty of
extra-curricular activity with Mr Bench Press,' I say.

'Ra-ther! Jake is so totally fuckable – he's got big
brown eyes and a stomach you could bounce twopence

pieces off. And actually he's rather good company too. It's just a pity there's no future in it.'

'Why do you say that, darling? The man sounds divine,' drawls Patti, vainly trying to attract Philippe's attention by snapping her fingers in the air.

'No money,' says Angela dismissively. 'The man doesn't own a single gold card, his car is six years old, he shops in Gap and, worst of all, he lives above a shop.' The last three words are said in an embarrassed whisper.

'But apart from all that you like the guy, right?' I ask her.

'Oh yes, I like him very much. But let's face it, unless he gets Elton John as a client, he's never ever going to be able to earn enough money to keep me in the style to which I am accustomed. It's all that bastard judge's fault. If it wasn't for him, I'd be rolling in it.'

I should explain at this point that Angela's divorce settlement was finalized a couple of weeks ago. Instead of the £2 million payout she was hoping for, Lord Chief Justice Boothby awarded her a modest fifty grand – 'Not enough to keep me in nail polish,' as she told Nigel Dempster.

'Have you thought about going back to work?' I ask her.

She looks aghast. 'You *must* be joking. I wouldn't go back to being a receptionist for all the slingbacks in Prada. No, I shall just keep looking until I find me a rich man. Stella's promised to set me up with Roger

Bowles, haven't you, babe?' she says, simpering at her friend.

'He'll be a pushover,' says Stella of the eminent BBC broadcaster. 'According to Titus, he's a sucker – and I mean that quite literally – for a big pair of knockers – and Angie's certainly not lacking in that department,' she says, gesturing at Angela's generous cleavage.

'But isn't he a little old? He must be getting near retirement.'

'He's sixty-one,' says Stella matter-of-factly. 'But she won't have to have sex with him, everyone knows he's impotent. He's into infantilism. You know the kind of thing . . . all she'll be required to do is wipe his arse, pin him into a giant nappy, *breastfeed* him.' As if acting on some invisible cue, she and Angela fall about laughing.

'That is utterly revolting,' says Patti, who has finally caught Philippe's attention. 'Angela, you can't possibly consider dating this deviant. I'm sure we can come up with somebody more suitable. Thea, you must know lots of eligible young men,' she says, emphasizing the 'young'.

'Erm, I'm not sure really, I'll have to have a think.' There is no way I'd stitch up one of my friends by setting him up with Angela. The woman is a total parasite.

Philippe is standing at the table, waiting patiently to take our order. The others have unimaginatively settled on consommé to start, followed by a selection of warm salads and a steamed vegetable medley to share. Everything on the menu looks so delicious, I just can't make up my mind, so I ask Philippe for his recommendations.

'The goat's cheese and sundried tomato tart would be an excellent choice to start with, madame,' he says. 'And for a main course, I would recommend the calves' liver in cream and brandy sauce.'

'Sounds good to me. And is the raspberry millefeuille still gracing your dessert menu?'

'Certainly, or perhaps madame would prefer today's special: caramel profiteroles with crème anglaise.'

'Ooh, it's gonna be a tough choice,' I say, smiling at him. At this point I notice that Stella is staring at me with a barely concealed expression of disgust.

'Is something wrong?' I ask her.

'Not at all. I just wish I could put it away like you do,' she says cattily. 'I've never known anyone with such a, how can I put it – *healthy* appetite. Don't take this the wrong way, Thea, but maybe you should think about cutting down on your calorie intake. I do think self-restraint is so important for women in our position. After all, you can hardly blame Toby for looking elsewhere if you're piling on the pounds, now can you?'

I am speechless with indignation. The fucking bitch. As I listen to them wittering away, I wonder why the hell I bother maintaining a friendship with these harpies. Mind you, it's not the first time I've thought that – and I dare say it won't be the last.

TWELVE

I arrive at Maze Hill station in Greenwich just after seven-thirty. Now that I'm actually here the butterflies have started. Kim offered to come with me and right now I'd be glad of her support, but I can't rely on other people my whole life; this is something I must do on my own. Of course, I don't seriously believe that 'Kevin' will still be living at 83 Hermitage Road after nearly three decades, but the current occupants may have some faint recollection of him or, if I'm really lucky, a forwarding address. I walk towards Trafalgar Road, zipping up my polar fleece against the chilly evening air. I deliberately didn't wear anything too flash – this part of Greenwich is a bit rough round the edges – even as a kid Mum didn't like me coming down here on my own. We lived further west, on the border with Lewisham – not more upmarket, exactly, but a bit more characterful at least.

When I reach Greenwich Hospital, an ugly grey

monolith squatting malevolently at the foot of Van-
brugh Hill, I take a quick look at the A–Z in my
shoulderbag to refresh my memory, before crossing the
road and taking the first turning on the left. Hermitage
Road is a narrow, treeless street of Victorian dockers'
cottages. As I count the numbers off one by one, I am
conscious of a loosening in my bowels. What if Kevin
does still live here? What if the man who opens the door
has my eyes or my nose? Should I invent an excuse
about trying to track down an old friend or come clean
immediately? I don't want to give him a heart attack.
Come to think of it, I don't know that Kevin ever
actually lived at 83 Hermitage Road – just that he once
met Mum there. It suddenly strikes me that I haven't
thought this madcap scheme through properly at all.

Ridiculously, I feel a small glow of pride when I
discover that Number 83 is one of the smarter cottages
in the street. A low picket fence encloses the small but
neat front garden and the front door is painted a sunny
yellow. Someone is at home because, through the chink
in the curtains, I can see that the lights are on. God, do
I really want to put myself through this? I wonder what
Mum would say if she could see me now. She never
encouraged me to make contact with my dad, but I
don't think she'd have stood in my way if I'd shown any
real interest. 'Whatever makes you happy, Thea love,'
that was her catchphrase. So before I can change my
mind, I push open the little wooden gate, walk up to the
yellow door, smooth my hair flat, take a deep breath

and push the doorbell hard. After a few seconds it opens to reveal a beefy man in his mid-thirties with a florid complexion and a stainless steel ladle in his hand.

'Yes?' he says rather irritably. 'If you're a Jehovah's Witness, I'm not interested.'

'Oh no, I'm trying to track down an old friend of my mother's,' I say trying to sound confident, even though my legs have turned to jelly. 'He used to live here a long time ago. I was wondering if you knew him.'

'Goodness, I doubt it very much. We only moved in last summer,' he says a little more kindly. 'Listen, I don't mean to be rude, but I've got a pan of spaghetti bolognese back there and an unsupervised eight-year-old, so I'd better get back indoors.'

'Please, I'd be ever so grateful if you could just spare me two minutes,' I plead.

I must look dead pathetic because he gives a kind of half-smile and says, 'Well, you'd better come in, then.'

I step inside and he gestures to a room just off the hallway. 'Do you want to wait in the living room with Ben while I switch off the spag bol? I won't be a sec.'

He bustles off up the hall and I walk into the lounge, where a small blond-haired boy is sitting on his heels in front of the TV, engrossed in *Power Rangers*.

'Hello there,' I say to the kid, as I perch one buttock on the arm of a brown velvet sofa. He turns his head a fraction, gives me a small, shy smile then turns back to the screen. I look around the room, checking out the candelabra wall lights and the heavy William Morrisprint curtains. A bit twee for my taste, but it's all expensive stuff. Then the man reappears minus the ladle.

'I'm Alan, by the way,' he says, wiping his hand on the side of his jeans before extending it towards me.

'Thea, Thea Carson,' I say shaking his hand. 'It's terribly kind of you to invite me in like this.'

'Well, I can see this is important to you – although, like I say, I don't think I'll be of much help. Now who's this chap you're looking for?'

'I don't have much to go on I'm afraid. He's called Kevin – I don't know his surname – and he lived here in the early Seventies.'

'That's going too far back for me,' he says, rubbing his chin. 'I'd never lived south of the river till we moved here. Cheryl, my wife, might be able to help you, though, she's lived in east Greenwich her whole life – grew up in the next street, in fact. And if *she* doesn't remember your Kevin, chances are she'll know a man who does. She'll be back any minute, she was catching the seven-fifty train. You're welcome to hang on for her.'

'I don't want to impose . . .'

'It's no problem, honestly.'

'Well, that'd be great. Thanks very much.'

Alan sits down in an armchair and we make strained conversation, while the Midwich Cuckoo continues to stare at the TV screen glassy-eyed. After ten minutes or so, I'm beginning to think about making my excuses and leaving when I hear the sound of a key turning in a lock. Alan springs up to meet his wife and I hear muted voices from the hallway. Moments later, a shortish, roundish, blonde woman in a putty-coloured mac appears at the lounge door.

'Mummy!' squeals the kid, who jumps up like he's just been zapped by 10,000 volts. He runs to her and wraps his arms around her midriff and, at the risk of sounding overly sentimental, I have to say I find it quite a touching scene. It must be amazing to have a little person so totally in love with you. Maybe one day I'll find out what it feels like for myself. The woman flashes me a hesitant smile and Alan introduces us. 'Love, this is . . .' he pauses. 'Thea,' I prompt him. 'Yes – Thea – of course. She's trying to trace an old friend of her mother's who once lived here, in our house. I was absolutely no use whatsoever, but I thought you might know something, being a local girl and all.'

'Well, I'll certainly do my best,' she says.

I give her the spiel and add that Kevin would probably have been in his twenties or thirties when he inhabited their home.

'Gosh, that's not much to go on,' she says. 'I grew up in the next street, but I can't say I ever met any of this house's previous occupants – except the ones before us, of course, and they'd only been here a couple of years themselves. *Kevin* – no, I'm sorry, I don't know any Kevins.'

My disappointment is obvious. 'Well, thanks anyway,' I say dejectedly, standing up and hooking my bag over my shoulder. 'I guess I'll just have to draw a line under this one.'

'Hang on a mo,' says Cheryl suddenly. 'There is one person round here who might be able to help you.'

'Oh?' I say, my eyes lighting up.

'Tom Bailey at Number 22 has lived in this street since the Sixties, believe it or not, so he knows pretty much everything that goes on round here. He's probably your best bet.'

'He's a leading light in Neighbourhood Watch and the resident busybody,' says Alan, raising his eyes skywards. 'You can't walk past his house without the curtains twitching.'

'Now, now, Alan,' Cheryl reprimands him gently. Then she turns back to me and says, 'You'll probably catch Tom at home if you go round there now, he rarely goes out in the evenings.'

After thanking them both profusely, I head off back down the street to Number 22. All the lights are off, but behind the net curtains I can make out the bluish flicker of a television screen. This cottage isn't as well looked after as Cheryl and Alan's place. An overgrown privet threatens to flatten the rickety fence and the windowsills are desperately in need of a lick of paint. Still, he's an old guy so DIY probably isn't high on his list of priorities. I walk up to the shabby front door, which bears a Neighbourhood Watch sticker and a neat handwritten sign Sellotaped next to the letterbox saying, 'No flyers or circulars please'.

There doesn't appear to be a bell or a door knocker, so I rap sharply on the door with my knuckles. After three or four minutes there's still no reply, so I flick the letter-box flap a couple of times. At last I hear signs of movement, a shuffling noise, followed by the rattle of deadbolts being pulled back. Finally, the door itself creaks slowly open and a withered head with two sunken eyes appears over the top of a brass chain.

'Can I help you?' he says in a genteel voice that bears no trace of a south-east London twang.

'Mr Bailey?' I ask.

'That's me.'

'I'm so sorry to bother you, but I'm trying to trace an old friend of my mother's who once lived in this street. Alan and Cheryl at Number 83 said you might remember him.'

'Did they now?' he says suspiciously.

'I won't take up much of your time, I promise.'

'I don't usually let strangers in the house, you can't be too careful these days. I'm chairman of the local Neighbourhood Watch, you know,'

'Yes, yes, I do know actually. Alan and Cheryl spoke very highly of you. They said if anyone could help me it would be you,' I say, batting my eyelashes in a blatant display of flattery.

'Well, seeing as you've been recommended, I'll make an exception just this once.'

The door shuts and I hear him fumble with the chain, then it opens again and I see that, despite his advanced age, he cuts rather a dapper figure in tweedy trousers and braces over a light-coloured shirt. He ushers me into the dark living room, where *Brookside* is blasting out and switches on an old-fashioned standard lamp with a ruched fabric shade.

'Can I get you something – a cup of tea, perhaps, or a glass of lemon barley?'

'No, thank you. I'm fine.'

'Chocolate digestive, slice of Battenberg?'

'Really, I don't want to put you to any trouble.'

'Oh it's no trouble dear, no trouble at all. I don't get many visitors you see, so I like to make a fuss of the ones I do have.' He picks up the remote control from the arm of his chair and jabs at it randomly until the TV goes quiet, then sits down on the chintzy two-seater sofa and invites me to join him.

'I've lived in this street more than forty years,' he says proudly.

'I guess you must really love this part of Greenwich.'

'I suppose I do, although it's changed beyond all recognition over the past twenty years. There's no sense of neighbourliness any more, people are too wrapped up in their own lives to bother about anybody else. If it wasn't for Neighbourhood Watch nobody round here would even know my name,' he grumbles. 'To be honest, it's the house that keeps me here; this place holds a lot of happy memories. After my wife died twelve years ago, I knew I would never move. I like it here, surrounded by all her things. If they want to cart me off to an old people's home, they'll have to take me kicking and screaming.'

'You must miss her an awful lot.'

'You can say that again. Cancer stole her from me – three months from diagnosis to death, three short months to say goodbye. It was too quick, too damn quick.'

To my horror, a fat tear springs from his eye and begins a slow descent down his cheek. He wipes it away and clears his throat noisily.

'My mum died of cancer a couple of years ago,' I say quickly in an attempt to spare his discomfiture. 'I know how it feels to lose someone you love.'

'I'm sorry to hear that, she can't have been very old.'

'Fifty-nine. I thought my world had ended, but it's true what they say about time being a great healer. The pain hasn't gone away, it just gets easier to cope with.'

He nods sadly, acknowledging our shared emotion. 'So why are you so keen to track down this friend of hers after all this time?

Shit. I wasn't prepared for that, so I just say the first thing that comes to mind.

'My mum left him some bits and pieces in her will, jewellery and, erm, books. I wanted to give them to him personally.'

'I see. And this chap used to live here in Hermitage Road, you say.'

'I believe so – Number 83. It was a long time ago, the early Seventies.'

'And his name?'

'Kevin.'

'Kevin what?'

'I don't know his surname I'm afraid.'

'Surely your mother wrote his full name in her will – the solicitor will have asked her for it.'

'Oh, it wasn't an official will,' I hastily ad-lib. 'Just a handwritten letter to me, with a list of friends and what she wanted them to have. I've managed to track down most of the others, but I've drawn a complete blank with Kevin.'

'You know something? I think your luck just might be in.'

'You do!' I exclaim, leaning forward in my seat.

'Because as it happens I do recall a gentleman called Kevin living at Number 83.'

'Ohmigod, that's amazing!'

'He and his wife moved in around . . . let's see, my son had just emigrated to Australia, so it would've been 1973. He was a nice chap, always had time for a *good morning* and a *how are you?*'

'He had a wife, you say.'

'That's right, Jenny – and very pretty she was too. Huge brown eyes and long curly hair, almost down to her waist.'

Which means, of course, that Kevin was married when he was seeing Mum.

'Now what was their surname?' says Tom, leaning back against the lace-trimmed antimacassar and closing his eyes. 'Something Italian it was, beginning with an

F . . . Franco, Franconi, no – Fanconi, that was it. Fanconi!' he says jabbing a finger triumphantly in the air.

'Fan-con-i,' I say the word slowly, rolling it round
in my mouth. 'Did they stay in Greenwich when they
left Hermitage Road do you know?'

'No, they went north – to Turnpike Lane, I think,
or was it Tufnell Park? Something to do with his work
I seem to remember. He was a heating engineer – once
fixed my boiler for cost price, very good of him.'

I can hardly believe it, the first piece of the jigsaw
falling beautifully into place. And now that I know his
surname, the task of tracking him down will be infinitely
easier. Kevin Fanconi . . . I can almost picture him,
dark-skinned and swarthy with heavy eyebrows and
thick wavy hair.

'What did Kevin look like? Do you remember?' I
ask Tom gently.

'I can do better than remember, I've got a photograph somewhere I shouldn't wonder,' he says, getting
slowly to his feet and shuffling over to a dark wooden
bureau in the corner of the room. 'We had lots of
neighbourly get-togethers back in those days, not like
nowadays when nobody even bothers to acknowledge
you in the street.'

Watching him rummage through a large shallow
drawer in the bureau, I can feel my excitement building.
Just think, in a couple of minutes' time I could be about
to come face to face with my dad for the very first time.

'Here we are,' he says, holding up a dog-eared print.

'The Hermitage Road street party for the queen's Silver Jubilee.' I get up and join him by the bureau. The colour photo shows a line of long trestle tables, decked out in red, white and blue bunting and laden with wine and Coke bottles, cheese and pineapple hedgehogs and slices of gateau. There are three men in the shot and it's not immediately obvious which one is Kevin.

'That's your man,' says Tom, gesturing at a blond man in a pink shirt and a Starsky-style belted cardigan, who is raising a Babycham glass to the camera. He's short, fair-skinned and thickset; nothing like me at all. Squinting at the picture, I scan his face for some resemblance – my high cheekbones or arched eyebrows, but there's nothing discernible. Still that doesn't prove anything. Plenty of people look nothing like their parents.

'Did they have any kids – Kevin and his wife?' I ask.

'No, at least not while I knew them. They were newly-weds and only in their middle twenties when they moved into the street. That's Jenny Fanconi there,' he says pointing at a slim, dark-haired woman in the foreground. Her head is slightly cocked to one side and she's smiling, her eyes half-closed against the sun. Tom's right, she *is* pretty.

'You've been a big help,' I say, handing back the photograph. 'Thank you so much.'

'Good. I do so like to be useful,' he says with a twinkly smile. 'Be sure to pass on my regards if and when you run Kevin to ground, won't you now?'

'Of course I will. And thanks again, Tom. I don't know what I would've done without you.'

As we say goodbye on the doorstep, he suddenly reaches out and squeezes my hand. 'I hope you find what you're looking for,' he says.

'So do I,' I say, squeezing his hand back. 'So do I.'

Travelling back across London by minicab, I feel quite proud of myself. Besides the fact that I'm one step closer to finding Kevin, I'm amazed that I had the confidence to knock on two strangers' doors and extract some sort of useful information from them. I'm not usually very good at asserting myself, I've always been too dependent on other people for my own good.

I'm on such a high when I arrive back at Kim's that I head straight for her office to see if I can take my investigation one step further. She and Tim have gone to a dinner party tonight and won't be back for ages. Flinging my bag on the floor, I fire up the Mac, log onto Internet Explorer and key in the URL for BT's online phone directory. Thank goodness Kevin's got such an unusual name, I wouldn't have a hope of finding him if he was a Brown or a Jones. The search page flashes up and I quickly key in the blanks:

NAME: Fanconi
INITIAL: K
AREA: London

I hit the *RESIDENTIAL* search button, sit back and cross my fingers. A few seconds later a new page flashes up: 'Sorry, we were unable to complete your enquiry.' Damn. That means he's either ex-directory or he's moved out of the city altogether. I'm about to disconnect, when I have another idea. Returning to the search page, I hit the *BUSINESS* button. Come on, come on . . . why is this stupid thing so slow?

While I'm waiting for the information to download, I start sifting through the tray of filing on Kim's desk, sorting into it piles – invoices, correspondence, VAT receipts, and so on. I can't resist reading the personal letter of thanks from Amba Lazenby. Handwritten on a gold monogrammed card it reads: 'Dear Kim, I just wanted to thank you for staging such a spectacular party. It was a night I'll never forget . . .' That's a joke, given that she was stoned and/or unconscious for most of it. I stick it in the correspondence pile and glance up at the computer screen. Fucking hell. I don't believe it. The little beauty's found something:

Fanconi, K. Heating Contractor,
35 Quentin Road, N7.

Everything fits: the name, the job, the Tufnell Park postcode. I'm so excited, I grab the phone and dial the number straight away without a thought as to what I might say. After two rings an answerphone picks up:

'Fanconi Heating is now closed,' says a nondescript male voice. 'Please call again between nine a.m. and six p.m. or, if you require our emergency callout service, please call Kevin on . . .' I jot down the mobile number that follows before replacing the handset. Should I wait until tomorrow when I'm feeling cool, calm and rational or call him now when I'm fired up and ready for action? Checking my watch, I see that it's just before ten . . . oh, fuck it, there's no time like the present.

My fingers are trembling as I punch out the number. When the ringing tone kicks in, I almost jump out of my skin. Deep breaths, Thea, stay calm; you're so close, don't blow it now.

'Hello, Kevin speaking,' says a male voice.

I am suddenly struck dumb.

'Hello?' the voice says again.

'Er, Kevin Fanconi, heating contractor?' I say, sounding like a right idiot.

'That's me. Do you need help?'

'Help? What kind of help?'

'You tell me,' he says, laughing good-naturedly. 'Boiler conked out, blocked flue, no hot water?'

'Oh, right. No. I mean yes. I mean you *can* help me, but not in the way you think.'

'Sorry, love, you've lost me.'

I take a deep breath and in the few seconds it takes to exhale I formulate my next, critical sentence.

'You don't know me, but my name's Thea Carson.

I'm not sure if I'm speaking to the right Kevin Fanconi, but a long time ago – twenty-eight years to be exact – I think you knew my mother.'

A long silence follows. I begin to wonder if he's put the phone down, when I hear him say, 'I'm racking my brains here love, but I'm afraid the name Carson doesn't ring any bells. Was your mum a client of mine or did I know her socially?'

I laugh with relief, a silly nervous giggle. 'Oh no, Carson's my married name. My maiden name is Parkinson.'

'Shirley Parkinson!' the words practically explode out of his mouth.

'Yes, yes, that's her. You do remember her then?'

'Remember her? How could I possibly forget Shirley Parkinson, the woman who changed the course of my life?' he says excitedly. 'How the hell is she? Still living in Greenwich?'

'No, no she's not. Actually, she's dead; she died of cancer nearly two years ago.'

'Oh no, I *am* sorry to hear that. Your mother was a good friend to me when I was going through a difficult time, a very good friend indeed. I haven't seen her in years, mind you, but she was often in my thoughts.'

Wow. Sounds like they were pretty close, and they obviously parted on good terms.

'I'm in the process of tracking down a few of my Mum's old friends – and it took quite a bit of detective work to find you – because she left some bits and pieces in her will and I know she'd want you to have something. Would you be interested in meeting up one day, just for coffee or a quick drink?' I venture.

'Why not? When are you free?'

'Any time really.'

'It's all right for some . . . got a rich husband have you?' he says with a laugh – not a nasty snide laugh, but a really big belly laugh like he really is joking . . . if only he knew.

I laugh along with him. 'I'm lucky enough to have flexible working hours,' I explain.

'Well evenings are best for me. I'm on callout tomorrow and Wednesday, so how about Thursday, around six-thirty?'

'That'd be great. We're both in north London, so let's meet somewhere central, like Islington.'

'OK . . . do you know the Prince of Wales on Upper Street?'

'I certainly do; I'll meet you in there.'

'Perfect. Oh, how will we recognize each other?'

'What do you look like?' I say. I'd better not let on that I've seen a photo of him, not yet anyway.

'Well I've got blond hair, receding a bit now . . . and I'm on the short side. And I've got a beer belly – the wife keeps telling me I should get down the gym. I'm not painting a very flattering portrait of myself, am I?'

We laugh simultaneously. 'I'll find you,' I say.

'Well, Thea Carson, I look forward to meeting you.'

I replace the handset and punch the air in triumph.

In two days' time I will meet the man who could just possibly be my father. My story about Mum's will sounds convincing enough and Kevin didn't seem in the least bit suspicious. Actually, he sounded like a really nice guy, I can't wait to meet him. Switching off the computer, I release a big noisy yawn. I'm not used to so much excitement in one day. And, as I make my way upstairs to bed, I suddenly realize that I haven't thought about Toby once since lunchtime.

THIRTEEN

When I woke up this morning and went down to breakfast, there was a wonderful surprise waiting for me on Kim's kitchen table. A huge bunch of flowers – and I'm not talking about a poxy bunch of long-stemmed roses, I mean a seriously expensive, over-the-top, mother-fucker of a bouquet – with lilies and orchids and great green ferny things I don't even know the name of. *To my gorgeous wife*, read the little card. *Out of sight, but not definitely not out of mind. All my love, babe, Toby.*

After our row on the telephone, I had imagined that Toby would put me firmly to the back of his mind. That's his usual way of coping with a problem: ignore it and hope someone else will eventually take responsibility for sorting it out. But maybe I misjudged him. I was really touched by his thoughtfulness. Not that a bunch of flowers will heal the hurt I feel, but it's a sign that he wants forgiveness – isn't it? I was half tempted to use the gift as an excuse to ring him; to be honest, I've been gagging to call him for days, but Kim urged me to stand firm.

'You agreed to have a complete break from one another until he gets back from tour and there's only another week to go,' she said. 'If you call him now, it'll look like you're backing down and he'll know he's got you by the short and curlies.'

She's right, of course. And I *am* still smarting from that Alexa Hunt business. But the truth is I miss him like crazy. So I've decided that if he comes back from the tour suitably contrite and makes a real effort to spend more time at home, I'm prepared to let bygones be bygones. Even if he did sleep with that girl, I can't let one mistake ruin our marriage. Patti's right, a celebrity wife has to be flexible – although I do think there's a fine line between being flexible and being a doormat.

I can't wait to tell Toby about the search for my father. He's going to be stunned at how much I've managed to achieve in such a short space of time; I certainly am. In the two days since I spoke to Kevin, all I've done is fantasize about our meeting, which will take place this evening. Wouldn't it be the most amazing thing if he did turn out to be my father? We'd have to do a DNA test, of course, just to make sure, but that's straightforward enough. Kim is as excited as me. We should have spent the day brainstorming ideas for an uber-cool PR company's tenth birthday party, but all we've done is discuss tonight's rendezvous – what I should wear, what I should say, how I'm going to broach the delicate subject of paternity. We both agree that I shouldn't mention my famous connection, not at our first meeting, anyway. 'You don't want celebrity clouding the issue,' Kim warned. 'You want Kevin to like you for yourself, not for who your husband is.'

By the time the cab arrives to take me to the Prince of Wales at ten past six, I'm in a state of nervous anticipation. I agonized over what to wear, but in the end I plumped for a pink Whistles dress with knee-high brown leather boots and my tan leather coat.

'Good luck,' says Kim, giving me a big hug as she sees me off. 'And remember, don't you leave that pub with him, however nice he seems, because at the end of the day you don't know him from Adam. And call me if there are any problems at all.'

'Yes, Mum,' I say cheekily as I climb into the cab.

Arriving at the Prince of Wales five minutes early, I have a quick scout around just in case Kevin's early too, but the place is only half full and there's no sign of an overweight blond fifty-something male, so I order a double gin and bitter lemon to calm my nerves and settle down in a corner seat. After twenty minutes and a second gin (just a single this time), I'm beginning to think he's not going to show. Why are all the men in my life so bloody unreliable? I'm wondering whether to call his mobile when suddenly he walks in. I know it's him straight away. He may be twenty-five years older than the man in Tom's photo, but he's barely changed, if you ignore the laughter lines around his eyes and the thinning hair. Oh, and the navy blue boiler suit's a bit of a giveaway. He scans the bar until finally his eyes settle on me. I smile hesitantly and give a little wave and he breaks into the most enormous grin and comes striding over.

'Thea?' he says.

I nod.

'You've got your mother's eyes,' he says.

'Really? I never thought we looked at all alike.'

'No, I can see her in you, I really can.'

Immediately I feel more relaxed.

'It was bumper to bumper on the North Circular,' he explains. 'I came straight here after my last job, I didn't even have time to go home and change,' he says gesturing at his navy overalls.

'It's wonderful to meet you,' I say, extending my hand.

'Likewise,' he says, giving me a firm handshake.

After he's furnished himself with a half of Guinness, we begin the awkward business of getting acquainted. I tell him I'm married and that my husband 'works for a record company', which is bending the truth only ever so slightly and he in turn reveals that he's still married to Jenny, although they remain childless. They live in a three-bedroom semi off the Holloway Road, from where Kevin has been running his own business for the past twenty years and doing very well for himself by all accounts. He asks me how I managed to track him down and I provide an edited version of my trip to Hermitage Road.

'Bloody hell, Tom's not still there, is he? How wonderful that he remembered me after all this time. I'll have to drop him a line,' he says. 'It sounds like you went to an awful lot of trouble to find me.'

'I quite enjoyed it, actually,' I say. 'I'm just sorry it took me so long to get round to making contact with you. After Mum died I managed to get in touch with most of the friends she'd listed in her letter, so I could give them the little mementos she wanted them to have. But she'd only written down your Christian name – and no address – so I didn't think I'd ever be able to find you. Then I was going through some of her old diaries recently and I found a reference to a "Kevin" at the Hermitage Road address and put two and two together.'

'Well, it was very clever of you, although I must say I'm surprised Shirley bothered to leave me something. What was it?'

'Oh, nothing very valuable I'm afraid. Just a, er, chiffon scarf. I meant to bring it with me, but I was so excited about meeting you I left it back at home. I can always put it in the post.'

'A chiffon scarf . . . how wonderfully appropriate of her,' he says. I can't imagine why he would consider it a particularly fitting gift. It was simply the first thing that popped into my head.

'Shirley was a lovely woman,' he continues. 'And

always buzzing with energy; I never knew anyone with so much joie de vivre.'

I nod and take a gulp of gin, feeling emotion start to bubble up inside me.

'Are you all right, love?' Kevin asks me gently. 'I'm sorry, I didn't mean to upset you.'

'I'm fine, really,' I tell him. 'It's just that it's been a while since I've discussed Mum with someone who knew her – I mean really knew her intimately like you obviously did.'

He seems a bit taken aback by that. 'Well, you know, we didn't know each other that long, just a matter of months really. But in that time I suppose we did get pretty close. It was quite an intense sort of relationship.'

'Why did you split up, if you don't mind me asking?'

'Split up? Oh no, I think you've got the wrong end of the stick,' he says in a tone that's more amused than offended. 'We were never a couple, goodness me, no. Our friendship was purely platonic. I'd just got married when I met Shirley, and the fact that we're still together is all down to your mum, quite honestly.'

Shit. How embarrassing. I naturally assumed there had been a romance of sorts. Why else would Mum and Kevin have shared an evening rendezvous every two weeks, regular as clockwork? My confusion must be obvious because Kevin leans towards me and says in a stagy whisper, 'I take it Shirley never told you about my

. . . how can I put this? – I hate the word *deviancy* – *tendencies*, how about that?' He throws back his head and gives a great fruity chuckle.

Tendencies – what the fuck's he on about? Unpleasant images of sado-masochism and indecent exposure float before my eyes.

'To be honest, she never even mentioned you,' I say defensively.

'Well, let me get the next round in and when I come back all will be revealed,' he says mysteriously.

As soon as he's safely at the bar, I dig my mobile out of my bag and call up Kim's number from the phone book, so if need be I can contact her by pressing a single button. Oops, he's coming back. I shove the primed phone in my pocket, so it's close to hand and force a smile as Kevin puts my drink down in front of me. He sits down and without any sort of preamble, launches right into the story of how he met Mum.

'I'd been called out to a flat conversion in Lewisham to fix a leaking radiator,' he begins. 'On the way back to Hermitage Road I stopped off at a newsagent's on Blackheath Hill to buy a packet of mints. Some strange force – I don't know what, I like to call it fate – made me glance at the cards displayed in the window. One in particular caught my eye: *Skilled dressmaker available. All work considered. Contact Shirley Parkinson* – or words to that effect. It was the *all work considered* that clinched it; so I went back to the van for a pen and jotted down the number.'

I don't know where on earth this is leading and I'm bursting to go to the loo, but I don't want to interrupt Kevin's flow so I just nod encouragingly.

'It took me several days to pluck up the courage to make the call, but when I did and I outlined to Shirley what I wanted, she didn't sound in the least bit surprised; well, maybe just a tiny bit. She took it all in her stride and said that yes of course she was happy to do the job and why didn't we meet sometime to go through designs and colours and so on. She even offered to bring along some fabrics to show me.' At this point, he pauses and takes a big swallow of Guinness. Then he looks me right in the eye and says, 'The thing is, Thea, I'm a cross-dresser, have been since the age of eight. And I'm not ashamed of myself; I used to be, but not any more.'

Well, that's a bloody relief; I had imagined something infinitely worse. I have absolutely nothing to fear from a man who dresses in women's undies. I might have been a bit freaked a few years ago, but let's just say my experiences in the world of showbiz have broadened my horizons. Take Danny Newman, for example: he's sexier than most women I know. But I have to say I don't imagine Kevin scrubs up terrifically well. I give him an appraising look ... no, I can't picture this chunky, broad-shouldered, frankly hirsute man (judging by his forearms, he'd give Robin Williams a run for his money) in drag. He's so totally not feminine.

'What's up? Trying to imagine me in a frock?' he says, smiling.

'Something like that,' I laugh.

'Well, at least you're not on your way out the door. A lot of people find it very hard to deal with. I was nineteen when my dad found out – he called me a "bleeding queer" and swore he'd never speak to me again.'

'And did he?'

'Never got the chance. He died of a heart attack three weeks later. My mother said it was the shock of my revelation, never mind that he'd suffered from angina for years. After that I didn't dare share that part of my life with anyone. I kept it secret, locked away deep inside me. Until I met Shirley, that is.'

'Hang on a minute, I thought you said you'd just got married when you met Mum.'

'That's right.'

'So Jenny didn't know about the cross-dressing?'

'Not then she didn't. We'd been together nearly two years before we got married, but I'd gone to enormous lengths to hide it from her. All my gear – the clothes, the make-up, the wigs – were kept in the loft, where I knew she'd never venture, and I only slipped into my glad rags when she was safely out of the house. I hated myself for deceiving her, but I was desperately in love and couldn't bear the thought of losing her. I was so convinced she wouldn't be able to handle the truth, that she'd think I fancied men or wanted to have a sex change. But like a lot of transvestites I'm *not* gay – I fancy women as much as the next bloke. For me, cross-dressing isn't a sexual thing, it doesn't turn me on. It's just a release from pressure, a way of expressing emotions that I normally keep bottled up. I've always had a strong feminine side to my character and wearing a dress makes me feel more relaxed. I know it's probably hard for you to understand, but it's just the way I am.'

'No, no, I do understand,' I reassure him. 'But what I don't understand is what on earth persuaded you to confide in a virtual stranger like my mum.'

He smiles. 'At first it was just a business relationship with Shirley and me. You see, I commissioned her to make Natasha an entire wardrobe.'

'Natasha?' I say frowning.

'My female alter ego.'

'Right . . . nice name.'

'Thanks, I put a lot of thought into it.'

'Anyway, go on.'

'I wanted the works – lacy slips, elegant sheath dresses, pretty high-necked blouses and smart pencil skirts, none of your pie-crust collar and pleated skirt malarkey. It took Shirley months to make and she did a bloody brilliant job. The quality of workmanship was second to none and everything fitted beautifully. I'd never felt so feminine, so fulfilled.'

'Yeah, I suppose it must've been awkward for you having to buy women's clothes in shops. I mean you couldn't exactly try anything on could you?'

'Absolutely. Nowadays, of course, cross-dressing

has become more mainstream – and there are all kinds of websites where you can buy clothes and prosthetics and so on. But back then it was a different story. God, I used to skulk round House of Fraser like a shoplifter, pretending I was buying stuff for my wife. That's why meeting your mum was the answer to my prayers.

'We used to meet once a fortnight, always on a Thursday because that's the day Jenny would go and visit her sister in Bexleyheath. Usually I would go to Shirley's house, but once or twice she came to mine. She had such a good eye, she'd suggest styles and colours I'd never even considered. She knew instinctively what designs would flatter me and draw attention away from my masculine features. Right from the beginning we clicked. She was a very warm woman and a good listener, and as we got to know each other better, I found myself confiding in her more and more. In fact, I started to really look forward to our fittings because I knew I could unburden myself – selfish, I know, but Shirley didn't seem to mind. She couldn't believe it when I told her my own wife didn't even know about Natasha; not that she was judgemental or anything, she just said it must be an awful burden for me to bear. And it was. Our marriage was starting to show the signs of strain after just a few months. I think Jenny suspected I was having an affair. My behaviour must've seemed quite furtive on occasions and once she found an eye-liner pencil in the bathroom. Only of course it wasn't another woman's eyeliner – it was mine. I'd stupidly forgotten to clear it away when I'd been putting on my make-up one afternoon when Jenny was out shopping.'

'Gosh, what on earth did you tell her?'

'I said I'd been doing some work on a female customer's boiler and I must have picked it up by mistake, thinking it was my biro. I don't think Jenny believed me, but she didn't say anything. I wanted to tell her the truth, but after seeing how badly my mum and dad had taken it I couldn't bear to go through a similar trauma with Jenny. I would probably never have come clean if Shirley hadn't persuaded me that honesty really was the best policy.'

I am literally on the edge of my seat as Kevin reveals how, during those fortnightly fittings, Mum helped build his confidence and convince him that Jenny might be able to handle the revelation that she was married to a closet cross-dresser. She also pointed out that he wasn't doing himself any favours by keeping such a massive secret bottled up inside him and that he alone had the power to change things. I thought Toby and I had 'issues' to work through, but our problems are a piss in the ocean compared to the dilemma that Kevin faced all those years ago.

'After weeks and weeks of talking things through with Shirley, I realized that I simply had to tell Jenny the truth – for my own sanity and the sake of our marriage.'

'How did she react?' I ask him, desperate to know how the drama unfolded.

'She was stunned, hurt, angry . . . but I think a part of her was also relieved that I wasn't having an affair, after all. After the initial shock, there were two inevitable questions: "Are you gay?" And, "Do you want to be a woman?" I had quite a job persuading her that the answer to both questions was an unequivocal *no*. Then she asked me why I hadn't told her sooner and what else was I hiding from her? I did everything I could to reassure her, but I could see where she was coming from – after all, buying women's clothes and dressing up in secret was hardly behaviour likely to inspire trust between us.'

'But she didn't say she was going to leave you?'

'No, she never once threatened to do that. We talked right through the night and by morning I think she was beginning to understand why I had acted the way I did. However, it was months before she fully accepted my cross-dressing – well, not so much accepted, more resigned herself to it. She said she could cope with "Natasha" only if we laid down some ground rules. So I was only allowed to dress up at weekends and only in the house. She knew I'd discussed my cross-dressing with Shirley and, even though they never met, I knew she was grateful to your mum for making me see sense. That said, she made me promise not to tell another soul . . . she couldn't bear the shame, she said.'

He looks down at his pint glass and sighs. I reach across and give his hand a little squeeze.

'But you're still together after all these years. She must really love you, to take Natasha on board like that.'

'Oh yes, in fact Jenny and Natasha have become best friends. The first time she saw me dressed up she burst out laughing; I suppose I must've looked very odd to her. But as time went on she began to really warm to Natasha. She was more sensitive than Kevin and easier to talk to. It was like having a sister or a very good friend, she said. She and Natasha have had some great conversations, more intimate than anything she could've had with Kevin. And we've had great fun together – she gave me make-up tips, helped style my wigs, she even accompanied me on shopping trips to pick out clothes for Natasha. I really am a very lucky man.

'So, you see, I owe your mum a huge debt of thanks. If it wasn't for her, I'm quite sure my marriage would've fallen apart within a couple of years. There's one thing this whole experience has taught me – and that's that you have to have total honesty between two people in a relationship.'

He's so right. What a pity Toby and I don't have that level of trust. I've been over and over it in my mind and his account of what happened with Alexa Hunt still doesn't ring true.

'Did you and Mum keep in touch after she'd finished making your outfits?'

'For a little while, yes. I told her how Jenny and I had managed to work things out and she was really pleased for me. But gradually we lost touch and then, of course, I left Greenwich and moved to north London. I should've made more of an effort; she was a very special lady, Shirley. Your dad is a very lucky man . . . I take it he's still alive?'

'Oh er, yes. He and Mum split up when I was tiny and we're not that close. I haven't spoken to him in years.'

'That's a shame. I'd be very proud to have a daughter like you – attractive, intelligent and, if I may say so, a good listener, just like your mum.'

I smile shyly, basking in his flattery. What a very nice man he is. Indeed, by the time the barman calls last orders, Kevin and I are chatting away like old friends. When we say our goodbyes on Upper Street, we share a hug and I promise to put Mum's scarf in the post. I'll have to buy one and crumple it up a bit so it looks old. I feel a bit mean duping him like that, but he won't know the difference.

Later, recounting the evening for Kim over a cup of hot chocolate, I realize that I'm more than a little disappointed that Kevin didn't turn out to be my dad – cross-dresser or not – but I'm glad we met. I thought I knew Mum inside out, but Kevin's story has made me see her in a different light. She was such a social butterfly, forever flitting here and there, liking to be at the centre of things. She had an ever-changing group of mates and I always imagined her friendships existed on quite a superficial level. I didn't know she was capable of such deep empathy and understanding and I can't help feeling a warm glow of pride on her behalf. God-damn it, she saved a man's marriage – how amazing is that?

FOURTEEN

Last Friday Drift played the final date of their UK tour. By lunchtime the following day nme.com had posted a glowing critique: 'Drift flooded Edinburgh's famous Corn Exchange with vibes, energy and heartbreaking rushes of vibrating guitar noise,' gushed the reviewer. And I adored the description of Toby as 'a curious bloke-angel hybrid . . . macho and fragile all at once', which is how I think of him myself. I know it sounds silly, but I couldn't help reaching out a hand to stroke the website's photo of my denim-clad, sweaty-browed love god of a husband. So when the phone rang, it was like some kind of freaky telekinesis.

I felt the most unbelievable sense of relief when I heard Toby's voice. You see, apart from those lovely flowers he sent me, we haven't communicated since our row on the phone and I was beginning to wonder what would happen when the tour ended. Would he simply arrive at Itchycoo unannounced – or might he have decided to decamp to Callum's? I even fantasized about him appearing on the doorstep with Alexa Hunt to tell me our marriage was over. Foolishly I tuned in to MTV last night, just in time to see her counting down the European Top Twenty. And fucking gorgeous she looked too. Bitch.

I felt a smug shiver of pleasure as Toby asked, 'How come you never phoned me? I checked my voicemail every day, but you didn't call, not once.' His plaintive tone pulled at my heartstrings and I found myself offering an apology and muttering something about needing time to think. 'I really missed you, babe,' he continued. 'Am I forgiven? Can I come home?'

'Of course you can, I'm dying to see you,' I said. I had been determined not to give him an easy ride on his return, but my resolve was crumbling fast. He told me he was booked on the four p.m. flight to Stansted – that was the good news. The bad news was that instead of coming straight home, he was stopping off at Stefan's place in Ladbroke Grove en route – Stefan being a sometime DJ and also Toby's dealer. I didn't want to start an argument, not on the phone, so I said that was fine, so long as he was back at Itchycoo in time for his dinner. Ivy had prepared her sensational baked chicken with olives and lemon, and all I had to do was stick it in the oven at 180 degrees for an hour and a half. I got the local vintner to drop off a couple of bottles of Batard Montrachet and then spent ages fussing over the dining table with flowers and candles to set the stage for a romantic reunion.

My big mistake was not qualifying what the phrase 'in time for dinner' actually meant. By the time Toby eventually walked through the front door just after ten p.m., the food was ruined and I'd glugged down three-quarters of a bottle of very expensive wine. I was drunk, he was stoned, I was fuming, he was unapologetic, he shouted, I cried, we drank the rest of the wine, we made up (sort of) and fell into bed. Isn't it weird how angry sex is always the most satisfying kind – physically, I mean?

The next day Toby surprised me by suggesting a picnic in Regent's Park. I had a throbbing hangover, but this wasn't an opportunity I was going to miss. I can't remember the last time Toby and I did something so, well, normal. We couldn't be bothered to assemble a hamper, so we stopped off at the McDonald's in Camden. Despite the baseball cap and the Gucci shades, Toby was instantly recognizable, not that anybody quite had the nerve to ask for an autograph but we got plenty of sidelong glances, and the spotty herbert behind the counter stammered, 'I saw you at the Brixton Academy and you fucking blew me away, man,' as he handed over our cheeseburgers. He practically keeled over when Toby pulled off the baseball cap and jammed it on his head, over the top of his Mickey D's hat; I thought that was a really sweet gesture.

I was determined not to waste this chance of a heart-to-heart and as we strolled arm in arm through the park. I asked Toby again about his relationship with Alexa Hunt. He repeated his earlier claim that nothing untoward had occurred at the Malmaison and told me not to be so paranoid. So I guess I'm going to have to let it lie. I can't keep on and on at him, he'll just resent me for it. Then I confronted Toby on the issue of what I consider to be his excessive socializing. Calmly and rationally, I explained why I hate it when he's missing in action because: *a*) I worry that something might have happened to him; *b*) I get lonely; and *c*) it's just not normal behaviour, not for a married man any road, rock star or not. He in turn explained why it's impossible to have a really good night out unless you do exactly that – spend the entire night out. Maybe he just didn't articulate it very well, but I really didn't get it; I, for one, can leave the house at eight p.m. and return by one a.m. feeling perfectly satisfied that I've had a good time. Anyhow, he agreed to limit his all-nighters to once a fortnight, but even then he must return home no later than twenty-four hours after his original departure from Itchycoo. In return, I have promised to make more of an effort to accompany him to awards ceremonies and industry parties. So I think we're back on an even keel. I'm certainly feeling much more optimistic about our relationship than I was three weeks ago. And, God, it's *so* good to have him back. I can't keep my hands off him – and he's the same.

The one disappointment was Toby's reaction when I told him that I'm looking for my father. I had been dying to tell him about my project, thinking he would be pleased for me and impressed with my ingenuity. But instead he seemed more concerned about the whole thing rebounding on him.

'Don't go dragging *my* name into the frame, whatever you do,' he said. 'The last thing I need is some bloody newspaper concocting a story about me and my long-lost father-in-law.'

I understand why Toby feels that way: when you're in the public eye the media seize on every little thing and twist it out of all recognition – and although you try your best to ignore it, it does start to grate after a while. I just wish he wasn't so scathing.

'You don't honestly think you're going to find your dad, do you?' he asked me.

'Why do you have to put it like that?' I replied crossly.

'Like what?'

'In that negative way. Why couldn't you have said, "Do you think you're going to find your dad?"'

'Does it really matter?'

'Yes, it does, actually. Clearly you're assuming that this whole project is doomed to failure.'

'*Project*. Bloody hell, we *are* taking this seriously, aren't we?'

'Well it's something that's very close to my heart. Why shouldn't I take it seriously?'

To demonstrate just how committed I was to finding my father, I told Toby about my meeting with Kevin. I should've known better. He pissed himself laughing when I got to the cross-dressing bit. 'You can't half pick 'em, Thea,' he chuckled, as if I had somehow selected these candidates for fatherhood instead of simply discovering their names in Mum's diary. In the end I didn't want to talk about it any more so I changed the subject. But he hasn't put me off, not a bit of it; his mockery has only hardened my resolve. I shall continue with my investigations and if and when I do find my dad, I shall be vindicated.

Last night Toby and I spent the evening with Drift's guitarist Luke and his new girlfriend, Lucy, who works in the press office at Run Records. Luke is my favourite among the guys in the band (next to my husband, of course!). He's so gentle and unassuming, no wonder the teenage Drift chicks love him. He hasn't had a proper girlfriend for months – not since he split with a well-known soap temptress, who really gave him the run-around – so I'm pleased he's hooked up with someone really down to earth like Lucy. Actually, I think she could prove a useful ally, someone to gossip with when we all go out as part of a big gang, because I don't really get on with any of the other girlfriends. Steve, Drift's bass player, is sporting a different piece of arm candy every time I see him and I don't have an awful lot in common with Callum's airhead model girlfriend,

Chantal. Even Callum takes the piss out of her. The last time the four of us met up – some record-company do at Sugar Reef, I think it was – he made her repeat the most embarrassing story. I could tell she didn't really want to, but Callum can be a bit of a bully when he wants.

'I was doing this shoot in a derelict warehouse on the Mile End Road,' she began hesitantly. 'And I was absolutely dying for a wee, so I asked the make-up girl where the toilet was . . .' At this point she looked at Callum, as if seeking his permission not to go any further, but all he said was, 'Go on, Chantal,' his voice tinged with irritation.

So she was forced to continue. 'And she said, "It's down the corridor, first door on the left – but there's no door."' At this point Callum began grinning like a maniac, in anticipation of the punch line.

'And I said, "Well, how the fuck am I supposed to get in then?"'

Callum and Toby were in fits, like it was the most hysterical thing they'd ever heard. I didn't laugh. It was a funny story, but I didn't find Callum's public humiliation of his girlfriend remotely amusing.

Thankfully Luke hadn't invited Callum and Chantal to his Thames-side loft, so it was just the four of us. Lucy cooked all these amazing tapas dishes and we shared a few bottles of Rioja. Almost unbelievably, Toby didn't get drunk, just a bit happy. In fact he was up at nine this morning, volunteering to get the papers and some croissants from the bakers. I'm looking forward to a relaxing Sunday morning, just the two of us. I've brewed a pot of Espresso on the hob, nice and strong, just the way Toby likes it and Earl Grey for me. When I hear the front door go, I hastily lay out the side plates and mugs on the breakfast bar and a big china platter for the croissants.

'Stick the croissants in the oven to warm up – it's already switched on,' I say, as he walks into the kitchen.

'I haven't got any fucking croissants,' he snaps.

'Why the hell not?' I say in a jokey way, spinning round to confront him.

'This is why not,' he says, holding up a copy of *News of the World*.

'Don't tell me you're in that bloody rag again, I wish these papers would find some proper news for a change. What is it this time? No, don't tell me, let me guess. Let's see . . . *Drift frontman in drugs bust*? Or how about, *Toby admits to wearing wife's knickers*? Now that *would* be news!' I giggle as I rummage in the freezer, hoping to rediscover some half-forgotten crumpets.

'Try: *Star's wife has secret abortion*.'

The words hit me like a slap in the face. 'How the hell . . . let me see that,' I say, yanking the paper out of his hand and tearing the front page in the process.

'Page nine,' says Toby in a flat voice.

The wife of Drift star Toby Carson was recently admitted to a private clinic for an abortion. According to an insider, Thea Carson, 27, was just over two months' pregnant with her first child when she underwent the operation at the exclusive Riverview Hospital in Middlesex, fuelling speculation that the couple's one-year marriage is under strain. Last month, Toby shared a night of passion with MTV presenter Alexa Hunt at Manchester's trendy Malmaison hotel during Drift's UK tour . . .

I can't read any more because my eyes are brimming with tears. Toby is standing there stony-faced, just looking at me. 'Come on, then. Who did you go shooting your mouth off to?' he demands.

I am incredulous. 'What? Surely you don't think I'm responsible for this?'

'Well, it certainly wasn't me. I know you weren't exactly thrilled at the idea of an abortion, but if this is your way at getting back at me . . .'

'You fucking shitbag!' I scream, launching myself at him and pounding his chest with my fists. For a few seconds he stands there passively and takes it, but when I show no sign of letting up, he catches hold of my wrists and pins my arms down at my sides until I go limp. He grabs my shoulders and pulls me towards him like a rag doll.

'Who did you tell?' he says with sudden intensity, his face contorted with ugly emotion.

'Only Kim, I swear,' I stammer.

'Well, if the story didn't come from you, it came from your so-called best mate,' he says, spitting out the words in disgust. 'She's never liked me has she?'

'Don't be ridiculous. Kim would never do a thing like that, never.'

He lets go of my arms and walks out of the kitchen. Seconds later I hear the slam of the front door. Wrapping my arms around my shoulders I close my eyes and take some deep, calming breaths. Whoever said being a celebrity's wife was easy should be shot.

It's been three days since Toby walked out and that's a record, even for him. I have made no attempt to contact him and vice versa. I am angry, hurt, betrayed – but, above all, exhausted. I've put so much energy into maintaining this relationship and I don't feel as if I have anything left to give. Nothing I say or do seems to make the slightest difference; Toby just carries on in his own sweet way, existing at the centre of his universe with everybody else orbiting him like satellites.

Kim was speechless when I told her about the newspaper story and Toby's reaction to it. She didn't see the weekend papers because she was in France with Tim, combining a romantic mini-break with sourcing props for a St Tropez party she's organizing to celebrate the launch of a designer swimwear shop. She was furious with Toby for suggesting that I – or indeed she – could be responsible for the story and outraged by his disappearance.

'That man is so predictable,' she said, her voice dripping with contempt. 'After all, why stay and face the music when you can run away like a little kid? You're a bloody saint, Thea. I swear to God I would've killed him by now if he were my husband. I mean, fancy suspecting his own wife of planting a story like that . . . You know who I reckon it was?'

'Who?'

'Think about it: it wasn't me and it wasn't you. If Toby really didn't tell anybody else about the pregnancy, there's only one name left in the frame and that's the Riverview.'

'You're joking; it's one of the most exclusive clinics in the country, Toby couldn't believe it when he got their bill.'

'I just don't see who else it could be.'

'Fucking hell. So much for patient confidentiality.'

'I can phone them up if you like, speak to their head of public relations and give him or her a good bollocking on your behalf.'

'Thanks, Kim, but there's no need. I suppose I shouldn't be surprised. Having no private life whatsoever is just the price you pay for having a famous husband. I ought to be used to it by now,' I said wearily, knowing that I will never, *ever* get used to it. 'Do you know what the most hurtful thing about that stupid story was? Not the fact that the whole country knows I had an abortion – although that's bad enough – but the suggestion that my marriage is on the rocks. J.C. has forwarded a whole bunch of sympathy cards from clients at the agency who think I'm one step away from the divorce courts.'

Finally, on the fourth day, Toby returns – and there's something very odd about him. He's clean-shaven, sweet-smelling (an unfamiliar aftershave, not his usual Hugo Boss) and he's wearing clothes I've never seen before – a Ted Baker T-shirt and some leather trousers. That's odd; he used to say only poofs wore leather trousers. He breezes in around lunchtime as I'm sitting in front of the box eating Ritz crackers and watching some crappy DIY show. That's all I seem to do these days – eat and watch TV. I should be out there trying to find my father, but I've been far too stressed and unable to get into the right frame of mind.

'Hey, babe,' Toby says and kisses me on the top of my head before flopping into an armchair.

'Long time no see,' I say, my voice thick with sarcasm.

'I've been at Callum's,' he says nonchalantly.

'Really?' I say, equally nonchalantly.

'Listen, I'm sorry I accused you of feeding that story to the newspapers. I know you'd never do something like that, or Kim for that matter. I was just feeling a bit emotional. You know the way I get after a tour – irritable and edgy. It's hard coming back to real life after a month of total hedonism, of not having to worry about anything except tuning your guitar and making sure you've got enough weed to last the night. But I should learn to deal with it and not take it out on you.'

'And it's taken you four whole days to compose that speech?'

'Yes . . . I mean no. I mean it's taken me four days to get my head together.'

I raise my eyebrows in open disbelief and turn my gaze back to the TV like I'm desperate to learn how to fit tongue-and-groove panelling on a bathroom wall; when all the while I'm willing Toby to come up with a better excuse, something more convincing, more loving, so that I can fall into his arms and tell him I forgive him.

'Anyway,' he says, reaching into the fruit bowl on the table and picking out a nectarine, 'I reckon I know where that story came from.'

'Really?' I say boredly.

'It's got to be the Riverview – some nurse or receptionist must've spoken to the press.'

'That's what Kim reckons.'

'Oh, so you've discussed it with her then?'

'Yes, Toby, I *have* discussed it with my best friend – seeing as she's one of the few people round here who actually listens to me.'

'Easy, babe, no need to go off on one,' he says with a mouthful of nectarine.

God give me strength.

'Anyway, that's the last time you're going to that fucking hospital.'

'Well, I wasn't planning on having another abortion.'

'No, no, of course not. That's not what I was saying. I just meant . . . Well, I just meant I'm sorry – about everything.'

And with that, he wanders off to the kitchen to make a coffee, so I guess that's conversation *finito*. I got my apology, but I can't help feeling short-changed; he didn't seem terribly sincere and I still don't understand why he had to disappear for four whole days. I'd like to discuss it some more, but I can't handle another argument.

Toby spends the rest of the day mooching around the house like Kevin the Teenager. I suggest we get a video out or go for a walk, but he's not interested, so I busy myself dead-heading the roses that line the front path.

'Leave it, babe, that's what we pay the gardener for,' Toby says.

'I happen to find it therapeutic,' comes my terse reply.

Around five p.m. I've settled into some knitting and he's reading an old copy of *Vanity Fair* when his mobile goes off. He's got the Small Faces 'All or Nothing' as his ring tone and I always sing along to it. It's our little joke because I'm a crap singer – seriously, I can barely hold a note. So even though I've still got a strop on, I can't resist warbling away; it's a Pavlovian response. 'Things could work out/just like I want them to/If I could have/the other half of you,' I sing as he fishes the phone out of his suede jacket, which is draped across the back of the sofa. He looks to see if he recognizes the number, then he frowns slightly and walks out of the room with it. 'A-llll or nothing,' I sing as the tune continues. Bloody hell, he's going up the stairs now. Isn't he going to answer the damn thing? 'A-llll or nothing.' A couple of seconds later, the tune stops and I hear Toby say, 'Hi, what you up to?' in a soft voice that's kind of – well, kind of flirty actually. Then I hear the sound of a door closing and then silence. I shrug to myself and carry on with my knitting. Toby's jumper is coming along nicely. The left sleeve is slightly longer than the right one, but I don't think anybody will notice. After five minutes or so I decide I'm thirsty, so I go to the kitchen for a glass of cranberry juice. As I'm carrying it back to the lounge, Toby comes bounding down the stairs two at a time and I see he's got his denim jacket on.

'That was Jason, he wants me to stop by his office. There's some tax stuff he needs me to sign or I'm gonna get fined for missing the deadline,' he says. Toby's accountant is forever chasing him about something or other. It's all very well earning shed-loads of money, but Toby's tax bills are enormous. 'I'll catch a cab on Haverstock Hill. I'll only be a couple of hours, promise – or three hours tops, depending on whether we go for a drink,' he says, hooking an arm behind my neck and kissing my forehead. 'See ya.'

'See ya,' I say to his departing back.

That's a shame. I thought we might go to the cinema tonight, there's a new Pedro Almodovar I want to see, but I doubt Toby will be back in time for the eight o'clock show at Screen on the Hill. Never mind, maybe tomorrow. What shall I do now? I know, I'll sort out some hand-washing. My pink lambswool cardie has been languishing at the bottom of the laundry basket for weeks. Upstairs in the bedroom I fish out the cardie, plus a couple of pairs of stockings and a silk shirt of Toby's. As I'm walking out of the room, I catch sight of Toby's mobile lying on the bed amid the rumpled quilt. Damn, that means I can't get hold of him if I need to.

Depositing the laundry on the bed, I pick up the phone, intending to put it on Toby's bedside table out of harm's way. Now, I'm not a naturally suspicious person, but as soon as that top-of-the-range Siemens is in my grasp, some primeval instinct takes over and almost before I know what I'm doing, I've pressed the menu key and scrolled down to *calls received*. At this juncture, I hesitate for a second, aware that what I'm about to do equates to rummaging through Toby's pockets or reading his secret diary – if he kept one, that is. Having made a conscious decision to proceed, I hit the *OK* key and a list of numbers pops up, with the most recent caller at the top.

I can see straight away that it's not Jason's number. His office is in Bloomsbury and has an 0207 code. This number is 0208, which means Toby lied to me. Why on earth would he do that? Perhaps it was Stefan, ringing to tell Toby of a consignment of some new skunk derivative he just *has* to sample. I'm always telling Toby he smokes too much dope, so it's possible he told a little white lie. But Stefan lives in Ladbroke Grove, so he's 0207 as well. I am gripped by the desire – no, the *need* – to know who Toby's mystery caller was and why he lied to me, so without further consideration, I press the call key. After two rings, a woman's voice answers:

Hi, you've reached Alexa. Sorry I can't talk to you right now, but if you leave your name, number and any message I'll call you back as soon as I can.

Exactly three hours and eighteen minutes after leaving for his alleged appointment with his accountant, Toby returns home. I turn my face towards him as he gives me a welcoming kiss, but inside, my vital organs seem to shrink from his embrace.

'Sorry I was so long, babe. I would've called to let you know I was going for a drink with Jason, but I left my mobile here,' he says casually.

'Did you?' I say.

'Yeah, I must've left it in the bedroom.'

'I didn't notice, I haven't been upstairs,' I say, trying to sound indifferent. I left the phone where I found it, lying in the middle of the bed. I even returned the hand-washing to the laundry basket, so Toby would have no reason to suspect I was telling an untruth.

'Which pub did you go to?' I ask.

'Erm, that one round the corner from Jason's office, the one with all the books round the walls.'

Is it my imagination or does my husband look a tad uncomfortable – and why didn't he look me in the eye when he answered that question?

Toby settles down to watch *Who Wants to Be a Millionaire?* on TV and I subject him to a covert appraisal while pretending to be engrossed in the *Radio Times*. Is his hair more rumpled than usual? Are the buttons on his shirt done up the right way? Is his skin suffused with a post-coital flush? But no, there's nothing to give the game away. I wonder if he spent those four days with her and not with Callum like he said. In which case, why the hell did he bother coming back home to me?

FIFTEEN

J.C. Riley's office is awash with wannabes. Last week, in a bid to attract new clients, he placed an advertisement in *The Stage*, inviting newcomers to attend a drop-in day. Only trouble is, they've all decided to drop in at the same time. Half a dozen individuals are currently huddled on the sofa in the small reception area, while another three are perched awkwardly on the windowsill. I do wish J.C. would get a move on; he arrived at the office more than twenty minutes ago and he still hasn't started the interviews. If anyone else arrives, I'm going to have to ask them to wait in the hallway.

'Won't be long now,' I tell the people in reception, as I walk past them en route to J.C.'s office. After knocking on the door, I go straight in like I always do. J.C. is sitting at his desk with his head thrown back, gulping hungrily from a bottle of Gaviscon.

'Everything OK?' I ask him.

'Just a touch of heartburn,' he says, dabbing at his

mouth with a big white handkerchief. 'How many of them are there now?'

'Nine,' I say. 'But one's a chaperone.'

'Don't tell me there's a kid out there.'

''Fraid so. A regular little Shirley Temple with ringlets and a gingham dress.'

J.C. sighs. He hates children. Let me rephrase that: he hates *working* with children; he doesn't think they're a good business proposition, given all the rules and regulations governing their employment.

'I knew I should have put *over-eighteens only* on that ad,' he says, pulling open a drawer and putting the bottle of Gaviscon out of sight. 'Give me five minutes then show the first one in, will you? After that just keep them coming.'

I return to my cubbyhole (*office* is really too grand a word), which is situated directly opposite reception. Leaving the door open, I switch on my computer and tilt the screen so that the sofa of wannabes is no longer in view. I'm beginning to regret agreeing to work a full day. Normally I don't mind doing a few extra hours, but today I can't help wondering if Toby is using my absence to steal some time with Alexa. In spite of his earlier denials, I always suspected there was something going on between them. I had hoped it was nothing more than a one-night stand, but obviously it's a bit more than that. I don't think it's serious, though; Toby is as affectionate towards me as ever and he does always come home in the end. In the high-pressure world of the rock star, Alexa is probably just another form of release; like drink or drugs – an attractive but essentially meaningless diversion. If I can only come to terms with that, then maybe our marriage will survive; maybe it will even be stronger as a result. Not that I'm prepared to put up with Toby's infidelity indefinitely. No way. I have decided to give him precisely one month to get the little groupie out of his system, and in the meantime I'm not going to let on that I know what he's up to. In fact, I'm not going to discuss it with anyone at all; not those self-professed experts in the art of celebrity husbandry, Patti, Stella and Angela; not even Kim. I shall simply pretend Alexa Hunt doesn't exist and if, by the end of my deadline, Toby has failed to excrete her, then I might just ask Patti for the name of that lawyer.

The intercom on my desk buzzes. 'Thea, I'm waiting . . .'

'Sorry, J.C. I was miles away.'

I step into reception and ask the skinny guy with the unicycle to follow me. He's been here since seven-thirty, and we don't open till ten. He was waiting outside with the milk when I arrived to open up. I lead the way to J.C.'s office and hold open the door while he wheels in aboard the unicycle. J.C.'s gonna love this one. Not.

Back at my desk I start opening the post, but it's not long before my thoughts turn once again to the state of my marriage. In my view, the problem is one of integration – or rather the lack of it. For the most part

Toby exists in a fluffy white cocoon, where he is cushioned and cosseted and protected from the harsh realities of life, like having to queue to get into a nightclub or pay cash money for a new pair of Nikes. My life by contrast is rooted firmly in the mundane and revolves around the house (buying new curtains/waiting in for the gas man/making sure the bills are paid on time) and J.C. Riley's office (typing, filing and dealing with arseholes). Given this disparity in our lifestyles, is it any wonder we've drifted apart?

We are both guilty of indifference, of not working hard enough to ensure that our two worlds regularly converge. My crime is my reluctance to engage in celebrity-related pursuits – and so I am going to make a conscious effort to accompany Toby to more showbiz parties, willingly as opposed to grudgingly, and I shall have the perfect opportunity to display my new-found enthusiasm at next week's Indie Music Awards.

The door of J.C.'s office opens and the skinny guy walks out. He looks dejected. I guess the unicycle failed to impress. I follow him into reception and smile at a man of indeterminate age sporting an ill-fitting toupée.

'Would you like to come through?'

In an instant Shirley Temple's overweight mother is staggering to her feet. 'Hang on a minute,' she says angrily. 'We were here before *him*. In any case, Candice-Louise has a Dairylea casting at eleven-thirty, and if we don't see Mr Riley next we'll be late.'

I roll my eyes skywards. I know it looks rude, but I

can't help it. I hate pushy stage mothers, and I saw plenty of them when I was a child actor.

'I'm quite sure this gentleman was here first,' I say firmly.

'It's OK, I don't mind,' says the man in a hoarse voice. He seems very nervous. His forehead is glistening with perspiration and he smells of damp duffel coats.

'That's very kind of you,' I say through gritted teeth. 'If you'd like to follow me, ladies?'

The mother and daughter safely deposited in J.C.'s office, I return to my desk to continue opening the post and contemplate Toby's principal shortcoming, which as I see it consists of a general apathy towards any matter concerning my work, my friends or my desire to find my father; although I must admit I think I'm partly to blame for his studied lack of interest in the last. My mistake was not discussing it with him right from the beginning. OK, so he was tied up with rehearsals and then he went off on tour and of course we weren't on speaking terms for a couple of weeks, but I could've at least mentioned it to him. He probably feels a bit left out and perhaps even a little jealous that the search for my father is taking me away from him. When you're married to man with a large ego, you have to work hard to make him feel loved. From now on I'm going to make a real effort to involve Toby in my little project.

Speaking of which, I have already decided that my next target will be Barney. He seems to have had a longer relationship with Mum than Roy and anyway, I like the name. I just wish I had a bit more to go on. Kevin had an address at least, but the only clue to Barney's identity is those three restaurants noted in Mum's diary: Rules, Simpson's-in-the-Strand and Pierce & Hussey. I wonder what kind of place Pierce & Hussey was – a pretty expensive one, if the other two are anything to go by.

J.C.'s door bursts open and out comes the fat lady with a face like thunder. Two steps behind her, blubbing noisily, is the little girl. 'Come on, Candice-Louise. Just ignore the nasty little man,' the mother is saying as she drags the kid through reception. 'He obviously wouldn't recognize talent if it stood up and punched him in the face.'

I step into reception. 'Right, who's next then?' I say breezily.

By five o'clock, more than forty hopefuls have passed through J.C.'s door. Most were despatched after less than ten minutes. I can't say I'm surprised, I know one shouldn't judge by appearances, but they looked like a pretty useless bunch, although there *was* one guy who caught my eye. He was the last to arrive and he didn't have quite the same air of desperation as the others. He just sat there on the sofa, reading his mountain-bike magazine and looking totally chilled, and just now, when he came out of J.C.'s office, he smiled at me and said, 'Thanks very much,' a simple courtesy that none of the others had bothered with.

I spend half an hour tidying up reception and finishing off some filing, then I stick my head round J.C.'s door to tell him I'm going.

'Good day?' I ask him.

'Quite disappointing really,' he says gloomily. 'I very much doubt I'll be taking on any of *those* amateurs.'

'What about that last guy? I liked the look of him.'

'Rubber Rick? Yeah, he had talent, but I can't do anything for him. The kid's too specialized.'

'Oh?'

'He's a contortionist.' J.C. pushes a video tape across the desk. 'Here, he left his showreel. Take a look if you like.'

'Thanks, I will,' I say, stuffing the tape into my bag.

The Northern Line is even more fucked up than usual and it takes me ages to get home. At least Toby's had the common sense to stick a couple of supermarket curries in the oven. 'What did you get up to today?' I ask him casually as I lay out knives and forks on the kitchen table.

'Not much. Listened to some music, smoked some weed . . .'

'By yourself?'

'Yeah. By myself. Why d'you ask?'

'No reason.'

Later, over dinner, I introduce the subject of my father. 'I don't suppose you've heard of a restaurant called Pierce & Hussey have you?' I ask Toby.

'Nah,' he says through a mouthful of chicken jalfrezi. 'Why d'ya wanna know?'

I explain that I'm trying to track down potential dad number two and that Pierce & Hussey is one of the meeting places listed in Mum's diary.

'I'm sure we've got an Egon Ronay guide knocking about somewhere,' he says helpfully.

'I've already checked – it's not in there.'

'Maybe it closed down,' he says, breaking off a piece of nan. 'Or maybe it was never a restaurant in the first place. Why don't you check the net, see what comes up?'

Keen to capitalize on Toby's unexpected show of interest, I persuade him to join me for a spot of surfing after dinner. He spent a packet on our state-of-the-art PC and all the accoutrements: digital camera, flatbed scanner, DVD and tons of software. He likes to have the best of everything. Perhaps that's why he has acquired Alexa Hunt as his latest accessory. After all, she is one of the best-dressed, most attractive under-25s in the public eye – and she's involved, after a fashion, in the music business, so her cool quotient is pretty high . . . Fuck it, I'm supposed to be pretending that the bitch doesn't exist. As I wait for the modem to dial up, I imagine a giant stiletto descending from the heavens and squishing Alexa into the ground.

Once the Freeserve homepage appears, I execute a UK search on the keywords *Pierce* and *Hussey*. A solitary website match appears: *www.piercehussey.co.uk*.

'That was a piece of piss,' says Toby. 'Go to the home page.'

Far from being a fine dining establishment, it turns out that Pierce & Hussey is a firm of solicitors, *specializing in media, entertainment and licensing law*. And judging by their slickly designed website and Aldgate HQ, they're at the top end of the business.

Reaching over my shoulder Toby clicks the *About us* button on the home page and begins to read aloud from the lengthy and self-congratulatory history of the firm: 'Pierce & Hussey's fifty years of diligent client service have given it a unique position as a firm which successfully combines traditional values with the progressive practices of a modern commercial organization. Established in 1952 by best friends John Pierce and Daniel Hussey, the firm quickly established itself as one of the Square Mile's premier media law firms—'

Wresting the mouse from Toby, I hit the back browser, convinced that this pompous firm of legal eagles cannot possibly be the same Pierce & Hussey noted in Mum's diary.

'Hang on,' says Toby. 'I thought I saw something there.'

I hit *About us* again. Toby's eyes flit across the screen.

'There you go,' he says gleefully, pointing at a paragraph halfway down the screen.

I read the sentence aloud: 'In 1969 they were joined by John Pierce's nephew, Barnabas Russell, who occupied a key position in the firm until his retirement in 1999 . . .' I stop and do a double take. 'Oh my God, Barnabas – Barney, do you think it's the same guy?'

'Could be,' says Toby. 'The dates certainly add up and if Barney worked at Pierce & Hussey, it would make perfect sense for your mum to have met him there.'

'Toby, you're a genius!' I squeal, spinning round in the black leather executive chair.

He smiles bashfully, 'It was nothing.'

'How many B. Russell's do you think there are in the phone book?'

'Hundreds probably.'

'Do you think Barney will have maintained some sort of connection to Pierce & Hussey, even though he's retired?'

'Definitely. He's the founder's nephew isn't he? Why don't you give them a ring in the morning? Or if you can't wait till then send them an email.' He starts walking towards the door.

'Where are you going? Don't you want to help me write the email?'

'No can do. I said I'd meet Callum for a quick drink in Camden, I'll only be a couple of hours.'

'Oh, OK,' I say, disappointed that he's lost interest already.

A couple of minutes later I hear the front door slam. I wonder if he's really meeting Callum or if he's gone round to Alexa's. Maybe if I give it half an hour or so and then call his mobile . . . I should be able to tell from the background noise whether he's in the pub or not. 'Stop it!' I scream out loud with sudden fury, bashing the mouse mat with my fist. I shake my head in an attempt to banish all thoughts of *that* woman and start to compose my email. I keep it short, saying simply that I am trying to get in touch with a former employee, Barnabas Russell, as my mother, Shirley Parkinson, made him a small bequest in her will and I only have his old workplace as a contact address. I ask if they would kindly forward my mobile number and email address and ask Mr Russell to get in touch as soon as is convenient.

The email safely dispatched, I settle down in front of the TV and prepare for yet another evening without Toby. Oh well, at least I'm not entirely alone; I still have Rubber Rick for company.

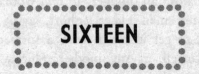

SIXTEEN

If I didn't know any better, I would say my husband was a paragon of virtue. In the three days since his mobile phone revealed his lying, cheating ways, there have been no more suspicious calls, no new aftershaves, no unaccounted-for absences, no indication whatsoever that he's playing away. In fact, we've been in each other's company almost continuously and he hasn't shown the slightest inclination to leave my side. He actually begged me to accompany him to yesterday's celebrity five-a-side at Stamford Bridge, where I cheered him on from the sidelines. Afterwards, instead of going on the piss with the others, he took me out to dinner at Nobu. Gwyneth Paltrow was sitting at the next table and I couldn't stop looking at her all evening. Toby hates it when I'm openly awe-struck – he kept kicking me under the table and hissing, 'Do you have to?' through gritted teeth. He'd forgiven me by the time we got back to Itchycoo, where we shagged with gusto on the dining-room table.

And there's more good news. It came in a phone call this morning. 'It's Barnabas Russell here,' said the voice at the end of my mobile. 'I'm responding to your charming email. The office has just forwarded it to me.'

'Barney!' I said in an embarrassingly schoolgirl squeal.

He responded by chortling poshly – *haw, haw, haw*. 'I'm sorry to laugh, I must sound dreadfully impolite. It's just that it's so strange to be called Barney again after all these years. Nobody in my entire life has ever called me Barney – with one notable exception, of course, and that's your dear mother. Now let's arrange a meeting, shall we? I'm dying to meet you.'

'You are?' I said stupidly.

'Most definitely. I wondered if you were free this afternoon.'

'Oh, oh yes, that would be wonderful.'

'Why don't we go for a nice afternoon tea? Claridge's is always horribly decadent – my treat.'

So this is the reason I am sitting in the back of a cab heading for Mayfair. I've even remembered to bring one of Mum's books with me – a battered copy of William Faulkner's *As I Lay Dying* – which I shall present as her bequest to Barney. It's a shame to give it away, but I can't turn up empty-handed. I had been hoping Toby would offer to come for moral support, but he had a hair appointment with some cutting-edge stylist he met on a magazine shoot. He did wish me luck, however, and said he was looking forward to hearing all about it when I got back.

By the time I walk into Claridge's elegant art-deco foyer, my stomach is doing back flips. I really shouldn't get my hopes up, but I have a good feeling about Barney. I've deliberately arrived a few minutes late to give him a chance to get there first. Glancing around the room, it doesn't take me long to spot the solitary man. He's dressed in a well-cut charcoal-grey suit and pink open-necked shirt and he looks almost celestial, bathed as he is in the brightness from the elaborate Dale Chihuly light sculpture directly above his head. Lying on the white-linen-clothed table in front of him is a broadsheet, although I'm too far away to see if it's the *Telegraph*, which he promised to bring for identification purposes. I smile tentatively and he picks up the newspaper and raises it discreetly in the air like a bidder at Sotheby's. As I make my way over to him, he stands up to greet me and I see that he's tall, over six feet, and very distinguished. Hmm, I could do an awful lot worse than discover I was the fruit of *his* loins, although there's no obvious physical resemblance between us, except for the height, I suppose.

'Thea, I presume,' he says, extending a liver-spotted hand.

I smile and shake his hand. 'Thank you for agreeing to meet me. I was so pleased that you decided to get in touch,' I say, sitting down on the gilded chair that

Barney has pulled out for me and smoothing out my Dolce & Gabbana pencil skirt.

'How could I resist? Your email was so delightful and your mother . . . well, it's no exaggeration to say that she was the great love of my life.'

Goodness. I hadn't expected such a frank admission so early in the proceedings, but I'm delighted at the same time . . . a bona fide boyf at last!

'I was devastated when Shirley passed away,' he continues. 'Of course our relationship ended before you were born, but I never forgot her and the special time we spent together.'

'So you did know she had cancer then . . . I wasn't sure.'

'Not until after she'd died. We hadn't been in touch for many years, but I heard the sad news via a mutual friend. It was a shocking waste of life. Your mother was the most amazing woman I ever met and to be cut down in her prime like that . . .' The words seem to choke him and he takes a second to compose himself. 'I sent a wreath to the funeral, but I didn't feel it was appropriate to attend in person – I am, after all, a complete stranger to you. I must say I'm very touched that Shirley left me something to remember her by. After all these years I rather thought she would have forgotten me.'

'Oh yes, I've brought it with me. It's not very much I'm afraid, just a book, but it was one of her favourites,' I say, unzipping my Prada tote and sending up a silent prayer to Mum, asking forgiveness for this small but necessary deception. At the same time a waiter appears at my elbow and starts to offload his tray of tiny sandwiches, scones, pastries, a pot of tea and two glasses of champagne.

'I took the liberty of ordering for both of us,' says Barney. 'I plumped for the Champagne Tea, it was your mother's favourite.'

'Were you two regulars here then?' I ask, handing over the dog-eared paperback.

'We certainly were,' he says, taking the book and running a hand over its faded cover. 'Which is why this place will always have special memories for me. Let's drink a toast to her memory shall we?' He hands me a champagne flute and we chink glasses. 'To Shirley, a truly wonderful woman.'

'Mum,' I say. I don't want to get all misty-eyed, not yet anyway, so as a distraction I help myself to a fat sultana scone and begin purposefully heaping it with jam and cream. 'How did you two meet, if you don't mind me asking? I must admit Mum never talked about you, so I was rather intrigued when I saw your name on her will.'

'At a dinner party, hosted by one of my colleagues at Pierce & Hussey. It was love at first sight – at least for me,' he says, smiling like a self-conscious schoolboy. 'My colleague was friendly with your mother's then boyfriend – some long-haired social-worker chap – and I was accompanied that night by my on–off girlfriend

Diana – a lovely woman, but not a patch on your mother. By dessert Shirley and I were flirting quite openly, by coffee I was smitten.' He chuckles. 'When I left with a sulking Diana at the end of the evening I had your mother's phone number, surreptitiously scrawled across my linen handkerchief. I called her the very next day, we met for cocktails at the Savoy and by midnight we'd pledged to ditch our respective partners, mad impetuous fools that we were!'

'How terribly romantic,' I say, dabbing at my mouth with my napkin to remove any stray scone crumbs.

'Oh Thea, you've no idea,' he exclaims. 'I was in seventh heaven, she was quite the most exciting woman I'd ever met. I had a very conventional upbringing . . . public school, law at St Andrews, a cushy well-paid job in my uncle's firm, so meeting a bohemian young woman like Shirley was truly magical. She made me feel so very alive. It was as if my existence up to then had only been half a life. I could never understand what she saw in me, especially considering I was four or five years older than her. I suppose it was a case of opposites attracting, we each opened the other's eyes – I introduced her to fine wines and gourmet food, she took me dancing in smoky jazz clubs.'

I can almost imagine them, smooching on some darkened Soho dance floor, and what an eye-catching couple they must've been. Mum, plumply pretty in a multi-layered skirt and off-the-shoulder cheesecloth top she'd have made herself. Barney, tall and debonair, slightly more formal in corduroy slacks and a polo-neck sweater. What a pity their relationship didn't work out.

Helping myself to a second scone, I suddenly realize that Barney hasn't eaten a single thing since we arrived. I do hope he doesn't think me piggish.

'Would you like a scone?' I say, holding out the oval plate towards him.

'Thank you, I don't mind if I do,' he says, delicately lifting one onto his plate. 'I'll have some of that jam too, and maybe just a tiny dollop of cream ... I shouldn't really, cholesterol levels and all that, but a scone without cream just isn't worth having,' he says, giving me a conspiratorial smile.

'My feelings exactly,' I say, pushing the pot of clotted cream towards him.

'You know, Thea, you remind me a lot of your mother; not so much in looks as style. You have her grace, her elegance ... and I see that you're wearing a wedding ring – your husband must be counting his lucky stars!'

I can feel myself blushing. 'That's kind of you to say so.'

'Have you been married long?'

'Just over a year.'

'Aah, so you'll still be in the honeymoon phase, where you can't bear to let each other out of your sight.'

'Not exactly. His job takes him away from home,

so we don't spend as much time together as we'd both like.'

'That's unfortunate. What line of business is he in?'

'He's a musician. He plays guitar . . . and sings.'

'How wonderful. I'm a fan of the big bands myself, Glenn Miller et al. No doubt your husband's taste in music is more modern.'

'Yes, you could say that.'

For obvious reasons I am unwilling to pursue this line of conversation, so there is a brief lull. We've finished our champagne, or at least I have – Barney's glass is still half full – so I pour a cup of tea for us both, giving me time to formulate a way to steer the conversation towards the question of my paternity.

'So why did you and Mum split up, if you don't mind me asking?' I venture. 'It sounds as if you had the perfect relationship.'

'I wish I knew. We spent six blissful months together – one minute everything in the garden was rosy, the next Shirley was telling me she needed some "breathing space", as she put it. Actually, that's rather naive of me . . . I suppose the truth was that she never loved me as much as I loved her. Looking back, the disparity in the strength of our feelings was obvious from the outset, but it was something I foolishly elected to ignore. Given the choice, I would've spent every spare minute with your mother, but she was always more circumspect – one or two meetings a week was more than enough for her. I think that in the end I suffocated her. I was ready to settle down, you see, but she was too much of a free spirit. I cried for a week, I didn't know what to do with myself. I bombarded her with flowers, phone calls, love letters, but she had made up her mind and insisted that she was acting in *my* best interests, as well as hers. At the time I didn't have a clue what she was talking about, but it soon became clear.'

He pauses and takes a slow, deliberate sip of tea. 'Anyway, it's all water under the bridge now.'

'What do you mean by – "it soon became clear"?'

'Oh, don't listen to me, Thea. I'm just a silly old fool who got his heart broken a long time ago.'

Barney looks distinctly uncomfortable, as if he's worried he's said something he shouldn't have.

'Please tell me the whole story, Barney,' I say gently. 'I so rarely get the opportunity to talk about Mum with the people who knew her . . . please don't worry about being indiscreet; you won't offend me, honestly.'

'Very well, if you're sure . . .'

'Quite sure.'

He clears his throat and stares fixedly into the middle distance as if he's summoning up some inner courage. 'About a month after we'd broken up, I heard on the grapevine that your mother was pregnant with you. Apparently she had another boyfriend, although nobody seemed to know who he was.'

'Gosh, she was a fast worker!' I exclaim. Then, worried Barney might think my remark in poor taste, I add, 'It must've been very upsetting for you – the fact that she'd seemingly managed to get over you so quickly.'

'Quite. But it was worse than that.'

'Oh?'

'You see, Shirley was already *three* months' pregnant, which means—'

I finish his sentence. 'Which means she must have been sleeping with somebody else while she was seeing you.'

'That was certainly my understanding of the situation. And the thought that Shirley had been unfaithful to me was like a knife twisting in my heart. I vowed never to contact her again and I was true to my word.'

Wow, this is getting heavy, *really* heavy. If Mum was sleeping with two guys at the same time, how could she be certain which one was the father? I don't think they had DNA tests in those days. Although there is another possibility: maybe Mum *was* carrying Barney's child, but put the word out that she had another lover, fearing that Barney might do something silly like insist they got married, or try to assert some kind of parental rights over me. I have no doubt that Mum would rather have trodden the difficult path of single motherhood than be beholden to a man she wasn't in love with. If I am to discover the truth, I had better proceed with care.

'How awful for you, I can't imagine how you must've felt,' I say, frowning sympathetically. 'Actually,

I know exactly how you felt ... I'm going through something similar myself. You see, I recently discovered my husband is having an affair.' Shit, I'm not supposed to be talking about myself. That just slipped out.

Barney looks at me aghast. 'You poor child. Here I am, wittering on about old wounds while you're going through hell right at this very moment.'

'It's fine, honestly,' I say unconvincingly. 'I think it was just a casual thing, I'm pretty sure it's fizzled out now.'

'I'm glad to hear it, although I can't imagine why your husband would've been tempted to stray in the first place ... anyway, it's not for me to judge. I just hope you two can get your marriage back on track. I sometimes wish I'd tried a bit harder to win Shirley back, particularly when I heard that she'd broken up with your father before you were even born. But at least he had given her the thing she longed for – the one thing I knew I could never provide.'

'I'm sorry, Barney, you've lost me. What could that other man – I mean, my father – possibly have given her that you couldn't?'

'Silly me, expecting you to read my mind – I meant a baby. Shirley always wanted children, I knew that.'

'But you weren't so keen?' I ask.

'Quite the opposite. You see, I'm infertile – the result of a particularly nasty bout of mumps in my early twenties. I had lots of tests, but the doctors said I was incapable of fathering a child.'

Clunk. Everything is falling into place – and I don't mind admitting that I'm pretty gutted. I really hoped Barney would turn out to be the One, but clearly it's a biological impossibility.

'Did my mother know you couldn't have kids?'

'Yes, we discussed it very soon after we met. It was never an obvious source of tension, but I did wonder if it might have contributed to the eventual failure of our relationship,' he says in a regretful tone.

'Well, if it's any comfort, the thing with my dad was pretty casual – Mum never even told him she was pregnant.'

'Yes, I did hear that he scarpered pretty sharpish. Do you have any contact with him at all?'

'No, nothing. Never have.'

'That's a shame. Listen, Thea, this is going to sound rather silly, but I've often wondered whether your father was somebody I knew, especially as Shirley was so secretive about him. Goodness, how I tortured myself with the thought that I might even have introduced them myself. I suppose it doesn't make much difference now; all the same, I wonder if you'd mind putting an end to the mystery for me.'

If only . . . But hang on a minute, maybe I *can* help ease an old man's heartache.

'It was nobody special, just some guy she met in Ronnie Scott's,' I tell him. My eyes, casting around the room for inspiration, alight on the huge glass sculpture suspended above us. 'His name was Dale. Dale

Brightman. It wasn't love or anything, just a fling. Whereas you . . . you she really cared about. Or she wouldn't have left you that book would she?'

'Yes, yes, you're probably right. I can't tell you what a comfort that is to me, even now, all these years later. I shall treasure that book till my dying day.' He looks down at the book, still sitting on his lap, and points at the title. 'Rather an appropriate choice of phrase as it turns out.' We both laugh, which helps to diffuse the melancholy.

'I see that you're married too,' I say, nodding at the slim gold band around his left index finger. 'You obviously found love again.'

'Not really,' he says sadly. 'I tied the knot a mere six months after your mother and I broke up. It was too soon, far too soon – and it's a decision I've lived to regret for the rest of my life.'

'You're still married to the same woman then?'

'Yes, Diana and I are still together.'

'Diana – the girl you took to the dinner party where you met Mum?'

'The very same. She'd always made it clear I'd only have to snap my fingers and she'd come running and that's exactly what happened. I suppose it was a silly sort of revenge. I even sent your mother a wedding invitation, which was very childish of me. She didn't reply and I don't blame her. In the event, the only person I was hurting was myself. I tried to convince myself that I loved Diana and in a funny sort of way I suppose I do – but it's a comfy, companionable sort of love, it was never the grand passion I had with your mother. I kept hoping things would change, that the more time I spent with Diana the more love I would feel for her, but it didn't work out like that. I should never have married her, I should have stuck it out on my own and waited until I found true love again.'

'Why didn't you just file for divorce as soon as you'd realized you made a mistake?'

'I would have done, had it just been Diana and me. But things were a little more complicated than that. Two years after our marriage we adopted a baby – Alice – followed by a little boy, Edward, a year later. I could never have left Diana after that; those two children have given me more joy that anything else in my life. Of course they're both grown up now and doing very well for themselves. Alice is a teacher in Surrey and Edward's training to be a barrister, both married, both very happy. But I can't see the point of upsetting the apple-cart now, it wouldn't be fair on Diana. So we carry on as we are, living in our nice detached home in Wimbledon – she with her Lady Taverners, me with my Sunday golf – and it's not such a bad life, I suppose. No doubt marriage to your mother would've been a little more exciting, but it wasn't to be.'

He tilts his head to one side, so that the soft yellow light from the Dale Chihuly sculpture catches the side of his face, and I suddenly get an impression of how he might have looked as a young man. I can see why Mum was attracted to him; he has such a kind face.

As we say goodbye outside at the taxi rank, Barney takes my hand in his. 'I'm so glad to have had the opportunity to meet you, Thea,' he says. 'And take some advice from an old codger – if you're truly in love with your husband, despite what he's done, then fight for him with every last breath in your body. But if you have any doubts, any doubts at all, then let him go. Take it from one who knows, a marriage without passion is like . . .' He hesitates and then smiles. 'A scone without cream.'

Back at Itchycoo, I find Toby in the living room, sprawled across the sofa and watching football on Sky Sports. Strangely, his hair doesn't look that much different, just a bit more tousled.

'How'd it go then?' he asks, turning down the volume on the TV.

I launch into a detailed account of my afternoon with Barney, but Toby appears only mildly interested and his eyes keep wandering back to the screen.

'So it was a complete waste of time then?' he says tersely when I get to the bit where Barney told me he couldn't have kids.

'I wouldn't put it like that,' I say. 'He was a lovely guy and he talked about Mum with such affection. In a funny sort of way, he brought her alive for me again.'

'That's nice,' says Toby. 'Listen, babe, don't take

this the wrong way, but I really think you should knock this stupid scheme on the head ... all this running around London meeting up with strange middle-aged men. You're never going to find your dad, never in a million years.' He reaches for the remote control and pumps up the volume on the TV.

SEVENTEEN

I'm torn between my Carlos Miele silk petal dress and the Ruti Danan black lace sheath. I think I'll go for the Ruti – it's slightly more risqué and, as the lady in Koh Samui pointed out, there's something reassuringly exclusive about a micro-label. Imagine how embarrassing it would be to see somebody else at tonight's Indie Music Awards wearing exactly the same outfit. Actually, *I* would probably see the funny side; Toby, however, would be mortified.

My appearance at the IMAs is a way of consolidating my position, of demonstrating that I *am* capable of being the perfect celebrity wife when the situation demands it. And what's more I'm going to make sure I look so goddamn hot that Toby won't be tempted to stray ever again. I'm quietly confident that his affair with Alexa Hunt has burned itself out – only two unexplained absences in the past ten days and neither one of them was an all-nighter. I think I did the right thing – not confronting him, but just quietly biding my time. Now it looks as if it's all blown over with the minimum of upset for everyone concerned.

I think Toby's really pleased I'm making the effort to go tonight. He asked me if I fancied it a couple of weeks back. 'Maybe,' I'd said, which usually translates to, 'You must be fucking joking.' So imagine how surprised he was this morning to hear me on the telephone, booking the car to take us to the Docklands Arena.

'You've decided to come then?' he said disbelievingly.

'Absolutely. I'm rather looking forward to it, as a matter of fact,' I replied.

'But you hate awards ceremonies.'

'I don't *hate* them, I just find them hard work – all that schmoozing with people from the record company, but Patti and Rich are going to be on our table, so at least I'll be among friends.'

'Rich Talbot, that old git. Why the fuck is he coming?'

'He's being presented with a Lifetime Achievement Award, that's why – and don't you dare be rude to him.'

He narrowed his eyes at me. 'You know there'll be loads of photographers there, don't you? And you know how much you hate having your picture taken.'

'Honestly, Toby, the way you're acting anyone would think you didn't want me to go!'

'Of course I do, babe. I'm just worried you won't enjoy yourself.'

'Don't you worry about me. Anyway, Drift are up for Best Band and I wouldn't miss your acceptance speech for the world.'

'We might not get it, you know. We're up against some stiff competition.'

'Of course you will,' I said reassuringly, planting a small kiss on the sexy brown mole to the left of his nose.

Just wait till he sees me in this black lace number. It fits in all the right places and now that I've slipped a couple of gel-filled inserts into my bra, I've even got a cleavage, sort of. My legs are brown enough to go without tights and I'm wearing the most fabulous Gina stilettos, which bring me up to a shade under six foot. Tiffany diamond earrings and the Asprey & Garrard charm bracelet Toby gave me before he went on tour are the final finishing touches.

I usually wear my hair loose, but I wanted to do something special for tonight. Earlier today, on Patti's recommendation, I paid a visit to Anthony at Nicky Clarke's and I must say he's done a fabulous job, dressing it into a smooth chignon, with a few delicate wisps escaping around my face. 'Not bad,' I say out loud as I scrutinize my reflection in the full-length mirror. I hope Toby likes the finished result; I made him promise to stay downstairs until I was ready.

The cab's due any minute, so I grab my Lulu

Guinness handbag and toss a few make-up essentials inside and a mini can of Elnett in case my 'do' starts drooping later in the evening. Now that I'm about to make my grand entrance I'm suddenly feeling nervous – how silly is that? I go to the top of the stairs and lean over the banister. 'Toby!' I shout down into the hall. 'I'm *read-eeee*!'

I watch as he emerges from the lounge. 'Well, hurry up and get your arse downstairs, will you? The cab's outside,' comes his rather irritable reply as he makes for the front door without even looking upwards. I expect he's just feeling a bit of pre-Awards tension.

'Turn around, Toby, I've got something to show you.'

He turns around, hands on hips like a stroppy teenager. Even from two flights up, I can see his eyes widening as I begin my descent. 'Wow,' he says when I reach the first-floor landing. 'You look amazing,' he says as I'm walking down the final flight. 'Fancy a quick knee-trembler?' he offers when I draw level with him at the foot of the staircase.

'I thought you said the cab was waiting,' I twirl a strand of hair around my finger in what I hope is a seductive fashion.

'Wait there,' he says and walks – no, jogs – towards the front door, pulls it open and shouts to the driver, 'Five minutes, mate.' Then he slams the door and comes walking back to me. 'Knickers. Off,' he commands.

Obediently I wriggle out of my lace-trimmed Collette

Dinnigan's. He pushes me against the wall and kisses me roughly, groping my gel-assisted right breast with one hand, while the other pushes up my dress. 'You want it, don't you?' he breathes into my ear. 'Yes,' I whimper. And I do want it – badly. He fumbles with the front of his Evisu jeans and presses his hardness against me. I grab his arse and, in one swift movement, push him deep inside me. He gives a low groan and begins frantically thrusting. Four minutes later and it's all over. He caresses the side of my face. 'I do love you, babe,' he says. 'You're the best.' Then he fastens his jeans, takes my hand and leads me to the waiting cab. My new dress is all creased and my lipstick is smudged, but I don't care. My work is done, there's no one else I need to impress tonight.

Outside the Arena a sizeable crowd is pinned behind the safety barriers and a bit of a frenzy breaks out when Toby and I appear. He smiles and signs a couple of autographs, while I hang around on the red carpet trying not to look too much like a spare part. On occasions like this, I always wonder if people realize that I *am* his wife and not just some dollybird on a promise. Probably not – and I don't suppose it really matters. As we approach the press pen, close to the entrance, a barrage of cameras go off. I make like Liz Hurley – big smile, chest out, one leg in front of the other (makes you look slimmer) – and then we're whisked inside by the security staff.

We've got a good table, close to the stage, but not so close we'll be craning our necks. Patti and Rich are already there, together with Callum and Steve (both unaccompanied and clearly pissed already), plus Luke and Lucy.

'Darling,' says Patti, kissing me on both cheeks. 'You look fabulous. I told you Anthony was a miracle worker.' She surveys my new hairstyle approvingly. 'And Toby, how nice to meet you at last.' Toby flashes her one of his most charming smiles and she practically melts to the floor right there in front of him. 'This is my husband, Rich,' she says. The two men shake hands.

'I liked the work you did with Santana last year,' says Toby graciously. Nice one, Toby!

'Thanks, man,' says Rich.

I walk round the table to greet the others. Callum and Steve are too busy chatting up two star-struck blondes at the next table – competition winners prob-ably – to pay me much attention, but Luke gives me a hug and Lucy compliments me on my dress.

'I like your trouser suit too,' I tell her.

'It's only French Connection,' she says in an embar-rassed whisper. 'I feel a bit under-dressed actually.'

'Well don't,' I say, knowing how disabling it can be when you feel out of place. 'I think you look very chic.'

A team of waiters has already started serving dinner, so I quickly take my seat in between Toby and Patti. Somebody fills my glass with champagne and pretty soon everyone's talking and laughing. By the time we get to coffee Toby and Lucy have swapped seats so us three girls can chat together, while Rich regales the guys with stories of life on the road that would put Spinal Tap to shame. The atmosphere is buoyant and good-natured and I'm almost disappointed when a faceless voice, booming out across the auditorium, announces the start of the awards ceremony, which means everyone has to shut up and face the stage.

For the next hour and a half I sit there bored shitless, but smiling and applauding politely, while the gongs for Best Newcomer, Best Solo Artist, Best Album, etc. etc. etc., are handed out. Our table goes wild when Rich goes up to collect his Lifetime Achievement Award, the one prize that is always announced in the music press in advance. Rather touchingly, he pays tribute to Patti in his acceptance speech – 'my precious muse' he calls her – and I watch as her eyes fill with tears. I guess he really must love her, despite all the infidelities.

Then comes the moment we've all been waiting for, the final and most prestigious award of the night: Best Band. Two gigantic plasma screens on either side of the stage screen video clips of the five short-listed groups and an expectant hush descends over the Arena as Danny Belmont, frontman of last year's winning band, The Belmonts, takes to the stage and tears open the big silver envelope. 'And the award for Best Band goes to . . . Drift!'

The whole place seems to erupt. Toby and Steve hi-five each other, Callum tries to jump onto the table, but is sensibly stopped in his tracks by Luke. I want to congratulate Toby before he goes onstage, but somehow in the melee I lose my chance and before I know it they're weaving their way between the tables to claim what is rightfully theirs. Lucy squeezes my hand under the table as Toby accepts the award on behalf of the band and the four of them cluster round the podium.

'We'd like to dedicate this to Sonny McGregor,' says Toby, raising the pewter and glass trophy above his head.

'And all our fans,' adds Steve.

'And our mums,' says Callum with a maniacal grin.

The audience cheers and whoops in appreciation and many are on their feet; Drift are clearly a popular choice. I can't tell you how proud I am, seeing *my* husband on *that* stage. Winning Best Band is such a testament to all his hard work and commitment. He really deserves it, they all do.

I watch impatiently as they start to make their way back to the table. There's so much backslapping and hand-shaking en route that it takes them an age. Finally, Toby is within arm's reach, but just as I go to deliver my own special congratulations Sonny McGregor steps into the frame. 'Thanks for that, Toby. I really appreciate it, mate,' says Sonny and they give each other a macho embrace. Then Sonny's girlfriend, silly Tania with the endless legs, decides to get in on the action, grabbing Toby's arm and twittering away about how thrilled she is. I've spent a few painful evenings in her company and, believe me, that woman can bore for England. I try to catch Toby's eye over the top of her head. He sees me and gives a little wink, but it's another couple of minutes before he finally escapes.

'Well done, darling,' I say, hooking my hands behind his neck. 'I knew you'd get it.'

'It's amazing, I'm so bloody chuffed,' he says. 'We're gonna have one hell of a party tonight. Are you up for it or do you want me to find a car to take you home?'

'This is one of the biggest nights of your life, of course I'm up for it,' I say indignantly.

The sound system starts pumping out the Stereophonics and Arena staff begin clearing away the tables so that the after-party can begin. Callum and Steve have relocated to the toilets to begin their own personal celebrations and the rest of us head upstairs to the VIP area. We bag a velvet-upholstered booth and Toby and Luke take everyone's drinks orders and disappear to the bar, while I dash to the ladies'. I'm absolutely bursting and thankfully there's no queue for the cubicles; although in front of the mirrors it's every woman for herself. Afterwards, as I'm washing my hands, I notice that my chignon has slipped slightly, so I retrieve the emergency hairpins from my handbag and start tidying it up, which is quite a tricky operation, given the number of women jockeying for space. I'm just about done when suddenly I hear a distinctive husky voice that makes my blood run cold.

Glancing along the line of women, almost to the end, my worst fears are confirmed: Alexa Hunt, in the flesh. It never occurred to me that the silly little slag would be here, although I suppose I shouldn't be surprised. She's dusting blusher on her perfect cheekbones and chatting away to a petite redhead, who I recognize from some crappy kids' show on Channel 5. I'm pretty sure they haven't noticed me. Playing for time, I rummage in my handbag and pull out a tube of mascara. As I coat my lashes, I strain to hear what they're saying above the noise of toilets flushing and women chattering.

'How did the shoot go?' the redhead's saying.

'It was cool, Bob Parker-Thomas is one of my favourite photographers,' says The Slapper. 'I think he really captured my essence, if you know what I mean.'

'Yeah,' nods the redhead sagely, as she applies lipgloss.

'And the best part was, not only did I get a monster fee, I also got to spend ten days in Mauritius, courtesy of *Upfront* magazine. I only got back yesterday – check out my tan.' She extends a smooth bronzed limb and strokes it narcissistically.

'You're sooo lucky, Lexy,' says the redhead adoringly. 'How come the lads' mags never want to shoot me?'

I don't hear Alexa's response as they're moving towards the exit. Hurriedly I stuff my mascara in my bag and follow them out, my head down to avoid recognition – not that The Slapper would even know, or indeed care, what Mrs Toby Carson looks like. They're heading straight for the bar, I wonder if Toby's still there. Glancing over at our booth in the corner, I see the familiar red-gold shock of hair and breathe a sigh of relief. I hope she walks past us later on, sees how happy we are together as we celebrate Toby's success. That would wipe the smile off the bitch's face.

Making my way through the crowds back to the booth, I am suddenly struck by a vile coincidence. How long has it been since Toby became more loving, more attentive, more . . . well, more like a husband? Ten days. Exactly. And by her own admission it's ten days since Alexa Hunt jetted off to Mauritius to bear her smooth, freshly waxed loins to some salivating snapper.

I don't have time to ponder the 'coincidence' any further because Patti yanks me down beside her. 'I was wondering where on earth you'd got to,' she says. 'Still, I can't complain – while you've been gone I've been getting acquainted with your darling husband. He really is adorable; Stella and Angie are going to be green with envy when I tell them I've finally met the love god in person!'

'Yeah, well looks can be deceiving,' I mutter, glowering at Toby, who is chatting away to Rich like butter wouldn't melt.

'What was that?' says Patti, as she pushes a glass of champagne towards me.

'Nothing,' I say sulkily.

As the evening wears on, I get progressively drunker. I only picked at the mediocre beef in red wine dinner earlier, so I'm drinking on an empty stomach – champagne, then gin, then tequila slammers. Everybody's going for it; except Rich, who is practically comatose, his head lolling at an awkward angle against the wall. The wild man of rock is obviously getting soft in his old age. Patti, meanwhile, is in her element, fluttering around like a butterfly on speed. It's a long time since she's been to a high-profile event like the IMAs. 'It's just like the old days,' she squeals, leering at some pre-pubescent who wafts past on his way to the bar. 'I'm suddenly feeling awful thirsty. I'll just get a drink – see if the old girl's still got what it takes,' she says, winking lewdly and nudging me in the ribs before following in the youth's wake.

I've hardly had a chance to talk to Toby all night. Every few minutes a fresh acolyte appears at our table to pay court to the newly crowned king of indie. Lucy keeps trying to engage me in conversation, but I'm not in the mood for small talk. I've got other things on my mind. Eventually she gives up and turns back to Luke. They can't keep their hands off each other. I wonder if Toby is – *was* – like that with Alexa. I keep scanning the crowd, looking for her and that sycophantic mate of hers, but they're nowhere in sight. Maybe they've gone back downstairs to the party. Actually, now I come to think of it, I quite fancy a dance myself.

'Toby,' I say, tweaking his shirtsleeve. He's deep in conversation with some skinny geezer smoking a cigar. 'Toby,' I say again. Still he ignores me. 'Oi!' I say loudly, simultaneously punching him on the arm – hard. He stops talking and turns round to look at me, clearly irritated at the interruption.

'Do you mind – I'm talking,' he hisses.

'I know. You've been talking all evening, talking to everyone but me,' I say.

'Sorry, babe, but there's a lot of important people here tonight.' Then in a louder voice, he says, 'Thea, I'd like you to meet Dave Scully, head of A&R at EMI. Dave, this is my wife, Thea.'

I manage a forced smile and a half-hearted hand-shake. Then I turn back to Toby. 'I want to dance,' I say petulantly.

'So go dance,' he says.

'On my own?'

'Luke 'n' Lucy'll go with you, won't you, guys?' he says, signalling to the engrossed pair. 'Downstairs, with Thea to dance?'

'Yeah, sure,' says Luke, ever the gent. 'C'mon Thea.'

I give Toby a final disapproving frown before heading downstairs with the others. The place is heaving. I lead Luke and Lucy to a tiny unclaimed space on the dance floor just below the stage and begin moving to the music. Damn, these shoes really weren't made for comfort. I bend down, pull them off and toss them to the edge of the dance floor. Bare feet, that's better, now I can really dance. After fifteen minutes or so Luke and Lucy say they're going to take a breather and I wave them away, insisting I'll be fine on my own. Now that I'm obviously unattached, a couple of guys try to move in on me, but I give them the cold shoulder. Not only am I perfectly happy dancing on my own, but Toby would kill me if he saw me with another man.

After thirty-five sweat-drenched minutes I'm dying for a drink. It takes me ages to find my shoes and when I do they're completely trashed, having been trampled on by my fellow dancers. Oh well, that's a couple of hundred quid down the drain. Never mind, I can always buy another pair – half a dozen pairs – if I want.

Looking around, I can't see a single familiar face, which reminds me why I usually avoid events like these. I get a Coke at the bar and mooch around a bit. There's still no sign of Luke and Lucy, although I do spot Callum, with his tongue down the throat of one of the blonde competition winners. I decide to head back upstairs to Toby, but when I get there I discover that our booth has been taken over by another noisy group. Rich is still there, still comatose, but Toby is nowhere in sight. I check Rich, just to make sure he's still breathing. He rolls his head and mutters something unintelligible when I touch his shoulder, so I think he's OK. I wish I knew where Toby had got to. How selfish of him just to leave like that. I do a thorough recce of the VIP area in case he's lurking in some darkened corner. I spot Patti deep in conversation with the youth, but still no Toby.

I head for the men's toilets in case he decided to go for a quick pick-me-up. Dave Scully is just exiting. 'I don't suppose Toby's in there is he?' I ask him.

'I don't think so,' says Dave, as he adjusts his fly. 'Last time I saw him he said he was going outside for a breath of fresh air.'

Strange, Toby's not usually such a lightweight. I head back downstairs and wend my way through the mass of bodies. I feel faintly ridiculous. Here I am, Thea Carson, wife of the Best Band frontman, wandering around barefoot looking for my husband and master like a lost puppy.

It's two a.m. and I can feel my hangover starting to kick in already. Sod it, I've had enough, I'm going home. I'm sure there'll be dozens of cabs outside. En route for the exit I walk past a glass booth with a sign outside that says 'Security'. I might just pop in, tell them who I am and where I'm going, just in case Toby comes looking for me later. Maybe they can do a tannoy announcement or something: 'Will Mr Toby Carson, looking for his missing wife, please contact security . . .' Hah, imagine how embarrassed he'd be.

I stick my head round the corner of the booth. 'Excuse me,' I say to one of the blue-suited guards. 'I just wanted to let you know that I'm going home now.'

'Righty-ho, love,' he says. 'Cabs are waiting at the main entrance.'

'The thing is I've lost my husband. Can I leave my name with you just in case he comes looking for me?'

'Yes, love, just a minute.' He turns around to rummage in a drawer for a pen and a piece of paper and as he does so, I get a clear view of the bank of CCTV screens behind him. Each of the half dozen or so screens shows a different view of the outside of the building, pretty boring really. But then a movement on one of the screens catches my eye. It's a man and a woman shagging up against the cold metal facade of the Arena. Bloody hell, it's brass monkeys out there; they must be desperate. The guard turns back to me, pen at the ready. 'Now what did you say your name was?' Over his left shoulder I can still see the shagging couple. The girl's got long blonde hair and her head is thrown back in ecstasy while the bare-buttocked bloke pumps away in faintly comedic fashion. She looks vaguely familiar. Actually, they both look familiar . . . Shit.

'Love . . . your name?'

'Mrs Fucking Mug,' I say, my voice trembling with emotion, before running out into the night.

EIGHTEEN

Today is the first day I've felt remotely normal since the night of the IMAs. In the past two and a half weeks I have lurched from gibbering wreck to hysterical diva to vengeful bunny-boiler and back again. The pain's still there, raw and suppurating, but I'm beginning to deal with it . . . that's if you can call holing up in Kim's spare room and refusing to set foot outside the house dealing with it.

The one saving grace in all this is that the story never made the papers; which is pretty miraculous when you consider that *my* husband was fucking a no-brain MTV presenter at a major showbiz event – OK, so it was *outside* a major showbiz event, but he was still bloody lucky no one else saw them. So at least I have been spared public humiliation and a plague of reporters on my doorstep.

When I saw that black and white image on the CCTV screen I didn't cry, I didn't fall apart and I certainly didn't consider confronting Toby there and then. I went into self-protection mode: caught a cab back to Itchycoo and then called Kim to ask if she'd take me in yet again. She did more than say 'yes' (never mind that I'd woken her up in the small hours), she drove round to pick me up, angel that she is. Within twenty minutes, I had packed a bag and was gone. But before I left I penned the Adulterer a quick note and stuck it on the fridge door with the pink loveheart magnet that Toby won in a Christmas cracker at his mum's house last year and then made a great show of presenting to me.

> *Hope Alexa enjoyed her 'knee-trembler' (two in one night – you must be very pleased with yourself). Have a shit life, you bastard.*

> *T*

I did think about doing something really vindictive, like trashing his sound system or taking a hammer to that fucking chandelier he loves so much, but I couldn't see the point, not when he could replace them the next day without even noticing a dent in his wallet.

The first night I didn't shed a single tear, I was far too angry for that. I just ranted and raved about what a bastard Toby was, while Kim produced suitable expressions of disgust and loathing. I think she was a bit hurt that I hadn't shared my suspicions about Alexa Hunt with her sooner, but she didn't question my motives, she's a better friend than that. We finally went to bed around five a.m., but I didn't sleep. I just lay there, wishing all manner of vile punishments on Toby and wondering what my next move would be. I was pretty pleased with myself for leaving Itchycoo like that and not sticking around to hear Toby try and talk his way out of it. In the past I've been very patient – meek, some might say – but this time, he had pushed me to the limit.

First contact came around four p.m. The call came through on Kim's home phone line and as she was closeted in her office, working on a fashion designer's hen night extravaganza, I answered it myself. I hardly recognized him. The confident, swaggering, self-assured pop star had gone and in his place was a pathetic, kowtowing, guilt-racked little boy. I think he'd been crying too – his voice had that thick, stuffy-nosed quality.

He begged me to come home, begged me to give him another chance, begged me not to go to the press with the story (I was actually quite insulted by that last request), but it was good to hear him grovelling like that and I felt superior in my role as 'the wronged wife'.

Of course, Toby didn't know that I had discovered he was carrying on with Alexa *before* last night, so I formulated a little test for him. If he came clean, I'd give him a fair hearing. If he lied, that would be it – for ever: *You are the Weakest Link, Toby. Goodbye.*

'So tell me, Toby, was it a drunken one-off with Alexa or are the two of you having an affair?' I said in my chilliest Anne Robinson voice.

There was silence for a second or two while he considered his answer.

'I'm going to be totally honest with you,' he said in a quiet voice. 'I've been seeing Lexy, er, Alexa for a while. It started when Drift guested on her MTV show, the week before the tour started. We went for a drink afterwards and she came on pretty strong. I was stupid and weak . . . I didn't set out to have a relationship with her, I swear, it just kind of happened.'

'And then it just kind of kept on happening, I suppose?'

'Yeah, sort of.'

'So that *Mirror* story was true – you did shag her in the Malmaison.'

'Yes, yes I did. I know I told you we just had a drink and fell asleep, but the thing was, that night in Manchester I told her it was over, that I couldn't go on seeing her any more because it was eating me up inside – being unfaithful to you, I mean.'

'Was that before or after you fucked her?'

'After – I mean before. Actually, I can't really remember, I was pretty trashed that night. So I didn't see the point in admitting it to you then, not when it was already over.'

'But it wasn't over, was it, because you carried on seeing her.'

'I didn't mean to, we just kept bumping into each other and, let me tell you, she's a pretty persistent woman.'

'And she's very attractive, of course.'

'Not half as attractive as you, babe – and not nearly as intelligent either. She's a bit of an airhead actually.'

'Well that makes me feel a whole lot better,' I said. 'Not only has my husband been unfaithful, he's not especially choosy where he sticks his knob.'

He gave a big sigh and said, 'The point I'm trying to make is that I'm not in love with her; it was just stupid, selfish sex. I should've finished it ages ago, but I was too spineless. She's been abroad for the past week or so, doing a photo shoot, and while she was gone I realized how stupid I was being – jeopardizing my marriage like that. I decided that when she came back I would end it once and for all.'

'So last night, you decided to give her one last poke for old time's sake?'

'Last night was a terrible mistake. I knew she'd be at the IMAs—'

'Which is why you tried to put me off going.'

'I guess, but I thought it would be OK. I knew Alexa wouldn't cause a scene or anything, I just didn't like the thought of you two being in the same building.'

'In case I picked up on the vibes between you?'

'No . . . I dunno, I just didn't like it that's all. Alexa seemed to be keeping her distance, but when you went off to dance she made a beeline for me and started flirting really obviously in front of Dave Scully, so I dragged her outside to tell her I wasn't going to see her again. But then she started kissing me and one thing led to another. Before I knew it, we were going at it hammer and tongs—'

'I can do without the details, thanks very much.'

'Sorry, babe. Anyhow, when I came back inside I saw Dave and found out he'd told you I'd gone outside for a breather. I guess you came looking and saw us, huh?'

'Something like that.'

'I know how I'd feel if I saw *you* with another man, you must've been sick to your stomach.'

'Sick's not the word. Try repulsed, revolted, appalled, disgusted—'

'Easy, babe . . . anyway, listen, I swear it's over with Alexa. I called her this morning and told her never to contact me again – and she was cool with that, she knows the game's up and she doesn't want to jeopardize her career by being labelled a marriage wrecker.'

'Goodness, how very selfish of me not to consider Lexy's feelings in all of this,' I said with as much sarcasm as I could muster. 'Here am I, feeling sorry for myself, when all I've got to lose is my marriage. I mean, Lexy's entire career is at stake!'

'All I'm saying is that she's accepted we're never gonna see each other again.'

'But how do I know you won't cheat on me with someone else?' I asked him.

'You just have to believe me, babe . . . Alexa was a silly one-off. I've never been unfaithful to you before and I never will be again.'

'But why did you have an affair with her in the first place? Our sex life has always been pretty good. One woman isn't enough for you, is that it?'

'It's not as simple as that. When I met Alexa I was going through a really stressful time, recording the album, preparing for the tour. I don't think you really understood just how difficult all that shit was for me, but she listened to me, she stroked my ego, she was *there* for me. Hey – it was flattering. What more can I say?'

For me that was the final straw. 'You really are a superficial little shit, aren't you?' I said with a scornful laugh. 'You don't seriously believe I'm going to have you back after the despicable way you've behaved. Nothing you've said has convinced me you value our marriage one iota. Don't bother to call me again; you'll be hearing from my lawyer shortly.'

With that I slammed down the phone and promptly burst into tears – big, ugly, snotty sobs. After a minute or so, Kim emerged from her office. 'Thea?' she called out from the hallway. 'Is that you?' When she saw the state I was in she threw her arms around me, not caring whether I covered her dry-clean-only cardie in mucus as only a true friend would. In a hiccuping voice I recounted the highlights – or should that be lowlights? – of my conversation with Toby.

'He's changed so much since he got famous,' I snivelled. 'He's not the man I fell in love with. He's . . . he's . . . he's . . . a fucking wanker and I hate him.' And my crying started afresh.

For the rest of the day and into the night I couldn't stop crying. It was embarrassing. Poor Tim didn't know what to say to me as I sat there howling in front of *ER* (not recommended viewing for anyone with an emotional disposition, never mind one as vulnerable as me). I must've looked a right state – my nose was red and bulbous, my eyes were like slits – and my temples were throbbing, but still I couldn't stop crying. After a while, Tim politely excused himself and went into the kitchen to study the FTSE.

Gradually, over the next week, I managed to get a grip. Toby made a couple of attempts to call me – I refused to speak to him – and he even came to the house on one occasion. Kim wouldn't let him in, but shouted up the stairs to ask me if I wanted to see him. I might have considered it, but peeking out from behind the curtain in the upstairs bedroom I saw that Toby had asked the cabby to wait in the street – so he obviously wasn't that hell-bent on seeing me.

'Tell him to go fuck himself,' I shouted back down – a message that Kim duly delivered, remarkably managing to keep a straight face.

The week after that I grew calmer still. I think the big turning point came a couple of days ago when I finally realized that Toby wasn't going to make some grand romantic gesture, like hire a plane to trail a banner across the sky, which read 'Thea, I'm sorry for being such a bastard'. Nor was I about to metamorphose into Jerry Hall and be prepared to forgive and forget (although in the end even she got fed up with turning a blind eye).

I've been asking myself, *Why am I so upset? Why don't I give him another chance?* After all, I knew Toby was having an affair and, in a sense, I had accepted it. Hindsight's a wonderful thing and maybe I should have confronted him right from the start, but I didn't – and I now acknowledge that was very stupid of me. But what I can't forgive him for is: *a*) shagging that little cow at an event that I was attending, *b*) lying to me about their night at the Malmaison, and *c*) being such a drivelling idiot on the phone – I mean, 'she was *there* for me' – I've never heard such a pile of shit in all my life. And let's face it, I put up with a lot in that marriage – the all-night binges, the lack of interest in my search for my father, that awful business with the abortion . . . I guess Alexa was simply the straw that broke the camel's back.

But what about the lovely house, the designer wardrobe, the fancy restaurants, I hear you say. Surely she can't really be prepared to give all that up? There's no doubt about it, I *will* miss the lifestyle – especially Itchycoo, I adore that place – but there are more important things in life than material possessions, such as happiness and trust and respect. And I didn't get much of that living with Toby. I don't mind admitting that the thought of being on my own scares me shitless, but in the words of the Small Faces, it's all or nothing. So I guess I'm picking the 'nothing' option.

Yesterday I was trying to remember all the good times we'd had together and do you know, there weren't that many; not since we've been married anyway. Fame *does* change people; I've seen that for myself. I guess it's easy to start believing your own hype, to think that you're some sort of untouchable, that you can treat people how you please because you're a star and your feelings are somehow more important than theirs. No wonder showbiz marriages are notoriously short-lived, I guess mine is just following in a grand tradition.

I may sound blasé, but I don't feel it. Coming to terms with the end of my marriage is one of the most distressing experiences I've ever been through and only slightly less painful than Mum's death. At least her cancer was an act of God and beyond my control, whereas the break-up of my marriage is entirely manmade. Am I about to call in the lawyers? Not yet. I need time to adjust to the situation first. I checked my bank account and Toby hasn't stopped his monthly direct debit. And I'm still using my credit card – not caning it though – because I can't expect Kim and Tim to support me. I suppose I'll have to work out a financial settlement with Toby eventually and maybe I should think about asking J.C. to let me go back full-time. But for now I'm just concentrating on getting through the day.

With all the trauma of the past couple of weeks, I've scarcely given a single thought to my long-lost father. But today, as part of my self-imposed returning-to-normality regime, I plan to begin looking for the final candidate – Roy. To be honest, even if I do succeed in finding Roy I don't hold out much hope of him being my dad. In fact, I've come to realize how extremely naive I was ever to imagine Mum's diaries could hold the key to his identity. Life is never that straightforward. Nevertheless I am determined to see this project through to the bitter end and hopefully, when Roy has been successfully eliminated, I shall be able to lay a ghost to rest and get on with the rest of my life – fatherless and husbandless, but thankfully not friendless too.

Having reread Mum's diary yet again, in the hope of gleaning further clues, I realize that this time I have nothing to go on bar a Christian name. I didn't especially want to involve anyone else in my search – it's a very private matter, after all – but it looks like this time I don't have a choice. After careful consideration, I come up with a couple of people who might be able to shed some light on Roy. One is Marty – he and Mum were exceptionally close, but I'm not sure she would have told him about an ex-boyfriend she dated only fleetingly and I wouldn't want to hurt his feelings by enquiring.

The other, more likely, source of information is Val, who ran the leather stall next to Mum's at Greenwich Market. I wouldn't say they were best friends, but they socialized a lot together before *and* after I arrived on the scene. I haven't seen Val since Mum's funeral, but I manage to find her number in my Filofax – not in the A to Z of addresses, but scrawled on the Birthdays and Anniversaries insert. I can remember Val writing it there herself during Mum's wake, an intimate and exceptionally emotional affair for a dozen or so of the Greenwich contingent, which I hosted in the back room of a local pub on the day of the funeral.

'Your mum was one in a million,' she'd said tearfully. 'We mustn't lose touch.' Inevitably, we did just that. In fact, I haven't kept in touch with any of those people who expressed their heartfelt condolences on that dreadful day – not even Marty – and they in turn would've lost track of me as I moved from Greenwich to Kilburn and thence to upper-crust Belsize Park. I should have made more of an effort. I was so devastated in those first months I couldn't bear to be around people who knew Mum, preferring to wallow in my own private grief. I've come through that now – a realization that only dawned on me when I met Kevin and Barney. Despite my disappointment at discovering I wasn't related to either of them, I was thrilled to hear them reminisce about her and they made me feel proud to be her daughter. If it wasn't for them, I don't think I'd have the nerve to contact Val. I just hope she isn't too put out by my sudden reappearance after two years of silence.

In the event she is disproportionately pleased to hear from me. 'Thea Parkinson, I don't believe it!' she exclaims. 'Of course, it's Thea Carson now, isn't it? I nearly had a heart attack when I saw your picture in the newspaper with your boyband-chappie husband. I took it straight round to show Eileen next door. "Look at this," I said, "it's Shirley's girl – all grown up and doing very well for herself." Ooh love, you have blossomed since I last saw you. Don't get me wrong, you were always a pretty little thing, but now, now you're a real beauty and no mistake.'

She pauses for breath and I seize the opportunity to get a word in edgeways. 'I'm sorry I haven't been in touch for so long,' I say. 'Especially after you were so kind when Mum died.'

'No need to apologize, Thea love, I'm sure you've been very busy with your new life,' she says generously. 'Ooh, you are a credit to your mum, it's such a shame she didn't live to see you so happy.'

I enquire about her own family – husband Mick has taken early retirement on the grounds of ill health, son Dominic is now in the final year of a business studies degree – and we chat about the ups and downs of the leather business (Val opened her own shop in the early Nineties and has now branched out into soft furnishings), and then I cut to the chase.

'It's great to catch up with you, Val, but I'm afraid I do have an ulterior motive.'

'Don't tell me, you're doing a feature for one of those lovely celebrity magazines and you want your Auntie Val to dig out some old photos,' she says with a chuckle. 'You'll be pleased to hear I've got some absolute corkers! Remember when your Mum and I left you playing nicely in the garden and came out half an hour later to find you'd taken off your shorts and T-shirt and put them on the cat. There you were, standing in your Victoria Plum knickers and vest, cradling your "baby" as you called poor old Ginge. I was laughing so much the camera was shaking.'

'Shit, I'd forgotten all about that – how old was I, six or seven? Promise me you'll destroy the negatives the minute you get off the phone or I'll never be able to show my face in public again,' I say, and we both have a good laugh about it. I'd forgotten how much fun Val could be.

'Seriously though, Val, I was hoping you could help me track down one of Mum's old friends.'

'Well, I will if I can,' she says. 'What's her name?'

'It's a *he* actually and his name's Roy,' I say. 'Ring any bells?'

'Roy,' she says. 'Hmm, it's vaguely familiar, but I'm not sure. Can you give me a bit more to go on?'

'I only know that he dated Mum the summer before I was born and I think it was a fairly casual relationship.'

'I've got it!' she says triumphantly. 'Roy Potter, local boy, good-looking chap, dark-skinned, father came from one of those Indian Ocean islands – Mauritius, I think. I only remember him because a couple of years later he married another stallholder, Debbie something.'

'Val, you are amazing!' I say excitedly. 'Does he still live in Greenwich?'

'Ooh, I wouldn't know, love. I haven't seen him for yonks. But Debbie still works the market, she's got a second-hand clothes stall. They're not together any more, mind; they had a couple of kids, I seem to remember, and then it all went pear-shaped.'

'But Debbie would know where to find him, wouldn't she, if they've got kids and stuff?'

'I s'pose so . . . if you don't mind me asking, why are you so keen to find Roy Potter? Shirley only went out with him a handful of times and I don't think they had much in common; he was a bit of a jack the lad, as I recall and frankly your mum deserved better.'

I can't see the point in lying, not when Val's been so helpful, so I tell her the whole story – finding Mum's diaries, compiling a shortlist of three, my fruitless, but highly enjoyable, meetings with Kevin and Barney.

'Goodness, you *have* gone to a lot of trouble,' she exclaims. 'I knew you had no contact with your dad, but I didn't realize you never even knew who he was. Did your mum never tell you?'

'Not exactly. It was a subject she was never very comfortable discussing . . . actually, she implied it could've been one of several men and she never even told any of them she was pregnant. I don't suppose she ever mentioned any names to *you*?'

''Fraid not. I didn't think it was any of my business – we were mates, but not bosom buddies. The only time we ever talked about it was when she was a bit hard up. You would've been about four and the Inland Revenue had just dumped a huge tax bill on her. I suggested she get in touch with your dad and ask him to lend her a few quid, just till she was back on her feet again.'

'What did she say to that?'

'She just brushed it off. I think she said something along the lines of: "Thea's father is not a part of our lives and never will be." I didn't like to bring the subject up again after that.'

Bloody hell, Mum played her cards close to her chest. It doesn't sound as if she confided in anyone – at least not as far as my dad was concerned.

'Val, can I ask you something?'

'Fire away, love.'

'Do I look like Roy Potter? I mean, even just a tiny bit?'

'Let's think . . . there's no obvious similarity, he is half-black, after all. But then you've got that lovely dark hair and you've always tanned very nicely, haven't you? I remember when you came back from those three weeks in Barbados with that Adam bloke you used to go out with – you were that dark, you could've been an Indian yourself!'

'Yeah, you have got a point there.' I'd never considered that I could be mixed race, but I suppose it is a possibility.

'How on earth are you going to find out if Roy *is* your dad, when your mum didn't even know who got her pregnant?' asks Val.

'A DNA test, it's quite straightforward.'

'Well, just you be careful ... the past can be a dangerous thing, you know,' she says gently.

'I will – and if I draw a blank with Roy then I'm just going to forget about the whole thing.'

'Well, I wish you the best of luck – and I know you've got a fancy new lifestyle a million miles away from a market stall in Greenwich, but don't you go forgetting about us, will you?'

If only Val knew how my 'fancy new lifestyle' has collapsed around my ears. But I don't want to shatter her illusions about my perfect existence, so I promise faithfully to keep in touch, give her my mobile number and omit any reference to the breakdown of my marriage and the fact that I am now single, depressed and homeless. Still, she'll be reading about it in the tabloids soon enough.

NINETEEN

This place has hardly changed in twenty years: more tourists and more tat by the look of things, but the vibe's the same and those familiar smells – home-made fudge, warm leather and damp canvas – bring a million memories flooding back. As a kid I knew this market like the back of my hand and every stallholder knew *me*. Saturdays and Sundays always followed the same routine: Mum and I would arrive at eight a.m. sharp, lugging three huge holdalls and the collapsible clothes rail that we'd brought in the minicab. Others were required to turn up hours earlier in order to secure a pitch, but Mum was one of the favoured few whose position was guaranteed – and ours was one of the most coveted pitches, nestling in the top left-hand corner of the covered market, next to the coffee bar and a row of overpriced antique shops.

While Mum erected the clothes rail, I would unpack the holdalls, separating the clothes into piles – trousers in one pile, skirts in another, and so on. Then Mum would hang the larger garments on the clothes rail, setting aside the best, most eye-catching pieces of handiwork to suspend from the stall's metal framework. The smaller items, T-shirts and scarves, were placed on a trestle table; not piled up one on top of another, but spread out nicely so people could see the quality of the design and the neatness of the stitching. 'It's all in the presentation,' Mum would say with a certain measure of pride and only when she was fully satisfied with her display were we permitted to open our little folding stools, unscrew our Thermos of tea and wait for the first punters to arrive.

Summer was the most lucrative season, thanks to the day trippers who flooded into historic Greenwich, come to admire the *Cutty Sark* or straddle the famous Meridian line. Of all the nationalities who clogged the tourist drag, the Americans were the biggest spenders. They would cluster around the stall and coo over Mum's 'cute' abstract print Ts and floaty see-through blouses and think nothing of buying seven or eight items at a time, gifts for the folks back home. How grown-up I felt, fishing in the cash box for change and folding customers' purchases into crinkly white carrier bags. Nowadays Mum would probably be prosecuted under some child labour law, but back then nobody looked twice at a skinny kid helping out her ma.

Today Mum's old pitch is occupied by a long-haired guy of nineteen or twenty whose trade is silver jewellery. It's still early and I watch from the doorway of a secondhand bookshop as he finesses his display, laying out rings and earrings in velveteen trays and hanging delicate necklaces on a revolving stand. Seeing me hovering there, he calls out apologetically, 'I'll be open for business in two ticks.' Now that he's noticed me, it seems churlish not to take a look, so I wander over to the trestle table and make a show of browsing. A pretty pair of earrings, little sterling silver starbursts, catch my eye and I buy two pairs – one for me and one for Kim.

'I don't suppose you know if Debbie's here today?' I ask him casually, as he wraps my purchases in tissue paper. 'She's got a clothes stall.'

'Debbie Potter?'

I nod.

'Should be, she's here most Sundays. Her pitch is out the front there, next to the health-food shop.'

I thank him, tuck the earrings safely into my jacket pocket, and make my way across the cobbles to the entrance of the market, where the stalls meet the traffic-choked road and a plaster arch bears the Victorian motto: *A false balance is an abomination to the Lord, but a just weight is his delight*. Thanks to Val's description, I spot Debbie almost immediately: 'mutton dressed as lamb' was the phrase she used and she wasn't wrong. The Lycra-clad woman with straw-coloured highlights and a tan the colour of a Vuitton fake would give Bet Lynch a run for her money.

'Debbie?' I say, injecting a false note of friendliness into my voice.

'Yeah,' she answers and continues pricing battered leather jackets without looking up.

'Sorry to bother you, but I'm a friend of Val Stephenson – she used to run a leather stall here,' I say hesitantly.

Debbie puts down the ticket gun and looks at me. 'Uh huh,' she says noncommittally.

'She said you might be able to help me,' I say. 'I'm trying to find someone, your ex-husband, actually – Roy.'

'Are you 'avin' a fuckin' laugh?' she says in broadest *sarf-east* London. 'I ain't seen Roy for months. What d'you want 'im for, anyway – owe you money does 'e?'

'No, no, nothing like that,' I say hastily and mutter something vague about him being a friend of my boyfriend.

'Like I said, I ain't seem 'im for ages, I ain't even got 'is number, but if yer desperate you'll probably find 'im at the station . . . that's if 'e's doing a shift today.'

'The DLR station?'

'Nah, the mainline station on the 'igh Road . . . I still can't believe 'e's finally got 'imself a proper job,' she says. 'Mind you, 'e's probably still pouring 'is money down 'is throat, like 'e did the whole time we wuz married; 'e wouldn't 'ave paid a single penny in maintenance for them kids if I 'adn't put the CSA onto 'im yer know.'

'Really? Oh dear,' I say lamely, unsure of the best way to react to this unsolicited disclosure. Debbie may have kept the marital surname, but it certainly doesn't sound like there's much love lost.

She looks over her shoulder at a customer rifling through a rail of vintage Levis. 'Be with you in a minute, love,' she tells him. 'Gotta go,' she says, turning back to me. 'Give Roy me best if you find 'im . . . on second thoughts, don't fuckin' bovver,' she cackles.

Greenwich station is only a few minutes' walk and as I make my way up the High Road I realize that I don't have a clue what Roy does – is he a train driver, a cleaner, a ticket inspector? With any luck, I shall soon find out.

At the entrance to the station a burly man in a Connex uniform is giving directions to a pack of foreign students – the kind I used to get really annoyed with when I lived here because of the way they seemed to take over the whole pavement with their bulging ruck-sacks and noisy jabbering. When he's sent them on their way, I approach him and enquire if Roy Potter is on duty today. 'Ticket office,' he says cursorily, nodding towards the foyer. Behind the glass screen I can just about make out an exotic-looking man of indeterminate age. I join the queue of customers – this apparently being the only way to get Roy's attention – and as the line moves forward I strain to get a better look at him. From what I can see, he's not bad looking and he seems to be smiling a lot, which is always a good sign.

Finally, it's my turn to be served. Before I open my mouth, I peer through the glass and check out his name badge . . . good, I've got the right man.

'Sorry to bother you,' I begin. 'I don't want a ticket, I just wanted to have a chat with you – later, I mean, not now.'

He looks bemused and the woman in the queue behind me kisses her teeth impatiently.

'I'll be quick because I can see you're busy . . .' I continue. 'My name's Thea Carson. You don't know me, but you knew my mother – a long time ago.'

'And was she as pretty as you, darling?' he asks in a lilting voice.

Is he flirting with me? How positively indecent. But then again he doesn't know what I know.

Nevertheless, I smile good-naturedly and say cheekily, 'How about it then?'

'Are you asking me out?' he says, leaning closer to the screen to look me up and down.

'Look, are you buying a ticket or what?' the woman behind me says irritably.

'Sorry, I won't be a second,' I say, before turning back to Roy. 'When's your lunch break? Maybe I could buy you a drink?'

'You *are* asking me out,' he says, looking very pleased with himself. 'D'you know the Anchor?'

I nod.

'I'll be there in my lunch break, I clock off at twelve-thirty,' he says. Then he adds playfully, 'Don't you go standing me up now.'

'I'll be there,' I say, as the woman shoulder-charges her way past me in her haste to the counter.

With a couple of hours to kill, I decide to head for Greenwich Park, former hunting ground of Henry VIII. It's also the place where I smoked my first illicit cigarette, drank my first under-age can of Diamond White and was groped in the rose garden by Ben Thomas, my first boyfriend (our relationship only lasted three weeks, I think he was disappointed by my lack of tits – but then again I *was* only twelve). Armed with a can of Diet Coke and a Belgian bun, I settle down on one of the benches overlooking the boating lake and begin to psych myself up for my meeting with Roy. I can't say I'm especially looking forward to it. He seems like a bit of a wide boy and hardly ideal father material. I'm half tempted to forget the whole thing and head back to Kim's, but I've come this far so I may as well see it through.

I know the Anchor well. It's probably Greenwich's least fashionable watering hole, tucked away in a semi-derelict side street close to Deptford Creek and away from the tourist thoroughfare. Kim and I used to go occasionally as teenagers to drink sickly rum and blacks and eye up the local rough trade from the notorious Pepys estate. It's a gloomy traditional pub with lots of dark wood and moth-eaten leather and huge picture windows overlooking the moody Thames.

When I arrive, at twelve-thirty sharp, the pub is half-empty. Half a dozen tables have been taken over by a party of dour-faced pensioners gobbling fish and chips, doubtless lured by the promise of cheap grub and guaranteed seating, and in the corner by the fruit machine a group of four middle-aged men are engrossed in a game of cards. It doesn't look like Roy's here yet, so I order a half of lager and lime and take a seat at a table by the window. A plaque on the wall reveals that the pub dates from 1870, when it was one of Greenwich's famous 'whitebait taverns', feeding government ministers and even, allegedly, Charles Dickens. Gazing out at the murky river, I try to imagine what it would've been like back then when Greenwich was a major maritime centre. This stretch of water would have been thick with working vessels, bringing goods and materials up into the docks, but not today – just ferryboats crowded with sightseers and the occasional dredger.

Five minutes pass, followed by ten and fifteen and then twenty. Maybe Roy was joking about meeting me; what am I going to do if he doesn't show?

Just as I'm thinking about leaving, he makes his entrance, a full thirty-five minutes late. He's still wearing his unflattering Connex uniform of navy trousers and white shirt, the garish blue jacket slung over one shoulder. He casually glances around the pub, we make eye contact and he raises his eyebrows at me. But, rather than coming straight over, he starts chatting to the barmaid and it's obvious from their banter that this is his local. For a minute or two I remain seated, just checking him out. He's average height and very slim – what you might call snake-hipped – and he really is quite good-looking for an old bloke; a mature version of Imran Khan. I wait until the barmaid has pulled his pint before walking over to him.

'Glad you could make it,' I say.

He smiles. 'My pleasure, darling,' he says, but makes no apology for his lateness. He rummages in his trouser pocket and pulls out a handful of coins, but I rest a hand on his arm. 'Allow me,' I say, drawing a fiver out my purse.

'It's a long time since a lady bought me a drink – especially one as beautiful as you,' he says in an embarrassingly loud voice.

I laugh nervously, noting that we've got an audience in the shape of the four blokes by the fruit machine, who have interrupted their card game to observe my exchange with Roy.

'She's well out of your league, Roy. You've got no chance!' one of them shouts and the others burst out laughing.

'My so-called friends are just jealous, ignore them,' says Roy with a wolfish grin, which shows off a row of even white teeth, offset by craggy, coffee-coloured skin. 'Let's make ourselves comfortable, shall we?'

I lead the way back to my table by the window and we sit down opposite each other. Roy seems incredibly relaxed. I wonder if he really thinks I'm trying to pull him. He's just sitting there with a sleepy smile on his face, looking at me looking at him and waiting for my opening gambit. I've already decided there's no point using Mum's imaginary bequest as an excuse for contacting him – after all, the two of them barely knew each other. What's more, I'm keen to make it clear to him that this is not a date in any way shape or form – and so, rather rashly, I plunge in head first.

'As I said before, we've never met,' I say, watching him carefully for the slightest reaction. 'However, I think there's a chance we may be related.'

His eyes widen and he shifts in his seat, clearly ill at ease.

'Really?' he says, picking up his pint and taking a long drink. I look at his hand, gripping the glass. Like mine, it is delicate and narrow with long tapering fingers, 'artist's hands' Mum used to call them. 'And what makes you think that, darling?'

I take a deep breath and launch into a monologue about my mother . . . her name, what she looked like, who her friends were, where she lived until her death two years ago. At first Roy says he doesn't remember a woman called Shirley Parkinson, but when I mention the market stall and the date at the Coronet nearly three decades ago he agrees that yes, he does recall a fleeting romance with such a woman. 'Bubbly girl, lots of fun, shame she died so young,' he says. 'Anyway, where does she fit in to all of this?'

'Well, the thing is, Roy . . .' I pause – rather cruelly

– for dramatic effect. 'I think there's a possibility you may be my father.'

I derive a strange pleasure from the look of abject horror that crosses his face. Not so cocky now, are you, I think to myself.

He leans across the table, narrows his eyes and gives me a long hard stare, as if searching out a family resemblance. Then he sits back in his chair and crosses his arms defensively in front of his chest.

'No, definitely not, you've got the wrong guy,' he says firmly, shaking his head, all trace of his earlier flirtatious intimacy gone. 'I don't know how you found me or what you're after, but you're wasting your time. I've got an ex-wife and two kids to support, I've got no money, nothing.'

'I don't want anything from you, Roy, especially not money,' I say indignantly. 'I don't expect you to welcome me with open arms or write me into your will, I just want to find out whether or not you're my dad.'

'Did Shirley tell you I got her pregnant?' he says, suddenly aggressive.

'No. To be perfectly honest with you, she wasn't a hundred per cent sure who got her pregnant and, frankly, I don't think she cared. She was more than happy to bring me up on her own and a very good job she did too.'

Suddenly his features relax.

'Aha, so I'm not the only guy in the frame then?' he says triumphantly.

'Not the *only* one . . . but I've narrowed it down and you're a strong contender. You were definitely seeing Mum around the time I was conceived and what's more I've got her old diaries to prove it.'

His eyes flicker across the room to where his mates are sitting, as if he's sending them a silent SOS.

'Look, darling, I'm telling you, you're barking up the wrong tree. We only went out a few times, in fact I'm not sure I even slept with her. Now, if you don't mind, I've got to get back to work.' He pushes aside his half-finished pint and stands up, knocking over a chair in his eagerness to escape.

I try a softer tactic. 'I know me turning up like this must have come as an awful shock to you, but please at least think about it. It's easy enough to establish paternity with a DNA test.' He eyes me suspiciously, but doesn't walk away. 'Here, take my mobile number and give me a call if you change your mind,' I say, scrabbling in my bag for a pen and scrawling the digits on the back of a beer mat. He hesitates for a moment, picks up the beer mat, gives me one final, doubtful look and walks towards the door.

'What's up? Don't she like older men?' one of his mates jeers at him as he walks past their table.

'Shut your damn face,' comes Roy's curt put down.

Thanks to a combination of engineering work and Sunday timetables, the journey back to north London takes over an hour, giving me plenty of time to reflect on my brief encounter with Roy. He certainly seemed very defensive and I got the distinct impression he wasn't telling me the full story. But what can I do? There seems no point in pursuing him – after all, I can't force him to have a DNA test – and, anyway, part of me is relieved that he hasn't claimed me as his long-lost daughter. I didn't like his manner – flirty and cocksure and far too full of himself. I don't know what Mum ever saw in him . . . well, actually, I do, he must've been drop-dead goregous in his youth, all smouldering eyes and thick chest hair. I wonder if he was good in the sack . . . I doubt it, he'd probably just lie there and let the woman do all the work.

TWENTY

It's official: Toby and I have separated. Our joint statement, issued through Run Records and approved by my solicitor, was brief, to the point and only slightly dishonest:

> *After thirteen months of marriage Toby and Thea Carson have decided to undergo a trial separation. The decision is mutual and amicable. The couple would be grateful if the media could respect their privacy during this difficult time.*

. . . fat chance – in the five days since the statement was released I have received more than a dozen interview requests. Not that I'll be talking – as part of the interim settlement drawn up by our respective solicitors I have agreed to 'refrain from giving any media interviews – print, broadcast or Internet – until further notice'. I did feel a bit miffed about signing on the dotted line; not that I would be tempted to wash my dirty linen in public, but it's always nice to know one has the option, particularly when one is the innocent party.

On the advice of Charles Henley, my solicitor, I've decided not to rush into divorce proceedings. 'Act in haste, repent at leisure,' he warned me. 'Wait for the dust to settle first and then you can make a rational, clear-headed decision. Who knows, there could even be a reconciliation.' I don't know if I can ever forgive Toby for betraying me, but I suppose it won't do any harm to wait a while.

Kim and Tim have said I can stay with them as long as I like, but it's not fair to keep imposing on them and I'll have to start looking for a place of my own pretty soon. Toby's generous allowance, negotiated by Charles and paid into my account on the first of every month, means I'll be able to rent a decent apartment – a spacious Kensington mansion flat or maybe even a Docklands loft – I haven't decided. To be honest, the idea of living on my own is so terrifying I don't even want to think about it.

Yesterday Kim and I went back to Itchycoo for the rest of my things – another arrangement made through our respective solicitors. Toby wasn't there, I'd made sure of that. I haven't seen him since the night of the IMAs; well, except for some old footage on GMTV. They did a silly puff piece about the shockingly short life-expectancy of celebrity marriages, complete with the inevitable relationship expert, smugly dispensing advice from the sofa.

Ivy was waiting to let us in. Despite her insider knowledge of the ups and downs of her employers' marriage, she seemed genuinely concerned by the split. 'I can't believe it's come to this,' she said in a strangulated voice. 'The house just isn't the same without you.' And she was right. The differences were subtle, but they still wrenched at my heart: the normally full fruit bowl contained a single shrivelled satsuma, the framed photographs had gone and, most hurtful of all, my découpage dressing table had been moved out of the master bedroom and carelessly shoved up against a wardrobe in the boxroom.

I was planning to take away as much as I could load into Kim's little Peugeot – the portable TV, a couple of art deco lamps, a heap of CDs . . . but in the event I was so desperate to get out of there that I just stuffed some clothes in a suitcase, shovelled a pile of toiletries into a carrier bag, picked out half a dozen pairs of shoes and left.

I didn't cry or make a fuss, but Kim could see it had hit me hard. 'You know what-you need?' she said in the car on the way back. 'A good night out. I've been given complimentary membership to Dowagers, that new private members' club in Hanover Square. I think they're hoping I'll use it as one of my party venues. It's Friday tomorrow; why don't we check it out, have a few drinks, maybe go dancing afterwards, just you and me?'

'What about Tim?' I ask.

'What about him? He can stick on a ready meal and watch Sky Sports, he'll be fine.'

I wasn't sure I could face going out in public, especially when my face had been splashed all over the papers only days earlier. Practically all of them used that photo of Toby and me at the Tom Cruise premiere; we were laughing and holding hands and I didn't have a care in the world. Who would've thought just a few months later our marriage would be another casualty of rock 'n' roll?

But Kim wasn't going to take no for an answer. She assured me that Dowagers was a very classy establishment and not the sort of place where I'd get any hassle.

'Believe me, nobody will even recognize you; you look totally different in photos and your hair's really grown since that premiere,' she said. 'You can't go on hiding away for ever, it's time to get your life back on track and start enjoying yourself again. Just think – you're a free agent now, you can do what you like, go where you like, not have to worry about doing something that might harm Toby's precious reputation.'

'Yeah, but the thing is I'm so used to being one half of a couple, I'm not sure how well I can function on my own,' I said sulkily.

'Don't be ridiculous,' she scolded. 'And, anyway, you won't stay single for long, trust me.'

In the end I gave in. And now that I've drunk two Smirnoff and cranberries and half a bottle of Shiraz I'm actually rather looking forward to my first night out as a newly single girl. Kim insisted that we really dress up, so I've gone for my Ossie Clark crepe suit and gold cone-heeled sandals.

'You should wear black more often, it really suits you,' says Kim, resting her chin on my shoulder and looking at my reflection in the full-length mirror. Toby always said black made my skin look sallow, but his opinion doesn't count any more . . . as Kim says, I can do what I like now.

Dowagers turns out to be a pleasant surprise, a freshly renovated nineteenth-century townhouse filled with antiques and open fireplaces. Kim tells me it has been restored by one of the country's finest interior designers and the head barman purports to be fresh off the plane from Manhattan. After perusing the extensive cocktail menu, I plump for a passion-fruit daiquiri and Kim plays safe with a cosmopolitan. We settle into a soft suede sofa and within half an hour I feel myself starting to relax. If anybody here recognizes me, they're keeping it to themselves – it's that kind of place, very expensive, very discreet. Even when two fairly well-known models teeter in and start talking in loud voices nobody gives them a second glance.

Kim and I are debating whether or not to continue on the cocktails or switch to shorts when a waiter appears at our side and offloads two glasses of champagne onto the glass table in front of us. 'Compliments of the gentleman over there,' he says, nodding towards a group of three men who are sitting on the sofas flanking the splendid Georgian fireplace. As I look across, the one nearest to me smiles and raises his wine glass in a toast.

'Oh, my God, we've pulled already!' Kim exclaims. 'Or rather *you've* pulled. I *thought* I saw that guy checking you out earlier.'

'Oh no, he's coming over,' I say as the man stands up.

'Don't complain, girl, he's fucking gorgeous,' says Kim out of the corner of her mouth.

She's right. He's tall, tanned and oozing class in his beautifully cut navy suit and Italian loafers, and he's got this amazing Antonio Banderas hair, thick and dark, the kind you can tug on in the throes of orgasm.

He's standing in front of us now and this sofa's so low I have to tilt my head right back to look at him.

'Good evening, ladies,' he says in a deep sexy voice. 'I have no intention of interrupting your conversation, I just wanted to introduce myself.' He extends a hand and I can't help noticing the Rolex peeking out of his shirt cuff. 'Cameron Kennedy and I'm delighted to make your acquaintance.'

'Amanda,' I say, shaking his hand and seeing Kim's eyebrows rise ever so slightly at my sudden name change. 'Thanks for the champagne.'

'You're most welcome,' he says. Then he looks me right in the eye and gives me the sexiest smile ever. My toilet parts twitch obligingly and for a second I imagine him standing there with no clothes on. I wouldn't have believed myself capable of such wanton lust in the wake of my recent marriage trauma. To be honest, I didn't think I'd ever fancy another man again, but here I am, all hot and bothered by the first guy who looks my way.

Kim's voice snaps me back to reality. 'And I'm Kim,' she says.

'Pleased to meet you, Kim,' he says, stretching across the table to shake her hand. He doesn't give her the smile though, that was just for me. 'I don't want to impose, so I'll leave you to enjoy the rest of your evening.'

Shit, he's walking away.

'Why don't you join us for a little while?' says Kim. She took the words right out of my mouth.

'Well, if you're sure . . .' he says, looking right at me. I notice that his lips are full and peony pink, a pleasing contrast to the dark tan of his face.

'Quite sure,' I say firmly, my eyes never leaving his.

I budge up along the sofa to make room for him. We're sitting so close together I can feel the heat of his thigh through two layers of fabric. It makes me feel unbelievably horny, like a bitch on a heat. I can barely concentrate, it must be the alcohol.

We chat a bit about the club and how nice it is – or rather he and Kim chat, I'm just staring – and Cameron says that he's having a night out with a few work colleagues.

'Where do you work?' asks Kim.

'KPMG, I'm a management consultant. There, I've rather killed the conversation now, haven't I?' he says, which makes Kim and I laugh. 'How about you two?'

'I run my own party planning business and Amanda is my senior designer,' Kim says without missing a beat. 'She's extremely talented, I'm very lucky to have her.'

'I don't doubt it for one second,' he says, somehow managing to make the innocuous words sound suggestive.

I suddenly panic that maybe I'm not looking my best. It's quite warm in here and I've probably developed an unattractive facial sheen. I excuse myself and head for the ladies'. Once in front of the mirror, I pull out my Clinique compact. A quick dust of powder and a fresh slick of lipstick and I'm ready for round two. As I make my way back to the bar, I see that Cameron's friends have joined us. One of them is whispering something in Kim's ear and now she's throwing her head back and laughing. Kim's good at small talk. She has to be in her line of work. Don't get me wrong – she's not a flirt, she'd never be unfaithful to Tim, not in a million years. But she's an extrovert, a social engineer.

'Amanda, I'd like you to meet my friends, Tom and Andrew,' says Cameron. I smile at them and say 'hi'. They're expensively dressed too. Management consultancy may be dull, but it's clearly lucrative work. An ice bucket has appeared in the middle of the table and Cameron pours me a glass of perfectly chilled Laurent-

Perrier. Kim leans across. 'Are you OK?' she whispers. 'Do say when you're ready to leave.'

'I'm doing just fine,' I whisper back.

Kim keeps Tom and Andrew talking, leaving me to concentrate on Cameron. When he asks me any personal questions I lie blatantly. So he thinks I was brought up in Surrey and enjoy horse riding and tai-chi. He in turn reveals that he's thirty-two, public-school educated, likes karting and water sports. Classic city boy. I'm not really listening to what he's saying, I'm just watching his full moist lips open and shut.

After a few more glasses of champagne, he makes his move.

'I'm sure you get guys coming on to you all the time,' he says. Our heads are so close they're practically touching. 'And I don't mean to sound like a total idiot, but I just wanted to say I think you're absolutely gorgeous.'

'Thanks,' I say. Well, give a girl a break . . . it's a long time since I've flirted with anyone, I'm out of practice.

'I noticed you as soon as you walked in. I told myself, "I *will* talk to that woman tonight if it's the last thing I do,"' he continues. 'Of course I expect you're already spoken for, that would be just my luck.'

Thank goodness I'm not wearing my engagement ring tonight. I dispensed with my wedding ring long ago – the night of the IMAs to be precise. It's lying at the bottom of the little ceramic jar filled with pens on top of the fridge at Itchycoo. I don't expect Toby's even realized it's there. But I've kept my engagement ring because it's so pretty, a little diamond cluster on a slim platinum band. I took it off this morning when I was applying some hand cream and forgot to put it back on.

'No actually. I'm between boyfriends at the moment,' I say. I know I sound cocky, but I don't care.

'Well, in that case, how would you fancy meeting up for dinner one night?'

Dinner? What's he on about? I hope he's not going to spoil the game. I'm not interested in his mind, only his body.

'Perhaps we could get to know each other a little better *tonight*?' I suggest. I'm not usually this forward, but I don't want a relationship, just straightforward, uncomplicated, down 'n' dirty sex.

He looks slightly taken aback and for a second I think I've blown it. He recovers quickly however and puts a warm hand on my thigh. 'I know it's a terrible cliché – but your place or mine?' he says in a low voice.

'Yours,' I say quickly. I don't think Kim would appreciate me using her home as a knocking shop.

'I only live in Clerkenwell, it won't take us long to get there,' he says. He's excited now, his pupils are massively dilated, he probably can't believe his luck.

'Let's leave now,' I tell him. 'I'll just have a word with my friend.'

I tell Kim I'm going home with Cameron, and she

makes me promise to leave my mobile switched on so she can contact me.

Outside in the street we manage to hail a black cab straight away. After giving the driver his address, Cameron wastes no time in getting to know me better. His kisses send tingles through my knickers, while his hands explore my breasts and the tops of my thighs. I can see the cab driver looking at us in his rear-view mirror. I wonder if we're turning him on. He catches my eye and doesn't even have the decency to look embarrassed. In fact, he actually winks at me.

Part of me doesn't believe I'm doing this. I've only had two one-night stands in my entire life and even they weren't intentional – that is to say, I fully expected to see the blokes in question again. Only thing was, they weren't interested in anything more than a quick shag: one tiptoed out of Mum's house while I was still asleep, the other gave me a made-up phone number. Bastards. And yet at the same time I feel extraordinarily liberated (not to mention massively turned on) by my single-minded pursuit of pleasure. I wish Toby could see me now ... Damn it, I came out tonight to forget about him, so I concentrate instead on Cameron's tongue, which is wetly probing my ear. He's got the most enormous erection, I can feel it pressing against my thigh. Should I attempt to unleash it here in the cab or wait till we get back to his place? Better wait, I don't want our voyeuristic cab driver to crash.

By the time we get to Cameron's home, an impressive fourth-floor factory conversion, I am, to put it bluntly, gagging for it. Waving aside my host's offer of a drink, I demand to be taken to the bedroom. We fall on each other hungrily and in less than a minute we're both naked.

Cameron proves himself a generous and imaginative lover: the foreplay is great, the sex sublime. His only shortfall is his inability to locate a condom. 'I know they're in here somewhere,' he says as he frantically rummages in a bedside cabinet. I can't wait any longer and drag him back towards me. 'Just be careful, that's all, I'm not on the pill,' I warn as he enters me. He is only too happy to oblige, ejaculating copiously onto my thigh just seconds after my own shuddering climax.

Sinking back on the damp sheets, I feel strangely triumphant. I shagged another man – and I enjoyed it, so maybe there is life after Toby. And Cameron certainly isn't complaining, 'Amanda, you are one hell of a woman,' he says, kissing me on the nose.

While Cameron goes into the living room to locate a post-coital cigarette, I avail myself of his Pegler power shower. When I emerge from the bathroom, draped in a soft burgundy bath sheet, he's lying in bed smoking and there are two glasses of wine on the bedside table.

'I thought you might fancy a drink,' he says. 'It's Chilean Chardonnay, damn good stuff. I bought two cases on the Internet.'

'No thanks,' I say, retrieving my crumpled clothes from the bedroom floor. 'Actually, would you mind calling me a cab?'

He looks confused. 'It's three in the morning. Aren't you going to stay the night?'

'No,' I say evenly. I must sound like an awful bitch, but I've got what I came for so what's the point in hanging around?

'Well, give me your number then and we can arrange to meet for dinner one night next week. I know a great modern European place in Shoreditch—'

'No thanks,' I say curtly, cutting him off mid-sentence. 'Listen, Cameron, I had a really nice time tonight, but that doesn't mean I want to get involved,' I say, sounding more confident than I feel.

His face falls. 'But I thought . . . never mind,' he says, shaking his head. 'I'll call that car.' He gets out of bed, pulling the top sheet around his waist, and picks up the phone. 'I'll put it on my account so you won't have to pay.'

Thankfully I don't have long to wait. As Cameron sees me to the front door, he presses his business card into my hand. 'Just in case you change your mind,' he says, pressing his lips to my cheek.

I give him a tight little smile and let myself out. As the cab makes its way northwards, I feel a tiny twinge of regret. Maybe I shouldn't have been so blunt with Cameron, he seems like a sweet guy. But there's no point running headlong into another relationship while

I'm still getting over the previous one. I've made that mistake too many times in the past.

Halfway home I suddenly realize that I forgot to switch my mobile on like I promised Kim. Checking my voicemail, I see that I have a message, left at ten p.m., and I don't recognize the number.

Hi, Thea, it's Roy. I'm sorry if I was a bit off with you the other day, it's just that it was such a shock . . . finding out that I might have a daughter I never even knew existed. But I've given it a lot of thought over the five days since we met and in spite of what I said to you earlier, I think there's every chance that I am your father. So, I was wondering if maybe we could meet up again. Here's my number . . . Hope to hear from you really soon.

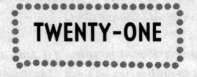

TWENTY-ONE

The prospect of another visit to the Anchor was far too depressing, so I persuaded Roy to meet me somewhere more salubrious – the bar at the Oxo Tower. This time he's not late; in fact, when I arrive at eight-fifty, ten minutes early myself, he has beaten me to it and is sitting at a table, sipping amber liquid from a chunky glass. Unsure of the most appropriate form of greeting – a handshake seems too informal, a kiss on the cheek too intimate – I finally settle for a simple 'hi'. Roy, however, is in a more effusive mood. Jumping to his feet, he locks me in a clumsy embrace, suffocating me in a cloud of lemony aftershave.

'It's great to see you, Thea,' he says in his sing-song voice. 'And may I say how gorgeous you're looking this evening?'

He's obviously being polite because I look like a dog. I'm wearing old Levi cords, my hair stinks of cigarettes and my make-up is non-existent. The truth is

I'm feeling shit after my night of drinking and casual sex and have spent most of the day nursing a vicious hangover.

'Can I get you a drink?' I ask him.

'No, no. I'll take care of that,' he says with mock formality. As he heads to the bar, I marvel at the transformation. The slick, flirty wide boy I met last week has metamorphosed into somebody altogether more tasteful. He even *looks* different. That Connex uniform did him no favours, but tonight he's straight out of the Next catalogue in his chinos and button-down shirt.

Roy's voicemail had intrigued and slightly disturbed me, so I called him first thing this morning . . . well, when I say first thing, I mean midday (don't forget, I didn't get home till three-thirty). Roy was about to leave for work, so there was no time to talk, we just arranged tonight's meeting.

I was full of expectations as I left the house. 'I know you're excited, but try to be objective,' Kim warned. 'Listen to what this Roy character's got to say and then consider the evidence . . . Just because he *thinks* he's your father doesn't mean he *is* your father.' She's right, but it's going to be hard to remain calm and rational if all the evidence is pointing in the same direction.

'There are so many questions I want to ask you,' I tell Roy when he returns with the drinks.

'You can ask me anything you like,' he says, licking his lips nervously. 'But, first off, I'd like to offer you my sincere apologies for the way I behaved when we first met, trying to brush you off like that. I wasn't thinking straight, I was in a state of shock. Imagine how I felt – a beautiful girl turns up out of the blue, offers to take me for a drink and then announces she could be my daughter.'

'I guess I was a bit heavy-handed, I can see that now,' I concede. 'But shock or not, how come you've changed your tune all of a sudden? What makes you think you might be my father after all?'

'I'd better start from the beginning.' He gulps from his glass hungrily, then draws the back of his hand across his mouth. 'It was a long time ago and some of the details are a little hazy,' he begins. 'I met Shirley at the Tunnel Club in Greenwich. I can't remember how we got talking, but we did – and she made quite an impression on me, I don't mind saying. She was such a pretty girl and very feisty, but I like 'em like that.' At this juncture he nudges me with his elbow as if sharing a private joke – only trouble is, I don't get it.

'She said she already had a boyfriend – an older bloke, I think – but I didn't let that put me off and I managed to persuade her to let me take her to the flicks a couple of days later. We had an OK time; at least I think we did. After that, we went on a couple more dates . . .' His sentence tails off and he starts swishing the whisky around in his glass. 'I'm pretty sure we did have sex – at least once, maybe more.'

'Pretty sure – but not totally sure?' I say, conscious of the supercilious tone in my voice.

'As sure as I can be,' he says, smiling apologetically. 'Back in the day, I put it about a bit and I didn't really keep score.'

'And did you use condoms *back in the day*?' I say disdainfully.

'Er, sometimes, but not always. I seem to remember Shirley telling me she was on the pill, so I don't think we bothered.'

'That's funny,' I say drily. 'Mum always told me she couldn't take the pill – it gave her terrible headaches.'

'Maybe she just pretended she was on the pill so she could trick me into getting her pregnant,' Roy says hopefully. 'There's no way I would've slept with her if I thought I was going to get her pregnant. I certainly didn't want to become a daddy, not at that stage in my life.'

It's just about plausible. I wouldn't say Mum was the scheming type, but what was it she had said to me all those years ago . . . ? *I desperately wanted a baby, but I'd given up hope of ever finding the right man . . . I threw caution to the wind, let things run their natural course.* Roy might have been an attractive proposition – good-looking, a bit of a rogue, the sort of man who would've run a mile if, by some chance, he subsequently discovered he had got her pregnant.

'But things didn't work out between you two . . .' I leave the words dangling between us.

'No, it just fizzled out,' he says with an embarrassed shrug. 'I don't think we had much in common. I didn't fit in with her crowd, all those weird hippy types.'

'Did you keep in touch with each other after you split up?'

'Nah. Once I bumped into her in the pub – it was a good while afterwards mind, more than a year. I said "hi" and asked her how she was doing, but she wasn't very pleased to see me; in fact, she acted like she couldn't wait to get away.'

My brain does some quick calculations . . . I would've been on the scene by that stage.

'Did you know Mum had had a baby?'

'Not then. I moved to Portsmouth soon after that. I owed a bloke some money and needed to get off the scene for a while,' he says with a self-conscious grin. 'It was a good few years before I came back to London and that's when I saw Shirley again – at Greenwich Market – and there was a little girl helping her on the stall. I suppose I assumed it was her kid, but I didn't really give it that much thought.'

'That was me all right,' I say, smiling at the memory. 'Did you talk to Mum that day?'

'No way, I was with Debbie and she didn't like me talking to other women, especially ex-girlfriends . . . she's always been the jealous type. We're divorced now.'

'I know.'

His eyes widen. 'You do?'

'Yeah. She's the one who told me where to find you.'

'Did you tell her why you were looking for me?' he says, a worried look crossing his face.

'No, I just made out you were a friend of a friend,' I say.

'I'm surprised she was so helpful,' he grimaces. 'We didn't exactly part on the best of terms.'

'Yeah, I kind of got that impression. But you've got a couple of kids together haven't you?'

'That's right, a boy and a girl. They're grown up now, of course.'

'D'you see much of them?'

He purses his lips. 'Not as much as I'd like, their mum's poisoned them against me. Hey, why don't I arrange a night out for us all? Not Debbie – just you, me and the kids. After all, there's every chance they could be your brother and sister,' he says excitedly.

'One step at a time,' I say, holding up my hands defensively. 'Let's not play happy families until we know the score.'

'But we do look a bit alike, don't we?' he says. 'I don't expect you've ever considered the possibility that you could be mixed race, but you are kind of dusky, aren't you? And don't forget I'm only half-Mauritian myself, my dad was from Dublin.'

'I suppose so,' I admit grudgingly, while my eyes are drawn to his delicate, long-fingered hands.

'Didn't you say there were a couple of other names in the frame . . . some other guys Shirley was seeing around the same time as me?' he asks.

'That's right.'

'And have any of them owned up?'

'Er, no. Actually, I've managed to rule both of them out.'

'So I'm your main man then,' he says eagerly. 'I know Shirley and I only got together a couple of times, but that's all it takes . . . Debbie certainly got pregnant pretty easily. *Mr Super Sperm* she called me.'

I suppress a shudder. 'Are you involved with anyone at the moment?'

He shakes his head. 'I've had a few girlfriends over the years, but nobody serious.'

'Do you think you'll ever get married again?'

'I'm not sure. Breaking up with Debbie near enough broke my heart; the divorce was the most difficult thing I've ever had to go through – and the fact we had kids together made things ten times worse . . . just be thankful *you* haven't got any.'

I put a comforting hand on Roy's forearm; maybe he's more sensitive than I'd given him credit for. Suddenly I snatch my hand away. 'What did you just say?' I ask sharply.

'Er, nothing. I dunno, I've forgotten.'

'You said, "Just be thankful *you* haven't got any . . ." How the hell would you know whether I have or haven't got children?' I stare at him accusingly. 'You know about me, about my husband, don't you?'

He doesn't blush – his skin's too dark for that – but he avoids my gaze and starts poking at the ice in his whisky glass.

'Roy?'

He looks at me and nods his head sheepishly. 'I only realized who you were when I saw your photo in the *Sun* on Monday. I didn't recognize you at first; your hair was different, but obviously the name was the giveaway. I don't know much about pop music – I'm more of a ska man myself – but even *I've* heard of Drift . . . my Lisa's mad about them as a matter of fact.'

Shit. This is precisely the situation I wanted to avoid, but how naive of me to think Roy wouldn't have picked up a tabloid in the last week. This has changed everything. I've spent practically my whole married life trying to work out who's genuine and who's not, who really likes me and who just wants to get a piece of Toby. And now here I am facing the same dilemma yet again; only this time, the stakes are infinitely higher.

Roy has obviously read my mind. 'I hope you don't think I've changed my story about being your dad because I found out your husband's a big star,' he says.

'Well, you must admit it is a bit of a coincidence,' I snap.

'Yeah, I can see how it looks, but believe you me it doesn't make a blind bit of difference to me who your husband is. I'm a straightforward bloke; I take people as I find them. And listen, I'm really sorry to hear your marriage has gone down the pan, it must be hard for you. Still, I guess you won't be short of a bob or two, will you? I've read all about these pre-nuptial agreements.'

'I don't give a shit about the money,' I say coldly.

'Is that what you're after, Roy – money? Do you think that by claiming to be my father you can get a piece of the action?'

'No, you've got me all wrong,' he says, waving his hands in protest. 'I'm just trying to do the right thing. You were the one who searched me out, remember? You asked me if there was a chance I could be your dad and I'm just giving you the facts. But if you don't want to hear it, then fine. I'll go now and leave you to get on with your life.' He stands up and starts walking towards the door. For a moment I sit there, frozen, but then something jolts me into action.

'Roy, wait,' I call out to him. The couple at the table next to us stop talking and turn to see what's going on; I shoot them a mind-your-own-business look. Roy, meanwhile, has stopped in his tracks. 'I'm sorry,' I say. 'Come back and let's finish what we started.'

One hour later and Roy and I have come to a mutual agreement. We will both undergo a DNA test as soon as it can be arranged and I will foot the bill. Roy's only concern is his fear of needles but, thanks to the research I did on the net in preparation for this eventuality, I am able to reassure him that a cell swab from the inside of the cheek is just as reliable as a blood sample. As for what will happen once we get the results . . . we don't consider that outcome.

The following week, Roy and I meet at a discreet private clinic in Harley Street. I had half expected him to get cold feet and blow me out. I guess his appearance proves that he isn't just some gold digger, that he really believes he could be my father. All the same, I'm under no illusions. Now that Roy knows of my connection to Toby, my value as a potential offspring is infinitely higher. It's like the thrill when you bite into a KitKat and realize it's solid chocolate, or you walk out of the newsagent's and discover the assistant's given you change for a tenner instead of a five.

The procedure is simple and painless and the consultant explains that, while a paternity test can prove with 100 per cent cast-iron certainty that Roy is *not* my biological parent, it can only prove with 99.9 per cent certainty that he *is* my father – but frankly, if it's good enough for the courts, it's good enough for me. The results, we are told, will be available in two days' time. The clinic has agreed to call me first with the news and then Roy.

As we walk towards Regent's Park Tube, Roy suggests going for a coffee. I'm not desperately keen to spend any more time in his company than absolutely necessary, so I palm him off by saying I have to meet a friend in town.

'Let's hope we get some good news in two days' time,' says Roy as we go our separate ways.

I smile and nod and wave goodbye, but the trouble is I don't really know what *would* constitute good news. I do desperately want to find my father; with Mum gone and now Toby, I feel like I'm floating in a vacuum, desperate for someone to claim me as their own and yank me back down to earth. And yet somehow I can't imagine discovering that I'm Roy's daughter would send me into raptures. I would far rather be the product of some long and meaningful relationship, the daughter of a man who was interesting and cultured – somebody like Barney, say – rather than the loin fruit of the smooth-talking but utterly unsophisticated Roy, who shared a few forgettable dates with Mum. But in the words of the old adage, you can choose your friends, but you can't choose your family. And even if Roy does turn out to be Mr Super Sperm, it doesn't mean I have to like him.

TWENTY-TWO

It's that time of the month again. I missed the last wives' lunch. It was right after the IMAs and I wasn't in a fit state for socializing of any kind. Kim made my excuses to Patti over the phone, telling her I was chained to the toilet following a particularly violent bout of gastro-enteritis. Of course, when the news of the split hit the tabloids, the others discovered the real reason for my absence – and, I have to say, they've all been terribly kind.

Angela sent me a gorgeous bunch of long-stemmed yellow roses (according to tradition, of course, yellow roses are the flower of infidelity, but I'm assuming she doesn't know that), and I got a nice letter from Stella (although I didn't find her assertion that there were 'plenty more fish in the sea ... but probably none as good-looking as Toby', especially comforting). And good old Patti dispatched a Clarins gift voucher and a slick promotional leaflet for *Only Dinner*. I'm not entirely sure why she thought I would be interested in 'a bespoke introduction service for people of integrity', but I suppose it's the thought that counts.

To tell you the truth, I was surprised at their thoughtfulness. I had half expected to be dropped like a hot brick once they found out my marriage was dead in the water, but it seems I am still Somebody Worth Knowing. And God knows I'm going to need all the friends I can get if I'm to build a new life as a singleton. So when Patti rang me three days ago to see if I was up to lunch, I accepted immediately. But I'm not stupid, I know there's a pay-off: my marriage break-up gossip in return for their public show of support.

Sure enough, the minute I walk into the restaurant – a French eatery close to Cambridge Circus, enjoying something of a renaissance thanks to the patronage of a certain over-rated It girl – they pounce on me like a pack of hungry wolves.

'We've been *sooo* worried about you,' says Patti, as the maître d' unfurls my napkin with a flourish.

'Poor darling,' coos Angela, patting my hand sympathetically.

'You're looking awfully well – considering,' says Stella, sounding disappointed. She stares at my feet before enquiring, 'Are those shoes Miu Miu?'

'No, they're Nine West actually.'

She flares her nostrils in disgust. 'Does that mean Toby's stopped your credit card?'

'Yes, actually, but it's only what my solicitor

agreed,' I say breezily. 'It's perfectly reasonable . . . just think, otherwise I could be spending his money willy-nilly on clothes and jewellery and gorgeous little accessories.'

'Precisely,' says Angela. 'Milk the fucker for all he's worth while you still can, that's what I say.' I guess she still hasn't got over losing out in the divorce battle with Titus.

'He's giving me a decent monthly allowance, so I don't feel at all hard done by,' I reassure her.

'And what's going to happen to Itchycoo?' asks Patti. 'Surely you're not going to let the marital home slip through your fingers?'

'Toby's welcome to it,' I say – and I mean it. I wouldn't want to live there on my own; it holds too many memories.

She frowns disapprovingly. 'Nobody says you have to live there, darling. Just get him to hand it over and then put it up for auction; you'll make a killing, prices have rocketed in Belsize Park this past year. I know a fantastic estate agent—'

'And start compiling a list of expenses,' interrupts Angela. 'Personal styling, domestic services, pet care, etcetera. You'll need all that when it comes to finalizing the divorce settlement.'

'But, Angela, I haven't actually filed for divorce. And, anyway, I shan't be requiring any *domestic services*, I'm perfectly capable of cleaning up my own mess.'

She takes a sharp intake of breath. 'Never, ever let

me hear you say that in public again,' she scolds. 'As far as the judge is concerned, you can't even boil an egg . . . clean up your own mess indeed. You're going to be telling me you haven't got a pet in a minute.'

'Well no, I haven't actually.'

'Well get one pronto,' she hisses. 'And make sure it's the kind that needs an awful lot of looking after.'

Thankfully I am rescued by the waiter, come to take our order. The others are engaging their usual champagne-and-salad fest. I deliberately pick the most fattening dish on the menu – veal escalope with Dijon cream and rich dauphinoise potatoes with a Parmesan crust.

'Have you found yourself a new man?' asks Stella.

'Give me a chance,' I say. 'It's less than a month since I split up with Toby – far too early to get involved with anybody else.'

'Well, Toby certainly hasn't let the grass grow,' she says, a peculiar, twisted smile playing around her highly glossed lips.

'What on earth are you talking about?'

'You mean you haven't heard?' she says, all wide-eyed and innocent. 'Ouch!' she squeals suddenly and bends down under the table to rub her leg.

'I thought I told you to keep your trap shut,' says Patti, glaring at her.

'What?' I say, looking from one to the other.

'She'd have found out for herself soon enough,' says Stella. 'Far better that she hears it from a friend.'

'Will somebody please put me out of my misery?' I say bad-humouredly.

Patti nods her assent and Stella reaches into her soft leather Hermès handbag and produces a well-thumbed copy of *Wow!* 'It came out today,' she says. And then adds, somewhat unnecessarily, 'I have a subscription.'

I get a sickening sense of déjà vu. I've spent half my married life discovering stuff about Toby from the pages of magazines and tabloid newspapers. I wonder what's in store for me this time. Still, I reassure myself, I've got over Toby now . . . well, I'm *getting* over him anyway. Nothing he does now can hurt me. Famous last words.

The story is spread across not two, not four, but *nine* glossy pages.

EXCLUSIVE!
Alexa Hunt: Men, Marriage and Me
*The stunning MTV presenter talks for the
first time about the new man in her life,
Drift star Toby Carson*

My mouth opens and shuts like a stranded fish. I am dimly aware of Patti's hand squeezing my arm and some muffled words of consolation, but I'm not listening to what she's saying, I'm too focused on the pages and pages of ghastly photographs in front of me: Alexa preparing an exotic fruit salad in her 'state-of-the-art' stainless steel kitchen; Alexa lighting candles for an impossibly romantic dinner for two in her 'elegant' dining room; Alexa in a silky Janet Reger nightgown sprawled across a circular bed ('My custom-made bed is made for loving,' gushes the pull quote underneath). Most gut churning of all is a photograph on page five of Toby and Alexa together. It's not part of the *at home* set, it looks more like a snap. They're both on horseback and behind them I can see trees and blue sky dotted with cotton-wool clouds. Alexa is ravishing in skin-tight creamy jodhpurs, her loose blonde hair whipping across her tanned face, and as for Toby . . . I hardly recognize him; he looks so carefree and relaxed.

I glance down at the picture caption: 'As this photograph from Alexa's private collection shows, the couple like nothing better than escaping the stresses of their busy working lives with a spot of horse riding.' Horse riding . . . since when has Toby been into fresh air and exercise? And, more to the point, he hates animals – all of them. I begged him for a puppy, just to keep me company, but he refused, saying he didn't want to come home to hairs on the sofa and shit on the stairs.

Patti's voice breaks into my reverie. 'Darling, are you all right? You've gone awfully quiet.'

'Hang on a minute, I'm reading,' I say.

Random phrases jump out at me as my eyes scan the syrupy copy: *This time I really think I've found The One . . . I've kept a wedding scrapbook from the age of 12 . . . lots and lots of babies and a cottage in the country.* Somebody pass the sick bucket.

The waiter appears with our food and I lift up the magazine without taking my eyes off the page so he can slide the plate underneath. I see that my name has been relegated to a piddling paragraph at the bottom of page two. Well, it's only to be expected. *Wow!* doesn't want its beautiful, lovely, gorgeous story tarnished by a nasty, ugly marriage break-up, now does it? I bet they offered Toby bucketloads of money to pose alongside the 'effortlessly stylish' Lexy. I wonder if he was tempted . . . nah, he's smarter than that.

I see that Alexa is deliberately vague on the question of how long she and Toby have been an item. *We've only been seeing each other a few weeks, but it feels like much longer*, she gushes. Of course, thanks to that *Mirror* story about their liaison at the Malmaison all those months ago, it will be glaringly obvious to any celeb-watcher worth their salt that Toby was carrying on with Alexa while we were still living together. Absolutely bloody marvellous. It seems Alexa Hunt is determined to destroy any last vestige of dignity I may still possess.

'So that *Mirror* story was true then?' says Angela.

I nod my head.

'And *she's* the reason you split up?' asks Stella.

I nod again.

She looks at me smugly. 'I thought as much. I didn't buy that *mutual and amicable* bit in your joint statement.'

'Listen, Thea, I know this probably isn't what you

want to hear right now, but couldn't you have forced yourself to overlook one teensy little indiscretion?' asks Patti. 'It's nothing compared to what I've had to put up with from Rich, as well you know.'

'No way,' I say crossly. 'It's not just that Toby was unfaithful, it's that he lied to me when I asked him if he was having an affair. And this just proves he's even more of a liar than I thought,' I say, jabbing a finger at the magazine. 'He made me believe it was just sex, he promised me he'd finished with her . . . for God's sake, he even described the woman as an "airhead" – and now he's embroiled in a, a . . . what does the bitch call it?' I turn the pages over, searching out the monstrous cliché. 'Aah, here we are: *an intensely fulfilling and meaningful relationship*. So don't talk to me about "one teensy little indiscretion" when I could cut off his bloody balls with a blunt Stanley knife.'

I said that last sentence rather loudly and the two elderly and perfectly coiffed ladies at the next table have stopped eating and are staring at me quite aghast. 'Can I help you?' I say in a lairy fashion. They look away, embarrassed.

'I'm sorry, darling, that was dreadfully insensitive of me,' says Patti. 'I shouldn't assume you would want to follow my example . . . not every wife is as tolerant as I am.'

Or as stupid, I think to myself.

'God knows why you're worried about spending his

money while the two-faced shitbag is having the time of his life with some jumped-up pop tart,' spits Angela.

'And I guess the fact she's got a few years on you doesn't make things any easier,' says Stella, smiling evilly.

I squeeze the arms of my chair to stop myself punching her lights out.

'Listen, everyone,' I say. 'I'm awfully sorry, but would you mind if I left you to it? I've suddenly lost my appetite and I'd actually quite like to be on my own right now.'

Patti nods sympathetically. 'We understand perfectly, don't we, girls?' she says, looking at the others. Angela's smile signals her agreement, but Stella is wearing a slightly pained, struggling-with-haemorrhoids sort of expression – she clearly feels short-changed by the quantity and/or quality of my emotional outpourings. Well, that's just tough.

'Now don't go hiding yourself away,' says Patti bossily, waving aside my offer of cash for my uneaten lunch. 'And if you ever need somebody to talk to, you know where I am, but don't forget: Mondays are a no-no because it's hair, nails and shopping, although not necessarily in that order; Tuesday p.m. is aromatherapy, Wednesday is my writing day, Fridays are always a bit tricky because I see my psychotherapist first thing and that usually wipes me out for the rest of the day, and Saturday is polo – but apart from that, I'm all yours.'

I *would* laugh, were it not for the tears pricking the back of my eyelids. I swallow hard. 'Thanks, Patti, it's nice to know who my friends are,' I manage to squeeze out. The maître d' brings my coat from the cloakroom and I kiss each of the three women goodbye. As I make fleeting contact with Stella's perfumed cheek, she presses the heinous magazine into my hand.

'You take it – I can easily buy another one,' she says.

'Cheers, Stella,' I say, stuffing the offending article into my handbag.

Walking along Shaftesbury Avenue towards the Tube, I wonder why that stupid magazine article has got me so rattled. I already knew Toby was a lying, cheating bastard, so it shouldn't come as a massive surprise that he's still seeing Alexa. What really upsets me is the way they're flaunting their relationship, elevating it from the realms of grubby little shag into gorgeous, romantic love affair. And OK, so he didn't actually participate in that appalling nine-page spread, but he must've given her his blessing to talk about it. Why is he rubbing my nose in it? Hasn't he caused me enough pain already?

I haven't admitted this to anyone, but I was nurturing a tiny germ of hope that Toby and I might, just possibly, get back together. You see, I still miss him like crazy – and call me a fool, but despite everything that's happened I still love him.

*

I manage to contain my emotions for the most of the journey home, but as soon as I turn the corner into Kim's road the first hot tears begin to bubble up.

'You're back early,' Kim calls out from her office as the front door slams shut behind me. 'Don't tell me . . . the maître d' gave you a table with a wonky leg and you all stormed out in protest?' She snorts with laughter. 'Foie gras not up to scratch? Or did they dare to offer you Mumm instead of Krug? . . . Thea?'

When I fail to reply, she comes to find me.

'Hon, what on earth's happened?' she says, seeing me slumped on the bottom stair dabbing at my eyes with the rough wool belt of my coat, the contents of my bag scattered on the floor where I searched, unsuccessfully, for a tissue.

I gesture at the copy of *Wow!* lying at my feet.

She picks it up and studies the cover.

'*England soccer star's beautiful beach-front wedding*?' she says, looking at me quizzically.

'N-n-no, the other st-st-story,' I hiccup.

'Oh, *you* mean *MTV presenter opens her heart and the doors to her gorgeous home*,' she says grimly. 'I do hope this isn't what I think it is.'

She fans the pages until she spots Alexa reclining in her bubble-filled claw-foot bath, a glass of wine in her well-manicured hand. '*There's nothing I like better after a tough day at the studio than a long hot bath*,' Kim reads out loud. 'Bloody hell, this is Pulitzer

Prize-winning stuff. *But don't get me wrong . . . I love my job. After all, it's how I met Toby.*' Her eyes flicker from the page to me and back to the page again. 'Oh,' she says.

'It gets worse,' I say.

She raises her eyebrows in disbelief and continues reading. I wait silently while she digests the sycophantic questions and answers, watching her expression change from surprise to outrage.

'How very crass,' she says when she's finished, tossing the magazine to the floor in disgust. 'But I'd take it with a pinch of salt, if I were you. Alexa Hunt is a publicity junkie plain and simple; she gets panicky if a couple of days go by and she hasn't seen her face in a glossy mag. I wouldn't be surprised if she'd made half of it up.'

A faint glimmer of hope stirs in my guts. 'God, I didn't think of that,' I say excitedly. 'I just assumed Toby was a silent accomplice. Do you really think Alexa would lie so blatantly, pretend they were seeing each other when really he dumped her weeks ago?'

'Oh no, I'm sure they're still an item,' says Kim with unintentional brutality. 'Even *she's* not stupid enough to risk a libel action. What I meant was maybe she's exaggerating, making like they're love's young dream when really they're nothing more than fuck buddies.'

My face drops. 'Oh. Right,' I mumble. How pathetic I am, clutching at straws like that. Whichever way you look at it, my husband is a calculating shit who couldn't give a toss about me or my feelings.

'Don't take this personally, but that husband of yours really is a pig,' Kim says, echoing my thoughts. 'I wonder if he finished with Alexa and then got back with her after he found out you weren't going to have him back, or if he just didn't bother finishing with her at all.'

'Who knows?' I say, clenching my jaw in a vain attempt to stop my lower lip wobbling.

'This has really knocked you for six hasn't it?' says Kim, her voice softening.

I nod. 'I really thought I was getting over him,' I say, resting my chin on my hands. 'But right now I feel like my heart's been ripped out and fed through a food processor. God knows, I let him walk all over me when we were married, but even now we're separated he's still got so much power over me – and I hate that.'

'I know, hon,' she says, sitting down next to me and stroking my hair. 'It's only natural that you've still got feelings for him, but it will get better, I promise you. Just give it time. And it wouldn't hurt for you to get out a bit more, do something to take your mind off him.'

Later on, when I've washed my face and gulped down a comforting chicken noodle cup-a-soup I decide to begin house hunting. I can't impose on Kim and Tim any longer – it's embarrassing the way I always run to them when anything goes wrong – and besides which it'll stop me thinking about Toby.

While Kim is in her office trying to organize the importation of three thousand brown sugar candles from Thailand for a society wedding, I retire to the kitchen with the Yellow Pages and the free property supplement that dropped through Kim's letterbox yesterday morning. I've decided to stick to north London – Islington or Highgate – so I'll be close to Kim. And I'm going to have to rent rather than buy. Although Toby's monthly allowance is extremely generous, I don't have the necessary capital for a deposit. In fact, I don't have any capital at all. The revolting truth is that I am completely and utterly dependent on Toby.

For the next half-hour or so, I call each and every letting agency within my catchment area, stating my requirements: one to two bedrooms, built-in wardrobes and a high level of security. When I tell them the kind of money I'm looking to spend, they get terribly excited. Some get more excited still when I give them my name. It seems as if I have attained a certain notoriety thanks to my well-publicized marriage break-up.

'Are you *the* Thea Carson?' asks one. I wish people would mind their own fucking business.

'The one and only,' I say sarcastically. 'However, as I am sure you will appreciate, I'm very keen to maintain a low profile, so unless you can give me a cast-iron guarantee that my details will remain utterly confidential, I shan't be taking my enquiry any further.' Listen to me, getting all bolshy and self-important. It's not really me talking; I just don't want to be shat on from a great height. I've had enough of that to last me a lifetime.

'I can assure you of our utmost discretion,' smarms the estate agent. 'Winford, Warboys & Johnston would be honoured to take your instruction.'

Honoured indeed. What a pompous twat.

The second I put the phone down to William or Edward or whatever his name was – these estate agents all sound the same to me – it starts to ring.

'Hi, Thea speaking,' I say, thinking it might be one of the other agents calling back.

'Ms Carson, it's Dr D'Silva from the Regent's Park Clinic. Is this a convenient time to talk?'

Shit. I've been so preoccupied by that bloody magazine article, I totally forgot the DNA test results were due today.

'Yes it is.' My mouth has suddenly gone quite dry.

'I have your test results here.' He pauses for a second, letting the words sink in.

'And?'

'And I am able to tell you, quite categorically, that Roy Potter is *not* your father.'

I was expecting to experience a great rush of something . . . anger, disappointment, relief even. But all I feel is a strange cold emptiness, as if I had been disembowelled under anaesthetic and all my emotions Hoovered out.

'I see,' I say calmly. 'And you're a hundred per cent sure of that?'

'Totally. The gene patterns are completely different.'

'Well thanks very much for letting me know Dr D'Silva. Will you call Roy right away with the news?'

'Certainly,' says the good doctor. 'And do bear in mind that we offer a full range of counselling services should you require them,' he says hastily, giving it the hard sell before I have a chance to put the phone down.

'Thanks – but that won't be necessary,' I tell him.

So there it is. All doors are shut, all avenues have been blocked. I shall never discover my father's identity; I am now officially motherless, husbandless and father-less. But I mustn't feel sorry for myself. From this moment on, it's onwards and upwards. God knows, I can't sink any lower.

TWENTY-THREE

I have just been to see the most divine flat – or should I say *superior duplex apartment*, as William from Winford, Arsehole & Bumlick lovingly described it. It's a beautiful Georgian conversion in the heart of Highgate Village – video entryphone, high ceilings, original fireplaces and a walk-in wardrobe that could double as a third bedroom. I put down a deposit there and then, before I could chicken out. The decor is pretty dull, consisting mainly of no-imagination creams and browns, but I'll get to work on it as soon as I move in next month. Jewel colours, that's what I fancy; shimmering emerald-green sofa throws and curtains of amber damask. And I can guarantee there won't be a single fucking chandelier in the whole place.

I was feeling so pleased with myself that when I got back to Kim's I decided to take the bull by the horns and call Roy, a task I'd been putting off since the DNA results came through three days ago (not that he had made any attempt to contact me either . . . I was hoping his silence wasn't an indication that he was hatching some twisted blackmail plot). To be brutally honest, as soon as I knew Roy wasn't my long-lost pa, I just wanted to forget about him. It's not as if we have anything in common and I still have my suspicions about his motives. But I thought I owed him a courtesy call at least.

In the event, he was pretty stoical about the whole thing – nonchalant even.

'Sure I'm a bit disappointed, darling, but it wasn't to be,' he said laconically, before adding that we must keep in touch.

'Yeah, I'd like that,' I replied without enthusiasm. I suppose I might stick him on my Christmas card list if he's lucky.

Before I put down the phone, I had one last request of Roy.

'You won't go to the press will you – about me, I mean, and the fact that I was trying to find my father? It's such a personal thing and I couldn't bear seeing it splashed all over some tabloid gossip column.'

'What do you take me for?' he said, and for a second I thought I had seriously pissed him off. But then he gave a low chuckle. 'I may be short of cash, darling, but I ain't no low life.'

I can't help my cynicism. If there's one thing I've learned during my year as a celebrity's wife, it's that you can't trust most people as far as you can throw them.

On the subject of trust, I have just made a shocking discovery regarding my employer, J.C. Riley. The first hint that something was wrong came last week when J.C. called me late one night in a high state of anxiety.

'Don't bother coming into work tomorrow,' he said. 'In fact don't bother coming in again until further notice. I'm having a few problems with the business.'

He was unwilling to elaborate and I have since learned – via the Inland Revenue – that J.C. has spent the last ten years embezzling money from his clients. Apparently it only came to light when Alex Gaffney's accountant noticed some sort of discrepancy. I would never have believed J.C. capable of such a thing; although, looking back, he obviously led a very comfortable lifestyle with his flash car, designer suits and four-bedroom home in the poshest part of Dulwich. The business was never *that* successful so I always assumed he had some sort of private income. Now, of course, he's looking at a prison sentence.

Losing my job has come as quite a blow, especially as I was just about to ask J.C. if I could start working full-time. I'll have to start looking for something else soon, but in the meantime I've been helping Kim. She's putting together an Asylum party for one of those annoying pop psychologists they wheel out on reality TV shows and Channel 5 documentaries to say stuff that you or I or anyone else with a modicum of common sense would be able to articulate just as easily. The venue is booked, as is the team of designers who will transform the place into a gigantic padded cell for the night and Kim's regular seamstress has been commissioned to make dozens of pairs of prison-style pyjamas for the waiters and waitresses. What Kim is desperate to find now is a performance artist who will complement the 'mental' theme and amaze the 200 guests, a motley assortment of C-list TV types who would turn up to the opening of a motorway service station if it meant a free glass of champagne and an unflattering photograph in *Wow!* magazine.

'I've been racking my brains for days,' says Kim. 'Chainsaw juggling is too dangerous, mime artistry too tame and fire-eaters are a definite no-no with all that combustible padding round the walls. I think what it needs is a fresh pair of eyes.'

She hands me a sheaf of names and telephone numbers. 'You might want to start by calling a few agents; talk them through the brief and see if they've got anyone suitable on their books.'

An hour later and I'm despairing of finding anyone who fits the bill. I thought I'd hit the jackpot with a sword-swallowing duo called the Nutter Brothers, but then their agent realized they'd be halfway through a circus tour on the night of the party. But then I have a sudden flash of inspiration in the shape-shifting form of Rubber Rick. The ten-minute showreel he brought to J.C.'s office was amazing: not only did he show off his ability to squeeze himself through a whole range of impossibly small objects, including a toilet seat and the head of a tennis racket, but most impressive of all he donned a straitjacket and then proceeded to fold his entire body into a large suitcase ... the perfect act for Kim's Asylum. I left the video at Itchycoo, but I kept the little business card that came with it and stuck it in my Filofax for safekeeping; don't ask me why, just call it instinct. Ten minutes later and I have managed to secure a provisional booking for Rubber Rick. What's more, I got him for seven hundred quid – that's three hundred under budget – plus travel expenses from Leeds.

Kim is over the moon. 'You're a genius! He's perfect, they won't believe their eyes,' she squeals. 'You know, Thea, you've got a real talent for this.'

I positively glow with pleasure. This is turning out to be a really good day.

After lunch, Kim assures me that she doesn't require my services any more, so I decide to indulge in a spot of retail therapy at Portobello. I *was* hoping to pick up some nice bits and pieces for my new flat – sorry, *superior duplex apartment.* Of course, what I actually end up doing is spending a hundred quid on a vintage dress and a pretty floral-print handbag. But what the hell, I deserve it. And there's another thing I deserve even more – and that's a nice milky cappuccino with three sugars.

Sitting in Costa Coffee, resting my elbows on the long counter under the window, I realize that for the first time in ages I feel totally stress free. Kim was right; I needed to get out, take control of my life, start meeting new people. Speaking of which, there's a really cute guy with dreadlocks and Dairy Milk eyes at the other end of the counter and he keeps glancing in my direction. Just now I caught his eye and he flashed me a cheeky little grin, but I didn't smile back, I just looked away. How can I be sure of his motives? You see, it could be that he simply likes the look of me, but I can't rule out the possibility he's only smiling because he's recognized me; it's impossible to tell. God, I hate this stupid situation . . . famous for being somebody's wife, it's crazy. I'm going to have to think about dyeing my hair or growing a beard or something.

Suddenly my mobile – nestling in the bag on my lap – gives a little cheep, signalling the arrival of a text message.

> HEY KIDDO, LONG TIME NO C.
> VAL SAYS YR LOOKING 4 YR DAD.
> I THINK I CAN HELP. U NO
> WHERE I AM. TAKE CARE.
> MARTY X

My initial reaction is one of guilt: this is the man who has religiously sent me a birthday card every year since I turned eleven and I haven't called or written to him since the day of Mum's funeral. I kept meaning to, but somehow I just never got round to it; not even when I heard that Alison, Marty's much younger girlfriend of the past eight years, had given birth to a baby girl –

Bonnie, I think they called her. Imagine that: Marty, a first-time dad at the age of fifty-nine. I really should have offered my congratulations. Looking back, I realize how insular I became after I met Toby. I became a willing prisoner in a gilded cage, not a healthy state of affairs at all.

A few seconds later a big jolt of excitement hits me square in the guts; suddenly my brain is writhing with questions . . . Fucking hell, what does Marty know that I don't? Could *he* be the key to finding my dad? If Mum didn't know which young stud had fertilized her ovum, how could Marty possibly be any the wiser?

Retrieving Marty's number from my phone's *calls received* menu, I listen impatiently to the ringing tone. Come on Marty, pick up, this is urgent.

'Marty-it's-me-Thea-I-called-as-soon-as-I-got-your-message,' I burst out when finally he answers.

'Thea, how wonderful to hear from you,' he says warmly.

'I'm so sorry I haven't been in touch sooner,' I grovel. 'I meant to send some flowers when Alison had the baby, but it sort of slipped my mind. That sounds really crap, doesn't it?'

'Don't worry, love. I'm sure you've had more important things on your mind, especially since you split up with Toby,' says Marty generously.

I give a little snort. 'You heard about it then.'

Suddenly aware that Mr Dreadlocks is earwigging on my conversation, while pretending to be engrossed in shredding a paper napkin, I gather up my shopping bags and walk out of the shop, the phone cradled to my ear.

'Couldn't help it really – it was in every newspaper,' Marty is saying. 'I thought about getting in touch but I figured you'd have enough people fussing around you and anyway I didn't know where you were living. Then last week I bumped into Val at the big Sainsbury's in Greenwich and she told me you'd got in touch to say you were looking for your dad. She said that you'd already investigated a couple of possibilities and needed her help to track down some chap named Roy Potter. She also gave me your mobile number.'

Val never could keep her mouth shut . . . heart of gold and all that, but discreet? You must be joking.

'That's right, I did think about asking you for help, but I thought it might seem a bit insensitive – you being Mum's ex and all,' I say, perching on a low wall outside a newsagent's shop and trying not to get bird shit all over my Earl jeans.

'Well, I haven't got a clue who Roy Potter is,' says Marty. 'But he isn't your dad, I do know that much.'

Momentarily, I am stunned. I went to all that effort to track down Roy, agonized over what I would do if he did turn out to be my father, spent five hundred quid on a DNA test – when Marty knew it was a wild goose chase all along.

'Sorry love, I shouldn't have blurted it out like that.

Has it come as a bit of a shock?' says Marty, misinterpreting my silence.

'Oh no, it's not that,' I say hastily. 'I know Roy isn't my father. He seemed like a likely contender at first – right time, right place, I even convinced myself we looked a little bit alike – but the DNA test said different.'

'Bloody hell, you went to all the bother of a DNA test? I wish I'd bumped into Val sooner, I could've saved you a few bob.'

Now I'm really confused. 'Marty, I can't quite get my head round this,' I say. 'How did you know that Roy isn't my father? Even Mum didn't know who got her pregnant – at least that's what she always told me.'

He responds with a question of his own.

'Listen, Thea, how serious *are* you about finding your dad?' he says, suddenly earnest. 'I mean, is it just idle curiosity or are you really committed?'

'Well, I must admit it started out as a bit of a hobby. I was having a spring clean and I came across some of Mum's old diaries – that's what sparked it off,' I explain. 'But then the more I thought about my dad – what he looks like, where he lives, whether or not he's got another family – the more I wanted to find him. It's not that I want to have a relationship with him exactly . . . according to Mum, he doesn't even know he's got a daughter; it's just that I feel there's a whole chunk of me I know nothing about.' I pause, struggling to channel my emotions into a coherent stream. It's suddenly vital that Marty understands the way I feel.

'When I was growing up I never wanted for anything, materially or emotionally, and yet I always felt incomplete somehow. It's like I'm a jigsaw puzzle with a few pieces missing around the edge of the frame. I'm happy with who I am at the core. I just wish I could fill in the frame. I suppose what I'm trying to say is doesn't every person have a right to know their family history, to know where they come from? And that's all I'm asking for really.'

These are feelings I have never articulated – not out loud, not even in my private thoughts. How strange that it should all come gushing out now. For a moment neither one of us speaks – and then I break the silence.

'You know who he is, don't you?' I say. 'My father, I mean.'

'Not exactly.' He hesitates. 'But I can certainly point you in the right direction.'

At this, the hairs on the back of my neck stand to attention. 'Does that mean Mum lied to me . . . when she said she didn't know who my father was?' I say, knowing the answer already.

'I really don't want to get into this over the phone,' he says. 'Can we meet up and talk face to face?'

'Of course. It would be great to see you,' I say. 'I'm staying with my friend Kim at the moment; you remember her, don't you – blonde Kim, from Lucy Jaeger's?'

'Aah, the lovely Kim. How could I forget her? You two were practically joined at the hip.'

'We still are. She's been a brilliant friend since I split up with Toby. I'd still be an emotional wreck if it weren't for her. Why don't you come over for lunch one day this week – tomorrow, if you can make it?'

Mercifully, Marty *can* make it – I think I would explode if I had to wait any longer – but that doesn't stop me making one last attempt to extract some information.

'Can't you give me a clue, just something to keep me going?' I plead.

He laughs. 'You always were impatient, even as a little girl,' he says. 'Just hang on until tomorrow and then all will be revealed. This is a very big deal and I want to do things properly.'

'OK then, I'll see you tomorrow,' I say. 'And Marty – thanks for getting in touch. This really means a lot to me.'

Lying in bed that night, I fantasize about the various possibilities. Maybe the man who spawned me was younger than Mum – and I mean an awful lot younger – a teenager, say. It's a vile thought and I would never have had Mum down as a cradle snatcher, but it would at least go some way towards explaining why she didn't feel able to tell me. Could he have been a friend's husband? A second cousin once removed? Or was he –

and this one makes my blood run cold – a rapist? I even consider briefly the romantic notion that Marty himself had fathered me, conveniently managing to overlook the fact that he and Mum didn't actually get together until I was ten years old.

By the time Marty arrives for our lunch date I'm a bag of nerves. I get quite emotional when I see him standing there outside Kim's front door. He's put a bit of weight on his lanky frame, but the old hippy is still sporting a neat ponytail, now turned grey. He smiles at me and I step over the lintel and throw my arms around his neck, breathing in his signature Paco Rabanne.

'It's so good to see you,' I tell him. 'You look well, really well. Fatherhood obviously agrees with you.'

'I'm loving every minute of it,' he says. 'Bonnie's a real little daddy's girl. You'll have to come round and meet her one of these days.'

'Oh, I will, I can't wait, and in the meantime you'll have to tell me all about her,' I say, ushering him into the house. I've got the place to myself this afternoon. Tim is at work in the City as usual and Kim has taken herself off for a blow-dry and a manicure. She doesn't normally indulge in beauty treatments on a weekday, so I think she's just being considerate. She is as eager as I am to hear Marty's revelation and I did tell her she was welcome to join us for lunch, but she said no, this was a private matter between Marty and myself and if I wanted to share the news with her later on, in my own good time, then that was up to me.

Courtesy dictates that I must spend an agonizing twenty minutes catching up with Marty's news over our pizza and salad lunch. Despite his advanced years, he's clearly revelling in the role of fatherhood. He has another exciting piece of news too – he and Alison are getting married the month after next. 'We've been together eight years and now that we've got Bonnie I think it's the right time to make the commitment,' he says. 'It's only a register office do, but we'll be having a big knees-up afterwards. You'll be getting an invitation, of course. I want all my special girls around me on my big day.'

He says it quite casually, but that comment really touches me. For a few years Marty, Mum and I were a little family, and when they broke up I was devastated. Marty made a real effort to keep in touch with me, with both of us. I kept hoping he and Mum would get back together, but it wasn't to be. So it's nice to know he still thinks of me as 'special', even now that he's got a family of his own. And it somehow seems fitting that, in Mum's absence, he will be the one to impart the vital news that will lead me to my father.

When all the pleasantries are out of the way, we get down to the real business of the day.

'Stick the kettle on,' says Marty, when he's polished off the last slice of pizza. 'And I'll tell you everything I know.'

I brew up and set two mugs of coffee on the table, returning to the larder for the sugar bowl and then deciding on the spur of the moment to arrange a few coconut macaroons on a plate. I can feel myself deferring the moment of truth – like when you're really parched and you open a can of 7UP and for a few seconds you just stare at it, delaying the pleasure, that delicious moment when the ice-cold liquid slides down your throat. Marty watches me fussing around, but makes no attempt to hurry me. When at last I go to sit back down on the far side of the table, he says, 'You're too far away there, love. Come and sit here next to me.'

I do as requested. Then Marty clears his throat, moves his chair round forty-five degrees so he's facing me and takes both my hands in his.

'I want to warn you that what you're about to hear may come as quite a shock,' he begins.

'I promise you I'm ready for it,' I reassure him.

'It's something your mum told me one January night about eighteen months after we started seeing each other. We were at your place; you were safely tucked up in bed and we were downstairs, sharing a bottle of wine and a joint.'

I can picture it now. Our multi-coloured living room, a fat candle flickering in the hearth, Mum and Marty sprawled across a couple of floor cushions, passing a jazz fag back and forth between them.

'We were very much in love, soul mates, and I really thought we'd be together for ever,' Marty says, a little sadly. 'I don't know what prompted her to tell me about your dad, but I think she was tired of holding the secret inside her for so long; she needed someone to share it with. I know this might sound odd to you, but up till that night your mum and I had never really discussed the subject of your paternity, at least not in any great detail. I just assumed your dad was some old boyfriend of hers, I wasn't really bothered who he was or what became of him. I knew he didn't have any contact with you and that was all that was important to me. You see, by that point I almost looked on you as my own daughter. So there we were, half-cut and half-stoned and suddenly your Mum says, "Marty, there's something I want to tell you." Just like that, no forewarning at all – and she made me promise not to tell another living soul, not even you.'

'Uh huh,' I say slowly through a mouthful of macaroon, trying not to betray my disappointment that Mum had confided in Marty something she couldn't tell me. I think I would have preferred it if he had somehow stumbled on the truth – by coming across a forgotten love letter at the back of a drawer, say, or a packet of incriminating photographs.

'I had every intention of taking her secret to my grave,' Marty continues. 'But when I heard that you were looking for your dad and that you were on the trail of some no-hoper, I was forced to review the situation. I think you're absolutely right when you say that every person has a right to know where they come from – and now that your mum's gone I think it's time for you to know the truth. It's not a decision I've taken lightly, but I know Shirley wouldn't want to see you unhappy, fruitlessly chasing after a string of blokes because you think one of them might be your dad and being disappointed time and time again.'

The tension is becoming unbearable. I feel like I'm on a movie set. I'm almost waiting for the dramatic music to kick in – something jagged and high-pitched – like when the *Psycho* girl's about to get stabbed in the shower. Marty's just staring at me, a slight frown on his face, as though he's checking to make sure I've got the strength of character to deal with what he's about to reveal.

'Ooh, come on, Marty. Don't keep me in suspense,' I say, laughing nervously. 'I'm on pins here.'

He looks away, out through the window at the big apple tree in Kim's back garden, then turns back to face me.

'The thing is, Thea, your mum was desperate for a baby. She was already in her thirties and there didn't seem to be any prospect of a long-term relationship on the horizon.'

'Yeah, she told me that bit.'

'And she wasn't lying when she said she didn't know who your father was—'

'It was a one-night stand, you mean?' I interrupt.

'Not in the way you think. He was anonymous—'

'You mean she didn't even ask the guy's name?'

'Thea, you've got the wrong end of the stick completely,' he says gently. 'If you'll just let me finish.'

'Sorry, Marty,' I say contritely. 'Go on.'

He grips my hands so tightly I can feel his signet ring cutting into the soft flesh of my palm.

'There's no easy way to break this to you, love, so I'll just come right out with it—'

Cue drum roll.

He says the words slowly and with great care, as if he's explaining it to a child.

'She conceived you using sperm from an anonymous donor.'

A split second later everything goes weird. It's like I'm having an out-of-body experience. I can see my head lolling back on my shoulders, hear the loud thud of my heart rattling against my ribcage. My eyelids flicker shut and I put both hands up to my temples. Even though my eyes are closed, I can see Marty's hands on my shoulders. His lips are moving, but I can't make out the words, and then suddenly I'm choking; coughing and spluttering and gasping for air.

TWENTY-FOUR

The truth was so much worse than anything I could have imagined. Poor Marty was horrified that he'd brought on some sort of panic attack, but he kept his cool, grabbing the paper bag that the macaroons had been in and instructing me to breathe deeply into it. And when I'd calmed down he made me lie on the sofa and force-fed me gallons of hot sweet tea.

'You mustn't think badly of Shirley,' he kept saying. 'She was a wonderful mother to you and that's the most important thing to remember in all of this.'

'But weren't you horrified when she told you? Didn't you ask her why she'd done it?' I demanded, my voice high-pitched with emotion. 'Fucking hell, Marty, that was one hell of a secret to keep. I bet you looked at me in a different way after that, didn't you? *Poor little Thea, donor-sperm girl.*'

I cross-examined Marty for over an hour in a highly accusatory fashion. I couldn't help it. I was desperate to understand Mum's motives, to put her actions into some sort of context and, rather cruelly, I cast Marty in the role of accomplice. He wasn't around when she conceived, sure, but he knew more about that period of her life than any other living person, and now that he'd opened this can of worms he was damn well going to help me put the lid back on.

In fact, there wasn't much more to tell. Marty had seemingly taken Mum's news quite calmly. 'It was *her* life, Thea, *her* decision – a decision she'd made more than a decade before I even met her,' he said evenly, as my questioning grew increasingly hysterical. 'She did it because she was desperate for a child, simple as that, and in her eyes donor insemination was the most efficient option. And no, I didn't look at you in a different way after I found out, although I suppose I did feel more protective towards you.'

'*Efficient*,' I spat scornfully. 'Did she actually use that word?'

'It might not have been that word exactly,' admitted Marty, 'but that was her gist.'

I was filled with a sudden and shocking loathing for the woman who had brought me into the world in such a calculating fashion. To have been created from a single night of passion, however unloving, would have been preferable to a man in a white coat with a turkey baster full of some strange bloke's seed, produced from a wank in a cubicle with a copy of *Razzle* and a glass beaker . . . however goddamn 'efficient' it might have been.

I begged Marty to rack his brains for any more details about the insemination, but he didn't even know the name of the place where I was conceived, just that it had been some private clinic in west London. He did, however, recall Mum saying that it had taken two sessions to impregnate her.

When I had bled Marty dry, I just wanted to be left alone to reflect and gnash my teeth in private. But he refused point-blank to leave me – 'not when you're in such a state,' he said. And what state was that? Disgusted, angry, but most of all betrayed.

He stayed with me until Kim returned, freshly coiffed and manicured from the salon. She took one look at me and said, 'Bad news, I presume.'

'You can say that again,' I said bitterly.

And when Marty left, promising to call me in a couple of days, 'to see how you're coping', I knew that he regretted his decision to share Mum's secret, I could see it in his eyes.

'It's not so much the *conception* – but the *deception* that I'm having difficulty coming to terms with,' I tell Kim and Tim, after giving them the edited highlights of my startling conversation with Marty. 'Nobody stopped to think how I might feel in all of this. All these people – Mum, my father, the clinic – deliberately set out to create me, but they apparently thought it was OK to withhold information that every other child has the right to.'

'But that's because they never imagined you'd find out,' Tim says diplomatically.

'And that's another thing,' I rant. 'Why the hell didn't Mum tell me the truth, instead of letting me believe I was the result of a *normal relationship*? Every time I asked about my dad, she just brushed my questions aside. I can't believe she took that secret to her grave ... meanwhile, there's me trying to track down total strangers and wasting money on DNA tests. I feel like such a fool.'

'She was just trying to protect you, that's all,' says Kim. 'And I'm sure she thought she was acting in your best interests. I knew Shirley too, don't forget. And she would never knowingly have done anything to cause you pain.'

'Why did she have to use a fucking anonymous donor? Couldn't she have just had sex with some bloke? At least then I'd know his name,' I say rattily. '*And* I'd know how tall he was and what colour his eyes were.'

'Well, if you think it'll help you achieve some kind of closure, why don't you see if you can track down the clinic where you were conceived?' Tim suggests. 'Maybe they'll have kept a file on your dad. I don't suppose they'll be able to give you his name, but they might have a few details – age, occupation, that kind of thing.'

'Yeah, right, and how exactly am I supposed to do that?' I snap. 'All Marty knows is that the clinic Mum used was somewhere in west London. I don't even know if the place still exists.'

'You managed to track down three of your mother's old boyfriends or whatever, didn't you? And what did you have to go on? Just a bunch of old diaries,' Tim points out. 'Give yourself some credit, Thea. I bet that, if you really put your mind to it, you could find that clinic.'

That night, after I've eaten dinner with Kim and Tim and watched one of those crappy *Before They Were Famous* things on TV, I excuse myself, saying I fancy an early night. But instead of going to sleep I sit for ages on the end of the bed, staring at myself in the full-length mirror, searching my face for some evidence of a stranger's genetic inheritance. I try to imagine Mum desperate for a baby and considering the various alternatives. However much the idea revolts me, it must've taken some guts to opt for donor insemination, especially all those years ago when the practice must have been even more taboo than it is today. Given time, I think I'll probably be able to come to terms with that part of it. What I'm having more trouble dealing with is Mum's deliberate deceit.

'Oh, Mum,' I say out loud, 'why didn't you tell me? It would've been so much better coming from you.'

I feel empty and abandoned, a true orphan. With tears streaming down my face, I realize that I'm never going to be able to fill in the frame of the jigsaw now. I think about what Tim said, about trying to discover more about my donor father. I wonder if there's any clue in Mum's diary, the one for the year of my conception. I doubt it, I've read those pages so many times I must know every entry by heart.

Getting up from the bed, I slide open my underwear drawer, where the slim black volumes are stashed, and pick out the top diary. Flicking through the pages, I stop at August. Now, did I miss anything? Roy, Kevin, Barney, yeah, yeah, yeah . . . hairdresser's appointment, trip to Brighton, gig at Ronnie Scott's. I flip through August and into September but there's nothing I haven't seen before. Think, Thea, think laterally. Mum wrote everything in those diaries. Her clinic appointment would have been a very important date for her. Surely she would have jotted down a reminder. Turning back to the beginning of August, I methodically scan each page again. This time one entry catches my eye.

5 September
11a.m. Gunnersbury FC

I never knew Mum was a footie fan. In fact, I'm sure she hated football; she didn't even watch the World Cup on TV. Where is Gunnersbury, anyway? Somewhere near Chiswick, I think. I didn't even know it had a football club; it must be non-league. Hang on a minute, maybe I'm jumping to conclusions. Who said FC stood for *football club*? Could it possibly be . . . *fertility clinic*? I struggle to recall Marty's words . . . *your Mum's first insemination attempt failed, but the following month, when she was ovulating again, she went back for a second go and this time it was successful.*

Frantically, I flick back through the pages to the beginning of August.

7 August
11a.m. Gunnersbury FC

Fuck me, I've found it. The dates are spot on. I can see now that Roy was well and truly out of the picture before I was conceived on 5 September – which would mean I was born two . . . no, nearly three weeks premature. I also see that Mum was going out with Barney the whole time she was trying to get pregnant. Why did she string him along like that, only to dump him two whole months after conception, after telling him she needed some 'breathing space'? I guess I'll never know. But I'm not surprised she didn't tell him the truth. He would've freaked – what man wouldn't? Mind you, it might have been easier for him to come to terms with than his eventual conclusion – that she had been unfaithful to him.

Eager to confirm my theory, I go into Kim's bedroom and pick up the phone. Heart galloping, I dial Directory Enquiries and ask for the Gunnersbury Fertility Clinic in west London.

The operator clicks away at her computer for a couple of seconds. 'Sorry, there's no listing under that name,' she says.

Shit. I must have got it wrong – either that or the place has closed.

'However, I do have a Gunnersbury Fertility *Centre* – could that be it?' she asks.

'Yes!' I cry with relief.

'Here's your number now, caller . . .'

The staccato voice starts to spit out the number, but stupidly I am unprepared. Glancing around the room, I spy one of those stumpy red biros you get in betting shops, lying on top of a *Financial Times* on Tim's bedside table. Lunging across the bed – and practically pulling the phone out of the wall at the same time – I grab the pen and manage to scrawl the numbers on the back of my hand as the robot voice repeats them for a second time.

It's late, but I can't resist trying the number, just to make sure the place where my life began is still operational. An answerphone, asking me to call back between the hours of nine a.m. and seven p.m., puts my mind at rest.

Two days later and I am trundling down the District Line, heading for my appointment with Judy Mabb, senior administrator at the Gunnersbury Fertility Centre. I was terribly nervous on the phone, stammering and apologetic, but Judy, with her rasping sixty-a-day

voice, was a model of patience and understanding . . .
I'm sure I'm not the first donor kid to come knocking
on her door, looking for dad. After a ten-minute chat,
in which I told her everything I had managed to piece
together about the circumstances of my birth, she agreed
to look into my case. However, she warned me not to
get my hopes up as it seems that before 1990 there was
no legal obligation to keep records on sperm donors.

Judy's earliest available appointment was an excru-
ciating two days away. I spent an entire twenty-four
hours in obsessive fantasizing; imagining Judy lost in
some dusty labyrinthine archive, brushing the cobwebs
from battered manila folders desperately searching for
'the Parkinson file', when all along it had slipped down
between two shelves, never to be discovered. After a
sleepless night I attempted to distract myself by embarking on some research of my own, trawling the web for
every piece of information I could get my hands on.

I discovered some fascinating stuff. Did you know
that the first recorded case of donor insemination – or
DI as the experts call it – took place in Philadelphia in
1884? The process was shrouded in so much secrecy
that even the woman herself didn't know what was
going on. William Pancoast, a professor at the Jefferson
College of Medicine, had been trying to treat the wife of
a Quaker merchant for sterility. It was only when he
finally decided to examine the husband's semen under a
microscope that he discovered the guy was firing blanks.
Then, under the pretext of performing some minor

surgical procedure, our man Pancoast chloroformed the woman and inseminated her with the semen of one of his medical students. She conceived successfully, but neither her doctor nor her husband ever told her what had happened when she was unconscious.

In addition, I learned that the law now stipulates that no individual can father more than ten offspring by DI. However, back in the 1940s it was a different game and some champion donors contributed to the births of over a hundred children. What's more, in those early pioneering days when donors were in short supply, it wasn't uncommon for doctors to use their own sperm.

The most surprising and also the most comforting fact I gleaned was that, according to several studies, only around 10 to 20 per cent of parents who use sperm donors ever tell their children – so Mum's secrecy wasn't that unusual and maybe I'm not as much of a freak as I thought.

The Gunnersbury Fertility Centre turns out to be a smart, white-stuccoed building in a leafy residential street. Far from being the cold sterile setting I had imagined, populated by strutting Nurse Ratcheds and pervy-looking doctors with their hands in their pockets, the interior is warm and welcoming, although I daresay it's been redesigned a fair few times since Mum was here. The receptionist takes my name and directs me to the chic black couch under the bay window while she dials Judy's extension. I'm too nervous to sit and twiddle my thumbs, so I wander over to a large felt pinboard on the wall, on which dozens of photographs and cards are displayed.

As I get nearer, I see that each photograph depicts an infant – some sleeping, some cradled in an adult's arms, some propped up on the sofa next to an older sibling. I can't resist peeking inside one of the cards, a thick, creamy thing with a picture of cornflowers in a field on the front and *Thank You* embossed in gold letters.

'To all the doctors and staff,' it reads. 'Words can never express our gratitude for your terrific help and support. You have truly made our lives complete. Thank you from the bottom of our hearts for our wonderful baby girl. With very best wishes, William and Gina Sutcliffe.'

Paperclipped to the bottom edge of the card is a photograph of the cutest little thing you ever saw. A golden-haired, button-nosed angel with a big dribbly smile on her face and a Teletubby gripped tightly in one hand. Despite the fact that I don't even know these people, a tear springs to my eye.

'Miss Carson?' says a husky voice. I spin round to see a woman in her forties with hennaed hair piled up in a bun and a chunky ethnic necklace roped around her neck.

'I'm Judy Mabb,' she rasps. 'I see you've been admiring our success stories.'

She gestures at the pinboard. 'All born by donor insemination,' she says proudly.

'Oh, yes,' I say. 'It looks like you've made a lot of people very happy.'

She smiles appreciatively and leads the way past the reception desk and up a flight of stairs to a small but comfortably furnished room dominated by a giant castor-oil plant – a real one, not one of those nasty plastic dust traps – in a terracotta pot.

'Do take a seat,' she says. 'I'll be with you in one second.' I perch on one of the plush armchairs by the window and watch while she unlocks a filing cabinet and retrieves a blue cardboard folder from the top drawer.

'You said on the phone that you've only just discovered the truth about your conception,' she says, settling in the chair opposite mine. 'That must have come as a bit of a shock.'

'Yes,' I say, my eyes fixed on the blue folder now nestling in the folds of Judy's voluminous denim skirt. 'I'm still trying to get my head round it. I just wish Mum was still alive so we could discuss it together, then maybe I could understand why she did it.'

'She must have wanted you very badly – to have gone to all this trouble to conceive,' says Judy, pushing a stray auburn tendril out of her eyes.

'I suppose so,' I say a bit grudgingly. *Open the bloody folder*, my brain is screaming.

'It's only my opinion, but I think your mother's actions demonstrate a great sense of responsibility,' says Judy gently. 'I never met her, of course, I only joined the Centre four years ago, but I'm sure she thought long and hard before deciding on donor insemination.'

I nod politely, squeezing the sides of my chair to prevent me from grabbing the folder out of her lap.

'When an individual suddenly discovers that they've been born by donor insemination, it's quite common for them to feel that their whole identity is threatened, that their life up to that point has been based on a lie,' Judy continues, while she absent-mindedly rolls the wooden beads on her necklace. 'It's often worse for the ones who grew up with a mother – *and* a father. Imagine finding out that the man you thought was your father isn't even a blood relative.'

'Yeah, that would be really freaky,' I concede. I guess I should count myself lucky that I was never subjected to *that* level of deceit.

'Anyway,' she says briskly, opening the blue folder. 'I'm sure you're dying to know what information I've been able to find out about your donor father.'

I lean forward eagerly, as she selects a document.

'I can confirm that your mother – Shirley Parkinson – *was* an outpatient at the Centre on the dates you specified,' says Judy, glancing at the piece of paper.

Yeah, yeah, I know that bit already. Cut to the good stuff for chrissakes.

'Now, as I think I explained to you, before 1990, clinics like ours were not required by law to keep files on donors. However, Christopher Goodwin – the gynae-cologist who founded the Gunnersbury Fertility Centre in 1958 – was a pioneer in the field and felt very strongly that certain physical details of each donor should be logged, principally so that mothers-to-be and their partners could select a donor who shared some of their own physical characteristics. It's common practice now, but was quite unusual back then.'

She pulls out another document and holds it up to her face, leaving me looking at the blank underside. 'Your biological father was a final year medical student at St Luke's Hospital: white, 6ft 4in tall, with dark brown hair and brown eyes,' she says in a slow measured voice.

Each word is a revelation, a golden shimmering prize. A medical student – he must've been a brainy sod, then . . . a tall, brainy sod; now I know where I get my height from.

'What was his name?' I ask hopefully, well aware that such information is officially beyond my reach.

'I'm terribly sorry, but confidentiality laws prevent me from revealing the name of any donor,' says Judy. 'We generally use numbers for identification purposes. Your biological father was – let me see . . .' She licks her index finger and rifles through her notes. 'Donor number 148. And here's something else you might like to know: the same man fathered five other children by donor insemination.'

'Wow! So you mean I have five brothers and sisters out there?'

Judy nods. 'Half-siblings anyway.'

'Boys or girls?'

'I'm afraid the file doesn't say.'

'How totally fucking amazing!' My hand shoots to my mouth. 'Excuse my language,' I apologize hastily.

Judy smiles understandingly.

'I hated being an only child. I would've loved a sister – older or younger, either would've been fine. I don't suppose there's any way of tracing them is there?'

Judy shakes her head. 'Not unless they also approach the Centre for information about their donor father. In that event I could, with your agreement, pass on your contact details.'

'I don't suppose there's much chance of that is there?' I say, looking at her doubtfully.

'You never know, stranger things have happened,' she says.

Resting my elbows on my knees, I apply gentle pressure to my temples. After a lifetime of total and complete ignorance as far as my father is concerned, these few details are almost too much to take in. I feel strangely light-headed, almost dizzy.

'Who performed my mother's insemination? Do you know?' I ask Judy. 'I'd love to meet them.'

'The records don't say, but it would probably have been Mr Goodwin himself. He was pretty much operating a one-man practice until the late Seventies,' Judy explains. 'But I'm afraid you won't be able to meet him. He died two years ago; we have a splendid memorial plaque in reception.'

'That's a shame,' I say dejectedly.

'I do have one last piece of information about your donor father,' says Judy, rummaging in the blue folder. 'I've been saving the best till last.'

I look at her expectantly.

'He left you a small legacy, so to speak,' she says ambiguously, extracting a single sheet of paper folded in half.

'As I said, Mr Goodwin was a pioneer in his field. Not only did he record donors' physical characteristics, he also asked them, on a purely voluntary basis, to provide a written explanation of why they decided to become a donor. It's a procedure we continue to this day – it helps our clients feel they're dealing with a real person and not just a sample in a test tube. Some donors do it simply for the money – we currently pay forty pounds a sample – but others have more philanthropic motives. Of course, not everyone can be bothered to put pen to paper . . .' She pauses and hands me the piece of paper, still folded. 'Your donor was different.'

As my fingers reach out to take the paper, I notice that my hand is shaking visibly.

'I expect you'd like a few moments on your own,' Judy says tactfully. Then she gets up and leaves the room, taking the blue folder with her. For a couple of minutes I just stare at the back of the piece of paper. It's a single sheet of feint ruled, no margin, the left-hand edge still puckered where it was torn from a pad and I can just make out the shadow of black ink on the other side. Slowly I unfold it, holding it with the tips of my fingers so I don't crease or mark it in any way.

It's only a few lines long and Donor 148's handwriting is bold and slightly sloping. why have I decided to donate my sperm? it begins. Then two blank lines and a list of points, each beginning on a fresh line.

As a student of medicine, I am keen to advance the science of artificial insemination to help women who are unable to conceive by natural methods.

I would like to contribute to the genetic pool of the incoming generation.

It makes me feel good to donate and to feel that I am a part of someone else's – hopefully happy – life.

I flop back in the armchair, rest the paper carefully, almost reverentially, on my lap and close my eyes, letting the words float freestyle around my head. I feel such a jumble of emotions: pride, that my father was obviously an intelligent and articulate individual; relief, that even though he never knew my mother, in some small way he actually cared about her happiness; and sadness, that this is as far as it goes. Somehow this ending doesn't feel quite right. There are too many loose ends.

'Everything OK?'

I open my eyes to see Judy sitting on the corner of her desk. I was so absorbed I didn't even hear her come back in the room.

I nod. 'This is so amazing, to actually see his handwriting, to know what inspired him to become a sperm donor.'

'We have to keep the original for our files, but I can do a photocopy if you like.'

'Oh God, yes please.'

'The copier's down the hall, won't be a tick.' Judy takes the piece of paper from my outstretched hand and leaves the room, closing the door behind her.

I'm so excited by the prospect of taking a piece of my father home with me, that it's a good thirty seconds before I clock it. The blue folder. Lying on Judy's desk. Unattended. She set it down when she came back in the room and omitted to pick it up again when she went off to the photocopier. For her, an oversight; for me, a golden opportunity.

Without a nanosecond's hesitation, I lunge towards the desk, which is situated just a couple of feet from the door. Opening the folder with trembling fingers, I draw out the stack of notes. My heart is beating so fast it's threatening to erupt in my chest. *Is this an arrestable offence?* I wonder to myself as I scrabble through the half-dozen or so pages, each of which bears a *Strictly Private & Confidential* stamp in menacing red ink. I pounce on a document headed *Donor's Details,* desperately scanning the faded typescript for that all-important name. I almost pass out when the door starts to open. Fuck. She's going to catch me red-handed. The door opens a couple more inches, but Judy doesn't appear. I can see her hand on the brass doorknob, but it seems as if she's talking to somebody – an unseen colleague in the hallway outside. 'I'll just see my client out and then I'll be right with you,' she is saying. I bundle the notes back into the folder and cross the room in two giant strides, so by the time Judy enters I'm standing at the window, looking out onto the street below.

'I was just admiring the view,' I say through dry lips.

'Yes, it's not bad, is it?' she says, handing me the photocopy. 'I'm sorry I can't give you more information about your father, but we do have a moral and a legal obligation to protect our donors' identities.'

'I totally understand and I'm extremely grateful for your time,' I say. We shake hands and Judy sees me to the top of the stairs.

All the way home I repeat the same two words over and over again, lest I forget them: *Gareth Blake Gareth Blake Gareth Blake Gareth Blake.*

By the time I arrived back at Kim's, I was burning to tell of my triumph. Unfortunately she was still in the West End, where she had gone to recce a newly opened nightclub and potential party venue. However, Tim – home early from a business meeting and engaged in nothing more taxing than chopping vegetables for a casserole – proved a willing audience.

'So what's your next move?' he had asked, after I had regaled him with my act of daring in Judy Mabb's office.

'I'm going to try and find Gareth Blake, of course,' came my matter-of-fact reply.

I had already worked out a loose and frankly unimaginative course of action, which involved identifying possible candidates from a web search of the UK phone directory (Blake being a relatively common name, I expected these to run into the hundreds), followed by endless embarrassing phone calls while I weeded out the rejects. I hoped to speed up the process by simultaneously placing a series of carefully worded small ads in a handful of suitable publications.

I would probably have dashed headlong into that scheme that very evening, had Tim not drawn my attention to a vital clue that, in my excitement, I had completely overlooked.

'You say Judy told you Gareth Blake was a medical student?' he said.

I nodded and said that my father's old alma mater was the prestigious teaching hospital, St Luke's, on the south bank of the Thames.

'Well, if it's anything like my old college, they'll have kept tabs on their alumni, so's they can get in touch when they're staging reunions or setting up mentoring schemes,' said Tim. The penny was beginning to drop. 'Of course, they're hardly likely to give you Blakey's home address, no questions asked, but they might be willing to disclose information that will help you track him down – like where he's working or what his medical speciality is.'

Naturally, I was on the phone to St Luke's quicker than you can say *donor insemination*. The bad news was, the woman in the administrator's office refused to discuss 'any personal information pertaining to current or former students'. The good news was, she revealed that the college library maintained a database of published reports and articles written by or relating to graduates, which could be freely accessed by members of the public who had filled out the necessary visiting researcher's application form.

And so here I am, nearly a week later, settled in front of a computer terminal in the library at St Luke's, my visitor's pass clipped to the waistband of my jeans. I have decided that, unless the college database throws up a concrete lead, I'm going to call it a day. I could go on looking for my father for ever, but I fear it's starting to take over my life. It's all I seem to think about these days. Admittedly, it is a useful distraction; it helps keep my mind off Toby and how much I miss him. I know he's a bastard and I know I deserve better, but that doesn't stop me loving him. But all the same I can't spend the rest of my life wallowing in pointless fantasies about a man I've never met.

After a brief tutorial from one of the library assistants, I am ready to explore the database. All I have to do is key in Gareth's name and the year he qualified – Judy told me he had donated sperm during his final year, so I am assuming he qualified in the year of my conception. The advanced search facility allows me to select from a list of periodicals and time frames, but I want to keep my options open. I hit *enter* and pray that my father made some sort of contribution to medical research, however small.

A new page appears – a list of ten articles, all of which contain my father's name. In my delight, I can't help letting out a triumphant 'Yes!', which causes the man at the next terminal to shoot me a disapproving look over the top of his half-moon glasses. Muttering an apology, I turn back to the screen and begin to examine the ten entries one by one. While the database doesn't allow you to access the article itself, it does provide the name of the journal, the date of publication, and the title of the article, all listed in date order – oldest first.

Entry number one cites a report in *The Psychologist* by Dr Gareth Blake, MRCPsych on something called 'Attention Deficit Hyperactivity Disorder'; number two refers to a piece he wrote for the *Lancet* on the use of video surveillance in child abuse cases; number three is an article about aggressive behaviour in childhood in *Social Work Today*. It seems as if my father was some sort of child expert; how deliciously appropriate. Continuing down the list, I can't help congratulating myself on having been sired by such a patently erudite father and I am feeling quite optimistic as I arrive at the final citation, certain that one of these articles will yield a clue to my father's whereabouts. And that's when all my dreams disappear in a puff of smoke. Entry number ten is shocking both in its brevity and its content.

British Medical Journal, 18 Nov 2001, Obituary

I gawp at the words in disbelief, moving my face closer to the screen to read the entry a second time. I can hardly believe that fate could have delivered such a cruel blow, that the grim reaper would have cut down my father just three short months earlier, that all my efforts to find him have been utterly in vain. Then it occurs to me that perhaps this is another person's obituary, that Gareth Blake had simply been paying tribute to some eminent colleague or mentor. Jotting down the reference, I go to the help desk and ask where I can find the *British Medical Journal* for 18 November. The library assistant directs me to the periodicals section, where unbound copies of the current year's *BMJ* are displayed on aluminium racks.

It doesn't take me long to find what I'm looking for. I take the magazine to a nearby desk, turn to the obituary section and there, among the half dozen or so reported deaths, my worst fears are confirmed:

Dr Gareth Blake, a child psychiatrist and expert in the theory of residential child care, has died at the age of 51. Best known for his highly regarded report on child abuse, The Forgotten Children *(1992), Gareth always insisted on the need to listen to children and put their requirements first. In 1995 he submitted evidence to the Williams Committee into the selection and recruitment of staff in children's homes and was subsequently appointed as senior adviser to the National Society for the Prevention of Cruelty to Children, a post he held until his premature death. A self-effacing man who shunned the limelight, Gareth was also a sparkling conversationalist with a famously dry sense of humour. His many and varied hobbies included jazz music, gardening and walking the coastal paths near his beloved Broadstairs home. He died last week in hospital after a short battle with chronic myeloid leukaemia and is survived by his wife Linda.*

I stare at the page in a daze and am struck by an horrific irony: my father died just as I was embarking on the search to find him – perhaps in the very same week even. If only I had found Mum's diaries sooner. If only he had clung to life a few months longer. Fifty-one is too bloody young. As I read the obituary a second time, I take in more information: that he was a psychiatrist.

A highly regarded one at that. And self-effacing too. And I like the *famously dry sense of humour* bit. Unexpectedly, my eyes fill with water and the page in front of me turns blurry. I wipe away the tears quickly and take a few deep breaths. I had planned to read through all the articles my father wrote, but somehow I don't have the stomach for it any more. Gazing around the room, I look at all the students, some with heads bowed, some whispering in friends' ears, some staring distractedly into the middle distance and I try to imagine my father here, all those years ago, cramming for exams or trying to get his head round some turgid psychiatric theory. Rummaging in my purse for some coins, I walk over to the Xerox machine and take a photocopy of the obituary, before returning the journal to the bookshelf.

I am halfway to the exit when suddenly I stop, turn around and head for a row of Internet terminals I noticed earlier. Leaning over the back of the orange plastic chair, I type in the URL for BT's online phone directory. When the enquiry screen appears, I execute a residential search.

    NAME: Blake
    INITIAL: G
    AREA: Broadstairs

A second later I am rewarded with a single address and telephone number.

TWENTY-FIVE

The smell of the sea hits me the second I open the carriage door. It's nice to escape from London once in a while, especially on a day as beautiful as this. Toby and I used to go on day trips all the time before he got famous. We never made it to Broadstairs, but I had heard it was rather a genteel town and quite unlike its bawdy neighbour, Margate. Today I shall be able to judge for myself.

Leaving the station, I make my way down the High Street towards the sea front, pausing to admire the Regency terraces with their rusted iron balconies and the old-fashioned shop fronts, which give off an air of shabby grandeur. It's only just gone ten, but the place is already starting to fill with Saturday shoppers and tourists come to enjoy the watery sunshine. Once on the promenade, I sit down on one of the many wooden benches which overlook the wide sandy bay below. Consulting my street map, I see that West Cliff Road is only a short walk away, but I won't go there yet; it's too early. I'll leave it another half-hour or so.

I am well aware that what I'm about to do is somewhat unethical. I certainly don't want to cause Linda Blake any distress – nor, if everything goes according to plan, shall I. My aim today is not to stake my claim as a family member; what brings me here is a simple and perhaps slightly ghoulish thirst for knowledge. I can't bring my father back to life, but I still want – no, *need* – to find out more about the kind of person he was . . . the house he lived in, the woman he fell in love with, whether or not they had any children together.

My plan is simple. I shall present myself as one of Gareth's former colleagues, in the area by chance and wishing to pass on my condolences. For obvious reasons, I don't want to be identifiable as Thea Carson, and so I plan to use my maiden name of Parkinson. Furthermore, before leaving the house this morning, I scraped my hair back into a ponytail and applied minimal make-up so as to look as unlike my polished media-friendly self as possible. After graciously accepting the cup of tea that Linda Blake will doubtless offer, I shall make polite conversation, while absorbing my surroundings and trying to glean as much information about my late father as possible. It will have to be a sensitive performance, but, with my background in the dramatic arts, I'm certain I can pull it off. After twenty minutes or so in Linda's company I shall politely withdraw and be on my way. And that will be an end to it. The ghost will be laid to rest and I shall be able to get on with the rest of my life. Well, that's the theory, anyway.

Knowing full well that Kim and Tim would heartily disapprove of this fact-finding mission, I have deliberately chosen to keep them in the dark. When I got back from St Luke's on Wednesday night they were both suitably sympathetic when I showed them Gareth's obituary. Nonetheless, I sensed in Kim a certain relief that my search appeared to be at an end. Not that she hasn't been fully supportive of all my efforts to find my father, but I think she feared I had become unhealthily obsessed with the subject.

'I know you must be incredibly disappointed that your dad's dead, but you've done amazingly well to get this far,' she said. 'You should be proud of yourself.'

I had, however, omitted to tell her that I had managed to find Gareth's home address, specifically because I didn't want her to try and talk me out of coming here. *She* thinks I'm spending today shopping in Bond Street with Patti.

The house in West Cliff Road turns out to be a well-maintained semi with big picture windows overlooking the sea and there's a car in the driveway, a newish Clio, which is a good indication that someone is home. While I was hatching my plan, it did occur to me that Linda might have sold up and moved on, but I'm hoping the house will be too suffused with memories of her late husband for her to want to leave it. Walking up the crazy-paved pathway, I hesitate for just a second before pressing the doorbell. I'd be lying if I said I wasn't nervous, but there's no way I'm going to back out now. The door opens to reveal a bosomy, middle-aged woman with faded blonde hair and a slightly startled expression. Immediately I switch to actress mode.

'Mrs Blake?' I enquire.

'Yes,' she says.

'My name's Thea Parkinson,' I begin confidently. 'I knew Gareth.'

She presses her lips together and nods in understanding, as if she knows what's about to come next.

'I don't mean to intrude, but I was visiting some friends in the area and I very much wanted to pass on my condolences.'

'That's kind of you,' she says. 'Won't you come in?'

She shows me into a large open-plan living room, pleasantly decorated in soft shades of pink and beige.

'Do make yourself comfortable,' she says, gesturing at a smart three-piece suite. 'I've just made a cup of tea, will you join me?'

'That would be lovely, Mrs Blake.'

'Linda – please.'

I smile coyly. 'Linda.'

As soon as she's left the room, I seize the chance to snoop. My eye is drawn immediately to a small collection of photographs on the windowsill, the largest of which is a wedding photo in an oval brass frame.

Picking it up for closer inspection, I have no difficulty identifying the bride in her lacy Edwardian-style wedding gown as Linda, although she was much slimmer back then and her hair's a different style. The smiling dark-haired man beside her must therefore be Gareth, but before I can subject him to thorough scrutiny Linda returns with the tea.

Guiltily, I return the picture to the windowsill. 'I was just thinking what a handsome couple you made,' I say, my eyes lingering on Gareth's face.

'I know it's an awful cliché, but it really was the happiest day of my life,' she says, setting down two mugs on the glass-topped coffee table.

'Did you get married here in Broadstairs?' I ask chattily, as I make myself comfortable in an armchair.

'Oh no, we've only been here for twelve years. We tied the knot in York; it seemed to make sense to marry in Gareth's home town, given that he has such an enormous family, whereas I can count all *my* relatives on two hands.' She takes a sip of tea.

'It's funny you know, but even after all these years, I still find it hard to keep track of Gareth's relations and remember who's related to who – five brothers and one sister he had, quite amazing isn't it?' She looks at me thoughtfully and adds: 'Forgive me for asking, but have we met before – when you were much younger perhaps?'

The question throws me somewhat. 'No, I don't think so,' I say carefully.

'You didn't come to Gareth's funeral?'

I smile apologetically and shake my head. 'Unfortunately I was abroad.'

'But I take it you *are* on Bernadette's side?'

'You must be confusing me with someone else,' I say lightly. 'Gareth and I were colleagues. I met him through his work with the NSPCC. Like everyone else I had tremendous respect for him and, of course, his sense of humour was legendary,' I laugh half-heartedly, worried that I'm not convincing – and who on earth is Bernadette?

A look of confusion clouds her face. 'You *worked* with Gareth? I rather assumed you were some sort of relative.'

'Oh?' I say, feeling my pulse quicken and not wanting to say any more for fear of incriminating myself.

'It's just that you're the spitting image of Gareth's sister Bernadette,' she continues. 'That hair, those cheekbones . . . hang on a minute, I'll show you.'

She goes over to a bookshelf and pulls out a thick leather-bound photo album from the bottom shelf. 'Let's see,' she says, flipping over the pages. 'Aah, here we are. She was a bit older than you when this was taken – mid-thirties probably – but the resemblance is striking, I think you'll agree.' She hands me the album and points to a shot of a woman in a T-shirt and frayed denim shorts. Despite myself, I can't help giving a loud gasp – for the face staring back at me is unmistakably mine.

Even the long knock-kneed legs appearing from the end of her shorts are mine. She looks more like my mother than my mother did. But then, I suppose, she *is* my aunt.

'It's quite uncanny, don't you think?' Linda is saying.

In that instant, I realize that I can't continue with this hideous pantomime, that even *my* acting skills aren't going to be enough. Already this has gone too far; I should never have come here, forcing my way into someone else's life like this. I ought to make my apologies and leave, feign a headache, a forgotten appointment, anything . . . and yet I can't tear my eyes away Bernadette's face.

'Thea, are you all right? You look as if you've seen a ghost.'

'Al-most,' I reply without thinking.

'Sorry?'

'No, I'm the one who should be sorry,' I say, looking up at Linda. 'I should never have come . . .'

'Nonsense,' she says kindly. 'Gareth's friends are always welcome here.'

'No, you don't understand,' I say, almost pleading now. And then the words I thought I would never be able to say just slip out. 'I was lying, I'm not one of Gareth's old work colleagues. I'm . . . I'm his daughter.'

We stare at each other. Unable to believe my indiscretion, my face seems frozen in a mask of horror, while Linda's fist is pressed to her mouth. Desperately struggling for some words of reassurance, I finally blurt out, 'It's not what you think, I'm not some sort of secret love child.'

Slowly, she lifts her hand away from her face. 'Well, in that case, I think we should both sit down and talk about it, don't you?' she says with remarkable composure.

And so I tell her the whole story, from beginning to end: about growing up in south-east London never knowing who my father was, but always assuming he was somebody my mother had dated. I talk about Mum's death and the discovery of her diaries and how I managed to identify and then rule out three potential fathers. Throughout it all, Linda wears a deadpan expression, never interrupting, never asking where her late husband figures in my life story. It's only when I get to Marty's revelation that I was born by donor insemination that she reacts.

'I knew it,' she says, breaking into a wide smile. 'You're one of Gareth's donor babies, aren't you?'

Feeling extremely bewildered, I nod my head slowly. 'My mother was a patient at the Gunnersbury Fertility Centre in London.'

Linda claps her hands together delightedly, then jumps up from the sofa to embrace me. Things have suddenly turned surreal.

'You mean you knew your husband was a sperm donor?' I say, when she finally releases me.

'Certainly,' she says. 'He told me on our second

date. I was a psychiatric nurse at St Luke's and he was working in his first job in paediatrics. As I recall, we were in a pub in Charing Cross Road and we got into rather a heated debate about whether it was ever acceptable to discipline a child physically. I didn't think it was, while he was of the opinion that a judicious smack on the legs did no harm whatsoever. I asked him if he wanted kids of his own one day and he said, "I probably already do." '

'And then he told you he was a sperm donor?'

Linda nods. 'He told me he had donated three or four times the previous year.'

'Weren't you shocked?'

'A little, but at the same time I rather admired him. Unlike a lot of hard-up student donors, he didn't do it for the money, he did it because he wanted to help women who, for whatever reason, couldn't have children by natural methods.'

'I know. The Centre gave me a letter he'd written – well, more of a statement than a letter – laying out his reasons for donating. It was only a few lines, but I found it very comforting.'

'They still had that on file? How wonderful.'

'Do you know how many other women besides my mum Gareth was able to, er, help?' I ask, wondering if Linda is aware of the exact number of children her husband had fathered.

'Five,' she says proudly. 'Gareth made it his business to find out.'

'But doesn't that make you feel a bit weird – knowing that *your* husband fathered six kids by six different women?'

'It never bothered me, although I suppose it might have been different if we'd been able to have children of our own. It wasn't until after we were married that a gynaecologist told me I'd never be able to carry a pregnancy to full term – rather a cruel irony when you think that Gareth was a child psychiatrist. We did think about adopting, but in the end we decided against it.' She moistens her lips with the end of her tongue and then says, 'He never really articulated this to me – probably because he didn't want to hurt my feelings – but I think it meant a lot to him, knowing that the six of you were out there, his *donor babies* as he called you. Of course, what with the laws protecting donor's identities, he never dreamed he would ever get to meet any of you. Speaking of which, how *did* you manage to trace him?'

With a huge sense of embarrassment, I confess to sneaking a look in my file while Judy was out of the room. 'I know it was wrong of me, but I'd put so much time and energy into finding him that I couldn't let the opportunity slip through my fingers.'

'Do you know what Gareth told me?' says Linda. 'That he asked the doctor at the Gunnersbury to make his name and contact details available to any child of his born by donor insemination, should they ever request the information.'

'No way!'

'It's true. But the clinic refused, said it breached their code of conduct or some such.'

I shake my head sadly.

'Never mind, you found us in the end. How on earth did you track us to Broadstairs with only Gareth's name to go on?'

I tell her about my trip to the library at St Luke's and the discovery of Gareth's obituary.

'That must have been the most appalling shock for you,' she says.

'Yes, and the fact that he had died just a few months ago somehow made it much worse. I was so very close . . .' My voice tails off.

'His illness came like a bolt from the blue,' says Linda. 'First tiredness, then weight loss . . . I think he already suspected the worst and then blood tests confirmed that he was suffering from one of the most virulent forms of leukaemia.' She sniffs and swallows hard. 'He was my best friend; I miss him terribly.'

'Could I ask you where he's buried?' I say tentatively.

She gestures at the window. 'I scattered his ashes, out there, in the sea at Viking Bay. It was what he wanted; he did so love this place.' She pulls a tissue from her sleeve and dabs her eyes.

'I feel awful, coming here like this and lying to you,' I say. 'The last thing I wanted to do was upset you.'

'You mustn't apologize. I think you're quite a remarkable woman – the way you managed to find us.

And after losing Gareth it's wonderful to meet you; it makes me feel as if he's not so far away after all.' For a minute or two we sit there in silence, each lost in our own thoughts, until I pluck up the courage to ask, 'How do you think Gareth would have reacted if he'd still been alive when I turned up here?'

She doesn't miss a beat. 'He would have been thrilled, absolutely thrilled.'

I smile shyly. 'Do you really think so?'

'I know so, Thea.' She reaches across the coffee table and squeezes my hand.

By the time I left the house in West Cliff Road, darkness was closing in. Linda and I had so much to talk about. I filled her in on the rest of my life (I did mention in passing that my estranged husband was quite a well-known singer, but Linda said she had never heard of Drift). She in turn introduced me posthumously to my father – his career, his friends, his likes and dislikes. She told me his favourite jokes and showed me photos of his boyhood home, his mum and dad, his student flat-share . . . and on to foreign holidays with Linda, office parties and family Christmases. After lunch Linda took me to see some of Gareth's favourite places – the coastal pathway, the bandstand where he liked to listen to summer jazz, the cherry tree in the garden which he planted on their twenty-fifth wedding anniversary. And I know this is going to sound trite, but by the end of the day I really felt as if I had known him.

Just as we were saying goodbye to each other on Linda's doorstep, she suddenly asked me to wait while she dived into the house. When she came back, she had a small brown envelope in her hand. 'A keepsake,' she said as she handed it to me. I didn't open it until I was on the train back to London. It was a photograph of my father, taken on the day he graduated from St Luke's. He's smiling shyly, brown eyes twinkling, wisps of chestnut hair peeking out from underneath his mortar-board. Of all the pictures Linda had shown me, it's the one in which he looks most like me.

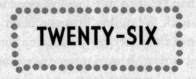

TWENTY-SIX

I'm not usually a gushy person; not someone given to great declarations or unnecessary displays of emotion. But I really do feel as if I've been . . . God, I'm going to sound like such a drama queen . . . *reborn*. Well, maybe not reborn, but risen from the ashes at least. Now, for the first time in my life, I have tangible evidence, irrefutable proof that I do have a father, that I'm not some strange hybrid girl with only half a genetic inheritance.

After much soul searching, I have even been able to come to terms with the fact that Mum concealed the truth about my father. I still feel hurt by her duplicitous behaviour, but the way I see it I have two choices: either I waste a lot of time and energy resenting her or I accept the decision she made all those years ago. I know she loved me and I know she thought she was acting in my best interests by not telling me I was born by donor insemination; so I'm going for the second option.

Linda and I have been in regular contact since our meeting last month and I have invited her to come and stay for the weekend when I am settled in my new flat. Kim and Tim were astounded when I told them about my visit to Broadstairs and I think Kim was also a little hurt that I hadn't shared my plans with her in advance. But, like true friends, they were thrilled that it had all worked out for me and they can't wait to meet Linda.

Last night, by way of celebration, I hosted a small dinner party at one of my favourite restaurants in Islington for the people who have helped and supported me during the journey to find my father: Kim and Tim and Marty, who came with his fiancée Alison (six-month-old Bonnie was left at home with the babysitter, but a formal introduction has been scheduled for later in the month). At the end of the meal, after the liqueurs had been served, I gave a little speech; nothing formal, just an off-the-cuff thing.

'I just wanted to thank everyone for coming tonight,' I say, looking at them all around the table. 'As you know, the last month or two have been very difficult for me and I couldn't have survived them without the support of my friends. So thank you to Kim and Tim for sharing their home with me for so long – and don't worry, guys, I'm moving out next week!' This makes everyone laugh. 'And Kim – I just want to say you're the best friend any girl could have.'

She reaches for my hand across the table. 'I'm really going to miss having you around the house, not to mention the office,' she says. 'Bet you didn't know Thea was an ace party planner did you, Marty?'

He shakes his head. 'She's obviously been hiding her light under a bushel. Maybe you should set up in business on your own, Thea.'

'Don't you dare!' Kim says with mock ferocity.

'As if.' I giggle into my Bailey's.

Then I turn to Marty, sitting on my left.

'And Marty, I'd like to thank *you* for having the courage to tell me the truth about my dad. I know it wasn't easy for you.'

He smiles. 'For a while there I really wondered if I'd made the right decision telling you the truth. I agonized over it for days afterwards, didn't I?' he says, looking at Ali, who nods vigorously in agreement.

'Then I thought maybe I should've told you years ago, when you were still a kid and it might have been easier for you to deal with, but that would have been very disrespectful to your mum. And, by the way, I'm dead impressed with how you managed to track down that clinic. I'm sure everyone here is very proud of you and I know your mum would be too if she was here today.'

'I hope so,' I say. 'Let's drink a toast to her, shall we?' Everybody raises their glasses over the flickering candle at the centre of the table.

'To Shirley,' I say. 'The best mum in the world.'

*

In many ways, last night signalled the relinquishing of my old life and the beginning of my new one. But before I can truly start afresh, I have one last piece of unfinished business to attend to.

My solicitor's appointment is scheduled for midday and for the occasion I have deliberately chosen to wear Toby's least favourite outfit, purchased last autumn for the occasion of his mum's sixtieth. To my eye, the slate-grey pencil skirt and matching fitted jacket was a classic piece, so imagine how crushed I was when, driving home at the end of a very pleasant evening, my husband told me I looked like a Latvian air hostess. I never had the guts to wear that suit again – until today, that is.

I arrive at Henley & Sons with twenty minutes to spare, which gives me plenty of time to read through the paperwork that Charles, my solicitor, has prepared.

'Are you sure this is what you want?' he asks, frowning at me across his desk. 'There'll be no going back after this.'

'Quite sure,' I say firmly, inking my name on the dotted line at the foot of the document.

At eleven fifty-eight, twenty-eight minutes later than requested (no surprise there), the intercom on Charles's desk buzzes into life.

'Mr Carson has arrived,' the receptionist announces.

Charles raises his eyebrows at me questioningly. I nod my approval and he asks the receptionist to show Toby in. I felt so strong and confident earlier, but now that it's time for the showdown I am suddenly nauseous.

The door swings open and there's Toby. It's the first time I've seen him in the flesh since the night of the IMAs. He's looking rough, really rough, but I suppose that's a rock star's prerogative. Five days' worth of stubble at least, battered old Diesel jeans and his favourite suede jacket. Nice to know he thinks I'm worth the effort. Actually, I'm glad; if he looked really hot, this would be an awful lot harder.

'Hi, babe,' he says, in an irritatingly casual fashion.

'Hello, Toby,' I say evenly.

'I'll leave you to it, then,' says Charles, gathering up some files from his desk. 'I'll be in the office next door if you need me.'

After he's left the room, Toby and I look wordlessly at each other for a few seconds. I notice that he's chewing gum, as if to emphasize that this whole thing doesn't really mean that much to him. I suppose I should be grateful that he managed to fit me into his oh-so-busy schedule.

'Shall we sit down?' I say, breaking the silence.

He shrugs his shoulders and collapses into the tan leather sofa behind him, while I opt for a high-backed swivel chair. Toby's face falls.

'Aw, don't be like that, babe. Come and sit here, next to me,' he says, patting the space next to him. 'I know you've missed me.'

'Pardon?' I say as icily as I can manage, while my heart lunges in my chest.

'Well I've certainly missed *you*,' he says. 'I've been gagging to see you, but after that day at Kim's when you told me to fuck off I didn't fancy another helping of humiliation. Luke said I should stop hassling you and give you some breathing space, that you'd get in touch in your own good time.' He smiles that lovely shy smile that used to turn my insides to goo. 'And it looks like he was right, 'cos here we are.'

'Well, at least you had the lovely Lexy to keep you company in your darkest hour,' I say sarcastically. 'I loved the nine-page spread in *Wow!* magazine, by the way. Very tasteful.'

He has the good grace to look embarrassed. 'Listen, I'm really sorry about that, babe. I should've stopped her, but she was desperate for the publicity, she reckoned it would help her get some kids' TV gig she was after. I didn't know they'd put it on the cover and use that stupid picture of us horse-riding together.'

'So did it work?' I ask. Like I fucking care.

'Nah, Cat Deeley got it.'

I release a derisive snort. So there is some justice in this world then.

'You know, Toby, that story really hurt me, all that crap about *lots of babies and a cottage in the country*. You said it was over between you two; why did you lie to me like that?'

'That day, after the IMAs, I did finish it with her, honestly, Thea. But when you walked out on me, I just sort of fell back into seeing her. I was so lonely without you and she was so, well, available. But she's ancient history now, I swear it.'

'You mean you've split up?' I say disbelievingly.

'Yeah, didn't you know? It was in the *Sun*'s 'Bizarre' column last week. I thought that's why you got in touch.'

'I had no idea,' I say. 'I haven't read a newspaper in ages.'

That's thrown him. He's got his bewildered-little-boy face on now – the one from Drift's first album cover.

'Whatever she told that magazine reporter, it was never serious between us. It's over; I swear on my mother's life.' He's never done that before – sworn on Lucy's life. Perhaps he actually means it this time. 'Look, babe, let's not beat around the bush any more. We need each other, don't we? We're no good on our own. All that stuff with the solicitors and the bloody *interim financial settlements* and refusing to take my calls . . . that was just to teach me a lesson, wasn't it?'

'For your information, I'm doing perfectly well on my own, thank you very much,' I say tightly. 'And I'm sure you'll cope just fine without me. Get yourself a good PA and you won't even notice I've gone.'

He looks confused. 'Sorry, babe?'

'Come on, Toby, don't play the innocent. Once

we'd moved into Itchycoo, I hardly saw you for dust. It didn't even feel like we were married half the time. Towards the end I began to feel like nothing more than a well-paid secretary. Seeing you shagging Lexy at the IMAs was the final straw, but if I'm honest I hadn't been happy in our relationship for ages. It was as if you – the great indie rock god – were the only one who mattered. You didn't seem to give a toss about *my* dreams and ambitions.'

'That's not fair,' he says lamely.

'It's true. You didn't show the slightest bit of interest in my work, you took the piss out of my friends, you thought it was hilarious when I told you I was trying to find my father . . . you knew how important that was to me, but you still treated it like a big joke.'

'C'mon, though, you must admit it was a bit of a wild goose chase.'

'For your information, I did find him in the end,' I snap.

'You're kidding,' he says. 'How the fuck did you manage that?'

'It's a long story and one I'm sure you're not really interested in hearing.'

A bruised look crosses his face. 'Of course I am. I'm interested in anything that concerns you, babe.'

He's not entirely convincing, but still I can't resist the chance to demonstrate to Toby that, far from falling to pieces following my departure from Itchycoo, I have actually been using the time at Kim's much more productively. And so, as coolly and dispassionately as I can, I give him the edited highlights. Even to my ears, the story sounds far-fetched and I half expect Toby to burst out laughing in his usual dismissive fashion. But to my surprise the disclosure that I was born by donor insemination seems to have affected him profoundly.

'Your dad was a sperm donor?' he says, his eyes as wide as saucers.

'You heard.'

'Un-fucking-believable.'

'Yes, it did come as quite a shock.'

'And you actually managed to find out his name, his address . . . you went to his house?'

'That's right.'

'That's amazing . . . that is *fucking* amazing.' He shakes his head in disbelief.

'You didn't think I could do it, did you? You didn't think I had it in me.'

'No, it's not that,' he says, lifting his head to look straight into my eyes. 'I know how determined you can be once you put your mind to something.'

'So what is it then?' I snap.

He hesitates. 'I did it once,' he says in an uncertain voice.

'*What* did you do?' I say, feeling my impatience mount.

'I donated sperm,' he says flatly. 'Just the once, mind you.'

I stare at him aghast. 'You didn't!'

'It was before we even met. I was a student; I needed the cash for some new guitar strings. I saw this ad in the paper and I thought it seemed like easy money.'

'How come you never told me before?'

'It sounds kinda sad, doesn't it? "Hey babe, I'm a sperm donor," and anyway I thought you might not like it.'

He's right. I would have been absolutely devastated at the thought of lots of little Tobys running around. 'Do you ever think about them?' I ask.

'Think about who?'

'All the children you might have fathered.'

'Nah. Anyway, they're not really *my* kids are they?' A look of fear crosses his beautiful face. 'Jesus Christ, I fucking hope none of them ever comes looking for me.'

Suddenly I realize that whatever he says to me, however much he asks for my forgiveness, the only person in this entire world Toby Carson really and truly cares about is himself.

'It seems terribly ironic that you were quite happy to dish out your sperm to all comers for forty quid and yet you didn't want to keep *our* baby,' I say spitefully.

'Why are you dragging that up now? I thought we agreed that having an abortion was the right thing.'

'No, Toby, *you* agreed and I, fool that I am, went along with it. I still think about that baby every hour of every day, you know.' The words nearly choke me and I struggle to maintain my composure.

He gets up from the sofa, kneels on the floor in front of my chair and takes my hands in his.

'I had no idea you felt that way, honest to God,' he says earnestly. 'You seemed to handle the abortion thing so well . . . OK, there were a few tears, but I thought that was just your hormones going into overdrive.'

'How the hell would you have known how I was handling it?' I say bitterly. 'You never tried to talk to me about it, you never even asked how I was feeling. It was as if you just didn't care.'

'Of course I cared,' he says, cupping the sides of my face with his hands. 'Don't you remember? I took time off, cancelled that shoot for *The Face* . . .'

'But it wasn't enough,' I say quietly. 'It felt like a token gesture.'

'Well, I'm sorry if that's the way it came across. I thought I was doing the right thing . . .' His voice trails off. He looks down at the floor, then back up at me.

'By the way, you might be interested to know it was Alexa who leaked the news of the abortion to the papers.'

I look at him aghast. 'What?'

'I only mentioned it to her in passing. I didn't think she'd go running off to the *News of the World*.'

'How dare you! You had no right discussing my personal business with that little slag.'

'I know, it was stupid of me. Alexa only admitted what she'd done after you and I had separated. She said it was her way of putting pressure on our relationship, of trying to split us up.'

'Well, she got her wish then, didn't she?'

'But it's not really over between us, is it? It's still not too late.'

'Yes, it is,' I say, swallowing hard.

He sighs impatiently. 'Look, if you need proof of my feelings for you, I've written a song dedicated to you; it's called "Dream Girl". It's all about how beautiful I think you are and how much I love you. It's my tribute to you, my way of saying thank you for everything you've done for me. I know I would never have achieved half as much with Drift if it wasn't for you creating a nice home life and patiently putting up with all my shit.'

It's funny, but I used to dream about Toby writing a song for me, like Noel Gallagher did for Meg with 'Wonderwall'. Of course, I would never have suggested it to him, that would defeat the object – songs like that have to be spontaneous – but I certainly fantasized about it. But, now that it's actually happened, I don't feel flattered or grateful; I feel gutted that he had to wait for us to split up before he was inspired to write the damn thing.

'It's on the new album,' Toby continues excitedly. 'I've persuaded the record label to release it as a single. It *was* supposed to be a surprise, but then my solicitor called me and said you wanted a meeting and I naturally assumed that meant we were getting back together.'

I look at Toby staring up at me, with as much devotion as a man like him is capable of; then I take a deep breath and gently extricate my hands from his. 'The reason I asked you here was to tell you I want a divorce.'

A look of utter shock crosses his face. 'You're not serious,' he says, his voice wavering.

'I'm afraid I am – deadly serious,' I say briskly, reaching across to Charles's desk and picking up the contract he has prepared. 'I'm sure your solicitor will want to go through it with a fine-tooth comb, but I'll just outline the main terms for you,' I say, staring intently at the papers so I don't have to witness Toby's hurt. 'I'm going to divorce you on the grounds of irreconcilable differences. I will agree to refrain from giving any interviews on the subject of our relationship in perpetuity and I'm asking you to do the same.' I glance up at him, but he seems to stare right through me, a stunned rabbit-caught-in-the-headlights look on his face.

'You can keep Itchycoo and all its contents, with the exception of my découpage dressing table, my clothes and jewellery. From a financial standpoint, I will accept a modest lump sum in full and final settlement.' I name the figure, but it doesn't seem to register with Toby; he just continues to shake his head despairingly. I press on: 'Charles tells me that even though we've only been married a year, I could probably get more money if I went to court, especially if I divorce you on the grounds of your adultery. But this isn't about money or revenge, Toby. It's about reaching a fair and equitable agreement for all concerned and pushing the divorce through as quickly and painlessly as possible.'

'Is that what you want?' he says quietly. 'To get rid of me as quickly as possible.'

'Yes, frankly, it is,' I say without rancour. 'I've wasted enough of my life, playing second fiddle to the men in my life and I think it's about time I put myself first.' I stand up and toss the document on the swivel chair behind me. 'Now, if you'll excuse me, I have a life to lead.'

As I sweep past him out of the office, he remains on his knees, staring at the floor. I don't look back.

EPILOGUE

Six months later

This morning I was giving the flat a lick and a polish when I heard Toby's song on the radio – the one he wrote for me, 'Dream Girl'. I put down my duster and my can of Windolene, walked over to the stereo and cranked the sound right up. I tried to listen to it objectively, as a punter would – and it was good; very good. At least the tune was. The lyrics . . . well, they were a bit slushy, but I guess Toby was feeling pretty emotional when he wrote them.

Afterwards I had to laugh when the DJ said, '. . . and that was "Dream Girl" by Drift, a song written by frontman Toby Carson for the lady in his life, the very sexy Stella Morrison . . .' I wonder whose idea *that* was. An over-zealous PR with an eye for a good story, or just Toby having a sly dig? Perhaps it had been Stella's own idea to claim to be the inspiration for *my* song. Whatever the truth, I think I can assume Toby has got over me.

I'm not bitter or jealous that my so-called friend has copped off with my ex-husband. On the contrary, I think they're very well suited, with their shared penchant for parties and posing and profligate spending. I hope it works out for the two of them, I really do. She's good value for money, old Stella, with her gift of the gab and her 23-inch waist and her swishy blonde hair. Not like me, who always tried to fade into the background at every opportunity. And now that my divorce from Toby has gone through uncontested and Stella's newsreader husband has finally come out of the closet and declared his love for a member of one of the nation's best-loved boybands, they're both free agents.

I believe they got together after being introduced at the Grand Prix, although I wouldn't be in the least bit surprised if Stella – who always professed to loathe motor sports – had engineered the whole thing. Looking back, it was obvious that she had designs on Toby . . . the gushy way she used to talk about him and her obvious delight when our relationship started to go off the rails.

Each and every stage of their five-month relationship has been slavishly reported by the media – the lavish gifts (a BMW Z3, no less, for her twenty-eighth birthday), the matching ankle tattoos (a cupid with each other's name written in Sanskrit underneath), and the artwork for Drift's new album cover, which was leaked to the *NME* (it was supposed to be *me* in silhouette of course, but Stella was kind enough to step into the breach).

As for me . . . well, I'm single – but happy. I hope to fall in love again one day in the not too distant future, but right now I have other priorities.

In approximately seven weeks' time I shall give birth to a baby; a little girl, according to the scan. I absolutely love being pregnant, my body feels so fantastically lush and fecund and, best of all, I've finally developed a cleavage. It was some surprise discovering I was pregnant. With all the mad stuff that was going on in my life – like finding my dad and getting a divorce and moving home – I had ignored my body's warning signals. I assumed my periods had stopped because of the stress and by the time I went to see my GP I was already three months' gone.

I'm not sure if Toby knows. I expect he does. There was a photo of me and my bulge in *Wow!* magazine, a paparazzi shot of me shopping in the King's Road – just a small one (after all, I'm practically a nobody these days).

Not that the baby is Toby's: it can't be, the dates are all wrong. It's Cameron Kennedy's – my one-night stand.

I thought long and hard before telling Cam I was expecting his child; even wondered if I might be doing him a kindness by keeping him in the dark. At least then he wouldn't have to wrestle with his conscience about whether or not to accept responsibility. But I know what it's like to grow up without a father and I didn't want my own daughter to be similarly deprived. So I upended three handbags until I found that long-forgotten KPMG business card, took a deep breath, and called him.

He was totally shocked; not just about the baby, but by the fact that 'Amanda' was in fact 'Thea' – former wife of Drift star Toby Carson. Quite a lot to take in, I think you'll agree. We met for lunch and I told him that I wasn't interested in money or maintenance, but that I *would* be putting his name on my daughter – on *our* daughter's – birth certificate and that if he was interested in visitation rights, I would happily get my solicitor to draft an agreement.

Cam mulled it over for a couple of weeks and then came back to me and said that yes, he *was* interested in sharing in our daughter's future. Whether or not that will actually happen remains to be seen, but we *have* built up a friendship of sorts, meeting up every couple of weeks or so. And he's bought me a top-of-the-range cot from Harvey Nichols and made me promise to call him the minute I go into labour, so the initial indications are good. And no, we're not about to fall in love and sail off into the sunset together. He's a nice guy and everything, but that kind of stuff only happens in movies.

Being a single mum won't be easy, I know that, but at least I've got plenty of back-up. Kim is in raptures at the prospect of becoming a godmother at last and Marty and Alison have already signed up as chief babysitters. I also kept my promise to Mum's old friend Val about staying in touch; she even sent her husband round to put up some shelves in what will be the nursery. As for Linda Blake, well, it's no exaggeration to say that she and I have become very close. We talk on the phone at least once a week and when I told her I was pregnant she gave me the most wonderful gift for the baby – an antique silver tankard that had belonged to Gareth. She's even talked about introducing me to some of his brothers and sisters, but I don't feel quite ready for that yet, especially when Linda told me that none of them was aware he had ever been a sperm donor.

As for the celebrity wives – Stella and I are no longer in contact, for obvious reasons, and Angela recently moved to Texas to marry an oil millionaire she met in the jacuzzi at Forest Mere. However, I *am* still in touch with Patti, who, despite my reservations, has proved herself a true friend. Not only did she concede that I made the right decision in leaving Toby, but she was genuinely horrified when he and Stella got together. Jaw set in an angry line, she declared, 'A celebrity wife should never shit on her own.' So now, whenever Patti sees Stella at a showbiz do, she cuts her dead, and I know she's used her influence to get her barred from half a dozen of the best day spas in London. Oh, and everybody now knows Stella's boobs are fake, which was news even to me.

Bringing up a child is an expensive business and Toby's lump sum won't last for ever. But I should be all right because I've got myself a full-time job; a proper, fulfilling career-girl job. Over the past six months, Party On! has gone into orbit and Kim just can't cope on her own any more. So she hired a secretary and set up a swanky new office in Muswell Hill and invited me to join as deputy director. I was worried she was just doing it as a favour – me being pregnant *and* unemployed – but she insisted that it was the other way round. She's even said I can work from home once the baby is born.

So you see, my life is really coming together. And OK, so there are still a few holes in the jigsaw frame, but all the key pieces are in place. Do I miss Toby? I sometimes get a tingle when I catch him on TV or see his face on the front of a magazine in Smith's and I imagine myself stroking that shaggy red-blond mane and kissing that cushiony mouth. But it's just lust, it's only the same thing those Drift chicks feel for him, it doesn't go any deeper; not any more.

The past year has been a real rollercoaster for me, but I don't have too many regrets. How can I when I've learned so much – not just about myself, but other people too? Never underestimate your own abilities, that's really important. *A friend in need is a friend indeed* – it might be a cliché, but by God it's true. And despite what you read in the magazines it *is* possible to be single and happy: I am living proof of that.

Oh, and I've also learned that every human being has their frailties . . . even indie rock gods.